AMBASSADOR 3:
CHANGING FATE

PATTY JANSEN

CAPRICORNICA PUBLICATIONS

GET FREE EBOOKS

Visit pattyjansen.com
or scan the QR code below with your phone to sign up for Patty's
mailing list. You get four series starter ebooks for free!

DID YOU KNOW?

Ambassador 3 is also available in audio. Click the image or visit https://pattyjansen.com to find out more.

1

———————

I WAS PRETTY GOOD at making an idiot of myself, but this had to be one of the most embarrassing things I'd done in my life.

The young man stood just inside the door, in my living room, not quite sure whether to hold his hands in front of him, behind his back or, heavens forbid, in his pockets. He seemed to settle on a little bit of each at different times, and never pulling off any of the positions with confidence. He looked and acted as awkward as I felt.

His name was Menor Ezmi. He came from Hedron—how could he not with a name like that?—and was in Barresh working on a temporary security contract. He was well-groomed and quite handsome, as far as I could judge other men for handsomeness: a well-shaped face, typical full Coldi lips, well-defined cheekbones and clear, alert eyes. He was athletic and lacked the chubbiness of so many Coldi people and, as was fairly common amongst Hedron Coldi, his hair was curly. He wore it in a big, bushy ponytail.

His education was impeccable; he was smart and articulate and had applied to my advertisement in the local news bulletin with the understanding that we would not be paying him, because this wasn't about money. In short, he ticked all the right boxes—for becoming the father of our child.

All the women in the house—and why were there so many of them all of a sudden?—stood or sat in the living room, looking at him, judging him as one judges a prize bull.

My housekeeper Eirani had something to say about his clothing. It was *too formal* according to her. She spoke keihu and he probably couldn't understand her, and I wondered what *too formal* meant anyway and why clothing mattered when we were judging what was underneath.

Sheydu feigned disinterest from the couch, but I could see her give the man curious glances when she thought I wasn't looking. It was hard to figure out what she thought at the best of times and this was not her favourite subject. With her greying hair and sun-spotted and wrinkled skin, under which her muscles rippled when she moved, she was easily the oldest person in the household, but I didn't think she had much experience in the matter of choice of mate or relationships. I suspected that her response to any man who showed interest in her in that way was a knee in the groin. Sheydu did not canoodle.

Xinanu was perhaps the biggest surprise of all the female members of my household. After we came back from our escapade on Asto, I had sent Nicha back there to find himself a pair of subordinate *zhaymas* to complete our association, since Thayu had taken on Sheydu and Veyada. He had done just that and brought two youngsters, but he had also come back with a woman with whom he had negotiated a contract for a child. Here she was on my couch, young, gorgeous, extremely sensual, seated next to Nicha, and very, very pregnant. She announced that our poor subject of interest had very nice muscles, but she disliked his hair.

"Do you ever straighten it?" She was from the Azimi clan, First Circle, and according to habit, she used subordinate *xayi* pronouns. I wasn't used to hearing that form in my apartment, and every time she used a *xayi* pronoun, as she did to the staff, I cringed a little.

Menor handled the subtle belittling without any reaction. "I quite like my hair. What is wrong with it?" He used colloquial *nyo* pronouns, as was standard at Hedron.

"Well . . ." Xinanu spread her hands. Her expression said, *Do I really have to explain that?* Then she said again, "Well. You're from Hedron, so I guess it doesn't matter."

Oh, those pronouns were really rubbing me up the wrong way.

As if she were the font of wisdom on all things concerning fashion. As if that even mattered. As if she had any say in the decision at hand.

I glanced at Thayu, who leaned against the doorframe with her arms crossed over her chest. Her face was very proper, unemotional. She hadn't said much yet, even though she would be the one carrying this man's child.

Xinanu pushed herself from the couch with a groan and walked around the young man, eying him from top to bottom. If I hadn't known that she had a good month to go still, I might have thought she'd be in danger of dropping the baby, but that was only the result of the fact that she liked wearing clothes at least two sizes too small.

"Hmm," she said, and looked first at Thayu, and then at me. "He's a nice specimen. Apart from that horrible hair, he's got nice shoulders, a good strong face, healthy legs and a butt to kill for, but tell me, why are you going for someone from outside?"

Thayu gave her the dead-fish stare. Her gold-flecked eyes were the only thing moving in her otherwise impassive face.

"Because," she said in her cold dead-fish voice. "Because there are far too many Inner and First Circle people trying to get a foot in our household already." She gave Xinanu a pointed look.

Oooo-er.

I waited for the return snipe, but Xinanu must have run out of pointed proverbs in this morning's snipe-fest with Eirani. Maybe her pregnancy had finally slowed her down. Heavens be praised.

"Apart from the hair, I don't mind him," Xinanu carried on. "Better than the other ones so far."

I cringed. That good old Coldi bluntness.

"Thank you," the young man said, and that only made her bluntness more cringe-worthy.

"Tell me, Menor, why would you do this thing," Sheydu asked him. She had twisted sideways on the couch and folded her legs under her. Sheydu had this uncanny ability to make the room go quiet when she spoke. "If there is to be no benefit to yourself and if, as you say, there will be no claims from you in regards to parentage of the child, even if it turns out to be a girl."

In most Coldi societies, boys inherited from their mothers and girls from their fathers, but I wasn't sure if Hedron adhered to this custom.

"I like to help other people."

"Hmph. Hedron isn't known for its soft heart."

"We're not at Hedron."

"No, well . . ."

"Maybe I left for a reason." He looked straight into her eyes. Not being from Asto, he could do that, and everything I'd seen so far confirmed that he completely lacked the *sheya* instinct requiring Coldi people to establish their rankings in relation to each other the first time they met another person.

I was beginning to quite like this young man. Polite, smart, with a healthy hint of sarcasm. Thayu's *sheya* instinct was not hugely strong, and any child of theirs would have it further watered down. From my personal point of view, the less *sheya* in my house, the better. It was one of those irrational things that truly baffled me about Coldi people.

Xinanu was right in that he was a lot better than any of the previous candidates, one of whom had expressed open disappointment that having his genetic material used for a child didn't mean that he was going to get any action in bed.

"Why are you in Barresh?" I asked him.

"We live in a very isolated community at Hedron. I wanted to see other places and understand the ways that people live there."

"Are you familiar with the Coldi contracts for parentage of children?"

"I am. I understand that the child will not be mine, and I have no right to claim it as mine for any purpose, be it legal or for the purpose of inheritance."

"You seem well prepared."

"Thank you, Delegate."

"I think we've exhausted our questions. Unless you have any . . ." Thayu made a *no* hand signal. "I will be in contact later."

"I'm looking forward to it, Delegate."

"I will let the young master out then," Eirani said.

He bowed politely to me before following Eirani out of the room. There were footsteps in the hall, and the sound of the front door opening and closing.

"So, what do you think?" I asked Thayu.

"I don't know. . . ." Thayu looked down.

Xinanu said, "I liked him better than the previous one. He was much too cocky and sleazy."

I gave her a *Shut up, woman, I didn't ask you anything* glare, knowing that the chance that she would get the message was slim.

"It's not about their behaviour," Thayu said primly. She didn't even look at Xinanu—

—who totally failed to get the message. "Of course it is. Do you want a child from a man who is a slob or who will be happy to settle for a spot in Eighth Circle?" When speaking to Thayu, she used the more respectful *chya* pronouns.

"And the state of curliness of his hair determines his suitability?" Thayu used *nyo* pronouns back at her.

"It determines whether he's a slob or not."

"He's from Hedron. They don't care about curly hair."

"It doesn't look good. It shows that he doesn't care about his appearance."

"How often do we have to yell at you: he's from Hedron. Things are different there."

"Since he's here, he has to live by our rules."

"And his status stands or falls by the curliness of his hair?"

I shouted, "Stop it!"

They did.

There was a moment of intense silence in which Thayu glared daggers at Xinanu and Xinanu returned a haughty look across the room and the couch where the other last two women in my household watched the proceedings with wide eyes.

Deyu sat on the couch closest to the window, watching in her typical timid fashion. She was also new to my household, but unlike Xinanu, she came from a poor family in the Outer Circle. She and her *zhayma*, a young *zeyshi* man called Reida, had been Nicha's selection as subordinates. Both were still in that stage in life where they watched the world with wide eyes. As yet, she lacked confidence to speak to most people in the household, especially Xinanu.

Raanu, on the other hand, sat next to Deyu with her back straight, no doubt drinking in all the detail of the discussions. She was extremely smart and knew very well that as soon as she said something, someone would send her out of the room, where proper eight-year-olds belonged. I still had no idea why Ezhya had sent us his daughter to look after with virtually no prior notice.

After the embarrassing incident in the *zeyshi* warren, I had tried to keep her away from things that Ezhya might judge inappropriate for his daughter, such as graphic details of relationships between men and women. I assumed that she had asked Deyu to take her into the living room when we were interviewing the applicant, and that, despite being twice Raanu's age, Deyu was distinctly subordinate in that relationship.

Now that the object of curiosity was gone from the room, the domestic staff went back to work. Xinanu waddled to the door. Nicha offered her his arm and gave me a *sorry about that* look over her shoulder, although I wasn't sure why he should be sorry. Having a child was his right, and Xinanu would not stay for long. But yes, I disliked her. I just tried not to let it show. But she made it hard at times. Very hard.

Thayu finally left her spot at the doorpost and joined me on the couch.

"You don't seem entirely happy," I said, closing her in my arms. "I think this was the best candidate I've seen so far. In fact, I'd be happy to use him."

She sighed. "You know, I keep looking at these men wanting them to look like you."

"None of the Coldi will ever look like me." Although he did have my curly hair, so that was a bonus.

She shook her head. She was quiet for a while, with a far-off look in her eyes. If I had been wearing my feeder, I could have heard what she was thinking, but I only wore it when I absolutely had to.

She sighed. "I just don't think it's fair for you."

"I told you not to worry about me."

She stroked my cheek. "But *I* worry. If we go ahead with this, you must promise me that you find a woman to have your child."

I laughed. I could just about see myself walking around the social scene of Nations of Earth with that mission. "The women who could do that for me don't work like that." I supposed I could find a surrogate if I really wanted, but I didn't.

"Yes, you told me, but I've also read that in your world you do have these services for people who can't have children."

"Listen, Thayu. It's not important to me. If you have this child, he or she will be mine as well. Nicha's son will be mine because he'll live with us. Heck, I even consider Raanu part of this family—"

And I'd forgotten about the little rascal. She was watching us from the door opening into the hall, having worked out that adult things were much more interesting than her lessons.

I glared at her, and where many Coldi would have cringed or avoided my eyes, she stared back unashamedly. Growing up with only adults in the Inner Circle, she was maturing fast, and would whup Ezhya's backside very soon if he gave her half a chance. Why ever he had sent his daughter here, I couldn't begin to guess—he knew we had the talks coming up.

I put on my Serious Adult voice. "Raanu, can you go back to your work?"

"But it's boring."

"Boring?" Thayu snorted and pushed herself out of my arms. "If you think that learning about all the *gamra* entities is boring, you know nothing about boring. In fact, I might teach you something about boring, if you really want to know."

Raanu shook her head, wide-eyed. Thayu's definition of boring was likely to be a thousand times more boring than hers.

Thayu smiled and stroked the top of Raanu's head. "Do your work, pebble, and I promise that if you can recite all the core *gamra* members and their representatives to me, I will take you for an interesting outing."

"Are we going to go on a boat?"

"Yes, we can go on a boat—if you behave and are careful." She was still from the generation that had been told to be afraid of open water. The saying went that the older Coldi people would drown in a teacup. The younger generation, however, considered regular rain, and even flooding, a normal thing. That was how quickly the planet was changing.

"I want to see the eels."

Those rare, huge creatures that lived in the waters surrounding the islands that made up Barresh.

"Do your work, and I'll see what I can do. I can't promise anything about the eels, though. Eels are wild creatures. We can go where they live, but I can't make them turn up. But we can do all the other things, once you have done your work."

Raanu drooped off to the room down the hall where she slept. Thayu smiled after her.

I said, "You still haven't answered my question about our latest candidate. I'm happy to use him. The decision is up to you."

She looked at her hands. "Oh, I don't know." Then she sighed and looked up at me. "I would like to have *your* child."

And that, of course, was impossible, and it was the thing she always said.

I didn't push her because Thayu disliked being pushed. This was probably as much of a reply as I'd get from her now. She'd think about it and would probably come around to my point of view after a few days. I thought that she liked him. At least she hadn't rolled her eyes as she had with the other candidates.

I'd send the young man a message letting him know we'd be in contact later.

It was probably better to let the matter rest until the negotiations about the *zeyshi* claim on Asto were over. I was going to need Thayu for however long that process would take.

We had taken some time off to meet the young man, but now it was time to get back to serious work. Thayu went to the hub and I wandered down the hall.

Last year, after I had saved Ezhya's position, he had paid me a substantial amount of money. I'd used some of it to knock out a wall between two adjoining rooms at the very end of the top floor corridor, creating one big office space where I could work with a few other people. I'd replaced the outer wall with a huge window that over-looked the marshland. It had become a light-filled, open room with locally-made furniture, including a big desk of solid timber made by one of Eirani's many cousins.

At the moment, this desk was covered in electronic devices, bits of paper and various plates and cups. Before Devlin came to tell me that Menor had turned up, I'd been reading through the text of the *zeyshi* claim for Asto for the umpteenth time, and the document was still open on my reader. The full text of the document took up only ten pages. It listed a number of references to witness accounts and studies on the history of Asto's treatment of the *zeyshi* people, who were, in short, people lacking the *sheya* association instinct that defined Coldi society. Studies had found that there was a spectrum of characteristics between Coldi and Aghyrian people, from muscular, broad-shouldered people with a strong *sheya* instinct, Coldi hair with its metallic sheen and gold-flecked eyes to taller people with dark eyes, dark hair, no *sheya* instinct. The most Aghyrian of all had even lost the Coldi ability to vary their body temperature. Most importantly, the distinction Coldi versus Aghyrian was not black and white and the document was written from that standpoint. In a nutshell, it said, *These are your own people and you have treated them like crap for millennia. They have the right to establish their own legal entity where they see fit and claim ownership of the products of their labour.*

The trouble with all of this was, of course, that *gamra* would absolutely agree with the statement, that *ownership of the products of their labour* could be taken to mean that they would control the Exchange, and that *wherever they see fit* could mean the entire greater Athyl basin, the home of close to one billion native Coldi people.

So we'd been testing the document for legal loopholes, of which there were many, and different interpretations, of which there were many as well.

There were two paper copies of it on the desk, one annotated with Chief Delegate Akhtari's notes, and the other full of legal references scribbled by Veyada.

I put them side by side.

If I'd learned anything about the claim document by going over it so many times in the last few months, it was that it had been written by a skilled lawyer and politician. The text was full of tricky wordings which could have different meanings depending on how you interpreted the surrounding text.

Yet the delegation that the *zeyshi* had sent, and that had arrived a few days ago, didn't match the calibre of the text, something Veyada and I had discussed a lot.

It included the *zeyshi* leader Nayu Omi and the Aghyrian woman Evala Sadet Arwan, whose temper didn't seem to have improved since I saw her in the *zeyshi* warren on Asto. The other delegation members, Chyana, Daranu and Emi, seemed little more than guards and scribes. I'd met the delegation briefly when taking them to their accommodation, and those three had barely said anything.

"None of these people are capable of writing an intricate legal claim like this," had been Veyada's first observation.

"They're negotiators, not lawyers."

"I know, but I don't think they even understand why the claim cannot so easily be dismissed. The sophistication is far beyond anything people without formal legal training could produce."

"Maybe it's s fluke."

Veyada laughed. "You're not a lawyer either, or you wouldn't say this."

True. "That's why I have you."

Veyada's words struck a chord with me and served as warning for the negotiations yet to come: these people were a scouting party for the real deal, and I hadn't a clue who these smart *zeyshi* lawyers could be. I suspected they had sent me the very people I had already met, presumably to make me feel at ease, and they clearly had some big guns kept under wraps until the real negotiations started.

In the past I might have felt sorry for the *zeyshi* and the tales of their mistreatment, but this reminded me to never, ever trust them.

The problem was that while I knew a fair bit about law, I wasn't a lawyer either. Veyada had combed over the document and all his notes made my head spin. They dealt with Asto law, *gamra* law and a little bit of Barresh law. Some of his comments were in direct conflict with what Delegate Akhtari had said. She was probably three times his age, and had lifelong experience at *gamra*. Who did I trust? Her or him?

She was Aghyrian; he was from Asto's Inner Circle. They were on opposite ends of the debate over this claim and let no opportunity go wasted to inform me of that fact. It made for an interesting negotiation environment.

And meanwhile, I was sitting here at my desk staring into the golden afternoon outside. A couple of lily harvesting boats returned from the fields with bulging nets of flowers. Some days, I would happily trade my position with theirs. My head was filled with worry, and I wasn't doing much work on this damn document that, to put it mildly, baffled me.

There was a small noise behind me. I turned around, expecting Eirani with tea. It was Eirani, but instead of tea, she had a *you have to come sort this thing out* expression on her face. Please, not another argument with Xinanu.

But she said, "Muri, Devlin needs you to come."

Devlin? That likely had something to do with the hub. Please not another Exchange outage. Or something else that we really, really couldn't use at the moment.

I left the office and walked down the corridor to the hub, which was off the main hall opposite the living room. Devlin sat in the semi-darkness on the main control bench, with the blue light from the screens and projections reflected over his oh-so-serious face.

He nodded when I came in. He was keihu, young and not as rotund as many of his kinsmen. He wore the hair around his face in little plaits of different lengths adorned with beads and ribbons in the colour of his family—golden yellow. The loose curls at the back of his head fell to his shoulders. The staff had insisted that they needed a house uniform, and I'd let Eirani choose what it would look like. A simple light grey tunic stitched through with thread in *gamra* cobalt blue. That thread looked black in the low light.

I sat on the bench next to him. "Is there a problem?"

He was looking at something on one of the screens. An Exchange log, I thought.

Devlin met my eyes with his dark brown ones. "It's that boy again."

2

———————

"THAT BOY", OF COURSE, was Reida, Deyu's *zhayma*. The two reported to Nicha, balancing Sheydu and Veyada who were subordinate to Thayu. I'd asked Veyada if the two lots of *zhayma*s weren't better off having similar experiences and being of similar age, but he'd said that large age and experience differences were very common.

Both youngsters were the result of Nicha's trip to the Outer Circle, where I'd suggested he find some people with knowledge of the *zeyshi* to complete our household. Both Reida and Deyu were Coldi, but had a fair bit of Aghyrian blood. Deyu came from a respected family in the Outer Circle. This was another surprise to me, that there *were* respected families in the Outer Circle. Sometimes the people in power spoke as if the lower-ranked citizens were all criminals, but in fact each Circle had its own ecosystem, and being the most populous of all, the Outer Circle's power structures were by far the most complex. Deyu's family owned businesses and there was food on the table in her house every night. Reida, however, was *zeyshi* and was proving all the bad clichés about those people to be true.

"What has he done this time?" I should have wondered why he wasn't in the room with us earlier, and sent someone out to check on him. With Reida, any absence was cause for suspicion.

Devlin said, "I just spoke to a city guard. They've detained him at the guard station."

"Again? Which councillor's daughter's bedroom did he climb into this time?" I spread my hands. I was getting pretty sick of this, to be honest.

"They didn't say. They requested that someone come to pick him up and sign for his release."

"*Pay* the bond more likely." And of course I had to go. Last time, Nicha had tried to collect him, but they wouldn't let him go until the person who was "the head of the household" signed that the miscreant would be berated and told not to do it again.

"What does he think he's doing? It's the third time they've locked him up. Does he think I have nothing better to do than go and rescue him?"

"I don't know, Muri. I'm just reporting what they said."

I sighed. "I know. Thank you, Devlin. Guess I'll have to get him, then."

I left the hub.

Deyu occupied the small bedroom opposite the entrance to the bathroom. She sat on the comfy chair next to the window studying.

When I came in, she flung her reader aside and rose to greet me in the subservient position. Because she was in training, she wasn't allowed to wear *gamra* colours yet, so she wore our house uniform.

"It's all right, relax," I said.

Her shoulders went down a tiny fraction.

"What did Reida say to you about where he went this morning?"

"Oh. He didn't say anything." Her cheeks went red. I told her repeatedly not to flinch when someone asked her a direct question, but that was proving very hard to unlearn. The instinct was very strong in her.

"You should ask him when he goes out. Where is he going, when is he planning on coming back? Does he need any help? Especially the latter. He's your *zhayma*."

"I . . . didn't think about that." She looked down. "I'm sorry. I'll do better next time."

"Never mind. Come with me."

"Where are we going?"

"He's got himself arrested."

"What? Again?"

The surprise was evident in her voice. He clearly hadn't communicated his intentions to her.

"We've got to go and pick him up. I want you to come with me. Maybe you can get some information out of him."

"Yes, yes. Sure." She hurried across the room and put on her sandals. "I'm ready."

Being Coldi and female made her smaller than me. As a healthy Coldi female, she would be a lot stronger than I was, but she cut a very timid figure while walking next to me. Her body temperature had long since dropped and she no longer wore her temperature retaining suit underneath the loose, local grey trousers and kaftan of our house uniform. As an Outer Circle inhabitant, she was used to spending a lot of time outdoors and her skin was still quite dark compared to that of Thayu or Xinanu.

Nicha told me that he had picked her up while working in one of the toughest bars in the Outer Circle. I'd asked her about it, but she didn't seem to want to talk about it, speaking in general platitudes like "It was all right," and "It was very busy." I never could get through that wall that she built inside her, behind which she'd hidden what had happened in this place, because obviously something had happened that had made her as jumpy and nervous as she was.

I didn't see Nicha anywhere, but I met Thayu in the corridor, and she asked if she needed to come.

"No, I want you to keep working." She was still doing background checks on the members of the *zeyshi* delegation. Their personal files hadn't been released to us—they probably never existed—and there were big gaps in their data. Thayu was scarily good at this type of work. I explained briefly to her what I was going to do and she gave me the *what, again?* eyeroll.

Sheydu came into the hall and said she'd come instead of Thayu. She had probably heard me talking to Devlin and had already strapped on a gun and put on her boots. And Sheydu was happiest when holding a gun or blowing something up.

The three of us left the apartment not much later, picking up Evi at the door. We crossed the wide avenues and courtyards of the *gamra* complex on the way to the station. It was mid-afternoon and the air had that pressing pre-monsoonal tension, the combination of high humidity and higher than average temperatures in which people sweltered and trees and plants let their leaves droop. Big clouds were building at the top of the escarpment in the distance, but they merely mocked us, because they would just hang around up there until they collapsed later in the day. It would be a couple of weeks yet before they developed enough strength to start rolling in and bringing the thunderstorms.

Trains were a recent addition to Barresh. Their most important function was to provide a link between the two natural and half a dozen artificial islands that made up the city-state, which lay in a vast marshy delta. As a result, all lines went over the water and all stations lay at the shore. Usually, there was also a harbour with jetties for ferries and water taxis and anchorage for private vessels and commercial agricultural or fishing boats. Commercial ships were absent from the jetty at the *gamra* island, but a tour boat lay moored on the other side of the station. One day, when all this madness was over, I would hire one of those and take the entire household for a trip to the beach. Maybe we could go to the Crystal Pools, too. If ever we got the time. I'd been promising everyone this trip for years. In fact, if ever we got the time, we should probably hire a larger boat and go right offshore to the tropical seas of the Thousand Island Ridge, where apparently you could swim with creatures that looked like scaled dinosaurs.

If only. *Stop daydreaming, Mr Wilson.*

A smattering of people milled around on the platform, mostly domestic staff going shopping in town. There was also a senior admin officer with an assistant, both carrying bags, probably on their way to the airport, and a couple of administrative workers on their way home. I was the only person in full blue uniform and got the polite treatment with little bows and nods that I had gotten used to, but couldn't say I liked.

The train arrived, a sleek affair with carriages that looked like bullets. There were only three. The morning, afternoon and early evening trains were the busiest and the trains usually had five or six carriages.

Inside the carriage, the air was cool and smelled of paint.

We sat down in one of the cubicles where seats faced each other. Deyu next to the window, me next to her, and Sheydu and Evi opposite us.

The train took off with a barely perceptible judder and soon we zoomed over the wetlands: marshy fields with reed clumps in shallow water, occasional small islands with megon trees with their characteristic drooping branches, and the occasional canal. Later, there were fields of floating lilies, their leaves bright green.

None of our group said anything.

I hadn't expected much conversation from Sheydu and Evi, and Deyu had a very strong *sheya* instinct and avoided looking me in the eye at the best of times, but today she seemed even more timid than usual.

"Do you know if Reida had any kind of problem?" I asked her.

"He didn't say," she said into the window.

"Deyu, I would like to remind you that you can always tell me or Nicha if anything is wrong."

"Yes. I know. Thank you very much." She glanced briefly at Sheydu who watched with her usual passive face. Sheydu's expression looked quite angry and disapproving in its relaxed state. She had never said so, but I had no doubt that she disapproved deeply of my appointing two Outer Circle people to the household. She had, however, complained openly about the two of them being *kids*, not even old enough to be provided with a feeder. Not old enough to receive weapons training and carry a proper gun.

My eyes met Sheydu's.

You're not helping. She's petrified of you. But I wasn't wearing my feeder and she couldn't hear me and that was probably just as well. *Petrified* of her was just the way Sheydu liked people.

In response to my question why Nicha had chosen such young people as subordinates, he had said that it was common practice amongst the middle classes on Asto to take trainees into an association, something Veyada had confirmed. Nicha's mother was Second Circle—a lot older than his father, who would have been an adolescent rising star at the time of Nicha's birth. Second Circle was solidly upper middle class in Athyl. They were the engine room of Coldi society, that hid behind the posturing of the Inner and First Circles. They were the people who controlled the assets that kept Asto running. If there was such a thing as philanthropy in Asto's society, Second, Third and Fourth Circles was where it could be found.

I liked Nicha's thoughts behind choosing the pair of them, but I wasn't sure if it was working as well as he'd hoped, and I had the feeling that we were headed for some sort of blow-up, which I was sure would come at the most inconvenient time for everybody.

The Barresh guard station was on the ground floor of one of the city's oldest buildings. It was a cramped, bare office with a tiny window under an overhanging balcony.

Besides a counter where a guard stood, there was no furniture. The only other door out of the room consisted of a metal grate, behind the counter that led to the dungeons. The concrete floor bore stains from the filth of ages.

The moment I stepped inside, and breathed the humid, stifling air with its stale smell, I was reminded of how much I hated this circus. The Barresh guards were going to play stupid games with us. They were a toothless tiger showing off dentures. They wouldn't charge, they would just make empty threats to show how much they disliked us. The stupidity of it hurt my brain.

The guard at the desk was the same guy from last time, too, a huge fellow with a shortage in the brains department that made him painfully slow at completing electronic questionnaires. A brain shortage which he took pride in displaying.

How long had Reida lived in my household?

I answered him, but his system should tell him from last time I'd collected the boy here.

Where did he normally live?

Previously on Asto, Outer Circle, now in my house. The system should tell him that, too, since I'd already answered that question twice in recent months.

Who employed him and in what capacity?

I did. He was Nicha's assistant. Same thing. I'd told him this twice before.

And so on and so forth. It was a surprise that the man could hear my replies through the gnashing of my teeth.

While he was picking out my responses on his screen with a single finger—whatever happened to thought readers or feeders?—I tried to get information out of him in return: what had the young man been arrested doing? What was the charge?

He said there would be no charge, as long as I could guarantee that it wouldn't happen again. I had to make an effort not to roll my eyes. I'd guaranteed this twice before. Why did they even believe me?

Oh, I understood it well enough, though. As my employee, Reida fell under *gamra* law. He'd been arrested in Barresh proper in an area that fell under their law. Barresh couldn't lock *gamra* people up for slight transgressions, because if it went to court, *gamra*'s pockets were much deeper than the council's. As to why they didn't simply extradite people to the *gamra* system, no one knew, but we suspected there was someone's loss of face involved. Probably some of the influential council families, those same ones who complained the loudest about "all kinds of criminals" being allowed to enter the city through the provision for *gamra* workers.

These guards were caught in the middle of that dispute, and I tried very hard to feel sympathy for them, but this particular man wasn't helping.

As to where Reida had been arrested doing what, the guards had been vague the previous two occasions he had been arrested, and this time was no different. The guard said he'd been caught climbing a first floor balcony of one of the commercial buildings. Apparently, one didn't climb balconies in Barresh. I didn't have the energy to argue about it. The best thing for me was just to answer his questions and ask the young man later. Last time it had been trying to climb into a councillor's daughter's bedroom window. Climbing things was obviously the young man's forte. Whatever happened to doors?

Evi and Sheydu had remained outside the office. Occasionally one of them would walk past the window. Deyu was standing in front of the tiny window—with metal bars—looking into the street.

By the time the guard was finally done, the light that fell through the tiny window had started to turn golden. He turned away from his screen and took his keys. I knew about the next bit, too. I gestured Deyu to come over.

The guard called a colleague to come to the other side of the metal grated door in the back of the room. The door opened with the aid of a really old-fashioned key and an even more old-fashioned creak, and the front office guard passed us onto the prison guard, who looked at me with a *not again* expression.

The door slammed shut behind me.

Let's just get this over and done with, right?

Deyu clamped her arms around herself. Unpleasant memories?

The old Barresh jail was located beneath the guard station, one of those secret corners of Barresh that a hundred years of rebuilding and reform had passed by.

For the sake of prison security and inmate discomfort, it was the only place in town that had been built entirely underground, and the humidity and mugginess closed in on us as soon as we were through that metal door.

Deyu and I followed the second guard down a set of dark and slippery stairs, our footsteps muffled in the constricted space. I could see little more than the back of the warden's uniform, broad and thick in the waist. He carried a light, which cast long shadows on the slime-covered walls.

At the bottom, we entered a second corridor with cells on both sides that disappeared into the darkness. The prison's stone walls were meant to keep out the rising water from outside, because we were well below the water table, but judging by the puddles on the floor, those old limestone blocks and the cement between them were no longer up to the task. The surface of the water reflected the sparse light with oily stains.

"Don't step in," the guard said in heavily accented Coldi.

Probably because of the risk of infection.

Deyu gave a tiny gasp.

"Are you all right?"

"I don't like it here." Her voice sounded small. Yes, I decided, definitely the result of some traumatic experience, maybe in the underground *zeyshi* warrens?

Something scuttled away in the dark space of one of the cells. Probably a ringgit or something similar. Those huge insectlike crabs lived in the reeds that surrounded the island. They had a habit of creeping into houses that were close to the water and building huge communal nests in the darkness under floorboards. They were fairly harmless, if messy and in possession of the loudest mating call I'd ever heard.

The warden stopped at a cell on the right hand side to open the door with a clanking of keys and creaking of metal on metal. Yup. Just like in a medieval movie set.

In the corner, on a bare wooden bed with a hard-looking mattress, sat the young man we had come to see: Reida.

As soon as the cell door was open, Deyu slipped past me and threw herself into his arms. He held her, softly speaking to her. At least this part of the association worked as it should. Their personalities might differ as night and day, but I had no doubt that they were true *zhayma*s.

A night in the cell had not been kind to Reida.

His face was pale, his cheeks smudged and his hair hung limp on both sides of his head. Loose. Very un-Coldilike. His upper arm bore a nasty bruise under his encircling black tattoo of thorns and leaves.

He did his best to maintain an angry glare, but I didn't miss the flicker of relief that washed over his young face as his eyes met mine. In the few months I'd known him, I'd learned that he was very bad at hiding his emotions.

"Get up," the warden said in keihu.

Deyu helped him up, but the warden shooed her out of the cell, and she retreated to the door. Reida stood forlorn in the middle of the cell. His traditional *shayka* was dirty and ripped at his left knee. He was wearing the cream yellow one—I liked that particular one. He wore metal braces around his ankles. Good grief. He was Coldi and stronger than most locals, but was that necessary?

The warden knelt, searching in his bundle of keys to undo the lock in the ankle braces.

"You're treating him like he's a dangerous criminal," I said, in keihu.

"All criminals are dangerous, Delegate."

"Your colleague said that he was climbing over a balcony. I guess he wasn't meant to be where he was arrested, but what else did he do that justifies this treatment?"

Reida said in Coldi, "It's because I'm Coldi and he hates Coldi." Oh no, I wasn't fooled. In the short time he'd been here, he'd picked up keihu and understood most conversations.

I frowned at Reida over the man's back in a look that hopefully said *Shut up while you're ahead.*

Reida averted his eyes. No, he wasn't stupid, if rash and entitled.

The ankle braces clinked on the floor. The warden stepped back. "Hands up and out."

Reida spread his hands wide. He walked stiffly to the door, where Deyu waited for him. She took his hand, and he stroked her cheek.

The guard said, "You're free to go, providing you behave yourself. The Delegate has been so kind to put up a bond but I'm sure he has a thing or two to say to you. So I don't want to see you back here again, right?"

Reida said nothing, his lips pressed together. I found out on a previous occasion that he had not a skerrick of shame in him. Because getting him out of jail was my task, right? Because I was the head of the association.

The warden sighed. He looked at me. "I can't keep reprimanding him, Delegate."

"I understand." He'd said that last time, too. Sooner or later, this young man was going to create a diplomatic incident. And yes, it would be my fault, and no, I had no idea why this young man kept doing this and why Nicha didn't seem to have any control over him.

In silence, we climbed the stairs, past the other guard into the little ground floor office, and then into the street, where Sheydu and Evi joined us, both with solemn nods. They knew the drill. They could probably tell from my expression that I wasn't happy.

Not fucking happy indeed.

We started walking. Evi went first, looking impressive in his black gear.

I walked behind him with Deyu and Reida, and Sheydu behind us.

I waited until we were well away from the guard station before I spoke. "What was it this time? The guard said they arrested you trying to climb on the balcony of the commercial building."

Reida looked down and mumbled something incoherent about helping a friend.

"What sort of friend and what did he want? Couldn't this friend climb the balcony for himself? What?"

He sniffed. "Nothing." He didn't meet my eyes.

"Reida, answer me."

He didn't look at me. "I thought the guard would have told you?"

"He did, but I want to hear it from you, because there were some large gaps in his story where I assume you can be more illuminating to me." I wasn't sure if he was just playing dumb or genuinely didn't know how little information those guards were willing to share, especially on matters of decency of female members of councillors' families. "Why were you trying to climb into that building?"

Another cringe. Then he looked at me, his expression defiant. "I was doing work for Nicha."

"Nicha would never send you on jobs that would involve your getting arrested. Don't try to jump around and don't try to blame this on anyone else, least of all my second." It still hurt me to say that, but I had come to accept that the current status of our relationship meant that Nicha was my second.

"All right then! I heard Thayu and Veyada say that they needed to get bugs into the merchanting office so I thought I'd do it for them, especially since I accidentally fried the previous ones."

Yes, that was another of the mishaps that plagued this young man. He'd accidentally routed a huge burst of data through those mostly dormant devices that were part of the security network that my staff tapped into, and taken all of them out. And he was right: he *did* always want to help, even if his *help* often made things worse.

I sighed. "Look, I think I've said this before, but I'll say it again: in case we need someone to go into buildings illegally, that is Sheydu and Veyada's task. Because they have the skill to get out of buildings again without being arrested."

Did I imagine things or did Sheydu wear a gloating grin on her face?

He shrugged. "I'm sorry."

"Reida, look at me."

We stopped in the street. While people walked past us on both sides, I faced him.

Recently, a storm had taken out a good number of the giant ancient trees in the old city, allowing the low sunlight to penetrate to street level.

Even with the sun in his eyes, his irises were eerie black, lacking the golden flecks that so many Coldi had. He displayed a kaleidoscope of emotion. Angry and sullen. Bored. Disappointed. Impatient.

"You cannot be sorry and expect it to be forgotten and forgiven, because that is not good enough. If it happened only once, all right, but I don't understand why you keep doing this. Why are you not listening to Nicha? Why did you—"

"I said I agreed that was stupid of me."

"Don't interrupt me."

He cringed again and a strange feeling struck me. He acted like a belligerent teenager. An *Earth human* teenager.

I had the right to hit him for his transgression, according to Coldi custom. But I couldn't do that, because hitting people for disobedience was not my thing and, besides, he was much stronger than I was; but it was clearly what he expected. My heart hammered against my ribs. Belting him here on the street would make me look bad. Letting his transgression slip would make me look weak in his eyes.

This young man was on the bottom tier of my association and was meant to obey me unconditionally. He was meant to perform a subservient greeting when I faced him. I'd told everyone in my house that I didn't care much for this custom and I really didn't, but everyone in my house had trouble weaning themselves off the habit. Except this young man. He did not act subservient and come to think of it, he had never acted subservient to me and, much as I hated it, he should have.

"Look, let's go home and deal with it there." Using that expression *dealing with* that held so much threat in Coldi. Dealing with often meant guns, violence. Death even.

Did I imagine it or did he cringe?

I should ask Nicha about this, because he had picked the pair of them out. Both of them were supposed to have the association instinct, but I wasn't sure about it anymore. Yet I couldn't imagine that Nicha would have made such a blatant mistake. I couldn't imagine why Nicha would have chosen someone whose only contribution to my household had been to create trouble from the very moment he walked in the door.

3

———————

W E WALKED THROUGH the main street, full of people having finished work at this time of the day, shopping at the little food stalls that spread a wonderful smell through the streets.

Groups of people streamed out of the airport building, talking and carrying bags. An army of young men with carts waited at the entrance, a highly organised fleet of motorised rickshaws that would take visitors with a lot of luggage to the guesthouses, their private accommodation or either of the two nearby railway stations that were not attached to the main building.

We walked along the fence to one of those stations, situated at the end of the jetty below the airport. It was hot here, and air shimmered above the paving.

The tarmac on the other side of the fence was a hive of activity. *Gamra* traffic had their own section at the very back, where arriving delegates could get straight to the station. Barresh was the first *gamra* seat where this infrastructure had been purpose-built, and it worked so well that it had been decided that when inevitably Chief Delegate Akhtari retired, the *gamra* seat would not move to another entity.

Since the assembly would be sitting in two days' time—and damn it, was that all we had to prepare?—there was a lot of activity at that end of the building. Many delegates travelled on shuttles, but some of the more important ones had their own transport. I glanced at all the craft parked there, half expecting Ezhya Palayi's craft to be there. A few days ago, it had come in unexpectedly to drop Raanu at our house. I had agreed to host her but would personally have picked a better time. Ezhya rarely divulged his reasons and since he barely acknowledged her as his daughter in public, I had accepted her visit. Raanu was cheeky, but smart; and I liked her. She behaved when she needed to, and she got on well with Thayu and the staff.

As of now, Ezhya's craft had not arrived, but the Damarcians were here, and so was the delegation from Hedron.

At the very back of the *gamra* allocated parking space stood a number of unmarked shuttles. They looked like commercial freight vessels, but they lacked the insignia of the Pilot's Guild or the Couriers' Guild. Otherwise, they were very plain and very non-descript, and some supplies of very ordinary goods stood on pallets waiting to be loaded. A couple of people stood talking next to one of those pallets. They wore plain, dark colours, which were clearly not uniforms.

My heart jumped.

There was only one organisation I knew that made a point of using unmarked transport and non-uniform dress in public: the Asto armed forces. It also made sense that they would be here. They would hang around in orbit, keeping an eye on the *zeyshi* group and the negotiations that concerned their world. But by the look of all the supplies being loaded, there was a large ship in orbit. A very large ship. Even the ship I'd travelled in to Asto had only one surface transport shuttle which was used sparsely. Most of the crew lived aboard and grew their own food. If they ever left the ship, it was to go into one of the orbiting stations. I didn't know where they got their supplies. They either grew their own or were supplied by even more secret military ships.

All of that raised the question: Why were they so blatant about their presence by coming down here for supplies?

The Coldi military only came out of the shadows for two reasons: bluff and armed action. I suspected they even preferred the latter from a position of cover.

Thayu might know what they were doing here, but then again, she might not. It often surprised me how little she knew of her father's activities.

We left the airport behind and walked down the hillside in full blast of the hot western sunlight. Those clouds we'd seen earlier had indeed collapsed, leaving a virtually clear sky.

Phew, it was hot. The sweat ran down my back under my shirt. That was one of the disadvantages of the cobalt blue: every little wet spot showed up on it.

I was alone in my suffering, because no one else cared. The others were all Coldi and the heat didn't bother them.

We entered the station just as a train arrived at the platform.

The carriage was about half full of people going back with shopping, *gamra* domestic staff with their purchases from the markets.

We sat in the aisle seats, near a group of children. There were six of them, of primary school age and dressed in prim dark blue uniforms, accompanied by one older girl. She told her companions, in Aghyrian and in a slightly too-loud voice, "That man is an official delegate for *gamra*. You have to greet them politely any time you see anyone wearing that colour blue in the street." She probably didn't realise that I understood her. Aghyrian shared some very basic grammatical structures with Coldi. The pronoun situation was a lot simpler, but oh the noun declensions!

The little ones turned around to gawk at me. Three were dark-haired and dark-eyed, one boy had auburn hair with hazel eyes and a distinctive olive complexion. A girl had hair as white as was common for upper class Mirani people, but her eyes were sand-coloured and the last one, a boy, almost radiated orange light for the colour of his hair. His eyes were intense green.

The children all gave me polite nods. *Delegate.* Then they returned their attention to the girl, who was now explaining about the history of the islands in the haughty way I'd come to associate with Aghyrians. For all I knew, she could be Marin Federza's daughter.

The train set off, gliding over the rails that connected the islands at high speed and with very little sound.

Occasionally, one of the children would frown at Reida who sat opposite me, doing his best, but failing, to cover the rip and muddy patches in his *shayka*.

The children were very polite and said nothing, and sat in their seats with their backs held straight. They didn't yell, they didn't fidget, they didn't fight. They listened to the older girl, who was still explaining, occasionally interspersed with remarks like *we built that* or *that was our design*.

I often wondered what their adults said about non-Aghyrian people, in that walled-off compound of theirs, where all the adults were Aghyrian and where they were taught that their home was Asto and that without their ancestors, the Exchange wouldn't exist, there would be no space travel, and basically none of the other people would exist because their ancestors had seeded all the other human populations. They learned that all science was Aghyrian and that the Coldi had tried to deny their status as artificial race for many years and had even gone as far as locking up Aghyrians as deranged freaks. Maybe they learned that if only the Aghyrians withdrew consent for everyone to use *their* technology, society would collapse.

The term "brainwashing" came to mind.

It was a wonder that not all of them turned out as arrogant as Trader Delegate Marin Federza.

We didn't speak much in our group on the ride home. Our fellow passengers were only children, but I felt uncomfortable discussing anything of importance in their presence. Aghyrians were very intelligent. They matured early. I didn't trust them.

Reida stared out the window, trying to avoid everyone's gazes. Sheydu was fiddling with something on her reader. Deyu pretended not to be there. Evi did what security did best: sat very still and watched.

The *gamra* island was at the end of the line, and lot of people, including the children, got off at the second-last stop, leaving only us and the other *gamra* personnel, two old men in admin uniforms. They raised eyebrows at Reida. He was that kind of young man, with his tattoos and wild hair and his sullen look.

I couldn't help the tattoos, but I could certainly do something about the hair and the defensive expression, yet getting angry at the young man hand-picked by Nicha was not something I looked forward to.

———

When we arrived at my apartment, Thayu came into the hall from the hub as soon as the door shut behind us. "Ah, there you are. Can you come in here for a moment—"

She looked from me to Reida and his muddied and ripped *shayka* and back again. "What a right state you're in, young man."

Reida cringed.

"I'm getting very sick of this," I said.

"I told you I was only trying to help—"

I turned to him. "Be quiet. Go to your room and stay there."

He nodded and drooped off. Deyu went with him, her arm over his shoulder.

Thayu watched him go, a troubled expression on her face. I knew what she was thinking. He was supposed to answer unconditionally to Nicha and certainly to me.

"All right, now, what did you want to tell me?" Was it even something I'd want to know?

"You need to come into the hub to see it."

Damn it, what now?

I followed her into the hub, where it was hot and stuffy and it smelled of keihu and Coldi sweat.

Devlin sat at the central control bench, working on something that I judged to be one of his study projects—he was still doing courses sent to him from Damarq. He flicked that projection aside where it hung, half finished, in the air. Not a study project, I saw, but a fact sheet on each of the Aghyrian delegates that would take part in the negotiations. We knew all the Barresh Aghyrians, but there were large gaps in the background of the *zeyshi* ones which it looked like Devlin was filling, probably with help from Thayu.

Good. I could use that.

He brought up the Exchange logo, which twirled in the centre of the room while the machines connected.

"Is there a problem?" I asked, liking this less and less.

"Not immediately, no, but this happened this afternoon." The projection showed that connection had been established. He flicked the main projector into life, found the news feed and moved the log slide back to this afternoon. The projection showed various types of communication going in and out. Veyada had been checking some law database. Thayu was on the central Athyl database. Data scrolled over each part of the projection. Devlin had been working on that same document that he'd shoved to the side when we came in.

All of a sudden, a strobe-like signal crossed the workspace. It flickered on and off for a few seconds and vanished.

In the replay, Thayu exclaimed, "What the hell. . . ?"

Devlin replayed it. We watched, and when he killed the playback, we all stared at each other.

"What was that?"

"Your guess is as good as mine," Thayu said in that dark tone that told me that she was thinking the same as I was: more tomfoolery by that Aghyrian ship that had caused the outage of the entire Exchange network.

"Do we know where it came from?"

"The Exchange is checking that," Devlin said.

"Do they suggest it could be that old ship?"

"They are investigating it. They won't say any more until they have more data." Devlin gave me a dark look. "They've suspended all travel in and out of Barresh until midnight. They'll make another decision by then."

"It's affected only Barresh?"

"At this point in time, yes."

Phew. "And it hasn't come back?"

He shook his head.

"That's a good thing, at least." But I remembered that the major burst of energy that had fried the Exchange had given a few warning blips in the days prior to the incident, too. They were right in suspending all non-essential travel. We couldn't have a repeat of that fiasco.

"Have they warned Damarq?" The main Exchange node.

"They have. Everyone's on standby."

Not that that would make a lot of difference. Building up the Exchange network had taken thousands of years. Re-establishing links, if they were broken, took weeks at the very least, no matter how prepared everyone was for the eventuality, and everyone had been very nervous since that disaster.

We'd since discovered the old Aghyrian ship that may or may not be the same one that went missing after the meteorite strike on Asto, but our complete failure to raise a response from this ship had made people question if this ship was even live or just an empty shell responding to automated processes set up years ago. Things didn't decay in space as they did on planets, and I had learned that people had found operational artefacts that were even older than this ship. It was just that most of them were harmless. They were satellites or probes that travelled on the course set out for them thousands of years ago. Occasionally, they would send a little blip to planet-based equipment that had long since stopped working to people who had died millennia ago. None of them caused large-scale Exchange failures.

While the people who tracked the ship were debating its status, it worried me that a few things were converging that had also been in place just before the outage: an important date for the *zeyshi* claim on Asto and a large presence of the Asto army. That reminded me. . . .

"Thay', do you know if your father is here?"

She looked up at me and frowned. "Here in Barresh?"

"No." I glanced at the ceiling. "Up there somewhere. In orbit." From my trip to Asto in the military ship, I'd learned that Asha Domiri spent very little time on the ground. He was either on a ship or in that mindbogglingly huge, amazing, frightening space station that orbited Asto.

"I don't know. Why should he be here?"

"Because of the negotiations?"

Her frown deepened. "But these are only preliminary talks. The *zeyshi* group is small, they have no military capacity and the military has no interest in them from that point of view. We don't even think these will be the people to conduct the main negotiations once it goes before the assembly. And we may have a huge army, but even they can't hang around forever everywhere."

"That's what I thought, but there are a couple of unmarked shuttles at the airport loading supplies. They look very much like Asto military stocking up for a large ship in orbit."

"That's . . . odd."

"My thought exactly."

She fingered her upper lip. "Well, I suppose he *could* be here, but I have no idea why he should be."

He'd be floating well out of the atmosphere.

She brought up the Exchange transfer log, and found nothing, but the airport log showed the four ships—two departed since I'd seen them. They were listed as *private transport*. Thayu looked up and met my eyes. She nodded. That was Asto military. She stared at the screen, fingered her lip and shook her head.

Ever since we first received the *zeyshi* claim, I'd had that niggling feeling that it was more than what it looked like on the surface. It was either a cover for something else, or there were important people involved. The quality of the legal text of the document seemed to suggest that. It also seemed like everyone else was already aware of this, but neglected to communicate this to us, the very people appointed to organise the negotiations. At some point in the future we were going to find out what was really going on, and hopefully that time would be early enough to avert most of the proverbial shit hitting the proverbial fan; but with every day that passed, that possibility receded.

Eirani called in the hall that she had dinner ready.

Thayu pushed herself up from the bench and we both went into the living room, where there were only three plates on the table. Eirani had brought the dinner trolley up and Raanu was with her, taking bowls off the trolley and carefully setting them on the table, her face screwed up with the effort.

"Where is everyone?" I asked Eirani while I sat down.

"I don't know why, but everyone wants to eat in their rooms. Reida says that you sent him to his room—"

"I did."

"—and the young lady is staying there with him. Nicha says that the lady is tired and they'll eat in his room. Veyada ate in the kitchen. He and Sheydu went into town for something. They seemed in a hurry." She counted off on her fingers.

I had to admit that this development worried me a bit, especially from Nicha, but I could understand it because a lot of people in the house made no attempt to be friendly to Xinanu.

"Can I put the bread on the plates now?" Raanu asked.

Eirani smiled. "You are getting to be such a good girl. Yes, you can do that, but do be careful with the sauce because it is very hot."

"I don't care!" Raanu said. She held her hand against the outside of the pot. It would have been sitting in near-boiling water to cook, but Raanu didn't even flinch. That was Coldi for you.

"That's a very handy thing to be able to do if you're a cook," Eirani said.

"I want to be a cook. Can I?"

"It will be a long time before you grow up, little miss. Come with me, and we'll get the drinks. I must be getting old because I forgot to put them on the trolley." She bustled out of the room, Raanu skipping along in her wake.

"I know what you're thinking," Thayu said, after they had gone from the room.

"How can you know that? I'm not even wearing a feeder."

"And why are you not wearing it? You should. I don't understand why you're always so stubborn about it."

"And I don't understand how many more times I have to explain that I don't like people invading my thoughts."

"Baaah, you're so transparent, it doesn't matter if you wear it or not. Anyway, I don't like her either. She's arrogant."

I had to think for a bit who she was talking about. Xinanu, I concluded. "Thay', do you think Nicha likes her?"

I could see on her face that the question disturbed her. "He has to, doesn't he? He chose her. He signed the contract."

"Maybe he made a mistake and he regrets it?"

"There are no mistakes when *sheya* is involved. You either feel it or you don't."

"How would you explain it, then? He's miserable and she is the cause."

"Yeah, I think so. Frankly, it's got me baffled. But there is no point worrying about it. She'll be gone soon. It's a pity I don't have the time to search for herbs or other stuff at the markets here to bring on the birth early. I'm sure Nicha would thank me." She grinned.

But the thought that Nicha had selected this person who made him miserable, and also selected the two youngsters who didn't seem to listen to him, disturbed me. Those were two substantial errors of judgment, and I had trouble believing that Nicha could be so careless.

4

———————

NICHA AND XINANU didn't come to breakfast either, but Nicha came out of his room as I went back to our bedroom to get changed into my formal outfit—I hadn't wanted to wear it to breakfast so as not to get food on it.

He was just closing the door behind him—it was dark inside his room and a stuffy smell spread from the door.

"Everything all right?" I asked.

"Yes, yes." He turned around, meeting my eyes. He seemed . . . flighty, for want of a better word. Nervous. Guess I would be nervous, too, when Thayu was about to give birth.

But since when had I felt so distant from him?

He nodded—I wasn't quite sure what the gesture meant. "You're getting ready for the meeting?"

"I am."

"Well, I better get dressed then, too." He retreated back into the stuffy darkness of his room.

What an awkward conversation. Whatever happened to the trust we shared? Hell, the bed we shared. And the comments we always got at the Exchange in Athens about how well our partnership worked.

When I finished dressing, he was still inside, but left the door open. By the morning light that flooded the room, I spotted him nuzzling the soft skin under Xinanu's ear, while bent forward over her extended belly. I imagined myself doing that to Thayu. I'd again mentioned using Menor's seed when we were in bed last night, but she still refused to give me a clear answer. Frustration grew inside me. I would like it if just one part of my life went to plan, even if it was only a little part.

This association wasn't working and I had little time to find out why. The negotiations would be very difficult unless I found out what underlying issue made people jockey for the best seats in the house, and after being all tearful about my agreement to use a seed donor for a child, Thayu seemed to have changed her mind. And now Nicha behaved strangely and, come to think of it, I hadn't spoken to him on a one-on-one basis for quite some time. For crying out loud, I was trying to do the right thing.

Nicha must have known that I was watching, because he turned around.

He came into the corridor, letting the door roll shut behind him with a clatter of the slats.

"Are you sure that everything is all right?" I asked.

"Yes. Everything on track." I couldn't help notice that he sounded tired. "She's just feeling tired and her adaptation is still bothering her." Adaptation happened when Coldi dropped or raised their body temperature according to the environment.

"What about Reida?"

He gave me a startled look before schooling his face into a neutral expression. "What about him?"

"Did you talk to him after I picked him up from the jail?"

"Yes." Again, an awkward reply.

"What did he have to say? He seemed very incoherent when I asked him. His story doesn't add up. Something about trying to replace the bugs that you lost when he fried your system."

"He says he's . . . sorry. And inexperienced, as you can appreciate."

"I can. I understand, but do get the truth out of him, whatever that truth is."

Nicha nodded. Not entirely comfortable, I thought, but I had to let it rest for the time being.

I walked into the hall, where the others were also getting ready.

Thayu arrived from the hub wearing her one-piece suit, armour and two guns. She also carried a bag on her belt with electronics, and handed me a feeder. I took it from her. Her expression was smug.

I lifted the feeder to the back of my head, where it climbed into my hair and settled on my skin with a burst of warmth. The flood of messages that went through my head made me dizzy. I took a while to regain my balance.

You really shouldn't take it off for so long, Thayu said.

Yeah, yeah, I know, I know.

Veyada, dressed entirely in white, came from the end of the corridor, where he and Sheydu shared a room. The suit and knee-length overcoat looked magnificent on him. White was the colour of court officials on Asto, and we'd agreed that he would wear the official outfit to show his status as lawyer. Deyu came as assistant. She wore the plainest, most junior *gamra* uniform with the khaki shirt and trousers edged in blue. Nicha also came in guard black, wearing armour and weaponry. We had agreed that Sheydu would stay behind to keep Reida in line.

———

Sadet, Nayu and the other three members of the *zeyshi* Aghyrian delegation had arrived in Barresh two days ago. They were staying in a visiting diplomats' unit, which, apart from three sleeping rooms spread over two floors, had a meeting room on the very top level which offered a sweeping view over the water.

The room was very nice, and *gamra* staff in charge of the accommodation had provided tea and snacks, mostly fruit and other sweet things neatly arranged on two plates that stood in the middle of the large table.

The members of the *zeyshi* delegation were already in the room and, apart from our group, people from the Barresh Aghyrians would attend, as well as people to represent Asto. Delegate Ayanu of Asto came with two of her assistants, and Trader Delegate Marin Federza surprised us by turning up himself, without assistant.

That was rather strange. In previous discussions he had not shown much respect for the *zeyshi* group, which he regarded as usurpers and rude blow-ins—not without reason. Turning up in person meant that he now regarded their claim as significant. I wondered what had changed.

Through the feeder, I gathered that Thayu shared my concern.

Let's hope we don't get caught in an all-Aghyrian conflict, Nicha added.

Exactly. We didn't need to know the details of how they decided which Aghyrian group had the right to speak for all of them.

We went through the ritual of extensive introductions that were common for *gamra* meetings. Whenever a delegate took part in a committee, it was customary that the other participants each received a fact sheet about the person in question.

I was impressed with the fact sheet that Devlin had given me. It made mention of the fact that Nayu had once worked in Fourth Circle and it listed all the associations that she had been in contact with. Thayu had done some good work here.

Sadet's history was plain: born in the *zeyshi* warren, and lived there all her life. She had tried to get into Eighth Circle, but realised that she would probably do better with the *zeyshi* so she had stayed there.

According to the sheet, Marin Federza was born in Barresh. He made a great point of the fact that he was the legendary Daya Ezmi's grandson. He'd lived in the Aghyrian compound in Barresh until going to the Trader Academy. I thought of the children I'd seen on the train yesterday. His biography spelled rich and privileged. The only thing he missed was a wife, something Thayu had noted as a weakness in a comment underneath.

Of Veyada, it said that he was the son of the chief administrator for the city of Athyl. I hadn't known that, and resolved to remember it as an example of cases where fathers looked after their male children. Usually it was fathers who looked after the girls and Nicha was going to be an exception. Veyada raised his eyebrows when I read the biography out to the assembled group.

Of Nicha, the document said that his mother was now chief officer at the Athyl Water Board, one of the most powerful civil organisations in the mega-city.

Thayu had written about herself that she used to work for Athyl's Internal Security Service, which was their main spy organisation. It surprised me that she was so open about this, because she normally kept it hidden. However she had done a fair bit of work related to the *zeyshi* and her statement was probably full of the usual Coldi bluff. To the *zeyshi* it would spell, *Don't fool with me because I know everything about you*. Her biography said nothing, however, about her military connection, and that omission was probably also strategic.

The three junior *zeyshi* delegates appeared to be lackeys, as I had suspected, their histories as unremarkable as their appearance. Significant only, I suspected, in that they brought the delegation size to five, and this was an important number for Aghyrians.

The meeting itself passed in a fairly harmless way, not in the least because we didn't touch on any of the claim. This preliminary meeting merely set a time frame and agenda for the talks. How long we would spend on what, and which topics needed to be addressed where.

Delegate Ayanu kept throwing in little sniping remarks about the intelligence of the *zeyshi*, but Nayu ignored them. She conducted this talk with an air of professionalism. Sadet, however, snorted and tensed at Delegate Ayanu's barbs and appeared to be bored. She looked out the window, she stifled yawns, and stared at Marin Federza, who didn't know where to look. It was amusing to watch.

She was an Aghyrian of the black-haired and dark-skinned variety. Her eyes were black without the typical Coldi gold flecking. For once Marin Federza looked distinctly uncomfortable. Halfway through our meeting, he rose and went to sit somewhere else, where he was no longer in direct view of her.

When the official meeting finished, Delegate Ayanu and Marin Federza were the first out of the door. I had intended to ask Federza what had happened to his usual entourage, but he was gone before I could catch him.

I stayed behind to check if the delegation was comfortable and if they happened to have any concerns.

Sadet dragged the jug of juice to her and poured a cup. "Would it be possible to get some real drinks?" Of the fermented or distilled kind, she meant. She drank half the cup and put it down with a clonk. "This is too sweet."

"We can't serve zixas," I said. Neglecting to say that some bars had it, but anyone who ordered it needed to be Coldi. Aghyrians could also tolerate red-coded food, but since many people couldn't tell the difference between some Aghyrians and Mirani, Aghyrians had been left off the allowable list. Unless they could produce a red-coded permit, which was a *gamra* issued document, and I was sure that these people wouldn't have it. Besides, I had no desire to defend the *gamra* bureaucracy.

"All this planning seems a bit obsessive," Nayu said to me. She was wearing a very pretty traditional black shayka with silver embroidery.

"Take it from me, it's not. We'll have a few more subjects to cover before we are ready to take the case to the general assembly."

One of the younger delegates said, "So you mean we're not going into the big hall tomorrow either?" She'd asked about this before. The three junior members of the delegation were definitely lightweight, as if put forward only to maintain the impression that the *zeyshi* were uncultured and dumb.

"Not yet."

I had no doubt that Nayu was the brains of this organisation. Sadet was there only to show off her tough image, and I strongly suspected that Veyada might yet be right that they had a high-profile person up their sleeve.

"Why can't we start the meeting now?" she asked.

Sadet said, "I don't get it either. I'd have been done with this whole thing yesterday. Done, finished and on our way back home. All we needed to do was get this signed."

"You'll find that there are a lot of people here who have different ideas."

She gave me an *are there any other ways?* look.

It was as if the *zeyshi* had on purpose sent the bluntest and most abrasive personality for us to deal with. And they seemed too naïve to be real. Just like I suspected that they'd bring in another and much more competent team member, I was sure that at some point a nasty cat was going to come out of a bag, but as yet, we hadn't even located the bag.

———

When we left the meeting room, Thayu informed me that the Barresh council had been called into a meeting by Yetaris Damaru, about a disturbance in the Exchange network.

"Is this about the same thing we witnessed?" I asked.

I don't know, but it seems likely. It's not like there are that many disturbances.

"We should go to that meeting," I said. "If it's important enough to call a council meeting, it means they've drawn a conclusion." That in itself was rare enough, as conservative as the Exchange liked to be.

We agreed that I'd go with Thayu and that Nicha, Veyada and Deyu would go back to the apartment, where there was a lot still to do.

According to Thayu's source, the meeting had already started, and since most trains to the island came in the mornings and afternoons, and there were fewer in the middle of the day, Thayu ordered a water taxi. It was a flat-bottomed boat with six seats and, at the back, a huge fan-driven jet engine. The driver was a Pengali female, young enough to lack the leathered skin common to the older Pengali. She was in traditional outfit—or rather, lack thereof. Because Pengali had striped skin they considered themselves above clothing. She only wore a belt, complete with "hunting trophies": skulls and insect wings and other bits of animals. Pengali didn't go around dressed up like this anymore —the young and hip wore bright-coloured belts and "clothing" made out of brightly-coloured fishing nets. They also tended to dye their tails with glow-in-the-dark paint.

This one was dressed up traditionally, for tourists.

She took Thayu's money with a broad grin on her face and, after tucking it into a pouch at her waist, revved the engine with a giant roar.

The boat spun away from the jetty and scooted over the surface at a crazy speed, blowing wind and spraying drops into our faces.

Thayu laughed aloud, and the driver whoop-whooped and whistled. Since coming to live in Barresh, she had shed some of her apprehension about large, open bodies of water, and didn't seem to mind being on a boat, as long as it had an engine.

It was amazing to see the joy on Thayu's face. She had been so serious lately. If all this was over, I had to make sure to take a trip in one of these boats out to the long sand bar that protected Barresh from the sea. There was a wide sandy beach on the ocean side, where the waves crashed on pristine sand. If we went with just the two of us, we could even fit a surfboard into this boat.

We came into town thoroughly windblown, at the jetty next to the airport, walking up the path that also led to the station. As we climbed the incline to the level of the airport's tarmac, I looked through the fence. Sunlight beat down on the paving and the air above the ground shimmered with the heat. All four of the Asto armed forces shuttles were gone.

From the airport, we walked across the dappled shade of the market square and into the council building. The council's assembly hall was at the back of the building, through a maze of corridors with mosaic floors. Every now and then we'd pass a domed hall with coloured glass ceiling windows and a fountain. In these domes, the sunlight would pierce the windows, sending shafts of light through the hall below. None of these majestic buildings had climate control, and they were all wonderfully cool, with humid breezes keeping the temperature down. The old city, with this building at its centre, was a little bit worn, ancient, rustic and incredibly beautiful.

The guard at the door to the council chambers informed us that the council was in sitting, but then let us in anyway.

The councillors sat at the central table in the hall. Yetaris Damaru had been speaking but fell silent as we came in.

"Ah, Delegate. I had been wondering why you weren't here. Come in, we've barely started."

Thayu and I found seats on the tiered benches. People turned to the door and nodded polite greetings.

"My apologies for coming late."

A serving robot trundled towards us with drinks and snacks. Thayu took a small plate of nut bread and two glasses of juice.

I wrapped my hands around the glass, cherishing the coolness of the chilled juice. Thank goodness for the food. There was no council meeting in Barresh without food.

Yetaris Damaru resumed his talk. "As I was just saying to the members of the council, there has been a significant development overnight in the case of the mysterious Aghyrian ship."

Yes, it was as I had thought.

Trouble had a habit of hitting all at once.

He flicked the projector into life.

Light from hundreds of little nozzles around the hall combined to form a three-dimensional picture that looked like a giant ball of hair such as one might find in the bathroom sink. The shape of it, however, was familiar to me. The structure of blue lines that looked like a web made by a drunk spider was the Exchange network: a continuous web of interlinked anpar lines which transported ships and communication. A broken line of white marked the known trajectory of the mysterious ship.

When we first observed the ship, immediately after the Exchange outage which it was said to have caused, it was on the outer edge of the galaxy. Since that time, it had come closer, but had jumped seemingly at random from one arm of the galaxy to the other, always staying far enough from inhabited *gamra* worlds to evade our telescopes, and because we had no one-way slings, or at least none that were not in military hands, we couldn't check it out. Maybe the Asto military had done that, because they had slings. In any case, if they had checked it out, they hadn't let us know the results, which I hoped meant that they were not significant.

Over the past months, when the ship had come closer, it had acquired a shape, albeit rather fuzzy still. It emitted no measurable electromagnetic radiation. It operated no outside lights and sent no communication. It had no wings and no rotating habitat either. The thing was a long cigar with flanges whose function we couldn't begin to guess. The only way we could tell its position was that it sent out a constant trail of visible light, not enough to be picked up with the naked eye, but strong enough to register on our instruments. Even at school on Taurus, my astrophysics teacher told us that visible light emissions meant that there was an antimatter engine at work. It had been during a curiosity lesson before the end of term, when he covered the subject, *Possible alien space ship propulsion*, and we had talked about theories of different ways of propulsion. It was a lesson that was strangely clear in my memory, even if the rest of my time on Taurus was not.

Visible light emission meant an antimatter engine. There was no other option. So the thing was definitely working, but whether it was *alive* was another matter.

Yetaris directed a laser pointer at a few spots in the network. "We've got new readings for the ship here and here." The projection extended the wriggly line that had expanded every day since we'd started having these meetings. The ship would continue moving in the same direction for a while and then jump an anpar line to another spot. Those lines would not be natural, but created by the ship much in the way the military sling worked—only much stronger.

"They've come a lot closer since the last time you reported on this," a councillor at the table said.

"Yes." In a grave tone.

"Still not responding to our communication packets?"

"No. But we picked up something last night." He flicked the laser and a dotted line cut across the projection of the "hairball" of active anpar lines. It bent around with the curve of the galaxy, crossing that vast space from the ship's position to us, Ceren, Beniz-Yaza system. Strong, even pulses with periods of silence in between. That was the same strobing signal that Devlin had shown me yesterday.

"This signal was emitted from the ship, we suspect through the same anpar sling they used to bring down the network. I'll play back a recording of events at the Exchange when it happened."

The sound system came on with a few crackles.

There was some static and then a woman was talking in Kedrasi, one of the Exchange operators, I assumed. Her voice was interrupted by a loud beep, followed by a burst of static.

The woman shouted, and an alarm went off.

Someone killed the alarm and a male voice—probably Yetaris Damaru—yelled in keihu, "Warn everyone. Get them on the ground!"

The woman's voice continued in Kedrasi, then switched to Coldi and told a passenger shuttle to come back to the airport—

A deep tone cut through the conversations, so loud and low in frequency that even the replay made the floor vibrate. It pulsated in strength, with the loudest points almost painful. Some councillors put their hands over their ears. And still the sound got louder. Now a hum merged into the pulsating sound, accompanied by blips of sound that went *whoop, whoop, whoop*. All of this in such low frequencies that if the sound had been any lower, my ears wouldn't have registered it. But my chest did. It was as if my heart slowed to match the pulses in the sound. The very air vibrated with it. Thayu's eyes were wide.

Can sound kill?

Then: a high-pitched multi-tonal shriek. Several people in the seats around me gasped or called out.

As soon as it had started, the sound was gone.

Silence.

For a few moments, no one in the hall said anything. My ears were ringing and my heart still pounding with the aftereffects of those vibrations.

I said, "What the hell was that?" and also, "That must have been frightening for the Exchange staff."

Yetaris Damaru nodded. "It was. I was on the floor. You can hear my voice in the recording. At one point, I thought the building would collapse."

Holy shit. This building was many hundreds of years old. The walls would easily crack under the influence of vibration.

"Could you turn it down?" I wasn't too sure about how that part of the Exchange operated.

"No. The operators have their individual controls, but the strength of the main signal is controlled by the core, and we are forever trying to increase the strength of that signal, never to mute it."

"So, what is your conclusion from this?" I stared at the intensity graph in the projection, where the sound levels of that communication were off the scale.

Yetaris Damaru switched off the projector and the hairball of lines vanished. I could see the other side of the hall again. "There is a lot we don't know or don't understand. Some things we can guess. At the beginning of the recording, we hear the low tone. It is, I'm guessing, a locator, a handshake signal. Then follows the low pulsating sound. It comes from the ship and it gets louder and louder until the humming starts. We're not sure where the humming comes from. Not the ship or the ground. It could be generated through the satellite that we know was targeted by the signal."

"What satellite?" a councillor asked.

"One that isn't on our books, because there is no known artefact at the location where the sound came from, but that is not so unusual in itself. There is a lot of undocumented space junk out there, and much of it could be prodded into action, given the right signals."

Asto liked keeping a register of every bit of junk around their planet, but had never shown as much care with other worlds. Early on, when they still thought they might annex Ceren as colony, they had placed a lot of satellites in orbit around Ceren. None of those were documented.

"Both the humming and pulsating sounds cut out all of a sudden to be replaced with a shriek."

"What is the meaning of the shriek?" a councillor asked.

"This is the significant thing. It's an information packet, sent from within Barresh in response to the handshake and exploratory signal."

Sent from within Barresh?

That was followed by a deep silence. The statement was highly significant, because it meant there was an Exchange-capable device somewhere in Barresh other than the Exchange. The experimental sling at the Aghyrian complex had been dismantled, I thought, after repeated run-ins with *gamra* law.

After a while, a councillor asked, "Whereabouts in Barresh?"

My first thought was *the Aghyrian compound* but he said, "A very unlikely place on the other side of the main island." He brought up a map showing the spot: in a street that ran along the water's edge. "We visited the houses in that street to investigate, but there is nothing unusual about any of them."

"Or their inhabitants?" someone in the audience said.

He shook his head. "Not the inhabitants either."

Thayu asked, "What was in the signal?" She rarely spoke up in meetings like this, but her keihu was passable.

"We're still decoding it. As is possible with the wake of the anpar lines, you can't just skim it and listen in. A good number of satellites encrypt their data, and this one appears to be very old and using a code that we're unfamiliar with."

I was keen to ask, *How about they send someone up there to look?* but a councillor asked another question.

Thayu answered it for me. *I have a suspicion it could be what my father is doing.*

I looked at Thayu. *If that's what he's doing, Asto would have known about this live satellite before now.*

True. And her expression turned to worry, because if the Asto military knew about the satellite, why hadn't anyone captured or destroyed it?

Who knew what sort of vessel this was? We couldn't have unspecified satellites relaying information to them. Thayu's father would definitely not allow that.

A councillor asked, "Apart from investigating this area, what else have you done? How likely is it that someone on the ground is actively talking to this satellite or even this ship?"

"Highly unlikely. We would have picked up the communication long before now. We scanned most of the island. Not just us—the entire Exchange network has undergone a full scan. The only information we have from the ship is the text we skimmed off the anpar wake."

I'd seen the translation of that snatch of text that had been hotly debated ever since the anpar line had disrupted the Exchange. It seemed a random snippet of text, a page from a diary or something similar. Its purpose was unclear, and certainly didn't seem to be part of a conversation or intended as such. It didn't even seem to be particularly relevant to anything. Just a random page ripped from a book and tossed on the wind. It mentioned the Aghyrian captain Kando Luczon, who had been captain of the ship when it left Asto. According to Yetaris Damaru, that was pretty typical of the type of information that one could gather from an anpar wake. Contemporary ships often left snatches of their maintenance logs. Thoroughly useless information, because it was never complete and often jumbled up.

The meeting concluded with the Barresh councillors congregating around the food trolley. I walked down the steps to the central floor of the hall and met Yetaris Damaru there.

"Many thanks for informing us about this meeting," I said.

"It is a pleasure."

"Keep me up to date when there is a new development. Could you send me the data you have on this shriek? I don't expect to have any answers, or to be able to decode it, but you can't have data like this in too many hands." I glanced at Thayu. She would remember the business with Sirkonen's datastick well enough. We'd been making triple, quadruple backups of everything ever since.

"Yes, I will send it." He made a note on his reader. After copying, I would have to look at it and give another copy to Devlin to play with, or Thayu. Did we have any code-breakers in the household? Veyada?

Veyada is pretty decent at code-breaking, Thayu said.

No one knew what to expect when that ship finally showed up here, as it seemed on its way to doing in a slow and roundabout way.

Heck, all the things we were discussing with the *zeyshi* claim might be futile once that ship was here. It might be an automated drone. There could be Aghyrian descendants aboard. The ship would be armed. It might be violent. The Aghyrians might want their planet back. One thing I knew for certain: if that ship was live, and if there were Aghyrian descendants aboard, we would not like what fifty thousand years' worth of development had done to a population that, fifty thousand years ago, built one-way slings that could transport them out of the galaxy.

But for now, they were playing a game of cat and mouse with us.

5

———————

WHEN WE CAME OUT of the meeting, the sunlight was turning golden and both suns hung low over the marshlands. In this part of the city, we were close enough to the markets that the air smelled of food.

Thayu said, "You know what? Let's eat here."

"Great idea." All of a sudden, I felt tired. I didn't want to go home to the problems that waited for me there: Xinanu's sniping to the staff, Eirani's complaining about it, Reida's sullen appearance, Nicha's apparent incapability of dealing with all of this.

"I'll let Eirani know that we're held up and don't need dinner."

I sent a message to the hub so that Devlin could let Eirani know.

We walked hand in hand along the main commercial street of Barresh. Market Street was a wide thoroughfare which held all the main administrative offices and a lot of commercial offices as well. It was a wide, tree-lined street with extensive dining areas on both sides, now fast filling up with people coming out of the offices. I spotted the occasional *gamra* blue glimpse in the crowd, but most of the diners were locals.

Thayu and I were quite fond of one of the quieter local eating-houses in an area that had been unaffected by the recent storms. The old trees here towered over the three and four storey commercial buildings on both sides. Wait staff at the eating houses underneath were frantically trying to clear the tables of little pink petals that fell from the canopy above. If you flew over Barresh at this time of the year, you could see the streets in the old city outlined in pink.

The serving staff at this place knew us and knew where we liked to sit. The business was unusual in that it was owned and run entirely by Pengali, and a group of young waiters and waitresses stood ready to take orders. Pengali were often referred to as a primitive race, but the ones I'd met were like these youngsters: confident, alert, smart and modern. They wore purple fish netting and had their tails dipped in purple paint.

Because it was early, we received a lot of attention, and had glasses and water and red-coded supplement pills for Thayu brought to us by three different people.

The dye on their tails glowed bright purple.

"Funky," Thayu said under her breath, while watching a young man walk past, tail waving behind him.

"What do you think about this Aghyrian communication?" I asked.

"I don't know." She returned her gaze to me, fingering her upper lip. "I'm trying to think up a thousand ways that this could be a hoax or some trick people play on us, but I'm not seeing any."

"I don't think it's a hoax. I *do* think that some people, like the military for example, know more than they are prepared to share."

"Oh, there's no doubt about that."

"Like your father for example."

"Of course. With his status, it's a surprise that he shows his face at all. He regularly turns up at Inner Circle meetings. People even know who he is and what he does. In the past, Asto would never have been so open."

It depended on your definition of *open*, I guessed.

"Could you guess how big the army is?" I suspected that she had visited some of these secret bases, even though she'd probably been instructed not to talk about them.

"They have their own associations." That was the standard reply to the question about the size of the army. More and more, I suspected that it meant that no one really knew and that the only place where the army was connected to the rest of Asto's associations was at the very top, which, to be honest, was the only way it would work. But it meant that no one except Ezhya knew of the size.

It was something that I'd not let myself get greatly worried about, but it tended to come out of dark corners sometimes to remind me that perhaps we *should* worry about it.

A waitress came to bring us two empty bowls and two sets of little tongs that locals used for eating. She placed these on a small glass plate—Pengali craftsmanship—while her tail swayed in a sensual rhythm behind her. I'd learned that there were two skin pattern types in the Pengali: zebra-striped and leopard-spotted. This woman was of the spotted variety and the pattern extended over her hands, shoulders, neck and lower legs. The Pengali tail was always black and white banded. Except when the white was dyed purple.

I picked up my water and cradled the cup in my hands. "It was a great idea to come here. This is a very relaxing place. We haven't done this for so long."

"Well, I hate to disappoint you, but that wasn't the reason I suggested it."

"Oh?"

"I wanted to talk to you for a bit."

Her expression was serious and my heart skipped. There was something that I had missed, I was certain. Something about her and my suggestion that we use a surrogate, or something about Nicha.

She said softly, "It's about this boy."

Boy? Then I realised. "Reida?"

She nodded. "What did the guards tell you about where he had been arrested, and for doing what?"

"Apparently, he was trying to climb the balcony of the old commercial building in Market Street." We'd just walked past it. "He said he was trying to replace the bugs that you lost."

"That's rubbish. We did have a bug there at one point in time, but that was during the council scandal and it was a long time ago."

"But what about the ones he fried?"

"Not in that building. But do you know what he was doing in that building?"

"I can make a decent guess. Merina Ramaru's house backs onto that building's yard. So her father has worked out how to stop him coming into the yard and using the ladder to climb into the window, so he climbs onto the balcony to—goodness knows what he'd been trying to do. Climb from the balcony over the fence?"

Thayu shook her head. "No. Do you know what is on the first floor of that building?"

I frowned at her. Did that matter?

She lowered her voice. "Yes, he was arrested climbing this balcony, and maybe councillor Ramaru and his big-bosomed daughter live adjacent to the complex, but our little rascal set off the alarm in one of the offices. He wouldn't have done that had he not been inside the office in question—"

"But the guard said nothing about this—"

"He wouldn't have, because the owner of that office doesn't want a fuss."

"All right. Now you have officially got me really curious. How do you know this?"

"First rule about spying: you never ask a spy where they get their material." She tapped me on the nose with a warm finger. A woman a few tables down from us frowned. I was still in *gamra* blue and Barresh people very much disapproved of open displays of affection. I could already hear the outraged calls *and these people do whatever they want wherever they want it.*

"All right then, madame spy, tell me whose office it is." And what was it with her flaunting her spy status anyway?

"Our friend Marin Federza."

"You're kidding."

"I never kid. I am the picture of seriousness." And she was, and she was not, because she smiled like the most gorgeous woman in the universe. My heart melted when she looked at me like that.

The sensual leopard-spotted waitress came to deliver our dinner: a bowl of glassy noodles, a bowl of sauce with fish pieces and a salad with nuts and red flowers. Thayu reached inside her pocket and pulled out a small bottle with a near-black fluid inside that looked like soy sauce but was so red-coded that it would probably kill me in five minutes. She sprinkled some over her sauce. Since she had started supplementing her food with this stuff, I'd noticed that her skin looked more alive, her hair had more lustre and she was not as tired. And she argued a lot more.

"But Marin Federza has an office at the *gamra* island in the plaza next to the station."

"He does. That's his *gamra* office. He's a Trader. He has a business office as well. Not a very large one, but, as is typical for him, it's in the most prestigious building in town."

Yes, that was true. Traders were inseparable from their profession and would probably rather die than give up the trappings associated with their status: an aircraft and office. I shouldn't have forgotten that.

"Why in all the worlds would Reida be interested in what is in Marin Federza's Trading office?" Then another thought. "Does that mean he was breaking in?"

"Whatever you want to call it, he definitely wasn't in there legally."

"But I still don't understand. Federza never misses the slightest opportunity to complain to me. Why hasn't he been at my doorstep to tell me about this?"

"That's the big question, isn't it?"

Holy shit. I leaned back in the chair, but I couldn't see the building from here. "Does he know that Reida was in there?"

"Most certainly. There is a recording, taken by his security cameras. Wait. I'll show it to you." She pulled out her reader and after some searching put it on the table facing me. On the screen I could make out a person carrying a light that made a glowing patch over a wall. The person walked slowly in the direction of the camera. When he passed, the light briefly reflected from the wall onto his side. He was Coldi, wearing a loose and light-coloured garment and a black tattoo of thorns encircled his upper arm. That was *zeyshi* and Reida was the only person in Barresh, at least that I knew, who had one of those tattoos. This was Reida. There was no doubt.

"What was he doing there? How long have you had this?" My heart was thudding. This was really much more trouble than I needed.

"I got this recording this morning. I haven't spoken to him yet. Nicha should do that, but I haven't spoken to Nicha either. You should do that."

She met my eyes. There was no playfulness in her expression now. I tried not to cringe.

She put a hand on my arm. The skin was so warm that the hair on the back of my arm stood up. "Nich' has fucked up. He knows it. I told you before that you should go hard on him and acknowledge that fact, so he can feel punished, and can move on to fix it."

"You know that's not my style. If he knows it, there is not much point in my yelling at him."

"Not yelling. Order him to fix it. You're the head of our association. You can't afford to let control slip, because someone else will take it." I was disturbed to see how angry she was. Here was a part of Coldi nature that would sneak away from me and then belt me over the head with vengeance. Nicha was her *brother*.

I sighed. "I can't just blame Nicha for something he hasn't done."

"He *has* done it. I don't know what clouded his mind when he selected this boy."

"He's just an adolescent rascal. We'll get sense into him eventually."

"No." Her eyes met mine in chilling intensity. "This is not your world. He is not immature or a child. All right, the first two escapades were immature, but we were meant to think that. They were probably diversions to distract us from the real action. Which is breaking into offices."

"Do you have any idea why he keeps behaving like this? Does he even have the instinct?"

"Oh, he does." Her eyes met mine. Clearly, Coldi could feel such a thing, while I was helplessly flailing around and surviving off guess-work. She came even closer and lowered her voice. "This is my theory: what likely causes his odd behaviour is that he has another superior somewhere else and he's acting on those orders."

Shit.

Her expression was serious. She nodded. No words were necessary. We both understood that danger.

I licked my lips. "You suggest that this other bond is stronger than ours?" That was something I didn't want to consider.

"It could be." I didn't like the frown on her face. "I've been thinking a lot about this recently."

And Thayu would not mention a suspicion unless she was quite certain that it was right. I'd run into that problem before, too. And now I was up against a brick wall by myself with no instinctive guidance for how to handle this situation.

I said, "I've been afraid of something like this happening. I don't understand why security doesn't vet people's associations." It was precisely why I had suggested that Nicha find someone from the

Outer Circle, because they were less likely to bring high-level unwanted listeners into the household. As it was, I already had to contend with the Asto army chief, who happened to be my father-in-law, but who also knew of most things in our household as soon as we decided on them. This was unavoidable. But as a silly Earth human, it made me uncomfortable, and I wanted to do whatever I could to limit this sort of thing happening. Coldi would go the other way. They'd collect as many ingoing and outgoing links as possible, and be proud of them, too. Look at who's spying into my household.

Thayu gave me a frustrated look. We'd discussed this subject many times, and I didn't feel I came any closer to understanding it or that they came any closer to understanding my concerns and discomfort. She continued in a low voice, "And to make matters worse, he comes back with this damn woman. *She* is an Azimi. And she's having a boy. Which also means that once she's had her child and she has left us, we'll still be living with an Azimi in our household."

"Only a baby, though."

"Babies grow up. No doubt that was exactly the purpose of this exercise. So we have someone from Azimi clan networks poking their fat noses in, as well as some unspecified network through Reida."

I took a deep breath. "All right. How can we find out who this superior of Reida's is?"

Wrong question. I knew it the moment I had asked it. I should have asked, *How can we make sure his loyalty to us is strong enough that he doesn't do anything that damages us?*

Thayu gave me that withering look that could make me crawl under the table. Coldi women did that look very well. I was sure that if I stepped back, or, heaven forbid, mucked up so badly that someone took a gun to me, she would take leadership of this pathetic semblance of an association in a heartbeat. In fact, I wasn't doing so well, so why didn't I hand over control to her straight away? Wouldn't it be great to just be told what to do?

"You're asking the wrong question."

"I know. I'm sorry. I'm busy and stressed out." I was dropping balls, but with Coldi, you could never, ever, afford to drop balls, because someone else would pick them up and run away with them. I took a sip from the water. It was sweet and wonderfully cold.

"You should have asked: why did Nicha choose this young man?"

What? "But I have been asking . . ." That was like . . . Did she really want to challenge her *zhayma?*

She came closer to me, enveloping me with her scent. I smelled it at night, when she slept in my arms. "This needs sorting out. Nich' has not been the same ever since he returned from custody after Sirkonen's murder."

In the deep, dark pit of my heart, I agreed with her. Nicha had been present, but not really *there* in the way he used to be. I'd thought that this was a result of my relationship with Thayu and the changing dynamic of our group, but those chilling moments in Ezhya Palayi's hub when I'd shot his challenger Taysha and realised that if I'd been Coldi I would have had Ezhya's position had left deep scars in me.

Hell, it had left deep scars in everyone who knew what had happened. Nicha was one of those people. I could still see his face when I told him what happened while we were sitting in Ezhya's aircraft on the way back from Asto to Barresh. When I'd just decided to accept inclusion in the Domiri clan, which was not *his* clan.

"We need to sort this out," she said in an even lower voice.

I nodded, feeling the stain of darkness creep into my heart. I loved Nicha. I didn't want to put pressure on him. I definitely didn't want to blame him for anything that had happened in the past.

"Do it. Sooner, rather than later. He needs to understand your position before he can discipline Reida. We need to know what Reida was doing there."

I nodded again.

"I'm not sure you fully understand the full implications of this." Again, that dead-serious look. A chill went over my back.

"Wait—are you suggesting that Nicha has selected Reida because *Nicha* still has some loyalty tangled up elsewhere?"

She let a deep, worrying silence lapse. I took it as a yes.

"But how can that be? He grew up in Athens, London and Rotterdam."

"He lived with our mother. How well do you know her?"

"Not well at all." I'd met their mother once, at the Exchange in Athens. She was a Palayi woman, who had, so far, been a bit of a mystery to me. An administrator for Asto's affairs. Had worked mostly on Earth, although I didn't think she was still there. At one point she must have liked Nicha and Thayu's father, Asha Domiri, having had two children with him, but I understood that the two had since fallen out badly. Over what, I had no idea, but let's just assume it had its roots in political or ideological differences. Asha was a military commander, as hardline as they came. His reaction to the *zeyshi* claim was *nuke from orbit*. That would make their mother . . . pro-cooperation or even pro-Aghyrian? So . . . let's assume that Nicha or Nicha's contact didn't like the influence Asha had on our association, so they ordered him to appoint someone who countered that influence.

Holy shit.

Thayu met my eyes. She only nodded.

"All right. I'll talk to him."

"No. Not talk. Order. Get it sorted. Find out where he stands. Find out where that boy's loyalties lie. Move him up, down or sideways in your association. As soon as possible."

A deep dread took hold of me. She was talking about *yedama*, a process I had only read about, where functions within an association were reassigned. Coldi people understood this instinctively, but how was I supposed to know whether Nicha and Thayu worked well as *zhayma*s or whether it would be better to, say, move Veyada up and Nicha to Veyada's position?

Damn. I *liked* having Thayu and Nicha together. I didn't want to change anything.

"Promise me." She grabbed my arm in a strong grip. "You wanted to understand us, live like us and do this right?"

It wasn't a question and I didn't need to answer it. It didn't even matter whether I wanted this. I was already in far too deep. There was no going back. The only way forward was to face the trouble.

I got the deep gut-churning realisation that this was probably why Nicha had suddenly decided to go into a contract with that woman, why he had been avoiding me. This had started happening not just recently, but ever since returning from custody on Earth.

And I had been too busy, too pre-occupied with his sister, to do anything about it.

I said softly to Thayu, "All right. This is what we'll do until it gets sorted. I don't want Reida on any task more sensitive than delivering messages. I'd prefer if he didn't leave the complex because we have no control over what he gets up to in town. We need to keep all our information close to our chest for the negotiations. As for Nicha: I think he'll understand the reasons if I prefer to take Veyada to meetings with the *zeyshi* delegation." Because of Veyada's extensive legal knowledge.

"Good. I'll tell both of them." She sounded a little too self-righteous for my liking. Did she really want her brother to get into trouble?

Most likely, she did not, but the enormously competitive society of Asto made the Coldi appear very hard-nosed at times. I had to force myself to remember that there was love underneath all that bluster and posturing. But right now, that was easy to forget.

6
______

WE FINISHED EATING, and all too soon it was time to
go. I felt like a coward for not wanting to return home,
but there was no delaying it.

"You know what else you should do?" Thayu said in a low voice as
we walked down the street on our way to the station.

No, I didn't know. My mind was numb from the revelations about
Nicha. It scarcely had room for anything else.

"Sooner or later, with your involvement in Coldi associations, you
will come across a situation where there will be a fight over a position.
Without training, with scrawny arms like yours, there is no chance
that you will survive."

Gee, thanks, Thay'. "I'm not Coldi. I can't win anyway."

"I wouldn't say that, and I'd very much hate for you to die because
you never trained."

As usual, Thayu was right. "So, what do you want me to do? Train
like a professional fighter?"

"That would be a start. I also want you to go armed at all times."

"But why—"

"No. For once, listen to what I say. Your status allows you to carry
arms. No one I know who has that status does not carry arms."

"I thought people frowned upon using anything except bare hands
in association fights?"

"No. There usually just isn't the time to draw a weapon."

That was true. I'd seen one of those fights once at the Exchange in Athens. Two Coldi people who were not associated with each other, but who had to work together met in the corridor. They looked each other in the eyes and lunged for each other without speaking a word. Everyone else in the group simply stepped aside and let it happen. The fight was over in seconds. Surprise and quick moves were everything. I guessed there would be no harm in learning to avoid being run into the ground by a bull with the agility of a panther and the strength of a bear. If I had time to draw a weapon, I might survive an attack like that. If I kept it at the stun setting, the other person would survive, too.

Still, the thought of always going armed didn't appeal to me. "All right. I'll do some training, but—"

"You will do both: get training and always have a gun on you. I want you to live. I want you to use the gun if necessary."

"Even against people I know?" Like Nicha, or heaven forbid, people high in the Asto hierarchy?

"Anyone who attacks. They won't be attacking because they dislike you. They'll be attacking because they have a reaction to you. If you avoided a fight, the instinct would keep firing each time you met this person and that would be far too distracting. If this person needs to work with you, they would never be loyal to you or the project, and would continue to undermine your position."

I knew that, but . . . "Why are you saying all this now? Is there someone you think might attack? I thought fights were rare."

"They are, in a stable environment. The current environment is not stable. In fact, there is a great unrest in the Coldi associations in Barresh. I haven't established the source, but it likely is some fallout from the changes in the top of Asto's leadership. You are directly involved through my father, so I assume you to be a target."

And here was another thing: because I had accepted Domiri clan membership from the leader of that clan, did that mean that I had some sort of relationship to him? Asha Domiri had moved up in the hierarchy, and there were likely to be people not happy with that.

I had gone a few paces before I realised that Thayu had stopped in the middle of the street. I turned back to her. "Thay'? What's going on?"

"This is the building." She jerked her head to the left-hand side of the street.

Total change of subject. It was the building where Reida had been arrested, the commercial building that held some of the oldest businesses in town. There were shops and eating-houses on the ground floor and the three floors above that contained individual units for business premises. A gallery-style balcony ran along the front of each floor, giving access to each of the business suites. The walls were made from limestone blocks and the floor plates from a kind of concrete containing white pebbles that used to be a commonly-used construction material in Barresh—the white pebble quarry had run out a long time ago. That concrete and the blackwood trimmings—from a tree on the rainforest plateau that had black wood stronger than steel— made the building over four hundred years old. It had withstood two wars and many storms and was elegant in that nonchalant Barresh way.

There were still some lights on in offices on all of the floors.

I asked, my voice low, "Should we have a look upstairs?"

"Yeah, why not?" Thayu led me up the steps to the first floor. Our footsteps echoed in the bare stairwell. There were two galleries along both sides of the building. We found Marin Federza's Trading office at the back, second last on the gallery. A curtain obscured the window, but judging from the distance between the next doors, the office didn't look very big. I could see no signs of breaking in. Neither could I see any signs of people having climbed up here. It would have been easy: there was a rubbish bin directly under the balcony. Something a bunch of drunk louts would do.

"Why make all that effort of climbing over the balustrade while you can just walk up here?"

"These galleries are closed at night. Didn't you see the gate at the bottom of the stairs?"

I hadn't. Dumb Mr Wilson.

We leaned on the railing. The building had a small yard ending in a jumble of mismatched walls that surrounded the private yards of the houses on the other side.

Thick canopies of overhanging trees made it very dark here. The trees were mostly in the yards that were on the other side of a wall, which were oases of fountains, clipped bushes, garden benches and mosaic paths, but right now, the ground was pink from a carpet of fallen petals.

Thayu said, "I truly don't know what Reida was doing here, and it disturbs me that Nicha hasn't said anything about it."

"Yeah, me, too. I also don't think that the councillor's daughter had anything to do with it. I think breaking into this office was his true aim."

"I wonder if he got what he wanted. Did the guards say anything?"

"I think the guards were silenced by Federza. They mentioned no specifics about where Reida was caught. They didn't mention Federza. They didn't mention breaking into the office. They just talked about climbing the balcony."

"Yeah," she said. "It's really hard for us to get information out of the Barresh guards as well. They're more protective of their damn council families than they are of the council's reputation."

There was nothing much to see here, so we went back downstairs.

We turned into the street and had walked a little distance towards the main square and airport, where we needed to get on the train, when Thayu glanced over her shoulder.

Anyone following us? I asked through the feeder.

"It seems so."

I peered into the darkness beyond the streetlights and the people who walked there. Tree branches hung over a wall that surrounded the compound that housed the council buildings. I didn't see anything unusual.

"How can you tell?" Her night vision was much worse than mine.

"Devlin told me just then. There are two people following us, and he tracked them back to the time we left the council building."

I'd had the hub upgraded and sometimes I wondered if the extra flood of information we got was beneficial or whether it made things more complicated. There were times like this when I thought we could well do without the extra information. If you were a reasonably high-profile *gamra* delegate, there were virtually always people following you. That didn't mean that they did so out of ill will. They would be people from the various news services, people who wanted to speak to you in private, investigators hired by your rivals to see if you did anything illegal that they could pin on you and, yes, security, too.

She grabbed my arm. "Come."

"Where to?" I wanted to go home. I didn't care about people following us.

"We're going to give them an excursion of the town."

Before I could protest, she took off in the opposite direction, back towards the eating-house.

I ran after her. "Who are these people? Are they dangerous?"

Thayu held her hand to her ear, listening to some security briefing. I opened all channels on my feeder, but whatever she was listening to was buried deep in the stream. She was worried, that was all I understood.

We don't know who they are, she said in response to my probing.

That in itself was cause for worry.

Thayu walked quickly and I had trouble keeping up with her. She was right that I could probably use some fitness training. Days spent sitting in meetings or at a desk did little good for me, and moving slowly into middle age didn't help either.

We went from one street to another and sometimes cut across using the alleys that ran behind the back yards of the stately houses, and that had originally been built for domestic staff and to collect rubbish.

Barresh was a low-lying city, with the highest point of the island a mere ten metres or so above sea level. This had, in the past, led to drainage problems when the rains came and big cascades of water fell into the delta from the escarpment. About fifty years ago, at the time when the *gamra* island was being built, someone had the idea of digging a network of canals through the problematic streets in lieu of the underground stormwater drains that forever backed up when they were most needed. The resulting canals crisscrossed that low-lying part of the city which stretched from a few blocks behind the council building to the eastern side of the island. Market Street itself mostly remained spared because it was the oldest and highest part of the old town. The canals were interconnected and closed off from the surrounding marshes by a set of locks that were usually closed to keep the water level in the canals high enough for boats, but that were opened after big rains. The network of waterways provided a public transport system.

As we came out of an alley, we arrived at one of the canals. There was a ferry stop here, a little jetty with a bench for people waiting, now bathed in greenish light from a street lamp. A boat was at the jetty, and the driver, a Pengali man, had just cast off the ropes.

"Wait!" Thayu called.

The driver and the two passengers turned around. The driver grabbed the jetty pylon with one hand while cutting the engine with the other.

We ran onto the jetty and into the boat. It was long and narrow like a broad canoe, and wobbled when we walked between the two rows of single seats. The two other passengers were a Pengali woman with a couple of baskets and a keihu young man who sat at the very front. He nodded at me when we passed. "Good evening, Delegate."

Thayu and I sat in seats across the centre aisle from each other. The driver gunned the engine, and the boat sped across the canal. Thayu studied the receding jetty and street behind us until we went around a corner.

She smiled. "That's them taken care of."

"Any idea yet who they were?"

"If I knew that, they wouldn't be following." Another security mantra.

"Where is this boat going?"

She looked around. "I don't know, but we'll get a water taxi back home from wherever we end up."

The boat stopped at another jetty surrounded by houses. I asked Thayu if we should get off, and she said to wait. The keihu man got off here, to be replaced with two chattering Pengali girls who sat at the front where he had been sitting. I was fascinated by how their tails moved when they spoke; that movement was extra-visible because of the dye that made the tips of their tails glow green in one girl and orange in the other.

After a few more stops, and having turned a good number of corners, I could see moonlight on the water ahead.

The last stop on the route was at the very edge of the island. The jetty was right next to the lock—now closed to keep the water level in the canal high enough for the boats.

The two Pengali girls got off and vanished into a dark street. Their glowing tails were the last I saw of them.

"Get off here, or go back," the driver said to me, in heavily accented Coldi.

"No, we'll get off." Thayu gave him some of the money pearls and we stepped onto the jetty. The boat turned around and zoomed back in the direction from which we had come, leaving us alone on the deserted street with the moonlight reflecting off the marshlands.

"Hmmm," Thayu said. "I'd have expected there to be a station here. Or some taxis."

Clearly, there weren't any.

"Where are we?"

She pulled out her reader and showed me on the screen. "There is a station over here." She pointed. "It's a bit of a walk, unfortunately."

I was going to say that I didn't mind but remembered how busy we were. I thought of Nicha, and the feeling of dread, which had evaporated during the boat ride, came back. Maybe we could do something else useful before returning home. "How far are we from this place where this reply signal to the Aghyrian ship was meant to have come from?"

She went back to her reader and zoomed out on the screen. "Not too far from here. There is another station in that direction, too. It's a better station, too. More frequent trains."

"Let's walk that way then. Let's see what's there."

We took the street that ran along the very edge of the island. It ran between houses with walled yards. In most places you couldn't tell that the water was close, because the walls on both sides of the street were too high. The trees were not as big here, because the houses were much closer together. Strangely enough, the increased density of buildings brought out their magnificent constructions, because the houses were closer to the street where the streetlights illuminated their centuries-old façades. Sometimes I would read bits on the history of Barresh, and it never failed to surprise me with its depth and colour. While it was easy to stick labels like "lazy", "fat" and "corrupt" on the heads of the keihu families in the council, they possessed a resilience that would be an inspiration to many other small entities, and, despite *gamra* trying to change the city, they stubbornly kept doing things the way they had done them for centuries.

I followed Thayu along the street and admired the houses, their cornices, columns and metalwork, their mosaic garden paths and coloured glass windows.

Sometimes there would be a little walkway between the houses to the left, showing us glimpses of the silver moonlit expanse of water. Once, I spotted a train zooming low over the water, giving me a clearer picture where we were. The *gamra* island was to the south of the main island. We were to the east of the main commercial district.

The road dipped down to a tiny harbour and jetty area. Besides pleasure craft, a number of fishing boats bobbed on the pylons of the jetty. Nets lay drying at the quay, big fuzzy-looking shapes hanging over posts or racks. The air smelled of fish.

The train line offshore was only visible as a line of tiny lights. It curved back to shore to the right of where we stood, but the station was around the point that jutted into the marshland.

"The location is over there." Thayu pointed at the peninsula ahead.

The street again plunged between houses. When we'd gone a little distance, Thayu stopped, looking at the screen on her reader.

"Here. This is where the reply signal came from."

The street here was quite narrow and sloped ever so slightly down to the tip of the peninsula. There were walls on both sides and houses behind those walls. Very ordinary and plain houses. There were no sounds, or signs of anything unusual.

"Well. That's . . . odd," I said. Although Yetaris Damaru had said it was just a normal part of town.

"Let's have a look over here," Thayu said.

She led me past the nearest house. A narrow alley ran between two walls. The surface was uneven and there were steps, invisible in the pitch darkness. If this was possible, Thayu, walking in front of me, saw even less than I did. She carried a tiny violet light that showed up blue through my spectrum-reducing contact lenses. The glow hardly reached the ground, but it made the moss on the walls glow pink. This confused me rather than helping me put my feet in safe places. I slipped and almost fell twice.

At the end, the alley opened up onto a sandy beach that sloped down to a moonlit reed field. The beach ran along the back walls and fences of houses.

"This is where that signal came from?"

"Yes, around here somewhere."

There was nothing here. Just a rocky knoll, some grass and bushes, and a few straggly wild megon nut trees. Those trees were now in flower and spread their heavy, fire-retardant scent in the air.

That smell typified Barresh. Even when I travelled, it seeped out of my luggage in hotel rooms and if I stayed long enough, it spread its fire-retardant mist over the room's contents. If there was a candle or oil light in the room, accommodation staff would be baffled that they couldn't light it anymore.

Ceren's moons were tiny, and didn't produce much light, but both of them were in the sky, with the broad ribbon of the Milky Way in the background. The ringgit made their usual racket in the reeds, almost drowning out the whoosh of the train that was just coming into the station. On the other side of the bay, the domes and towers of the old city protruded from the canopy of trees.

We picked our way to the tip of the peninsula, following the line of walled yards. The sand still radiated heat and the occasional breeze brought sounds of people talking from the houses.

"It's nice here," I said, but at the same time, Thayu said, "Shhh."

I listened. The train had gone and its whoosh over the rails was fast fading into the background noise. Closer by in the reeds, the ringgit were trying to outdo each other in their rattling mating calls. I picked up some humming sounds. "Am I hearing people talking?"

Shhh.

Then rustling of vegetation.

"Over there somewhere," Thayu said in a low voice.

I peered into the darkness and I noticed movement in the reed bed. Two people waded through the vegetation, silhouetted against the reflection of moonlight. One of them was holding some kind of equipment that let out little blips of yellow light. Sometimes it would produce a glow that illuminated a man's face. There might be a third person further down, I couldn't be sure.

"Any idea what they're doing?" I asked Thayu.

She was peering into the darkness.

Then there came the rustling sound of footsteps, much closer.

Careful, I sent through the feeder.

We ducked behind a bush. Thayu sank into a crouch. The moonlight glinted off the gleaming barrel of her gun. Her night vision was really poor, as with most Coldi people, and she would be at distinct disadvantage if it came to a fight.

A man's voice said, "Hello? Who's there?" He spoke keihu, his voice clipped and heavily accented.

A light flicked on.

The man in question wore a long-sleeved shirt that had seen better days, with the council symbol on the chest, and trousers that fishermen usually wore against the leeches that lived in the water.

Thayu came out from behind the bush. *Be careful,* she said.

He's a council worker.

Maybe. If he is, I don't really trust those, either.

The man's face was all angles: a strong chin, a straight nose, deep-set eyes and strong cheekbones. Not keihu. Not Aghyrian either. His eyes met mine. His irises were brown.

"Oh, good evening, Delegate." He gave a small bow. His Coldi was much better than his keihu. "It's a nice evening," he said.

"Are you looking for the origin of that signal that the Exchange picked up?" I asked, trying to sound as innocent as I could. The state of his shirt—all washed-out and worn at the collar—was really odd. "Finding anything?"

I could feel Thayu cringe through the feeder. She hated it when I did this.

"No. Is gone. Just once send signal, then gone."

A second person came behind him. This person was also in black overalls with the council insignia, but wore a full-face veil with a gauze panel over the eyes, probably against stinging insects. I couldn't even tell if it was a man or a woman. This person carried a piece of equipment on a strap slung over the shoulder.

"Is that for measuring radio waves?" I asked. I deliberately didn't use jargon.

Crap, at times I really can't believe you, Thayu said.

The man replied. "Yes. Nothing here at the moment." His companion pushed up the strap of the device that was in danger of sliding off his shoulder. The light from the screen flashed briefly. Its light glowed over the reed bed and the back walls of the houses that were behind us. The brief flash was enough to see that one of the walls immediately behind us had been reduced to a pile of rubble.

"Whoa, what happened there at that house?"

"Was a very strong sound. Walls are very old."

A chill crept over my back. When I heard that strong pulsating sound, I'd been afraid that the vibrations would break something, or cause someone to have a heart attack.

"Anyway, must keep working." He gave another respectful nod and continued into the reed bed with his colleague.

Thayu and I made our way to the pile of rubble. If this wall had broken, that would mean that the device that had sent the responding shriek was somewhere in the vicinity, right?

She flicked on her little light and directed its glow over the fallen stones. The inhabitants of the house had erected a temporary fence of poles with wire strung between them. All windows at the back of the house were dark.

"Why are these guys out here in the dark?" I asked Thayu in a low voice.

They've probably been here all the time, but I'm not sure if I like it either. They don't look like the regular council workers.

She was right. Their uniforms were much more scruffy than I would think acceptable for council workers. Maybe they were contractors. I didn't know. It didn't sit well with me.

"There are two possibilities about the origin of the sound." She crouched at the rubble. "One: the sound came from a person operating a portable device from here. When he was done, this person took his equipment and simply went home."

"That's not very likely. I wouldn't think you could carry equipment that produces strong waves like that in your back pocket."

"I agree."

I added the second possibility. "Two: whatever is communicating with the ship is hidden, for example inside one of the houses."

"Yeah." She shifted a block of stone. A bit of grit trickled off the jagged remains of the wall. "At any rate, it did a very good job at destroying the mortar. And our best chance to find out what it was and where it is has vanished unless it comes to life again." She looked over her shoulder, where the three council people had returned to the reed bed. They stood gathered around their equipment, talking in low voices. The hooded person had pushed up the hood, and it was clear now that all three were men. Dark-haired, sharp-nosed but otherwise rather nondescript.

"You know what I don't like," she said softly. "Those men are Tamerians. Why would the council hire Tamerians?"

Shit.

Somewhere in the mountain ranges of the non-*gamra* world of Tamer, someone was sending out a lot of mercenaries and spies. They were strong, well-trained and had the ability to blend in well enough to evade notice.

Many rumours circulated about Tamerians: that they were an artificial race, combining the strong points of all *gamra* peoples, and that they were "owned" by some kind of rich disenfranchised person who was following a political agenda.

Tamerians first started appearing—mainly as dead bodies in conflicts—a few years ago. We didn't yet know who the owners of these mercenaries were or whether their motivations were political or criminal. The issue was too new for an organisation as sluggish as the *gamra* assembly to get a grasp of the situation.

The most worrying thing was that they appeared to be resistant to Asto's heat and, now that I had officially visited Asto, and the official requirement that visitors were Coldi was dropped, people in power at Asto expected Tamerians to turn up and create trouble there.

Because of this, Asto had existed in a state of alertness and, for the first time ever, security checks had been put in place for flights bound for Athyl. They had never bothered previously, because any non-Coldi person would die pretty quickly on Asto, or at least without extensive protection.

And now we had Tamerians in Barresh. Hired by the council? Well, I expected the Barresh council to jump sideways at any time, but hiring Tamerians would be a highly controversial move. Yet here they were.

We walked around the site of the collapsed wall, using Thayu's light to study the ground. Thayu pointed out places where the young, probably Pengali, had met and sat around a hot water vent boiling illegally-caught fish—she could tell by the bones which fish they'd caught.

There were no obvious signs of technology.

"Could you scan for electronics under the ground?" Although I didn't imagine that there could be much. The water table was too high. The water was high in various salts and anything that came into contact with it would rust.

"I could, but I'd need to bring more powerful equipment."

I looked over the reed bed. "Like they have?" The three Tamerians walked through the reeds in single file, each carrying a tiny light.

"I don't know what that equipment is. I've never seen it before."

"Let's go home then and come back some other time when these guys are not here. They might find something and report it to the council anyway."

"I don't have high hopes that if they find anything, they'll report it."

"They should."

She nodded. "Yes, they *should*."

Which meant that they might not. I really didn't like this.

Should I mention to someone at *gamra* that the Barresh council was using Tamerians? Was it even important? *Gamra* had absolutely no say over what happened off the island. It was easy to forget that the organisation governed everything to do with the Exchange and wasn't a political body. If Barresh wanted to hire Tamerians, then that was their business.

But damn it, that still didn't mean that I had to like it. For one, there was no *need* for Barresh to hire Tamerians. They had plenty of people. Some really good people even. This smelled like someone's private project.

Federza? Looking for some transponder thing under the ground or in someone's back yard?

There was a jetty at the point, an extension of the main street that ran through the middle of the peninsula. From there, we walked back to the main part of the island, and then along the water until we came to the station.

We didn't say much. I was still mulling over the situation that got stranger and stranger by the minute.

The train took a while in coming—we were on the less-busy southern line—and we had to wait on the platform. The light here was much too strong to see if the three men still searched the reed bed.

I said, "I think I'll contact Yetaris Damaru tomorrow to see what those Tamerians are looking for and if they've found anything."

"Framed as an innocent question, right?" Thayu grinned.

"Because 'Why do you have Tamerians searching our town at night?' would be too confronting a question, don't you think?"

"I see you are learning."

"You can joke about it, but it concerns me."

"Yeah, me, too, but it's not our place to investigate. And it's not as if we haven't got enough worries of our own."

That was definitely true.

The train arrived and we took the short ride to the main station without saying much. Then we changed for the more crowded train out to the *gamra* island. The carriage was about half full, mostly with *gamra* delegates and their personnel returning from dinners and other trips into town. A bunch of young men and women, most likely domestic workers, were showing off purchases from the markets. One of them had bought a set of baby clothes, either for herself or a sister, and all the others remarked on how cute they were.

I glanced at Thayu as we unavoidably listened to this conversation, but she was doing something on her reader and ignored the subject of babies, although I knew her well enough to know that she would definitely notice it. Notice and say nothing.

I stared at my own reflection in the window, wishing I knew what to do about Nicha, about Reida, about Menor and Thayu's unwillingness to even discuss the matter further, about this general feeling of unease that crept up on me in the quiet moments, a feeling that some giant predator was watching all of us, be it the Asto army, the Tamerians, or something to do with that Aghyrian ship, or even all of those things. I wished I knew what it was so that I could do something about it. But I could only wait and pretend everything was fine.

The train stopped at the *gamra* island's station, the final stop before it would turn back to the city. Thayu and I got out with the other passengers and walked home through the tree-lined avenues and the courtyards.

We entered our building through the humidity-filled atrium, with its tinkling waterfall, and up the stairs to the gallery.

Evi had made his way back long before us, and he and Telaris sat in the little cubicle outside the door.

"Good evening, *mashara*. Everything all right?"

"*Mashara* is afraid that there may be a spot of trouble inside the apartment."

Damn it, what now? "Reida? More trouble between Xinanu and Eirani?"

"The Delegate has a visitor that *mashara* is quite certain the Delegate is not fond of." While he said this, Telaris' face came as close as I had ever seen to displaying a smile.

"*Mashara* is making fun of me."

"No, no, not at all."

Well, drat. "Let's go and see this unpopular visitor." As I walked past him, I whirled around at him. "But I bet it's Marin Federza."

"*Mashara* will not be betting with you, because *mashara* might lose."

I went into the apartment stifling laughter. It had taken me a long time, but I thought I was finally beginning to understand the subtle Indrahui humour.

7

———————

WHEN I STEPPED into the hall, Eirani came in from the other side. "Oh, there you are, Muri. We were worried about you when the others came back and—"

"Apparently Trader Delegate Federza is here."

"Yes, he came after the others had just come home, and wouldn't leave until he had seen you. I tried to get him to come back tomorrow, but I'm afraid he was very insistent." Very angry, more likely, about a junior staff member of mine breaking into his office.

"It's all right, Eirani, I'll go and see what he wants." Drat. I hadn't even spoken to Reida about it and was utterly unprepared for a conversation about that. Great.

"Will I bring you some tea?"

"Just leave it for now. He might not stay for long." Couldn't let the man think that he was welcome to disrupt my evening over this issue. I'd try to palm him off as soon as I could. "You're welcome to *make* some tea, though. I'll have it when he's gone." Hell, by that time I would need the tea.

"As you wish." Eirani gave a bow which was half-mocking.

"Where is Raanu?"

"The young lady has gone to bed after doing her work."

"Of her own volition? That's got to be a first." It had to have something to do with Thayu's promise of a day trip.

I walked down the corridor, wondering if I should drag Reida in with me, but I should really talk to the young man first to see if I could uncover a bit more of the reason for his transgression. And I should talk to Nicha. Somehow, I was going to get to the bottom of this, but Federza was not going to sit in the front row while that happened.

And while I was at it . . . I raked my hand through my hair. The feeder's legs attached to it and I pulled it free from my skin. That moment that it popped off always made me shudder. The background voices in my head fell silent. I put the thing in my pocket. There. Now I might not be able to listen to anyone, but no one could listen to me either.

The light was on in the office and Marin Federza sat in the chair that stood on the side of the desk. He rose when he saw me come in.

Every time I saw the man, I got a shock over how tall he was.

He nodded a polite greeting. "Delegate." He wore his full uniform, which, considering the fact that the assembly didn't sit, and the time of day, was a little odd.

"Good evening." I debated saying *good night*, because by the *gamra* clock it was well into midnight, but judged that a little *too* peeved.

"I do apologise about the hour, but I have a matter I need to discuss urgently."

From close up, his face seemed pale and his expression drawn.

"Sit down." Not in the mood for niceties. I let myself drop in my chair and gestured him to the chair on the other side of the desk. Behind him, I could see over the water where the lights from the main island of Barresh twinkled in the night and a train zoomed over the elevated track across the water.

He placed his fingers of one hand neatly meeting the corresponding fingers on the other, and then both hands on his knees. Was I imagining it or did his fingers tremble?

"Look, Delegate I understand you don't like me—"

"Who says I don't—"

His nostrils flared. "Oh, that's evident from everything you do or say. You don't need to apologise. Few people like me."

Well, whose fault is that? "Do tell me why you're here. I've been out most of the afternoon and evening, it's late and I have to prepare for tomorrow's meeting. If you are here for the reason I think you are, you're going to have to allow me some time to sort out this matter, because I'm not in the capacity to comment on it right now."

He raised his eyebrows and his expression was so genuinely surprised that it took me aback. He was a good actor.

"You're here because the commercial building's security camera shows my latest young employee breaking into your office in town. I'm going to have to apologise. I've only been notified of his transgression this afternoon, and I haven't been able to talk to the rascal. I will do that as soon as I can, and should bring him to apologise to you in person."

He nodded, and let a silence lapse. Not the reaction I'd expected, at all. I pressed on, despite the feeling that I was missing some important fact. "I understand you're angry, and I assure you that I want it cleared up."

"It's all right, really."

"No, it's not all right." Since when was breaking into offices all right? Seriously, what the hell was going on?

I stared at him, and the way he sat across the desk from me. Tired-looking, *defeated*.

"Then tell me why you're here."

He swallowed visibly and straightened his cloak. "The fact is, much as I dislike to admit it, I need your help."

Oh? I raised my eyebrows as far as they would go. "*My* help? This is something that you waited here for me to do? Something that absolutely can't wait until tomorrow?"

"I'm afraid it is."

"Something that only I can do?"

He looked at his hands and squirmed ever so slightly. "Well, much as we've disagreed on all kinds of matters, I respect your integrity. I have been suspicious of you ever since your arrival here—"

Well, that feeling was mutual—

"—but I've found not one reason that justified my doing so."

So what was this? Some kind of backhanded compliment?

"You have been, without exception, true to your word, transparent in your dealings with *gamra*. I don't like the fact that you work for the man I despise, but you have not made any missteps yourself."

He must not have been paying attention, because I could name plenty.

"And in the office you hold currently, I could imagine a thousand candidates that would have been a thousand times worse. Anyone from Asto's First and Second Circles, for example—"

"And all this is important because?"

"I'm explaining why I'm here." The tone of his voice acquired a little edge.

"Well, there is no need for explanation. I'd rather get to the main message."

He nodded, pressing his lips together and not meeting my eyes. "My life is in danger."

I almost laughed. And he came to *me*, and this household, the very epitome of risky politics? "We're all in danger, everyone who takes part in these negotiations."

"You don't understand."

"Tell me about it, then, because I'm stabbing in the dark." And I was getting extremely frustrated with his refusal to talk straight.

He looked up at the ceiling. "You've got bugs on."

"Of course I do."

"I want you to turn them off before I say anything."

"I can't do that, I'm afraid. My staff member who knows how to do that has already gone to bed, and I don't want to do it, because if this is as important as you say, I want a record of it."

"But my enemies will hear what I say."

"Of course not. No one hears what is said in these recordings unless I release them."

He looked at me. Blinked. Pearls of sweat glistened on his upper lip. He would know that what I said was not entirely true. If the news was juicy enough, it would find its way into the gossip circuit anyway. There was no secrecy.

"I want your guarantee that no one hears what I say in this room."

"You know I can't give that guarantee, for the safety of both of us."

"I am not your enemy." Spoken with an intensity that chilled me.

"Well, I don't know about that. You represent a group of people who have caused us no end of trouble. You provided the technology for people with political aims that allowed them to kill the president of my world. More recently, you were not particularly helpful during the Exchange outage."

"Please note that I represent the Trader Guild. I work for the Trader Ledger. No one else."

"As far as I could see, you were at the meeting this morning representing the Barresh Aghyrians. Are you now saying you don't really represent them?"

He hesitated. "I was . . . relieved from my position."

Well, what the hell. "Any reason?"

"The Barresh Aghyrians are not a homogenous group. I recently . . . disagreed with some of the more powerful members of that group."

"About what?" Who were these powerful members? Chief Delegate Akhtari?

He glanced aside. "That's why I wanted the listening bugs to be off. If they hear me talking about this—"

"—if I am to do something with the information, as I assume is your wish, I will have to justify my source. How can I do that without a recording?"

His nostrils flared. "You're a very hard-nosed diplomat."

"I can assure you, you have not experienced hard-nosed if you think that. I know that the Aghyrians are not a homogenous group. They've never presented themselves as otherwise. In fact they've never presented themselves as anything at all. They do their own thing in their own compound that's off-limits to any of the rest of us."

He met my eyes, his expression pained, hard, exhausted, contemptuous and a whole lot of other emotions all at once. "I would appreciate if for once you could set aside your vendetta against me."

"I have no vendetta against you." *Just get to the fucking point.*

Damn, I was getting angry and that was never helpful, especially without Thayu around. I wished to hell he'd just get to the point instead of dragging up all this nonsense.

I rose, breathing deeply to try and calm my rattled senses. I was going to tell him quietly to leave before I did something stupid and come back when he had decided to be more informative. He might be right about being in danger, but he should go to the guards if that was the case, because I couldn't help him.

I don't know what made me glance out the window, but I noticed a spot of light in the darkness of the marshland where there were only reeds. Pengali sometimes went fishing at night, but they never used light. My heart jumped. More Tamerians?

While Federza kept talking—something about trust and fellow delegates—I walked to the window. The light was gone now. Damn it. That wasn't a good sign. That meant there was someone out there—

A burst of fire flashed.

"Watch out!" I lunged, grabbed Federza's arm—

He called out, "Hey, what are you doing—"

—and pushed him face down on the carpet. I hit the floor a split second later.

Thump.

A flash engulfed the window. There was a loud crack. Lightning zapped across the opening, casting the room in hot white light. Glass shattered and sprayed through the room, hitting my back and the carpet with sharp thuds.

Then it was silent. Black spots danced before my eyes.

Holy shit. That was far too similar to a situation I was all too familiar with.

"Are you all right?" I asked Federza, forgetting to use formal pronouns. Forgetting that we'd just had a fight, damn it, forgetting about customs and formality, and just reaching out to him as a fellow human.

He said something in Aghyrian which I didn't understand. Likely a swear word. His face was pale and sweaty, and he breathed fast. He pulled at globs of glass which had melted onto his tunic. Then looked at me. Shaken. He might be a pompous prick, but damn it, I should have taken him a bit more seriously.

"Keep down!" Sheydu and Nicha ran in, both of them with guns in hand. They ran to the window, followed by Thayu. Deyu was with her.

"Get them out of here," Thayu said.

Deyu and Nicha helped me and Federza up and ushered us to the back of the room. Thayu and Sheydu each stood on either side of the molten hole in the glass. The charge had gone straight through the room and had hit the opposite wall, where I intended to put a bookshelf, but that was still empty. It had left a mark on the paint but had hit nothing important—because the important things it wanted to hit was us? Or rather, Federza?

Eirani ran in, all wide-eyed and panicked. "Oh, Muri, what

happened—oh." Nicha's outstretched arm stopped her. She covered her mouth with her hand. "Look at your clothes, Muri."

I looked. There were burn holes in my shirt and trousers. I had no idea if any of the glass had hit my skin. My mind was racing too much to feel anything.

"How dare they shoot at you? These criminals are getting away with everything. This is just outrageous. Not even in my time with—"

"Quiet." Sheydu cut off Eirani's flow of words. She wore her earpiece and was listening to something. Thayu held up her tracker. The screen flashed with a wriggly line.

Eirani glared sideways at the two Coldi women.

"Take them out of here," Thayu ordered in a low voice.

I protested. "Thay', you get yourself to safety, too."

She gave me a *don't argue* look.

Eirani muttered something in keihu about rudeness. "That's right, Muri. Do come with me. I will give you some tea to soothe the nerves. Let the soldiers do the shooting." She turned into the corridor, leaving us staring at her big backside.

Federza and I followed Eirani to the sitting room. My ears were still ringing and I felt unsteady on my feet, as if my knees would give away any moment. The corridor had never seemed so long.

Xinanu came out of Nicha's room in her nightshirt and stared at me, in particular at a spot on my side where the glass had burned through my shirt and that was now starting to hurt like blazes.

Damn it, damn it.

This apartment was meant to be a safe haven for me and everyone who lived here and was part of my staff or association, even Xinanu who annoyed the crap out of everyone. Eirani and the other local staff *deserved* a safe environment. Living on the island was about being safe. If I wanted break-ins, robberies and shootings, I would have moved to town.

That flash I'd seen would have been a long way off the island. *Gamra* security was strict and, so far, effective. They would patrol the waters around the island. They had warning systems set up if anyone crossed into the exclusion zone, and cameras, trip wires and infrared scanning equipment. Did that mean that the shot had been fired from outside the exclusion zone?

In the living room, we were met by the shocked stares of a

number of other members of my staff. Devlin, Yaris, all the kitchen staff. Reida was there, too, looking unimpressed, with his hair mussed from sleep. He sat with his hands clamped between his knees. He didn't meet my eyes when we came in. At some point I should speak to him, maybe even in the presence of Federza so that he could apologise straight away, but all that didn't seem so important now.

Xinanu came in after us, walking softly on her bare feet. Reida shuffled aside to make room for her on the couch. She sat down, placing both hands on top of her belly. Her dark eyes reflected the light as she glared at me, pursing her lips.

Raanu lay on the ground on a blanket, still asleep.

"Where are Evi and Telaris?" I asked in a low voice so as not to wake her up.

No one knew. On the ground floor, outside or otherwise on the case, I guessed.

"Does anyone know what's going on?" I looked at Devlin. But he was wearing his nightclothes and hadn't been at the hub. I leaned aside so that I could look out the door, through the hall. It was dark in the hub room, and I couldn't see anything, not even the faint glow of the screens that indicated that someone was at the central bench. "Is anything wrong with the hub?"

"We shut it down temporarily," Devlin said. "For security's sake." He yawned.

"Do you know why that was necessary?" Did this have something to do with that reply to the ship? With the fact that we went to look at the spot where the reply was said to have come from? With the *Tamerians*?

"No. Just that Sheydu was yelling at us to shut everything down." He used a pretty rude pronoun, which would have been the form Sheydu had used. "So I did."

Trust Sheydu to be rude about it.

Damn. What now? Sit here and wait until there was news? I stifled a yawn.

I didn't want to talk to Federza, whose prim uniform appeared to have acquired a good number of burn holes at his back. Surely he would have some idea who had fired the shot—

Tamerian mercenaries, hired by . . . whom exactly?

—but I didn't want the story in any other way than wrapped up and presented to me by security, with advice on precautions to take.

If Federza thought that only I could offer him safety, there was obviously something going on within the Aghyrian group. It was just a thing Aghyrians would do: hire others to do their fighting. The Aghyrian groups were parties in the claim and negotiations, and I couldn't get involved. Didn't want to be involved. Damn it, this was *my house* that had been attacked.

Eirani came in and set tea and fruit on the table. I poured some tea, for me and then Federza. He didn't want it so I left it on the table. He looked more shaken than I'd ever seen him.

"Drink the tea, please. I'll get my housekeeper to give you a snack." Otherwise he might faint.

He stared at me blankly, and didn't move. I put a cup on the table in front of him.

I took my cup anyway, got up from the couch again and looked into the hall.

Behind me, Eirani said, "They said we had to stay in here, Muri. For our safety."

I turned back from the door and sat on the couch again.

Federza must have changed his mind about the tea. He clutched his cup in both hands. Whenever he lifted it to his mouth, his hands trembled.

His eyes met mine.

"Is there anything we should know about the danger you're in at this point in time?"

He glanced around the room. "No."

Too quick? Afraid? I didn't know. It was hard to tell. He glanced at the cupboard against the back wall of the room. In most apartments, that was where the security recording equipment was. Maybe he still wanted me to turn it off. I didn't care. I wasn't going to and I was going to make sure that he was being watched.

The apartment's front door opened. There were footsteps in the hall and a moment later Telaris appeared in the door opening. He wore his armour over his uniform, and carried one of his guns in his hand.

I went to the door. "*Mashara*, any news?"

"*Mashara* did not find any trace of the culprits. They were too far away, and there is no trace of the attack in the garden. *Gamra* security are combing the reed fields." He came closer to me, enveloping me in his Indrahui onion-y scent. "This is confidential and the delegate didn't hear it: Trader Delegate Federza's apartment has been trashed. It seems that people broke in by blasting a hole in the façade."

Shit. I glanced over my shoulder at Federza. He didn't appear to have heard Telaris' news.

I lowered my voice. "So, *mashara* thinks that they were definitely after him and not me?"

He made a *who knows?* gesture. And then a *quiet* gesture.

I nodded.

"Can we move around inside this apartment?"

"*Mashara* advises waiting. The outside is not yet secure. Thayu and Sheydu are searching the garden and surrounding spaces. Then we will concentrate on resources inside this apartment."

"Thanks, *mashara*." They rarely gave me this much information about their operations. I guessed *concentrate on resources inside this apartment* meant the questioning of Federza and the staff.

"How much longer?" I stifled another yawn. I wanted Thayu and Nicha to come back to tell me what was going on elsewhere on the island.

"*Mashara* will notify everyone."

And he was gone again. I returned to my position on the couch, while avoiding Federza's questioning looks and Xinanu's angry glare.

Reida gave a soft snort. *He* had fallen asleep on the couch.

8

TELARIS WENT BACK to his work. He did give me permission to go into the hub as long as I didn't go to the ground floor, and I wandered into its darkness and sat down at the central bench. I needed time to think. I didn't want to face Federza and take part in the staring game between him and the rest of my staff, or suffer through prolonged uneasy silence or Xinanu's contempt. Or Eirani's fidgeting *because all the dishes still need to be done.* Apparently the hub had satisfied whatever my security had wanted to check, and the functionality had been returned. I stared at the flickering lights on the controls, barely registering their meaning.

Damn, I was tired.

How long before Thayu, Nicha, Veyada and Sheydu were finished going over the apartment and surrounding yard?

Every now and then I thought I heard footsteps coming closer through the corridor, but I was always mistaken or the person went somewhere else.

This was turning into a big, messy issue that was as clear as mud to me, and had dangerous elements if only I know what they were and who we faced.

Reida breaking into Federza's office, potentially under orders of another association.

Nicha potentially tangled up with that association.

Federza fearing for his life, a fear that was justified by this attack,

and this attack might have been carried out by Tamerians—hired by
. . . who exactly?

The same Tamerians who had been searching for the source of
that responding signal?

And the Asto army watched us all from above, sending warnings
about their presence in the form of not one, but four supply shuttles.

What a mess.

Above all, the thought that I had to speak to Nicha, and quite
urgently, sat as a brick in my stomach. Coldi people might be used to
the question *I know we've lived together for many years, but how well can I
actually trust you?* but I certainly wasn't. By my reckoning, Nicha
wouldn't be either, if I knew him well enough, which I *thought* I did.
But Coldi society had this habit of turning around and slapping me
around the ears with my own ignorance.

I'd never had a reason to investigate Nicha's mother's background.
He had said that he didn't have a lot of contact with her anymore, and
I believed him.

Most communication might have been disconnected from the
hub, but I still had access to all the information databases.

I brought up information about Nicha's parentage. His mother's
name was Tanayu and she came from the Inner Circle branch of the
Palayi clan. She was a very distant cousin to Ezhya, but too far
removed to have any importance in Coldi public life. I'd seen her once
—Nicha had kind of fallen out with her, too—and she was a polite,
very Coldi, unremarkable, high-ranking administrator.

There was nothing in her file that I didn't already know, and her
current employment—Asto's water authorities—gave away nothing of
her feelings, or the lack of them, towards the ruling leaders in the
Inner Circle. Or, for that matter, on the subject of *zeyshi* or their
claim. Apart from the fact that *zeyshi* lived in the aquifers, and that
she was responsible for those aquifers.

Hmmm.

Of course she was Thayu's mother, too, but Thayu had never lived
with her. And Thayu was younger than Nicha and had probably been
handed over to her father soon after birth. She had been raised by
military people. Their mother was an administrator and politician.
Thayu had been educated in a strict household, while Nicha's
upbringing had been much more relaxed. Brother and sister appeared

to never have spent much time together until Thayu came to live with me. Maybe it could be that Nicha . . . felt a little lost.

And that had left an opening for him to re-establish contact with his mother, who might then have roped him into a chain of command that I didn't want in my association. This could also be why Nicha had suddenly changed his contract and where Xinanu came into the picture. I definitely didn't trust her.

Did the link that ordered Reida to break into Federza's office come through Nicha or Reida?

Damn, my whole concept of safety had been overturned.

Who could I trust?

Nicha *should* be in that group, but at the moment he was not. Not until I had that talk with him, and to be honest I didn't know where he stood right now, especially if Federza chose to take the matter of Reida breaking into his office to court, as was his right. The only consolation was that it would be the Barresh court, which limited the damage to me, but would be worse for Reida. Having chosen the young man as subordinate, would Nicha defend him? And as superior of both of them, what was I supposed to do?

I felt sick.

So, the people I trusted were:

Thayu.

Veyada.

Sheydu.

Evi and Telaris.

That was it.

Bunker down and re-group. I had to sort this issue out. *Yedama*. Regrouping of the association.

Shit. My heart was hammering. I never left Nicha out of anything.

I took the reader from my pocket and sent each of those people on my list a message. *Meet as soon as possible to reconsolidate*. I didn't have to state the venue. The highest security meetings were always held in bathrooms. Part superstition and part because bugs had more trouble picking up clear recordings in large hollow-sounding rooms.

But before I met with the others, I had to make sure that Federza had left the apartment or at the very least left this floor. Then I'd make sure to put Nicha and Reida out of earshot by putting them on the door duty. It was a shitty arrangement, but I wasn't going to talk to Nicha unless I could get him alone. I was not going to embarrass him in front of the rest of the team, or Xinanu.

When Evi told me the apartment was secure, I went back into the living room where Raanu had just woken up and sat looking bleary-eyed on her blanket.

The soft conversation in the room died the moment I came through the door. All those people looked at me, people who I had considered part of my household—well, except Federza of course. But the kitchen staff and the office staff, and Reida and Deyu. They'd all been unfamiliar to me when I came, and I'd learned to work with them. Was I back to not knowing who I could trust? That shook me badly.

"*Mashara* says it is safe to move around in the apartment."

"Finally," Eirani said. She rose from the couch. "I was afraid we'd have to spend the night here. Come, young lady." She took Raanu's hand.

Raanu had her other hand in front of her mouth. She was yawning so much that tears rolled over her cheeks. For once, she had nothing smart to say.

The other staff also rose and went out.

Reida had woken up, and attempted to sneak out the door with the others.

"Reida."

The young man turned sharply to me. Oh, yes, he was expecting a good talking-to.

"Go and see Nicha. Tell him that I'd like you and him to relieve Evi and Telaris at the door. Tell both of them to see me."

He nodded, visibly relieved, and bolted from the room.

My eyes met Federza's, since he was only one left in the living room. "I've been informed that there has also been an attack on your apartment." I kept my pronouns as impersonal as possible.

His sand-coloured eyes met mine. He nodded, but said nothing.

"Were you aware of this?" A little bit more personal.

"No, Delegate, I was not." He pressed his lips together.

"Apparently, the front wall was blown out."

"It's all glass." He took a deep breath and let it back out. "I guess guards are swarming all over it and they have the area closed off."

"Probably. Will you have somewhere to stay safely overnight? I can get my people to escort you to alternate accommodation. We'll make sure that the area is safe and that—"

"It's all futile." The stress almost made his voice crack.

"Not if my security has anything to do with it."

He shook his head. "I can run, Delegate, but they will get me in the end."

"You're talking about Tamerians, right?"

He said nothing, but didn't deny it either.

"Tamerians who are here on the order of some of your kinsfolk who disagree with you for some reason that makes them very angry."

"Actually, it's me doing the disagreeing. It's no joking matter, Delegate."

"I wasn't suggesting that it was."

He breathed out a sigh. Relief? He took in another deep breath, shuddering.

He continued meeting my eyes in a kind of desperate way that told me that there was a lot more going on in that head of his and we kind of looked at each other like that, as if neither of us wanted to start, or to reach out a hand, or even show sympathy.

I disliked the man. Ever since I'd first met him, at the uniform shop on the ground floor of this building, he had behaved like a slippery snake and pompous arse. He talked over people's heads. He told half-truths, and never gave anyone any attention unless he thought that he could benefit from it.

And yet, here he was, broken and more afraid than I'd seen anyone in a long time. Too scared to tell me what was going on.

In the little sliver of the hall that I could see from my position, I noticed Thayu walk past in the direction of the bathroom. They'd be waiting for me. Evi and Telaris had already gone past and they were still officially on duty, and I couldn't allow Nicha and Reida too much time at the door wondering why they'd been put there.

I took a step towards the hall. "Look, I have to go for a little while now. If you are really too scared to leave, I can ask my staff to put a spare bed in one of the rooms downstairs. I have a room that doesn't have any windows, if that puts your mind at ease. I will come back later to talk."

"Accepted."

If he kept insisting on having the bugs turned off, I'd bring Thayu or Veyada into the room with me. Veyada probably. His memory was incredible.

I went into the hall, where I found one of the kitchen staff and asked him to instruct Eirani to take Federza down to the staff quarters and put him in the spare bedroom. The one without the windows, that the staff used as storage room. I debated asking the young man to lock the door behind him, but decided that would be a bit over the top and not appropriate for someone of Federza's status. I asked him to watch the stairs instead, to make sure that no one came back up.

"Not even Eirani?"

"Eirani is all right, and anyone else who works here. Just not him. No one else while he's watching."

I hoped he understood. I ran into the bathroom, where my team already sat in the water. The steamy air hit me in the face.

"Any problems?" Thayu asked after the door had rolled shut with a clatter of wooden slats.

"Federza. Is that enough of a problem for you?"

She rolled her eyes.

"We have to talk to him," Sheydu said. "I didn't like the way he was behaving at the meeting. I think he knows who shot at him."

"Tamerians," I said.

She gave me a sharp *how do you know that?* look.

I dropped my clothes on one of the benches that surrounded the bathing pool and slipped into the water. "Thayu and I went for dinner. Afterwards, we decided to have a look at the location where the reply signal to the ship was supposed to have come from. We found three Tamerians in black council uniform—" The one council badge I'd seen had been dirty. Not a state in which I would have expected council workers to wear their uniform to work. "—who were out there looking for the source of the signal."

"At this time of day?"

"It was immediately after dinner. Not terribly late yet."

"In the dark?"

"Yes, it was very dark out there."

"Tamerians have good night vision," Veyada reminded her.

"They'd better, because we couldn't see anything."

Sheydu interrupted, in her typical blunt way, "Does this have anything to do with us, because, you know, I have a lot of work still to do tomorrow, and there is another meeting, so I'd like to catch some sleep if I can."

"It does have something to do with us, in a roundabout way."

Sheydu snorted. She didn't like roundabout ways.

I told the assembled group about Reida, his break-in, his possible loyalty elsewhere and through him, Nicha. Thayu watched me, nodding occasionally, as if letting me know that I'd understood the matter correctly.

When I finished, there was an intense silence.

"Well, bugger that," Sheydu said. "I thought this arrangement with those youngsters was strange, but I wasn't going to say anything because, you know, you're not Coldi and you might do things differently."

Veyada snorted. "I've never known you not to say anything."

Thayu said, "We're not sure that there definitely is a problem, we only want you to be alert that there might be. If you find anything that points that way, report it to us."

I added, "The stability of our association will be of importance in the negotiations. This household will be at the centre of the negotiations that will, to some extent, determine the future of Asto. Many people want to influence us. The Barresh Aghyrians had expected to dictate the agenda, and they were thoroughly gazumped by the *zeyshi* claim. Everyone is jostling for the best positions, trying to gather as much knowledge, as many claims and counterclaims as they can. We are a target. Someone obviously wants to discredit us with the Barresh Aghyrians and sends Reida to break in . . ." I held up my hands. Federza's reaction didn't make much sense in that line of reasoning. He was supposed to have been furious at me for sending Reida, and I of course would be caught on the back foot because I hadn't sent Reida.

Sheydu still stared into my eyes in a kind of *and?* expression. I let my hands sink. "There are enough threats from outside our household. We don't need any from within."

She said, "Loyalty threats are hard. Because when loyalty is dubious, you can ask me many times are you still loyal, and I will say yes, even when we both know it's not the case. I have too much invested in being here and living in this house. I'll try to hang onto it for as long as I can. You won't want to upset the entire association, and also, the reason for diminished loyalty may be temporary. Doing nothing is usually a better option until it is not, but those resolutions are rarely easy. The outside threats are easier to deal with. Let us work on those first."

Veyada gave her a sharp look. "I presume we're going to question Federza about what Reida could possibly want."

I said, "It looks like Federza will be staying here tonight. Have you established anything about the state of his apartment?"

"The front has blown out. The *gamra* people are going over it now."

Sheydu made a noise that sounded like *idiots*.

"For what it's worth, I think that Cory's reasoning, even incomplete, makes sense," Thayu said. It was quite unnerving how the sound of her voice made Veyada and Sheydu take notice and how they didn't seem to have that reaction for me.

They will push me aside as soon as I become superfluous to their aims. In reality, Thayu was the leader of our association. I was just for show. That was why Nicha's half of the association wasn't working.

I said, "It's my guess that Federza is afraid of people he knows, maybe even those within the Aghyrian community."

"Why is that, do you think?" Veyada asked.

"I have no idea."

"Because Federza has something these people want, or want to destroy?" Sheydu said in a bored voice. "Like: money. That's always a good motive. We're not talking about Coldi here. Their motives for fighting each other will be strange like that." She glanced at Evi and Telaris, neither of whom had said anything so far.

Coldi didn't fight over money; they fought over loyalty, partnership contracts, and, oddly enough, what we would call petty crime. Theft was a breach of loyalty, a much more serious offense than in most other *gamra* entities. In Evi and Telaris' world of Indrahui, there were a lot of fights about honour and tribe. Indrahui were bigger experts on vendettas than the Sicilian mafia.

I said, "Whatever it is, we need to know with some urgency, because it will affect the negotiations, even if Federza has been relieved from his position as representative. We need to know why this happened."

There were silent, grave nods all around.

"All right. What do we do now?" Thayu asked.

I wasn't sure if she asked me or the group in general, but I had to think about it for a while. Everyone else was thinking, too, or maybe they waited for me to speak. Thayu gave a me a *why the hell do you keep taking off your feeder?* look. Everyone was tired and grumpy, and sure wouldn't like the conclusion I was reaching. Hell, I didn't like my conclusion.

I spoke in a low voice. "These people who have attacked both this apartment and Federza's apartment are obviously still around somewhere, probably around the apartment. The only way off the island is via the train—that doesn't run much at night—or the water. They may have shot from outside the exclusion zone, but guards would have picked up sound and movement in the reeds, especially if they used a boat."

"Don't overestimate the capabilities of the *gamra* guards," Sheydu said.

I ignored her comment. "They haven't reported anything, so it's my guess that at least some of these people are still here, or they may have left clues about what they were after."

She snorted. "Like what Reida was doing in that office."

"Yes, but I very much doubt that his loyalty would be mixed up with the Barresh Aghyrians."

"So that is coincidence that he was after Federza's stuff as well?" She flicked her eyebrows up.

"We simply don't know. But I'm saying that if we want to investigate, we should do that now, tired as I expect you all are." Hell, *I* was tired.

Veyada said, "There is no such thing as coincidence, only sheer luck and sheer stupidity."

Thayu and Sheydu simultaneously named the originator of the proverb, "Rimada Domiri, Commander of the armed forces."

I could have added my voice to that. I was starting to make serious inroads in recognising the authors of a good number of the thousands of Coldi proverbs.

Veyada grinned, and gave Sheydu a playful look. As usual, a recited proverb was a great tension breaker.

Sheydu stretched and yawned. Then she jumped out of the bath in one athletic movement. Stark naked, she grabbed her clothes and gun.

"Well, what the fuck, eh? Let's go and check on the work of those trusted *gamra* guards. Let's see if we can discover something that they didn't. That shouldn't be too hard." She pulled on her trousers without drying herself.

Veyada and Thayu also jumped out, leaving me in the water with Evi and Telaris.

"Does the delegate still require *mashara*'s services?" Evi asked in a low voice.

"No. I wanted to make sure that *mashara* knew what was going on."

"Is it official that Nicha cannot be trusted?"

I cringed. "Not official, and I intend to sort this out as soon as possible. For the time being, try to avoid involving him in sensitive situations. *Especially* don't involve Reida. Though only until I give the all clear. But I definitely want Federza watched at all times."

They nodded, and then we all got out.

Thayu pointed at me when we were leaving the bathroom. "Wear your armour. And your feeder."

Yeah, shit. Battle gear again.

9

———

A S GAMRA REPRESENTATIVE supposedly neutral in the Aghyrian case against Asto, I had the right to request information and to investigate the dealings and integrity of all parties in the negotiations. I intended to abuse the hell out of that right.

We moved like a well-oiled machine. I got dressed, went to the bedroom to put on the armour. I fished the feeder out of the pocket of my trousers and transferred it back into my hair, where it settled with the familiar burst of warmth.

Good to have you with us again, Thayu said.

I sent Devlin to bed, and told Telaris and Evi to resume their positions at the door and send Nicha and Reida back inside to rest.

I met Nicha crossing the hallway going back to his room. He was still not looking at me. Still expecting me to lash out, or maybe not, or afraid I would lash out. Nicha had been at my side for the best part of eight years. I did *not* want to do this.

How Coldi was Nicha, really? And how much of the societal structure was built into a Coldi person's genes and how much was learned? No one really knew.

I trusted Deyu with the special task of locking the door to Federza's room. I definitely did not want him to snoop around the apartment while I was away.

Thayu took me aside in the hall while we waited for Veyada to collect his gear. "What's this about, Cory? You've got that gleam in your eyes that you're up to something."

"Nothing too crazy or dangerous. We're going to pay a visit to Federza's apartment. I want to see if I can get anything out of the guards or bystanders. There is something going on with this Aghyrian group and I would like to know what it is before we get into the real negotiations."

"Well, we have until tomorrow morning." The agenda for the day's meeting would start to venture into subjects on which I expected substantial disagreement.

To my horror, it was already tomorrow morning, if very early, and there was too much still to be done. Talk to Nicha, talk to Reida, talk to Federza. Never mind prepare for the actual meeting. Oh and sleep. What was that again?

Thayu asked, "If Federza has fallen out with Barresh Aghyrians, who do you think they will send as replacement?"

There was that problem, too. "I have no idea. They don't exactly make a habit of being open." To be honest, I didn't even know too many other Aghyrians. They kept themselves well in the background.

"No, they don't."

"A replacement could be better, but it could also be a lot worse."

"I'm betting on the *worse* scenario."

I agreed. Federza might be an arrogant prick, but his experience as Trader meant that he had at least some appreciation of other people's living conditions. He'd been places, travelled a lot. "Federza says that he has a pretty good idea of who sent the people shooting at us, presumably the same ones causing all this other mischief, and he might tell me if I offer him sanctuary."

"Then why start investigating at Federza's apartment?"

"I'm hoping to learn something about Federza's motives. For all his unpleasant bluster, he sounds genuinely scared. There is something going on in that Aghyrian community that has perhaps been festering since Sirkonen's murder, or even before that. Someone is keen to settle some scores before the serious meeting rounds about the Aghyrian claim start. Well, that's my guess. I'm not sure how or even if it relates to the *zeyshi* Aghyrians or if the Barresh Aghyrian community is just supremely pissed off that with all their sophistication, breeding programs and money, they still couldn't secure a claim.

Maybe Federza is trying to come out with what's been happening behind the scenes. Maybe he's in the thick of it. I don't know. Then there is the issue of Reida. I think he's nothing more than a lackey, perhaps paying off a family debt by spying, but the person who sent him, and who may also be part of Nicha's network, is trying to prove or disprove something about the Barresh Aghyrians, or maybe just Federza. Well, all of that is my interpretation of the situation."

She nodded, slowly. "That's a fair enough conclusion." She smiled. "I'll tell Veyada that he may have found his match in unravelling political conspiracy theories."

"Did anyone mention my name?" Veyada came into the hall wearing his full armour. Like this, he looked so much like the Chief Coordinator's guard he had once been. The only thing missing from his appearance was the red sash that he used to wear. I'd hinted at him a few times that it was all right for him to feel bereaved over losing his high position, but Veyada was, as always, utterly focused and professional and wouldn't even flick his eyebrows at those awkward statements of mine.

Veyada was very quickly becoming one of my most important assets. Strangely enough, I felt that he was thoroughly enjoying himself. And I liked him immensely.

He reported for Thayu's benefit, and in code, that *gamra* security had declared the island safe for level five personnel, to which Thayu made the *We'll chance it* hand signal. They were both level five personnel: armed and trained, but *I* was level one: those in need of protection.

Not that we left too much to chance. Thayu had insisted I wear full battle gear. The armour was hot to wear, but at least after the recent escapades, Nicha had finally used his contacts and gotten some custom-made for me, so that I no longer had to make do with ill-fitting equipment.

Nicha.

Hopefully whatever we would find tonight would help solve that issue. Then I'd sit down with him and Reida and get all the issues on the table, including that of secondary networks which may or may not involve Nicha's mother. We'd sort it out. Things would be back to the way they were before.

We left the apartment in the company of Sheydu, her many

pockets bristling with explosives and other dangerous gadgetry, walked down the gallery and down the stairs. Normally the inner courtyard with the waterfall would bathe in muted light, but all the lights had been turned up to the max, producing an eerie, ugly greenish glow that cast harsh, lifeless shadows.

A bunch of *gamra* guards were milling around at the entrance to our building, wearing armour over their blue and grey uniforms. Thayu told Veyada to stay with me—not prepared to push the limits on level five personnel restrictions. She trotted over to them and spoke with them briefly. There were polite nods and serious faces. One of the men spoke into his comm unit.

"We're fine to go," Thayu said when she came back. She winked at me. "They didn't recognise you."

"Any news? Have they caught anyone?"

"Not so far."

There were a lot more guards around the building, most of them just standing around.

We continued on, through the abandoned courtyards in various states of lighting. Some had areas with seating, where light illuminated tables and chairs. A bunch of meili had landed on a table where the evacuate order had come in the middle of a meal and people had abandoned their plates. The animals—about the size of a rabbit—had pushed a couple of empty plates off the table and were fighting over the contents of another plate, a tangle of black fur and leathery wings.

With the lockdown following the security breach, the passageways that were normally full of people almost day and night were now completely empty. Occasionally I caught a glimpse of a couple of people silhouetted behind a window, curious to get a glimpse of whatever required such serious action.

As far as attacks went, the effort on my apartment was a rather lame one, either carried out by inexperienced people or with insufficient weaponry. Or maybe Veyada was right and it was a warning.

The density of *gamra* guards increased towards the eastern residential wings. A lot of them, as well as Barresh guards in black, milled about without much to do. Their communication was efficient, because no one asked us who we were and where we were going, but they all gestured greetings.

Federza's apartment faced the water, separated from the edge of the island only by a broad walkway, accessible to anyone who satisfied the entry guards to the island. The apartment was on the top floor, set back from the street atop a pyramid-shaped building.

Clearly, the side facing the water usually consisted of a glass wall, but that now showed a jagged hole.

"That shot has also been fired from the water," Veyada said.

Yes, and this made it likely that these were the same people who had also fired at my apartment. Two shots, both from a long distance off the water. Which made all those guards standing around look stupid. Had anyone even entered the island's perimeter? Someone had mentioned a break-in?

Veyada squinted into the darkness over the water, where he would see nothing with his poor night vision. Heck, I didn't even see much out there except for the glimmer where the moonlight reflected in the water. If there were any Tamerians in the darkness then the guards would need better equipment to find them. Most likely they were already far too late.

We went into the entrance of the apartment building, past another bevy of guards who greeted me with polite nods and let us through, up the stairs and onto the gallery.

The apartments along here were stylish affairs with open rooms, modern and spacious compared to mine. I suspected they came without the heritage listing of my apartment.

Where Coldi often used dark colours in furnishings, all Aghyrian buildings I had visited were wide, open, with a lot of glass and in light colours. People often made jokes regarding their concern about style and appearance, but the Aghyrian propensity for artistic pursuits was well-documented. In apartments we passed, fabric on chairs matched the carpet and the curtains. In one room, there was a strange contraption on the floor that looked like a hand half-clenched into a first and turned palm up. Little platforms rested on the "fingers". I decided the thing was a table. There were works of art on the walls. The doors were of the regular variety and not the rolling ones like the ones in my apartment. I had tried to get those damn things replaced, but had been informed that I couldn't, because modifications had to be within the guidelines of the building's historical value.

We reached Federza's apartment.

The entire front wall had blown out, leaving a gaping hole filled with molten glass.

A couple of investigators were walking around and taking pictures of peculiar details: not just the gouges in the wall, but also some kind of electronic device that had fallen off the table. They were a mix of *gamra* and privately employed guards. I guessed the privately-employed ones were Federza's. They wore dark clothing but no obvious uniform. They seemed to be working with the *gamra* guards, so I guessed that was all above-board.

As with my apartment, there were globs of glass everywhere, stuck to the carpet, the walls and ceiling.

The back of the couch in front of the window had blown off, spreading stuffing and shreds of fabric over the carpet.

A bookcase had toppled over, having spilled a layer of mangled of books over the floor. I spotted pages of Coldi, Mirani and Aghyrian.

Federza's bedroom looked out over the marshlands and was next to the living room. The charge had also shattered the window here, blowing a huge shower of glass onto the floor. The bed had received some of the debris. Globs of glass had melted onto the sheets that lay untouched from this morning. There were two impressions in the mattress.

What?

To the best of my knowledge, Federza lived alone. I frowned at Thayu and sent her a ping through the feeder, but she was studying something near the remains of the window, crouching with one of her many devices pointed at the carpet. A scent detector most likely. It helped identify explosives and sometimes even culprits.

She informed me of what she knew through the feeder.

The charge had hit in the centre of the living room window, blowing it inwards. Furniture, the carpet, ceiling and wall fixtures were damaged. There was no evidence that anyone had been inside the apartment.

Just like the attack on me, this appeared to be a lame operation. What could they possibly hope to achieve by shooting at our windows from great distance? As far as the guards had been able to establish, Federza had been out when it happened. He'd either been elsewhere or had just left for my apartment. At least at my apartment, they had attempted to hit us. This was just a random shooting at a non-random person's property.

I approached one of the *gamra* guards, Indrahui like so many of them. "Have you discovered anything of note yet?"

He eyed his colleagues as if consulting whether or not he was supposed to reply to me. Some unspoken communication went between them. I couldn't pick it up on my feeder, because it was probably well-shielded.

"It is not easy," he finally said in heavily-accented Coldi.

"How so?" Playing the innocent diplomat.

Thayu rolled her eyes at me. She disliked it when I tried chatting people up, because it *presented a security situation*, but it so happened that most *gamra* people were stronger than I was, so I'd become used to talking as a means of getting what I wanted. Both Sheydu and Thayu got annoyed with the degree of success I frequently had in this manner.

This guard happened to be the talkative sort. "They shoot from outside. Window blow in. Glass everywhere."

Yes, I could see that.

"But then maybe they come in through window."

"You think so? We're on the third floor."

"You and I care about third floor. Some people don't care about third floor. They climb in, steal—"

"Have you found hard evidence that anyone came in?" That would be a major finding.

"Could be." He glanced at his colleagues, who were clustered around the electronic device that lay on the floor.

"What's that thing?" I asked, innocent as I could.

"Communication."

I clearly wasn't going to get anywhere with him. He was too busy and his Coldi was too poor. "This apartment has a hub, doesn't it?"

"Yes, over there." He gestured into the hall.

I walked over to peek in. The room was about the same size as mine but more modern. The main light was on, casting the equipment in the wan greenish light given off by the pearls on the walls. Since the Exchange had locked down the island's communication, nothing was going on at the main projection area. The auxiliaries just gave dull information scrolling over a side screen. The temperature, the weather, news from town.

"Guards don't seem to know much," I said to Thayu in a low voice.

"They're administrators. Not paid to think. Not paid to be quick, or to draw their own conclusions. Sheydu is going to have a ball."

I couldn't restrain a brief chuckle. "What do you think? They seem to think someone came in."

"I can't see any evidence of that," Thayu said. "I think it's just one of the items on the list of things they've been instructed to look out for. Most of these kinds of things are done with robbery in mind."

"I still think it's some kind of warning," Veyada said behind us. "I mean—if they really wanted to destroy the place, they would have actually destroyed it."

"Not so easy when you can't count on fire to finish the job for you."

He gave me a sharp look. Yes, that was right. It was so easy to forget that nothing burned in Barresh. Probably nothing short of a very large bomb could destroy Barresh. It was a place with an annoyingly stubborn and rebellious streak.

Thayu said, "I agree with you. It doesn't look like a particularly well-thought-out attack. It looks like an impulse thing, not planned or carried out with adequate weapons."

"It could be a diversion," Sheydu said from the door.

Everyone turned to her. Sheydu was a quiet, thinking person. She could be moody, wasn't given to niceties, disliked chatter, jokes, children and gossip, but when she made a statement, people listened. Because it meant that she had thought about it for a long time.

"A diversion—what for?" Thayu asked.

But I saw what she'd been trying to say. "Someone trying to buy some time to search his office?"

"But . . ." Veyada hesitated. "Didn't Reida just get accused of breaking into that office?"

"Not that one. Reida was at his Trading office in town."

"Federza has two offices?"

"Yes." And that might have been the reason for some of the confusion.

Because whoever these people were, they were looking for something, maybe even the same thing Reida had been sent to steal. Reida would be able to tell me what it was and whether or not he got it. *After* I spoke to Nicha.

"Shit," Veyada said.

I nodded. Shit indeed. "We should go to that office. We probably won't find anything here."

Thayu stared at me. She grabbed for her comm reader. Hesitated.

"Should we call for backup?" She meant Nicha, who was a decent shot.

"No time." I really didn't want to have to go into my misgivings and tangled-up feelings about Nicha's loyalty, especially not when Reida's breaking in was involved. "If we're right, they'd be trying something right now. We have a chance at catching or at least seeing whoever it is."

There were nods at that, too.

Veyada tried again. "But wouldn't the guards have picked up intruders?"

Sheydu snorted. "The fact that the guards can't see them doesn't mean that intruders are not there. The security in this place is shit. I'm sure I told you that before."

She said that almost once every day. This was the part where we would all laugh and someone would tell her to relax, because this wasn't Asto. Except we all knew that she was right, and we had never thought that it mattered a great deal. The attacks on the *gamra* island were of the political type, so great amounts of money were spent on bugging and on show. On actual effective security for the island as a whole, not so much.

Thayu unclipped her spare gun from her belt. She undid the straps and rethreaded them through the bracket at the back so that it became an arm bracket. She handed it to me. "You take this."

I strapped the weapon on while we started walking. At Thayu's insistence, I had been taking some weapons training. *Because we can't keep relying on someone stupid enough to walk right into your path without seeing you.* She'd been talking about Taysha Palayi who hadn't known I was there until the very last moment, and hadn't seen me in the semi-darkness and chaos of Asto's central command hub because of the Coldi's poor night vision. I would not ever be an ace shot, but I felt a bit more comfortable with weapons.

We walked across the island, to the administration building in the forecourt, to the station where Federza had his office. To reach it, you had to go up a stairwell to the first floor, or you could walk along the central corridor that ran through the middle of the building. Thayu chose the corridor.

We walked as quietly as we could, but to me our footsteps still sounded like a horde of elephants approaching. Thayu's feeder told me that she'd chosen this path because if we flushed out someone, they'd have to flee down the stairs and into the open of the courtyard, rather than into the building, where the chance of hitting them with a shot was negligible.

I had been to this office before, having come up the stairs from the courtyard. I remembered the sophisticated furniture and the bookcases.

Thayu stopped abruptly in front of me. I had expected it, so stopped just as quickly behind her.

The door to the office had been kicked in and stood ajar.

We listened. I stood behind Thayu leaning against the wall, and Veyada and Sheydu against the opposite wall, holding their guns to take care of anyone who might come out. Coldi people had this eerie ability to breathe totally without noise, even if they had been running. I wasn't so lucky.

Thayu set her scanner to infrared and pointed it at the door. The little screen showed indistinct blobs of green and black. After a while, she shook her head. Sheydu pushed the door but stuff had been thrown against it from the inside and it wouldn't open.

She gestured *Is there another way out?*

Thayu shook her head.

Veyada gestured, *He's still in there.*

Maybe. Scan is negative. The office was on the first floor and it might be possible to escape through a window.

Veyada came to help Sheydu and together they shoved whatever was behind the door aside so that it would open. Thayu covered them, holding her gun in both hands and pointing it at the door.

There was a lot of stuff on the floor in the office: broken equipment, broken furniture, old documents. Everything had been overturned, all the shelves emptied. That picture of Daya Ezmi that had hung on his wall when I'd been here before going to Asto now lay on the floor.

Thayu scanned the room again. The window was intact. A door in the left hand wall went to a little kitchen and storage area.

Inconclusive, Thayu said of the scan results. Sheydu clicked her gun back into its bracket and exchanged it for the heavier weapon on her belt. Veyada did the same.

They inched forward into the office, backs facing each other, their dark eyes roving over every possible place that might present danger. I pressed myself against the wall in the corridor, knowing my utter uselessness in these situations. I barely dared breathe.

I could see Thayu's infrared screen, which showed no distinct shapes or heat sources, but they might have shielding. Our own armour wouldn't show much heat either, especially not when hidden, like in a cupboard. Apparently my body temperature was so low that I barely showed up on scans at all.

No one spoke. Veyada and Sheydu inched very slowly into the room until they were a good few paces in. Sheydu lowered her gun. She walked to the side wall and yanked open a door in a cupboard that stood out of my field of vision. She pointed her gun inside, waited, eying the contents of the cupboard.

Finding nothing in there that interested her, she shut the door, twisted a safe tie around the handles so the cupboard could not be opened from the inside in case she had overlooked something. She turned to the other side of the room and opened another door there, but also found nothing.

Veyada crouched behind the door to examine the debris they'd had to push aside to get the door to open. Veyada rarely shared his thoughts, but I picked up some of his deliberations about how someone could have dragged it with one hand reaching into the room and dropped it against the door to create the illusion that someone was still inside.

Sheydu went into the little kitchen and came out a moment later. *Nothing*, she gestured.

Thayu lowered her gun and also went into the room.

Now that the three of them had declared it safe enough to enter, I followed.

The office had been well and truly trashed. All of Federza's elegant furniture smashed to bits. They'd even put gouges in the wall. Why?

I stepped over the debris to the desk. In the wall behind it was a cupboard that had contained electronics. The pieces of equipment lay in fragments on the floor, readers and projectors and timers and Trader-related equipment which I didn't recognise, even a device that looked suspiciously Earth-made—

There was a tiny noise.

I froze and held my breath.

Veyada, next to me, also stopped and grabbed for his gun.

For several long moments, we stared around the room.

Any cupboard doors that Sheydu had not safe-tied stood open. There was no way that anyone hid in there. The door in the opposite wall led to a small kitchen where there was a bed along one wall. The little room had no windows. No one could hide in there either. Not after Sheydu had checked.

Thayu scanned the room with her infrared scanner again. I could see the screen over her shoulder—and then remembered the fight in the foyer in front of Ezhya's private apartment, where attackers had hidden in the dome.

There was a manhole in the ceiling. It was probably not obvious to people—and software—unfamiliar with Barresh architecture. Thayu used an Asto-made scanner.

I met Veyada's eyes and looked up.

He noticed the manhole. *Fuck*, he whispered soundlessly.

Sheydu and Thayu now also looked up.

Veyada sneaked around the room, carefully stepping over debris without making a single sound, keeping his gun pointed at the manhole. Thayu dialled up the sensitivity and scanned the ceiling. A very faint and indistinct lighter-coloured blob showed up. She showed it to Veyada, who aimed his gun and fired at the ceiling. The charge went straight through, and left a bright white trail on Thayu's scanner. It left a blackened hole in the plaster, but otherwise missed the lighter blob. On purpose, because Veyada wouldn't miss at this distance.

There was another scuffing noise. Now I could see clearly how the grey blob *moved*.

Veyada shot again, now hitting the ceiling on the other side of the blob. Bits of ceiling plaster rained down. "If you come out now, we'll let you live."

Nothing.

Sheydu dragged the desk under the manhole and found a chair

that still had enough legs to stay upright. She climbed on the desk, hauled the chair up, put it on the desk and climbed on. She had to bend her head to stop it from hitting the ceiling.

Thayu motioned me to the door with her gun.

I retreated into the corridor.

Then Sheydu punched the manhole cover upwards into the ceiling with both hands. A flash went off from inside. A man shouted and jumped from the manhole, shooting a wild spray of charges into the wall.

Sheydu fired once, a thick, white-hot beam of light that struck the attacker square in the back of the head.

The man hit the ground and crumpled. He did not get up.

Sheydu calmly stuck her gun back into the bracket at her belt. "I never thought those flashy firework shooters were any good."

She jumped down from the table with a solid *thud*.

Veyada had turned the man onto his back. His face was slack, his eyes unfocused, open and unmoving. He'd smeared his cheeks with dirt to make it stand out less in the darkness, but his skin was pale.

Sheydu snorted. "Tamerian. Hired muscle. They're supposed to be good." Clearly the operative word in that sentence was *supposed*. "Whoever sent him was even too cowardly to do the dirty work themselves."

Veyada searched the man's pockets, but found nothing. No ID, no loot, nothing to say who had sent this man.

"Well, that's annoying," he said.

I would call a death more than "annoying", but we were still wrestling with the question whether to call Tamerians human and if their deaths were real deaths, since they'd been bred for warfare, and their death would qualify as *hazards of the job*.

"Hmmm," Sheydu said. "If he's got nothing on him that means that either he didn't find what he was looking for, or the thing he was looking for can be sent electronically."

"We can get the building's hub logs," I said.

"Not until office hours."

"True."

Thayu had picked up his gun and studied the controls. "That's an unusual thing. I might keep that for a little investigation." She slid it into her belt.

As she did so, a flash erupted from a patch on the man's clothes.

"Shit, what's that?" Veyada kneeled next to him. The little patch had looked like a decoration attached to his shirt.

Sheydu whipped out her knife and cut the section of fabric that held the thing. She held it on her palm. The tiny device was only the size of a button and had a few tiny glass windows at the top. A spy camera?

"What was that?" came the voice of Devlin, who sat in the hub in my apartment and who was in contact with Thayu through the earpiece that dangled from her collar.

Thayu said, "I don't know. It's a thing stuck to his clothes. It appears to be some sort of spying device. It has a little glass eye."

"It just sent out a signal," Devlin said.

Thayu pulled the gun that she'd taken off the man from her belt again. "Could it be that it's a warning, slaved to his gun?" She frowned at the controls. "I'm pretty sure I'd turned it off, but this is some damn specialist gear. Look at the suit, too. These are professionals."

Sheydu snorted. Clearly *she* did not think so. Then again, she'd spent the prime years of her life guarding the most closely-guarded official in all of the *gamra* worlds and I'd bet the non-*gamra* worlds as well.

"I'm getting replies to that blip," Devlin said, a tinny voice through Thayu's earpiece.

"Where from?" she asked.

"A few places within the complex. One blip at a time each."

"Which places?" I leaned over Thayu's shoulder so that he could hear me.

"One of them was in the courtyard in front of the assembly hall. Another on the other side of our building, but it has since moved to the back."

"Shit," Veyada said.

I met his eyes, and we both knew that the problem was bigger than we'd realised. Because there wasn't just one or two Tamerians, there were loads of them, and likely they *hadn't* found what they were looking for, and I was starting to think that maybe Reida might have gotten to this thing first instead.

"We've got to go home."

10

____

WE WALKED BACK as fast as we could without running. Back through the building, down the stairs, through the quiet, leafy courtyards bathed in the harsh light from light pearls, past the guards. I had trouble keeping up, and Thayu, Veyada and Sheydu weren't even breathing fast.

Thayu, next to me, was fiddling with her comm reader.

"What are you doing?"

"I'm warning Evi and Telaris to put higher security on the door, and Nicha to keep an eye on what happens inside."

I felt cold. I would soon face the ultimate test of loyalty with Nicha.

The guards outside our building looked surprised to see us hurrying back. They hesitated, some reaching for their guns as if to look alert, even if they weren't sure what they were supposed to be alert about.

"Is there a problem?" their patrol leader asked when we were close enough.

"Have you seen anyone leave or enter the building?" Thayu asked.

There were headshakes to this question. The man gave me a *did we notice that you went out?* look.

"Have you run infrared scans of the area?"

They confirmed that they had, but had seen nothing abnormal.

Thayu briefly explained what we had seen.

"Several of them, on the island?" their patrol leader said. "Impossible. We've been standing here all night. I don't know where your data came from, but—"

"They're Tamerians."

He fell quiet. Met his colleague's eyes. The colleague pulled out his gun and dialled up the beam strength. The patrol leader nodded.

"Well . . . thank you. We'll keep an eye out."

We continued into the building, through the light-filled atrium. When we were climbing the stairs, Sheydu said in a low voice, "Idiots."

I was beginning to see what she meant.

Evi attended the guard post outside the door. I'd rarely known him to display any emotion and he looked most professional and unflappable, acknowledging us with a tiny nod.

"Everyone still here?" Veyada asked.

"*Mashara* has accompanied Trader Federza to a room in the guesthouse. *Mashara* received an order from *gamra* that Trader Federza was considered to be in danger. *Mashara* was asked to bring him to a safer building."

"Shit." Guess that was to be expected. I guess I really didn't want him in my house anyway. But damn. I'd hoped to have control over him.

The guesthouse was in the middle of the island, so there would be no risk of shooting from outside the exclusion zone. Still, I didn't like it. He had come to me even though he disliked me a great deal. There was a message in that. If he thought the guesthouse was a safer option, he would have gone there in the first place and would have avoided having to deal with me.

I'm not sure what to think of it either, Thayu said through the feeder. She asked, "Do you want me to go and check on him?"

No. I want you safe with me. "Let's deal with the issue of Reida first." I also needed her with me to face Nicha. The chilling suspicion grew that we were dealing with something much bigger than we first thought, and that an ill-considered move could do a huge amount of damage.

We went into the hall, where Yaris came in from the living room and Devlin from the hub.

"Muri, I've found some more people hiding in this area. They don't show up on the infrared scans because they're wearing insulation suits. But they use the small blips like the ones we saw to communicate. They don't register as radio waves, but once you know what you're looking at, it's obvious where they are."

"Good work. Make sure you liaise with *gamra* security."

"Already doing that." He moved to go back into the hub.

I asked his disappearing back, "Where is Nicha?"

But Nicha himself came running through the corridor. He stopped when he saw me. His cheeks went red.

His eyes met mine and I stared back at him. He didn't move. According to his position in our association, he was supposed to make the subservient greeting but I had never enforced the custom because I hated it. And even he had often told me about his dislike of the custom.

And indeed, he didn't look down, and didn't acknowledge the trouble in our relationship. "You went without me."

He sounded upset, and hell, I could understand that. I would be upset. I tried to probe his feeder, but he wasn't wearing one. "Yes, I did go without you."

"Why? What have I done?"

"It's because *you* employed in our association a young man whose loyalties to someone else take priority over ours. We can't trust him until we have secured his loyalty. By extrapolation, I need to re-establish your loyalty."

I'd used the official Coldi wording. My heart was hammering in my throat. I understood that when something like this happened, a Coldi association leader was allowed to use violence to settle the matter. That was out of the question for me, even if I hadn't been weak as a newborn lamb compared to Nicha.

He didn't respond. Didn't look down either.

I softened my voice. "What's going on, Nich'? You can talk to me, you know that."

Now he looked down. His voice was soft. "You know you are the most Coldi person I know without actually being Coldi?"

Thayu made a tiny hand gesture to Veyada and Sheydu to go and secure the apartment and the two disappeared without a sound.

I gestured for Thayu and Nicha to come with me to the living room, brother and sister, like little ducklings behind me. We sat on the couches in their perfect keihu triangular setting. Straight lines and right angles offended keihu people.

There was a moment of intense silence before I started. "I'm not a Coldi person. I'm floundering, Nich', but we need to get this sorted out quickly. We're all in danger because of that boy," I said, struggling to use the friendliest pronouns I could find. I was tired and cranky, and wanted to go to bed. And before that, talk to Reida.

"We're in danger because he can't be trusted. He is working for someone else, and breaking into offices in the city on behalf of someone else. We are not only getting the blame, but whatever he is doing appears to be linked to some of the problematic events of the last few days."

Again, no reaction. I longed to put my arms around Nicha's shoulders, and tell him something would be sorted out, but betrayal against trust was one of the worst offenses in Coldi society and forgive and forget was not an option. The other people in the household would hate me if I did that. It would destabilise our association.

"I'm sorry, Nich', but I need to know what's going on and what he's after. You didn't order him to break into Federza's office? Do you know who shot at my corner room? Do you know who the man is that Sheydu shot when we disturbed him breaking into Federza's *gamra* office? Where did Reida get these orders? What are his other loyalties? Tell me, Nich', because we need to know."

My heart was thudding so much that I was afraid I would faint.

Nicha pressed his lips together, twitched his mouth, wiped sweat from his upper lip. But he didn't look like he was going to fight. He took up a rather strange position, something that was a mix of the way he would greet someone on Earth and a subservient Coldi greeting.

"I feel . . . conflicted," he said after a long silence. "I'm aware that my position places us at a risk."

I moved closer to him so that I could put my hand on his shoulder. He felt very warm through his clothes. The hand that reached up to touch mine was even warmer.

A small sound near the door was of Thayu leaving. Having judged the conversation safe, she was probably going to do any of the million things that still needed doing.

"Is anything going on with Reida?"

"It goes back longer than that."

"This is about your other networks?"

He sighed, and I took that as a yes.

"Is anyone trying to manipulate you? Do you have links in a conflicting association?"

"Some. I've had those for years. I always wanted to cut them off, but I didn't, just to please my mother. It didn't use to be important because the links were very minor and they never called in much by way of favours."

He'd been sending his mother's acquaintances information about me? I pushed away that thought. Surely he hadn't done anything as serious as that.

"I'm guessing that these links have become important through Reida?"

"Yes, and Xinanu."

I frowned at him. Was she involved as well?

"I've been stupid, Cory. I was angry, and I was stupid."

"Tell me what the issues are, and we'll see what we can do." Although if he hadn't told me about these other links in the last few years, he had to have been ashamed of the connection and the problem was probably quite unsolvable.

Nicha shrugged but started talking. "I told you a while ago that I was negotiating a contract for a partnership for one child?"

Yes, he had spoken about that, at the time when I still feared that Thayu might be that person. Once it became clear that Thayu was his sister, the issue had been forgotten, and I had never heard him talk about it since.

"What happened?" Coldi partnership contracts were notoriously volatile. I'd seen that myself.

"Nothing. The woman was busy and I was busy and I didn't feel like taking up the contract when there was so much happening around me. But we kept postponing the arrangements, but never cancelling the contract, so when I was at Asto and you told me to look for *zhaymas* I thought to visit her, because you and Thay' were talking. . . ."

Yes, I'd talked about finding a donor so Thayu could have the second child she was entitled to, but likewise, I hadn't done much more than request a list of potential candidates and interview a couple of candidates. That issue still sat in the back of my mind like a hot potato. I wanted to use Menor. Thayu had reservations. We'd had little time to discuss the matter. I felt guilty about it, but we were so busy.

And the fact that Nicha found this embarrassing to talk about was telling in itself. Coldi people were not easily embarrassed by bodily functions. Hell, they'd have sex at a party in front of all their friends and think nothing of it. Both genders joked about it even. Being embarrassed was an *Earth* reaction. A chilling thought: how much was Nicha struggling with Coldi customs? How much was *my* training at Athens also *his* training?

Holy shit.

"Anyway, I visited this woman—"

"I didn't think the woman of your contract was Xinanu?" She didn't strike me as someone who would patiently wait for years after signing the contract.

"No." He looked at his hands.

"Then how did she come into the picture?"

Now he closed his eyes and breathed out, looking more intently at his hands. "It turned out that my contracted woman wanted to break the contract. There was a man who wanted to buy me out."

I'd done that with Thayu, a fucking fortune it had cost me, too, but I ended up getting my money back, because I'd shot the guy over a different issue. "So you went to negotiate."

"I thought it was only fair to her. Sorry, I know you don't like this custom."

It wasn't that I didn't like it, it was that I didn't think he liked it either.

"To be honest, I felt really terrible after that. I'd wanted to ask if she could come to Barresh to have the baby. She was really nice and polite. You would not have had all the trouble with her and Eirani that you're now having with Xinanu."

Let's not talk about Xinanu. The thought of her makes me grumpy. "So, what happened?"

"Well, I was lonely and I had a load of money. I was going to the Outer Circle bars to find *zhaymas*. Instead I got drunk. In fact, I got more drunk than I've been for a long time."

"Not even the time when we went to Damarq and started drinking that . . . what was it called again?"

One corner of his mouth moved up. "Well, maybe as drunk as that."

That was definitely not one of my most salubrious moments.

"Anyway, while I was being an idiot, this most beautiful woman comes up to me, starts talking to me, because *You look more intelligent than anyone else in this dump* and anyway, to cut a long and shameful story short, I was too drunk to use my brain. She tricked me."

Tricked you? But he wasn't wearing his feeder. It would have been damn handy if he had worn it. On the other hand, I didn't really need the feeder to figure it out.

"That was Xinanu?"

"Yes. She contacted me before I'd even left Asto. *I'm having your child. Do you want to negotiate about it?*"

I'd heard about these predators, usually women from lower families, who forced themselves into good contracts by feeding men liquor and seducing them. "But I don't understand. Usually the women who do this need money. She doesn't."

"Those do it for money. Others for some kind of bought loyalty."

"What, what, Nicha? Why haven't you told us anything about this earlier?"

Shit. I'd worried about having an Azimi in the house in the form of that baby Xinanu carried. A boy, who would take his mother's clan name. Turned out I needed to be worried about the rest of the clan first.

"I understand you're angry."

"I'm not angry. I'm trying to understand. We lived together. Hell, we shared the same bed at times. We were supposed to share everything. What's happened, Nich'?" All my pronouns were accusatory. I breathed in to calm myself.

"I deserve your anger. I'm not proud of it." He held his hands clasped together, the thumbs worrying at each other. "You haven't heard the rest of the story yet."

"You mean it gets worse?"

He nodded, once.

"All right then. Let's have it."

"Xinanu is Delegate Ayanu's daughter."

I sucked in a whistling breath. "You mean, she followed you into the bar with the specific reason of getting herself into our household?"

"That's what it appears to be, yes."

"And, it is Delegate Ayanu's association that is causing the conflict in you?"

I was used to people spying and listening to every word we said. But these were people we knew and trusted, and I had never encountered such blatant infiltration from all directions. And I didn't trust Delegate Ayanu. She was clearly trying to influence the outcome of the negotiations.

"I was in a loyalty network with her. Our mother is in it, too. It's mostly a group of very ambitious people. But I'm not so involved anymore. I don't really like her, but I have some ties because of my mother."

"What's the deal with your mother? I thought that you were trying to break free from her?"

"Yes, I was. I am. But if your father was very sick, wouldn't you go back to him and give him some comfort, even if you didn't like him very much?"

"Your mother is sick?"

He nodded, his lips pressed together. "Really not well at all. She's been pulling in all her networks and all favours that people owe her. I told her gently that I wanted to break with Delegate Ayanu and that whole association and she said just this one thing and then you're free to go."

"And the one thing was?"

"She said, 'Give this young fellow a chance. He's been wandering around and getting into trouble.' "

"I'm guessing that would be Reida."

"It was. I looked at his credentials and education and they were quite good."

"But who is he, really?"

"He's somewhere in the bottom of one of Delegate Ayanu's associations. For some reason she took a liking to him—"

"*Zeyshi?* In her association?"

"He's not *zeyshi*. He's just dresses as one. He does the ignorant Outer Circle thing quite well. No, don't look at me like that. He's done some work for Delegate Ayanu and my mother. My mother works for—used to work for," —his face took on a pained expression — "the water authority. *Zeyshi* live in the aquifers. That's why he dresses as one of them."

"You mean, he's a spy!" I could hit myself in the head. I should have picked up on that. The boy was too pale, too fine-skinned, to be a desert dweller. He was too over the top in acting as a playboy.

I forced myself to calm down. All right, Reida was a spy. Deep inside, I'd known that.

"What does she want from having him in my household?"

"Information. Something to pin you down or Federza or the *zeyshi* delegation. Anyone. As long as Asto gets what it wants."

This was not an uncommon practice amongst rival political camps. The fact that my household would become a focus point for this sort of jockeying shouldn't surprise me. In fact, it *didn't* surprise me, even if it surprised me what angle it came from.

"But. There is a but, right?"

Nicha nodded.

"Something went wrong?"

"I wouldn't call it wrong. Reida was doing some larking and behaving stupidly while collecting general information about all the parties in the negotiations. Just the regular stuff. He found something. He started behaving strangely and wouldn't tell me what it was. He said it was something that would be unwise to keep quiet, although nobody would like it. The more I pressured him on what it was, the more strangely he behaved. He said he didn't want to hand it to Delegate Ayanu. I told him if that was what he believed, he shouldn't." He looked at his hands.

"Reida found that hard enough. He said that if he disobeyed her, his family might suffer. I said, if he told me I'd make sure his discovery would not fall in the wrong hands."

"Did he show you?"

He nodded, but said nothing.

I prompted him. "What is it?"

"It's bad. You'll have to see it for yourself. I don't want to say anything here because . . ." He gestured at the back of the room.

"All right. Let's go and see it, then." I rose.

He hesitated.

"We need to go to the hub, right?"

"Yes, but . . ."

"What?"

"You're angry with me. You can tell me to . . . leave, you know."

"Nicha, why would I do that? You grew up on Earth. You, of all people, know about forgiveness and friendship with no strings attached. That's what I want from you, Nich'. Just be my friend. I understand how family can put pressure on you. What I heard, even about Xinanu or Reida, does not fall outside what I should have expected to happen to our association. We're the target for a lot of spying and I should have been more vigilant. If you think you are failing at this, you don't even begin to realise how much *I* am failing at it."

"But you're not—"

"You have the instinct. I'm doing everything blind."

"You're doing quite well. I'm messing everything up. I should have known better."

"Your first concern should be your mother. How bad is she? Do you want some time to go over there?"

"She's no longer working. She needs several expensive procedures. Some that are only available from the *zeyshi*." He looked down. "You know, I sort of fell out with her a bit, but we've made up. I like her better than my father. She and Thayu are the only family I have."

"I understand."

He stared at his hands. His eyes glittered.

I reached out and touched his arm, realising how long it was that I'd last done this. I'd failed him more than anything. I'd allowed him to become isolated. "Hey, Nich'. It's all right. We're still here. We can defend ourselves. Make our association stronger."

He nodded.

Next thing he hugged me so tight that I almost couldn't breathe. He had not allowed his temperature to go down since his extensive visit to Asto, and the heat of it radiated through the palms of his hands.

We sat like that for quite a while. Eventually, I wormed myself out of his arms. I was getting too hot.

"Let's go and look at this thing Reida has discovered."

"All right."

"No more secrets, especially not about something as important as having children."

"Just promise me one thing, Cory." He met my eyes in an intense look. "Take it to the assembly, this stuff that Reida found. Otherwise this problem will just continue to fester."

"What about your link to Delegate Ayanu?"

He grimaced.

"Is it perhaps something you could raise with Ezhya that Asto's delegate is blackmailing people?"

"Ezhya won't listen to me as much as he listens to her. Ezhya might listen to you. As for me, I'm less than a slug to him. He wouldn't listen to me if I stood in front of him holding a gun."

Whoa, why suddenly all this bitterness in his voice? Having tasted the equality and democracy of the Earth system, was he bitter about the rigid Coldi associations where he'd started off as my *zhayma* ready to take on the universe, and ended up somewhere in the middle with trouble directed at him from both sides?

"I'll raise it with him if you want." But that wasn't particularly helpful either. Any interclan networks needed to be discussed by the head of that clan. I was still feeling my way through the Domiri clan. Nicha was Palayi and the head of the Palayi clan was Ezhya. Dog, meet tail.

I pushed myself up. "We'll find some sort of solution for the next month. Then the baby will have been born and your contract with Delegate Ayanu's group will be finished."

He nodded, but didn't look convinced. "I'm sorry. I don't know what I was thinking."

"I know. Well, I think I know. You grew up on Earth. You went to school, a pretty good one, too. You rubbed shoulders with the free thinkers and children of politicians and heads of state. Now you've come to this point in your life, and things are not going as you wanted. You find that the culture that's supposed to be yours feels kind of alien. I know. I've felt the same my entire life. Nicha, the only thing I'm angry with is that you have said nothing about any of this before."

He let his head hang further.

And I did something I'd sworn never to do. I reached out and pushed his chin up with my hand. It was such a patronising Coldi gesture that I'd often felt revolted when I saw it, let alone when people did it to me.

But when Nicha looked up and met my eyes, I knew that it was absolutely the right thing to do. He'd been confused and needed firm guidance. His eyes brimmed with tears. I hugged him and he held me in a grip so tight that I could barely breathe.

After a short and comforting silence, I said, "Let's go and see what Reida has discovered, then."

"We'll need to talk to him."

"He's in his room. I sent him there last night."

We walked into the hallway, where it was dark and quiet. The part of the sky I could see through the ceiling windows had acquired a blue tinge. Dawn already. Eirani would get up soon. Maybe she was already up and in the kitchen. Her room was downstairs. I'd intended to do some reading before the meeting started.

Nicha went into Reida's room without knocking. The privileges of being a superior. He disappeared into the darkness.

He called. "Time to get up. We're here for the information." He flipped the switch that brought the light pearl in contact with the metal stand. Wan greenish light filled the room. The room was a mess. There were clothes on the floor and bundles of electronics spilling off his desk over the surrounding floor space.

The bedsheets hung half off the side of the bed. One of the pillows lay on the floor. The bed was empty.

11

WELL, BUGGER THAT.

"Shit," Nicha said. He took a few big steps to the bed and looked underneath, but that didn't make Reida appear. He repeated, "Shit." And a bit later, he added in a frustrated tone, "Evi said no one went out except Federza."

"Maybe he hasn't gone out." Although I had been pretty clear that he was to stay in his room—not that Reida had ever taken any notice of our orders. "Maybe he's just hiding from us."

We checked the cupboard, the passage to the tiny bathroom, under the beds, behind the curtains, under the couch. We checked the bathroom, the living room, and Deyu's room. She was asleep and none too happy about being woken up. But since this concerned her *zhayma* and because I was involved, she got dressed and helped look for him. But Reida was nowhere to be found.

"I don't understand," Nicha said. "Telaris has been in the corridor all that time."

"He obviously got called away for a moment." And not being considered any risk beyond the annoyance factor, Reida had not registered with security as needing surveillance.

Nicha said, "He's probably just gone to get something to eat."

But Reida was not in the kitchen. Nor was he in the downstairs living room where he often spent time with the kitchen staff. We went back upstairs, but no one there had seen him.

"*Mashara* was in the hallway the whole time. We did not see the young lad," Telaris said.

"You didn't leave at all?"

He shook his head. He didn't show it, but I could imagine the what-do-you-think-I-am expression on his face.

Deyu said, "He's not in the cupboard, or under the bed or anywhere else he could hide."

"The grate?" Telaris asked.

"Checked that. Too small."

We went back into the room and searched through all the corners where a person could hide and corners where a person couldn't hide, just in case. Since this was an older apartment, it still had the ceiling ducts that brought a soft whisper of cool moist air from the waterfall in the hall of the building, but the ducts were far too narrow for a person to crawl through. They were also covered in slimy vegetation, so it was just as well that there wouldn't be any duct-crawling involved. Ew.

"It beats me where he's gone," Thayu said. She had rejoined us as soon as we left the living room.

We went into the hub where I asked Devlin for the scan log to see who had gone out. Sure enough, Reida was on that list. He'd left the apartment not long after I'd gone to check on Federza's apartment, while I'd ordered him to stay in his room. I trusted that Telaris told me the truth that he hadn't seen Reida leave.

Damn.

The tracker showed him walking towards the main administration building. But the trail stopped suddenly in the courtyard.

Thayu and I looked at each other and then at Nicha.

Thayu asked, "Do you know of anything that he carries that can kill the signal so effectively?"

Nicha said, "No." But his face showed his horror. "Delegate Ayanu's office is in that courtyard."

"Do you think he's gone to deliver his information?"

He said nothing, but he obviously did think so.

"What sort of harm could this knowledge do in her hands?"

"Enough that I don't want to have to deal with it. Let's go," Nicha said.

"Go where?" Thayu replied a little more angry than normal. She must be tired, too. "I don't want anyone leaving this apartment without a good reason."

"This is a very good reason. Probably the reason why all these people are lurking around here."

I held him back. "Nich', please at least tell me the gist of what it is that Reida found."

"All right. The very short story is that the Aghyrian ship out there is live, and some people in the Barresh group of Aghyrians have been secretly communicating with them for quite some time."

I stopped walking and stared at him. "You're kidding."

"I wish I were, but wait until you see the data. It's unequivocal, and damning."

"What sort of people?"

"The descendants of the original crew of the ship, I'm guessing."

"Has Federza been talking to them, too?"

"I don't know about him personally, but yes, his group has been talking to that ship. It seems that some people within the Aghyrian groups want to share this information with *gamra* and others don't."

"Who is in which camp?" A chill went over my back. "What about Delegate Akhtari?"

"Who knows? We're only just scratching the surface of it."

"But then what is Delegate Ayanu going to do with this knowledge?"

"She knows about it because the military picked up the signals, but this evidence will give her irrefutable proof. She'll use it to put pressure on Chief Delegate Akhtari. She can make demands: do what we want or we'll make it public that your people have been negotiating in secret."

Shit. My head reeled. This was bad. This was bad enough to seriously undermine the integrity of the *gamra* assembly. What if Federza, and other Aghyrians, would be forced to step aside? What if it affected Chief Delegate Akhtari's authority? "I think anything as serious as that should definitely go before the assembly."

"I agree. That's why I wanted to keep it out of Delegate Ayanu's hands, because she is not going to do that."

"You would go against her? But she's in your network."

He winced. "Sometimes the choices you have are all equally dreadful. Then you have to take the one least dreadful to the community as a whole." One of the favourite Coldi proverbs.

"But I don't understand why *she* doesn't want to put it before the assembly. It would be pretty damning for her opponents. It would be a huge win for Asto."

"Yes, but admitting that they could listen to the data means admitting the existence of the military sling."

And the Asto military would rather die than do that. And the military were up in to their ears in this. *They* had known about the ship as well.

And now Reida had either fled or was going to deliver this material to Delegate Ayanu. He was in danger. And Federza . . . if he'd come to see me, I could only imagine that he belonged to the camp that wanted to take the matter to the general assembly, which meant that he was not my enemy, as he had already said, and that these guys hired by the other party—Tamerians!—were after him and he was in grave danger as well.

Damn it. Damn it. And I'd let him leave the apartment in the company of some random *gamra* security.

My first priority should be Reida, as part of my association, but I took out my reader to send Federza a message—and of course private traffic was restricted.

Triple damn it.

We left the apartment at a trot, meeting Eirani in the hallway, coming up the stairs. She said that breakfast would be served soon and looked wide-eyed as we all went for the door.

"But, Muri, breakfast!"

"Keep it until we come back."

We ran back down the gallery, not bothering to wait for the lift— did I ever have the patience these days? Down the stairs, into the hall and across the echoing space to the opposite entrance. The *gamra* guards still stood there.

"Seen anyone come this way?" Thayu asked.

Like Reida, like Federza.

There were shakes of heads all around.

"It's been very quiet," the leader said. "Command says that the alert will be downgraded at dawn so that people can go back to work."

I'd never heard a security guard use the word *mashara* when they spoke amongst themselves.

"Has anyone been caught?" Thayu asked. If they'd been catching Tamerians, we'd have a lot of dead bodies, prone as they were to kill themselves when captured.

"Apart from the individual struck in the Trader Delegate's office, no. We did a sweep of the island and found no trace of anyone else. As to his motives for being there, that will be investigated."

"You've been told about the signals we picked up, right?" From when she'd taken that gun.

"Yes, we investigated those, but have no reason to suspect a threat associated with them."

"Did you find the devices that were receiving the signals?"

He frowned at her.

"That device was sending signals to others!" She spread her hands. "The receiving parties were moving around."

"We found no evidence of that. The area has been extensively searched and cleared. Normal business can return soon."

She snorted. "We better go sort this out 'soon' then."

Oooh, that was a downright rude pronoun form. And Thayu wasn't often rude.

She set off at a brisk pace and we followed. I refrained from asking questions. It was rare enough that I was privy to discussions between security personnel, and to be honest, I could see why Thayu was balling her fists against her legs, but she knew her place, and that was with our household, and not to criticise *gamra* personnel.

When we were out of earshot of the guards, she muttered, "Fucking idiots." In military dialect.

Sheydu gave her an *I told you so* look, and Thayu snorted in response.

She would normally defend *gamra* security whenever the subject came up for discussion with Sheydu. But now Sheydu was actually right and by the look of things, it didn't put Thayu in a good mood.

We continued into the brooding atmosphere, through the passage-ways that led from the residential section to the main building. It occurred to me that on most days I didn't see as much of the island as I had this night.

"This is where he disappeared," Thayu said. We stood in the

middle of a spacious rectangular courtyard. There were a few benches to one side and a couple of trees randomly placed around the perimeter. "Delegate Ayanu's apartment is up there." She gestured with her eyes. Most of us knew where it was anyway. I had seen her go up there many times. A light was on behind the window.

"Do you think he's gone up there voluntarily?"

"With her, nothing is done voluntarily." Nicha shuddered.

"How do we get in?" Veyada asked.

Sheydu said, "We could just use the door, blast our way in and be done with it." Boy, she was in a foul mood today.

Veyada sniped back at her. "The Delegate would call the guards and rightly so. We have no valid reason to go in."

"She doesn't need a valid reason to hold him up there."

"If that's where he is indeed."

"Where else would he be?" Sheydu snorted. "I say we shoot our way up there and get the fuck out of here. I'm tired. I don't feel like chasing vague leads."

Everyone was tired. This had been one heck of a long night.

Thayu squinted into the light streaming from the window. It showed a patch of ceiling and a corner of a cupboard. The sky behind the building showed a distinct blue tinge. We wouldn't have much time until people started walking around. The all clear would be given at dawn, the guards had said, unless we could convince them that there was a real threat to public security.

There was nothing in the courtyard useful for climbing walls, just a few planter boxes with small trees for shade, and a couple of benches and stone walls for people to sit on. A fountain burbled in the pond in the middle of the open space. There wasn't even a café, as in so many of these courtyards. A quiet space to reflect. I looked around the surrounding part of the building. The windows that looked out over the courtyard were mostly from minor delegates' rooms. They were windows in bedrooms and the storerooms and staff rooms, since these apartments faced outwards, with views of the marches and the jetty. I couldn't see any movement up there, no one watching us.

"Up there," Sheydu said and gestured at the roof behind my back. Thayu, Veyada and Nicha all looked and nodded. I couldn't see what they were looking at. Sheydu walked to the wall and tested the down-pipe. Apparently it passed her scrutiny, because the next moment she jumped against the wall and hauled herself up, holding onto the pipe. She was on the roof in no time. Why did the sheer athletic strength of the Coldi always surprise me?

Nicha clambered up after her.

I said to Thayu, "If you think I'm going to climb up there—"

"Shhh."

The feeder channel opened.

There's a passage here, Sheydu said. She and Thayu used their feeders a lot more than I did with her or with Nicha.

From my position down in the courtyard, I could just see the top half of Nicha's body, and he now bent and folded something open. A window or an entry hatch.

Be careful, I said to him.

His head disappeared when he climbed down.

It's a kind of storage area, I heard Nicha's thoughts. *Not much here. Now walking through into the next room.*

"I got you," Thayu said. She bent to me so that I could see her screen, but she was using the ultrasound scanner and I found it hard to make sense of the diagrams. The scanner worked like a bat's sonar, and showed the position of walls and other solid objects. Something moved on the screen but it was hard to see if that was real or an artefact of the scan.

I felt rather useless. I had no idea why they thought that they could get into Delegate Ayanu's apartment through this building, but if there was one thing I'd learned, it was that security was best left to those trained for it. I lifted my hand up to my arm, feeling for the gun. Not sure whether it would protect me at all. All right, I had fired at Taysha Palayi when I had no choice, when he expected it and knew that it would happen. It still astonished me that I'd actually done that, and also that, even though he was right in front of me, I hadn't managed to miss.

Shooting rarely solved anything. At the very best, it made the situation a little bit less muddy for a bit.

Since coming back from that harebrained escapade, I had often lain awake at night experiencing that moment, over and over, like a horrifying, ever-repeating nightmare, as well as the moment that Ezhya came into the hub and I saw in his face that, had I been Coldi, I would have deposed him. Despite my assurances, he still didn't quite seem to have gotten over that and he seemed to have been avoiding me. I would see him for the upcoming assembly debate about the Aghyrian claim, but it would be the first time since that day.

We've found a way to get in, Nicha reported. *We're outside the back windows. Look, we've even found Reida.*

What is he doing there?

It seems they've locked him in a room. Ah, he's just seen us. Doesn't look too happy.

No, I was sure he wouldn't be happy. By the sound of things, Delegate Ayanu wasn't happy with him, either.

Sheydu said, *Shut your chatter and come help me open this window.*

All right. Reporting back later.

12

———————

E WAITED.

I sat down on one of the benches, looking into the fountain. I'd often wondered what Coldi would do when two of their multiple networks gave clashing signals. Thayu had looked puzzled when I asked her about it, as if that sort of thing never happened, but it must, and they must have some way of reconciling the less serious cases. For the more serious ones . . . I guessed we were about to find out.

It never ceased to amaze me what some people, Coldi or otherwise, would do for power. So, Delegate Ayanu was annoyed by my growing influence with Ezhya, and therefore she sent her daughter to prey on Nicha, to take advantage of him when he was down, just so that she had some strings to pull inside my association.

And there would be a little boy living in my household who was the result of that scheme. What a great start to life.

Thayu stood next to me, leaning against the trunk of a tree, listening to another news stream, if the screen on her reader was anything to go by. Veyada crouched nearby, continuously checking the building with his scanner. He would give periodic coded updates in what was apparently a delicate operation to get into Delegate Ayanu's office without triggering alarms.

I wished they'd hurry up.

The sky was fast becoming lighter. The *gamra* guards must have lifted the ban on going out, because people walked through the court-yard. At this time of day, they were mostly domestic staff with supplies. The breeze brought occasional wafts of cooking. I thought about Eirani and her wonderful breakfast that I didn't want to miss.

I hoped there would be time for a rest, too.

"Uh-oh," Thayu said next to me.

She grabbed my arm and pulled me into an entrance to a stairwell where the approaching dawn had not yet reached. The air here was cool and smelled of moist stone. There was a closed door at the top of the stairs and Thayu, Veyada and I pressed ourselves into the little alcove to the left of that door, which was probably built as a place where delivery people could leave their wares if the occupant of the office was out.

Footsteps echoed in the courtyard below. Through the arch-shaped entranceway to the stairwell I could see a group of four people: Delegate Ayanu with three guards. Not *gamra* guards, but Coldi ones, dressed in the grey-silver characteristic for Asto employees of the Inner and First Circles. Guns on both arms brackets. What were they even doing here? When Ezhya visited, yes, but Delegate Ayanu?

They didn't look our way and didn't show any sign that they knew we were there. The sound of their footsteps changed as they went past and then up the stairs, presumably into the next entrance, but I couldn't see that from where we were standing.

My feeder burst into life. *We're in.*

Thayu replied, *Get out now, Nich'. The Delegate is coming up with four guards.*

We'll grab Reida and go.

Please hurry up.

It would not be a good thing if Nicha and Sheydu were caught in there.

Veyada gestured for us to follow him. Quietly, we went back down the stairs, and ran along the wall of the building to the next entrance. Thayu unclipped the gun from her arm bracket. Veyada stopped at the bottom of the stairs, gesturing *quiet*. The guards' voices echoed from above, through the hall of stone and metal.

We went up, very quietly sneaking along the side wall in single file. First Veyada, then Thayu, and I came last.

Through the metalwork of the balustrade, I could see a narrow strip of a door where the group waited while the first of the guards disarmed all the locks.

Come on, Nicha, get out of there, quickly.

The door slid open.

The guards took one step inside—

There was a shout and someone shot out from the doorway, crashing into one of the guards. The two of them went toppling, the attacker pushing the guard flat on his back. The other two guards had their guns out in seconds.

Suddenly, the stairwell was full of shouting.

"Freeze!"

"Hands up!"

The landing in front of the apartment's door wasn't big enough for the guards to move far enough away for a clear shot. The attacker kicked out like a bucking horse and hit the gun out of one of the guards' hands. In the same movement, he swung his other leg aside, swiping a second guard off his feet.

While everyone was screaming, the attacker scrambled to his feet and pelted down the stairs—where we stood.

In the Delegate's office, someone yelled, "Stop him!" That sounded like Nicha.

The escapee was Reida, and he had already reached us.

Before I could say or do anything, Thayu grabbed him by his shayka and belted him across the head with such force that he gave one surprised squeak and collapsed against the wall.

The delegate's guards ran across the landing towards the stairs, and stopped dead when they saw us.

"What are you doing here?" one of them asked, his tone none too friendly.

Veyada stepped forward and conducted a conversation entirely in security code. The guards backed off a bit. They probably knew Veyada and knew about his previous employment.

I knelt next to Reida's crumpled form. His clothes were ripped and dirty, his hands bloodied from where he had torn his fingernails. Trying to get out of the room where he had been locked in? His eyes fluttered and opened to a hazy expression. "I'm all . . . finished with her," he said with a thick slur. "Sorry . . . sorry."

Veyada stopped his discussion with the guards to wave a finger at him. "Shut. Up."

This kind of callous-looking behaviour always disturbed me, no matter how often I experienced it. Coldi would tolerate a measure of poor behaviour from someone in their association and then all of a sudden they would lash out like this with excessive physical violence and callous remarks.

Maybe we humans were too soft, but damn it, belting someone senseless and then letting him recover on his own was not the way I liked to do things. Reida had been carrying a bag, and I used it as a pillow to support his head. Veyada was still talking to the guards and Reida didn't look like he'd be going anywhere for a while.

Damn, Thayu, what was that good for?

He wiped a trickle of blood that ran from his nose over his lip, resulting only in smearing it over his face and the back of his hand. He also had angry bruises on his arms that were definitely not a result of Thayu's belting. I searched my pockets for something to wipe the blood off, but came up with nothing.

"I'll take you to the med post." Better still, I sent them a quick message to come and collect him. Reida probably couldn't walk, or it wouldn't be a good idea for him to try.

"Leave him," Thayu said to me, softly.

What do you mean? He can't look after himself.

He's looked after himself ever since coming here and maybe even before. I need you to be alert. I want you to listen and watch. We're not safe here.

I looked up. Veyada was talking some bullshit about the reason for our presence being that we wanted to speak to the delegate before the meeting.

One of the delegate's guards said, "Your personnel was trespassing on our property."

Veyada said, "That person is also part of your association."

"I don't know anything about that."

"He's a spy for you. We can track and prove that. My leader is not impressed with this situation." Veyada's hand gestured behind his back for us to clear out.

I rose, because I trusted my association in matters of security.

Delegate Ayanu's guards had come down the stairs and surrounded

Veyada. They had their guns out of their arms brackets, ready to be used at the first opportunity.

"We'll take care of the young rascal now," one of the men said.

"No, he's mine." This was Nicha, at the door of the apartment. Sheydu was with him.

The guards whirled. Had they really been unaware that Nicha and Sheydu had been in the apartment as well? Sheydu held that fearsome gun in her left hand.

For a moment, I was afraid that there would be shots fired, but the delegate herself spoke up. She had been sheltering in the corner of the hallway.

Delegate Ayanu's face was round and the friendly expression belied the iron nature of her personality. She had the typical round-waisted look of a middle-aged Coldi woman. Because of her position, she was allowed to dress in all blue, which she did in style. "What is the meaning of this? Since when do we have break-ins from two sides at once? Nicha? Care to explain to me?"

"I don't think it needs any explanation," Nicha said, his tone subservient, but his word choice interesting. Why should anyone use the *zhyo* pronoun form? I'd learned it as a form of reverence, but he used it sarcastically. Was that something he'd learned when I'd sent him to Asto?

The delegate snorted, not entirely comfortable. "I would greatly like you to explain, dear second of mine. I'm disappointed. I would have thought my apartment was safe from you." Very sharp pronouns, those ones.

"I had my reasons."

I said, "Nicha is working for me."

Delegate Ayanu turned around. Her eyes met mine and her face showed a *I should have expected that you were involved* expression. "Is that so?"

I straightened. "He's been working for me for years. Surely that is not news to you, and I'd be happy if you stopped acting like it was. I would like to know why you're keeping one of our association locked up?"

"So, this good-for-nothing thief belongs with you as well?" She laughed. "You'll have to train him better so that he can get away without being caught." Her pronouns were all sneering and accusatory.

Thayu hissed next to me. *The hide of her. He did work for her. Now she's washing her hands off him.*

Calm down, I sent her. Reida had already said that he was finished with her. That was a good thing.

That's the most cowardly thing she could have done. I don't like the way she speaks to you.

Whoa, Thayu's anger almost bowled me flat. *Keep calm. I've grown used to her bluster.* It wasn't the rudest thing Delegate Ayanu had ever said to me either. Like most Coldi, she was all show and didn't often follow through on her statements.

Ezhya is right, you are much too soft on people who are rude.

Delegate Ayanu came slowly down the stairs. Her footsteps were deliberate, her face determined.

I continued, "To be honest, I think the boy belongs with you as much as he belongs with me. Since he came to live in my apartment, he's behaved strangely. At first, it seemed harmless. Breaking into councillors' daughters' bedrooms. Sure, their fathers were upset, but also smug that their daughters were so popular with a *gamra* official, even if only the most junior one possible. But you sent him to pretend he's after the girls, right? To put everyone on a wrong trail. To let everyone think that he's just a joker. Breaking into Federza's office was what you wanted him to do, right?" I used professional pronoun forms, because I didn't want to go into the question of whether she was a superior. With some people, I could make a reasonably accurate guess where I stood, but she wasn't one of those people.

Reida's voice came from behind, hoarse and slurred. "Ask her about the bugs she has all over the complex."

I turned around and frowned at him. *Bugs?*

His eyes still looked unfocused. Damn it, he should be taken to the hospital soon.

He nodded. "Ask her. My loyalty to her is done. Finished." A dribble of blood-stained saliva ran from his mouth.

I turned back to the delegate and frowned at her.

Her face had an expression of distaste. "He talks nonsense." Damn it, that was a downright abusive pronoun form. "He is nothing more than an insignificant slug, who will go back to being less than an insignificant slug. He can go and join those *zeyshi* whose outfits he wears."

Reida spat on the ground. "I'm not afraid of you. You should be afraid of me. I took the stuff that you were going to use to blackmail Federza. I know you got it on paper and destroyed the electronic copy, but it's never really destroyed. I have the document with your electronic signature all over it."

Whatever he had found had to be in the little bag that I'd been trying to use as pillow that now lay on the ground behind him.

He met my eyes and seemed to say *take it*.

Except I couldn't pick it up without drawing attention to it. If Delegate Ayanu noticed me taking it, she would ask for it to be handed back to her and I would have to give it up, because it had technically been stolen from her apartment and I had my conduct code to observe as *gamra* delegate.

I sent to Thayu, *Create a diversion. Draw her attention away from it.* But Thayu was in conversation with the Delegate's guards.

I had to do something. "I'm asking you to let the boy go. You are trespassing on my association." A typical Coldi phrase.

Delegate Ayanu laughed, looking at my Domiri earrings. "I see Asha has been teaching you well, Domiri pet." She snorted. "A pity that you're nothing but a thief and I want my possessions returned to me." She gestured and the guards came forward.

Immediately, regardless of what they'd been doing, Thayu, Veyada, Sheydu and Nicha sprang in front of me, guns drawn.

Thayu said, *Take that thing and run. Copy it before they can get their hands on it.*

What about you?

We'll hold them off. Go now, Cory, run.

I snatched up the bag and ran.

13

HOLY CRAP, I RAN. Down the stairs, where I narrowly avoided crashing into the two medical staff who had turned up to collect Reida. They greeted me with surprised looks.

One of them said, "We've come for an injured man."

"Up there," I replied, pointing at the entrance to the stairwell. Someone was shouting in the stairwell. I hoped Thayu and Nicha were all right. I hoped they could hold off any pursuit long enough for me to reach safety. Wherever that was.

I kept running, across the courtyard into the next courtyard, where people had returned to the outdoor eating-houses for breakfast and others were making their way to their various meetings.

My appearance drew a few raised eyebrows.

I turned into the first stairwell I encountered. This happened to be the building for minor delegates' offices. At the top of the stairs, I came out in a long passage on the first floor that was part-balcony, part-corridor, also a typical Barresh architectural feature. On one side, the gallery had a view into the courtyard and there were doors on the other.

I sat down on a bench that overlooked the courtyard, still breathing fast.

Thay' where are you?

There was no reply.

Maybe she'd closed the feeder. Delegate Ayanu's guards would be able to hear me, too, if they were tuned to the right frequency. They'd probably have broad-frequency sweeps to scan the area.

Running footsteps sounded down in the courtyard. Not Thayu or Veyada or Sheydu by the lightness of the tread.

I ducked below the potted bush that stood next to the bench, but the person walking through the courtyard at a good pace was only a delegate carrying a reader, who was probably late for a meeting.

I sat back down on the bench after he had passed and opened the bag. Inside a piece of cloth, a shawl of some kind, lay a comm reader. I activated my recording facility on my reader before turning it on.

The screen went dark and then a menu appeared. I stared at the list of documents on the screen, not even sure what I was looking for.

Meeting brief took me to a detailed description of everyone we knew who would be coming to the negotiations in the assembly and who had any kind of interest in the matter. Reida had listed all their attributes, memberships, known associations and positions they held, in the past and present.

I was impressed. For a young man giving the impression of being a lout, he was highly organised and methodical. He didn't misspell or make grammar mistakes either. It occurred to me that if I could remove the external pressure from him, if I could focus his loyalty solely on my association, then he could be extremely valuable.

But this was obviously not what I was looking for.

After going through a well-kept financial report of expenditures, including an entry that listed *fine for trespass*—seriously, what the hell— I opened a document entitled *plan and communication*.

The first page was in Aghyrian. Not phonetically written in Coldi characters, but with the proper characters. Which, obviously, he could read because why else would he keep the character set on his reader. Being used to the phonetic spelling, I could recognise a few words, but this was way too formal for me to understand it fully. The way the text was laid out made me think that it was a transcript from a conversation.

I would have to get someone to translate that, so I flicked to the next page, which was a page-filling image, a diagram of blue lines on a black background.

At first, I wasn't sure what I was looking at. Some kind of shape. I peered at it for a while before I realised that it was a line diagram of a space ship in exquisite detail.

I had never seen anything like this ship before. If those little rectangles on the plan were human-sized doors, then this thing was huge. Much bigger even than the hundred-year-old behemoths used by Earth to travel to what limited space settlements they had access to without using the Exchange. Ancient vessels like the *Venture* which had brought me to Midway Space Station as a boy. This ship was much bigger than that. The *Venture* had three levels of cabins and living quarters and carried about eighty passengers on long anpar flights, which was roughly 60% of capacity.

This ship, if it could even be called a ship, would carry thousands. An entire town. There were cabins for sleeping and larger rooms that might be used for recreation, schooling or other communal activities. There were two entire decks devoted to what looked like agriculture and food production.

The engine compartment was huge, much bigger than that of the Earth ships in comparison to ship size. You could probably fit the *Venture* inside the engine compartment of this ship three or four times. It contained two thick tubes, the function of which I could only guess. The legendary one-sided anpar generator? For a ship that size?

It had so little shielding, too. And what were the two flanges on the sides? Solar panels?

It had been a long time since I'd seen designs for ships like this. People on Earth used to love making plans for permanent live-aboard vessels that were self-sustaining floating towns. Getting to the natural anpar lines took a long time and the flight to Midway took three months. There had been talk of building bigger ships to forego the need of working with *gamra* and simply not using the anpar lines. I remembered competitions for the designs of such ships. I remembered poring over them as a little boy, to see where people would live their entire lives. The gardens fascinated me most of all. None had ever been built that I was aware of. With the anpar network, there was no need for long-haul vessels. Yet this looked like such a ship. Not only that, it looked like what people in my youth had called a *generation ship*.

Earth people had given up talking about generation ships long ago.

Designs like this were almost ancient history. It was just so much easier to sign all the *gamra* statements so that individuals could travel on the Anpar network. Just use *gamra* transport, never mind that Earth governments had no authority over it, never mind *gamra*'s stand on religion. Ideology could only take a person so far.

I flicked to the next image, which showed the ship from the inside. I'd been on board several ships. Other than the behemoth *Venture*, I'd taken the shuttles, usually Hedron-made models with panelling made of the ubiquitous Hedron steel, recognisable by its purple sheen. The interior of those ships usually involved brightly coloured furnishings, often bright orange. I'd been on board Asto-made ships with their functional elegance in white, silver and maroon. I'd been aboard Asto military ships with their bare walls, and old-style Mirani ships with their wooden panelling and well-crafted fittings. I'd even been to the Asto military's space station, with its broad walkways.

This ship was something different altogether. The image showed a broad but low-ceilinged corridor in which the floor was shining black. The walls looked like they were made from glass. Some were see-through, but others looked like screens. Strips of lighting were set in the ceilings and spread an even glow. The lighting was very blue, typical for Coldi or many other related *gamra* people, because they couldn't see red very well or not at all.

I flicked to the next image. This showed the control centre of the ship—I don't know if you would still call it "bridge"—a huge nerve centre two storeys high.

This ship would not be part of any modern fleet. The Asto military had an unspecified number of large ships, but they were nowhere near as elegant as this one. I had seen images of ships like this in only one place: the historical archives that contained all the information that was ever collected from the vast amounts of materials dug up from the aquifers underneath Athyl.

Veyada had shown me the few images that existed in those records of the large ship that the Aghyrians had built for what was to be their next wave of colonisation. He'd read out the passages about the legendary arrogance of the captain, a man named Kando Luczon, whose name had been mentioned in the snatch of information that the Exchange had skimmed off the mysterious ship's anpar wake.

Whose most famous deed had been to refuse to carry refugees from the impending disaster. And I remembered thinking that some people would have survived the initial impact hidden in their cellars, and they'd have chronicled the last days of the Aghyrian civilisation while slowly suffocating and dying of heat while the surface of their planet was pelted with dust and large sections of it liquefied with the heat of the impact.

I shivered.

Anyway, all of this data we had on the mysterious vessel so far pointed to the only conclusion: this was the ship, or a successor of it, that had taken those Aghyrians away all those years ago, the ship that had been piloted by Captain Kando Luczon.

Was it an empty shell or was there someone on board?

That first page of Aghyrian text, did it show a conversation between the ship and . . .

The Barresh Aghyrians?

Or Asto's armed forces?

Or who else would have the capacity to communicate with them directly?

A chill crept over my back.

There was something going on within the Barresh Aghyrian group. The army was taking in big supplies and sending warning signals that they were present and watching. But I hadn't seen Asha Domiri yet.

And Ezhya wasn't here yet, either, even if he had sent me his daughter to babysit.

Damn it.

I wanted to study the images but there was so much detail and not enough time.

My comm reader was much faster at copying this stuff than I could look at it. I really needed to get out of here. Also I heard a lot of yelling going on from the other side of the building. Delegate Ayanu's guards might have made it past Nicha and Thayu.

I closed the documents and was about to get up when there were footsteps behind me.

"Delegate."

My heart jumped. I turned around. Two *gamra* guards stood on the gallery.

"Yes? You want me?" I tried to keep calm, but my heart was

hammering. This looked like trouble. Not as bad as I expected, but still trouble.

One of the guards, a Coldi man, said, "I understand that you or your staff have unlawfully obtained some items from Delegate Ayanu's office. We have to ask you to come to the guard post with us to address the accusations."

Shit. Indeed. Unable to get past Thayu and Veyada, Delegate Ayanu had called the guards.

I held out the bag that Reida had carried. "If you're after this, a young member of my staff gave it to me. I have no idea what's in it."

He took the bag from me and looked inside. The reader was still on my lap. I coolly turned it off and stuck it into my inner pocket, as if it were mine. My pocket, of course, was already full with my own reader, so I had to put it in the other pocket. *Smart move, Mr Wilson.*

My hands were sweaty.

The guard rummaged through the bag, displaying the impassive face that Coldi did so well. "There is nothing of importance in here."

I hesitated. If they investigated or insisted on searching me, they would find out about the reader. I'd best hand it in now, before Delegate Ayanu got to tell them her version of the story. If ever there was a good reason to invoke the morality clause, certainly this was it?

I pulled out the reader. "This was also in the bag, but my staff member told me that it didn't come from Delegate Ayanu."

He took the reader from me, raising his eyebrows.

"Apparently, it belongs to Marin Federza. I've been told there is highly controversial material on it which I intend to take to the assembly under the morality clause."

He flicked up his eyebrows. "How did your staff member come by it?"

"You would have to ask him. I'm sure he will assist you with your inquiries." Deflecting the question. Poor Reida.

He nodded and switched the reader on, frowned at the menu screen and showed it to his colleague, who shook his head and said something in a low voice that I didn't catch. Hopefully the thing would come up with the nondescript menu that was harmless.

While they were looking at the screen, another group of people came onto the gallery: Delegate Ayanu and her guards, followed closely by Thayu, Sheydu and Veyada. Thayu's eyes met mine. Her expression was intense. Worried? Warning me? A sign of defeat? I couldn't tell.

Damn it, I needed to get that document translated as soon as possible.

The delegate stopped close to me, planting her hands at her hips. I don't know what she expected, but if she wanted me to perform a subservient greeting, she was going to have to wait a very long time.

I nodded to her. "Good day, Delegate."

"I'm not sure if it is such a good day. For me, perhaps, but not for you."

"It's a very nice morning for a meeting with some interesting people." If she was into posturing, I could do that, too.

"Whatever do you mean by that?" Oh, those pronouns of hers were worse than rude. She dared use *child*'s pronouns on me.

Thayu looked fit to explode, giving me the *you're not going to put up with this* look.

Well, actually, Thayu, I was, but that didn't mean I wasn't going to be rude in return.

"What I mean is that we will host the *zeyshi* Aghyrian delegation, who will have some interesting claims to make about the Barresh Aghyrian group. Claims that the assembly will find quite disturbing." I used the same pronoun form that she had used on me. I wasn't well-versed in the children's forms, but it probably didn't matter.

She did her impassive face expression.

I continued, "But I'm guessing you already know this, because the documentation that belongs to Marin Federza that details the explosive information came from your office, because you had asked Reida to steal it for you."

"Whatever are you talking about?"

"I'll tell you, and you can let me know if I'm right." A door opened on the gallery and a couple of people came out with curious expressions on their faces. Good. The more spectators, the better. We were all diplomats here, but I wouldn't put it beyond her to order a fight. Those Inner Circle guards with her could be pretty high-strung. "The situation is this: we have two groups of people who both claim to speak for the Aghyrians. We always assumed that we would be dealing with the group in Barresh here when the time came to allocate them land on Asto—"

She scoffed. "—Not just some land. They want all of it—"

"We have spent time talking to the Barresh Aghyrians. Their plans for a claim were moderate and concerned just sites of Aghyrian history." The aquifers, administered by the water board. "But then the *zeyshi* group makes a much more sweeping, much bigger claim on Asto. No one expected this. The Barresh Aghyrians are baffled. The Inner Circle is put on the back foot. No one knows what to do. We're doing our best to deal with it, but we don't understand the reason behind the claim. But then your lackey discovers something. Possibly the reason that the Barresh Aghyrians were content with making a modest claim is that they know what is about to happen and that whatever claim they make, successful or not, will be thrown out when this thing has happened."

The delegate snorted. "You love being vague. But if people are holding back important information, it should be reported."

"I fully agree. The evidence should go before the assembly, but that's not what you intended to do with it, right?" Oh, the hide of her.

"How do you know my intentions?"

"I'm right, aren't I?"

She snorted. "I don't have to reply to such stupid questions." Which probably meant yes.

"This issue is that someone has been talking to this ship that's out there stalking us. The issue is that no one at the Exchange knows for certain that the ship is live, but you've known for a while. The issue is that there is a recording of a conversation with the ship. By my reckoning you've had this controversial information for a number of days and have not yet taken the matter up with the assembly. You intended to use it for your own private purposes."

"Nonsense. I don't know where you get these silly theories."

"My association members aren't stupid. None of them is, not even the young fellow whom you underestimated so badly." Heck, we'd all underestimated Reida, thinking that he was after the girls. "Now, if you'll excuse me—if you don't have anything to add—I have a meeting to prepare for, and I'd like some breakfast before I faint." Judging by the light in the sky, the suns were about to clear the escarpment. "I presume you will be present. Your participation will be appreciated. I will take this to the assembly and will deflect any of your accusations or attempts by guards to arrest me by invoking the morality clause." I took the reader out of the guard's hands. "Thank you. I need this."

I bowed to her by way of goodbye and walked away. My heart was beating like crazy. I knew that my appeal to the morality clause was weak. With both her and Federza's offices involved, the issue would appear clear as mud to presiding authorities. She could easily press the break-in charges.

But no one said anything, and I managed to escape into the court-yard, with Thayu and Veyada on my heels.

14

"THAT WAS A very bold move," Veyada said.

"I would have called it crazy myself," Thayu said. "Where does she assume the right to talk to you like that?"

"Do you really think she's been using this data to blackmail people?" Veyada asked.

I met his eyes. "I think so. Within a day, we've had almost every party in this negotiation be the subject of an attack. Federza was shot at—and he was genuinely scared. He of course knew about his part, that they had this communication from the ship and had kept it secret. If we catch up with him, I wouldn't be surprised if he'd been trying to discreetly give the information to the assembly without getting killed by his kinsfolk. It would be fine if Delegate Ayanu had planned on using it in the assembly, but she would have called a sitting if that was the case."

"And get accused in the assembly of using the information to support her case," Thayu said. "Is it that easy?"

"It should have been easy, because if she had integrity, she would have called a sitting regardless of the possible accusations levelled at her."

Veyada nodded. "I agree. The fact that she kept this hidden for days doesn't speak well of her intentions."

I agreed. "It speaks well of no one's intentions, including Federza's"

"What is this morality clause?" Thayu asked.

Veyada said, "That you can claim, and this may be upheld in court, that you acted in the interest of society, even if you were caught performing an illegal act in order to get the proof you needed. It's mostly applied retroactively."

"I suppose we could use it to get out of any court action if anyone decides to charge Reida. I didn't know he was so smart."

"He's a fool," Thayu said. "Nicha is a fool for selecting him."

"I don't think he is. He acts like a lout, and his loyalties are messed up, but he's smart. I'll show you what he wrote about the meeting. For someone who came from a disadvantaged part of town—a downright poor part of town—he's very smart."

She frowned at me. "I'm not convinced that he actually comes from the Outer Circle. I know he's from the Ezmi clan, but not all of them live in the lower circles."

"Whatever he is, he's not dumb. If we can secure his loyalty and train him better, then he will be an asset to us."

"I agree with him," Veyada said. "Then again, money and family connections and upbringing do not guarantee intelligence. Hierarchies hold, even within the Outer Circle. They have their own microcosm of networks no different from ours. Maybe their networks are made even stronger by hardship, necessity and the desire to improve their lives. The only thing that worries me is that I'm not sure who has his main loyalty. He's been acting strangely, probably had conflicting orders."

"We should check on him that he's all right."

And, as usual, there was far too much going on, and I was dropping stitches.

The little voice inside me said, *That's why you have all these people, because you can't do it all alone.*

True, but I liked to feel *in control* and I felt far from that.

When we entered the hall to my apartment, Eirani came in from the corridor. "Oh, Muri, I didn't think you were still going to come. There were men here to fix the window, and I had to let them in. I didn't know what to do and you weren't here to ask. I guessed you had rather that the window was fixed what with the rains coming soon—"

"It's all right, Eirani." They'd be one of the normal maintenance crews.

Devlin came out of the hub. "The *zeyshi* delegation is getting ready for the meeting."

"Nicha has gone to meet them," Thayu said, before I could reply.

"We should go there soon, so we can brief them about the meeting." But all the notes we'd made would have to be thrown out in light of the recent discovery. And in all honesty, I thought we were better off postponing today's round of meetings until that document could be translated.

"Surely you will have some breakfast before you leave again?" Eirani asked. "I've already had to re-make the tea twice, because it had gone cold and no one wanted it."

"Not even Xinanu?"

"The lady complained of feeling sick and stayed in her room." Eirani sighed. "I know I shouldn't say this, but I don't understand why Asto ever had overpopulation problems if this is how much their women complain when they're having a baby."

I had to laugh at that. Xinanu was quite the drama queen, and if this meant that she was possibly having the baby early, then that could only be good news. "Yes, we'll have some of your lovely breakfast. Sorry, Eirani. Just let me do one thing."

I followed Devlin into the hub.

"There is a document I need translated with urgency. I want you to use a trusted translator only, and come back to me as soon as you have it."

He took the reader from me and said he would organise it.

I went to join Thayu and Veyada in the living room where the table was still set for breakfast although it was now well past breakfast time.

As I let myself fall into the chair, I felt so dizzy I was sure I'd faint unless I got something to eat soon. Eirani set about bustling with plates and bread and pouring tea. Raanu was with her, chatting away about the men who had replaced the big window, giving a blow-by-blow description on what they had done and how they'd gone about fitting the glass. I guessed that at home she never got to see any of this type of activity. I wasn't sure if she was aware why the window had to be replaced, but I wasn't going to enlighten her.

I took a slice of nut bread, ripped pieces off, dipping them in the bowl of jam before putting them in my mouth.

Damn it, that was good.

However, now that I wasn't so hungry anymore, fatigue took over. I wasn't sure that I could hold up for a whole day of meetings.

Both Thayu and Veyada looked tired as well.

For a while, we all ate and said nothing. Then Veyada pushed his chair back. "I better go and read up on the morality clause." He rose and walked to the door.

"Veyada."

He turned around.

"Don't try to be a hero. Have some rest."

"I have to read this before the meeting—"

"Have a rest. That's an order."

He nodded, the expression on his face blank, and left the room.

Thayu snorted. "Do you ever take your own advice?"

"I fully intend to. This meeting is too important."

"Well, let's go to the bedroom then."

But when we left the room, we met Devlin coming out of the hub. He had that *Big News* look on his face. My heart sank.

"Is there anything that can't wait?"

"Two lots of news. First, Ezhya Palayi is on his way here."

Damn. And yes, I had expected it. To be honest, did he ever expect Delegate Ayanu to act for him anymore? And could that be part of the problem? The ripples through society thing?

"All right. And secondly?"

"I've got the translation. You may want to have a read."

"That was quick."

"Yes, the translator she said she'd do it when she finished another job, took one look and translated it to me while I waited. She read it out and I took it down. I'm still waiting for a fully certified version; but though she said she might pretty it up a little bit, the meaning wouldn't change."

There went my rest.

I went after him into the hub. After we sat down on the bench, he pulled up a document.

"The translator reported that some of the language use was very unconventional."

"If it came from where I think it came from, I bet it would be." I dragged the projection over to the part of the bench where I sat.

It was indeed the transcript of a conversation. At the top, the translator had made a note that according to word use, one of the participants in the conversation was *contemporary* and the other was *aberrant* in the use of language, and she described *aberrant* as being formal, with the use of new and unknown phrases. The text was coloured in blue or green according to who was speaking. She had added the comment, *The difference in idiom, word use and pronunciation is very pronounced*.

The beginning of the document went like this:

Green, contemporary: This is a very sensitive issue at the moment. There is another group that has submitted a claim.

Blue: Were you not in contact with this group?

Green: We had no idea of their existence.

The green speaker went into some detail describing the *zeyshi*, their history and what their living conditions had been.

Blue: So you have mistreated this group often, then?

Green: Not us, the Coldi. They have systematically denied them rights, pushed them to the margins of society and disowned them. We have absorbed a fair few of them into our group.

Blue: Then why are you not working in conjunction with them to stop this abuse?

Green: We're a new group. We haven't been formed long, but I assure you that if we'd existed back then and had the means, we would have tried to stop them.

Blue: You would call yourself champions of all our people?

Green: We are the reason that Aghyrians still exist in our society.

Blue: You have the right to speak for all of them?

Green: we do indeed. Our leader is one of us. She will look favourably upon your request.

I stared at that last line. Was this person really talking about Chief Delegate Akhtari? What request?

The rest of the document went on in the same fashion. The person from the ship asking ever more pointed questions and seeming to obtain from the answers more information than the speaker wanted to divulge.

They hadn't travelled for four hundred ship years, the speaker said, to become involved in petty bickering.

The local Aghyrian wanted to know if the captain of the ship was really still Kando Luczon, and the prickly reply was that if, in the past fifty thousand years, the local Aghyrians hadn't been able to extend their technology to lengthen their lifetimes to four hundred years, just what had they been doing instead?

I read, with growing, albeit reluctant, appreciation for Marin Federza. *He* had seen the belittling and bullying, even if the local speaker had not. *He* had wanted to warn *gamra* about this.

I looked at Devlin. "This is a straight betrayal."

"What is?" This was Veyada at the door.

"I thought you were going to rest." Although now I was glad he hadn't yet gone to bed.

"I thought the same about you." He grinned.

Point taken.

I gestured at the projection. "Come and have a look at this."

He crossed the room and sat next to me on the bench. The scent of Coldi sweat enveloped me. I noticed a second person at the door. Veyada had brought Reida, wearing a clean tunic in my house colours. That was an improvement.

I gestured for him to come inside. He did so while looking at the ground in the fully submissive position. Amazingly, Thayu's belting had left no visible signs on him, and clearly the med post had found nothing wrong with him. Maybe I was the one overreacting. Maybe Coldi were even tougher than I had thought. Actually, scratch the *maybe*.

"Sit down," I said.

He did, clamping his hands between his knees. He said in a soft voice. "I have to apologise."

"It's all right. We'll talk more about it later."

He nodded, still not looking at me. "I want to make you understand that I am grateful to be accepted into your association. I'll do my best to serve the group as well as I can."

"I accept your apology."

"Thank you."

I touched his shoulder in the superior greeting, because he would expect me to do this, and he seemed relieved about it.

"We got the material you obtained translated. It's quite shocking. Veyada seems to think that your stealing the information might fall under the morality clause, which means you won't be charged."

"Thank you," he said again.

"Read the text," I told him. "This association of mine hangs together with politics. I hope you like politics."

"I don't mind it." He started reading.

Veyada was also still reading. I covered my mouth with my hand when I yawned. My eyes were gritty with the lack of sleep.

Veyada finished and met my eyes. For an intense moment, he said nothing.

"So, this ship is live, occupied, and they're trying to make deals with people here?"

"This comes from Federza's office. Somewhere in that arrogant mind of his, Federza realised that keeping this conversation from the assembly was not the right thing to do. So he copied this with the intention to . . . I don't know." Why hadn't Federza simply sent this material to all *gamra* delegates? He could have done so with one message. Maybe he didn't want to ruin his own career by incriminating himself.

"Shit." He stared.

"Reida stole this data. Delegate Ayanu was after it. We have the Asto military up there who are probably aware of it. And I don't think any of these people want this to become public knowledge."

Reida's face looked drawn.

Veyada said again, "Shit." And then, "Why? I could buy it if the Aghyrians wanted to keep the conversation secret, but why everyone else?"

"Think of it this way—and understand that this is my theory. These people left at the time of the meteorite strike. This was the time that the Aghyrian civilisation on Asto was at its zenith. They have been away for a long time. For us, an impossibly long time. They have obviously travelled at near-lightspeed and for them only four hundred years have passed."

His eyes widened. If you were like Earth and couldn't use the Exchange network, and were dependent on natural anpar lines, time dilation due to travel speeds could still be important. Every Earth child was taught about time dilation at school. The Coldi used the Exchange and had had not been taught to take it into consideration.

"In any case, however long they've been away, they've only started upsetting our system since that burst that caused the Exchange outage. That disturbance was caused by their anpar sling which they used to return from *outside the galaxy*. If that's what they can do, I would absolutely hate to think of all the technology that they've developed while they've been away. Not even to speak of anything they may have learned from other civilisations. They are likely to have all sorts of things we don't and know much that we haven't even scratched the surface of. Divided as we are, everyone is now trying to get into these people's pockets to see if they can get a favoured status. They don't *appear* hostile and appear to be open to talk to everyone. As long as it remains a secret. *Don't tell anyone and we'll give you some of our incredible technology.*"

Veyada said, "Shit. The army."

Well, yes, there was that, too. "All these people have figured out that the ship will eventually turn up here and want to get a piece of whatever loot they have to divide. Even if these people give us insignificant trinkets, their technology will make them superior trinkets. So everyone is hanging around here, pretending to negotiate while as soon as that ship turns up, all our negotiations will have been a waste of time. If these people want to resettle on Asto, they will just push us aside and do it."

Devlin asked, "You think the Asto army won't have anything to say about that?"

"Oh, yes of course they will. That's where the real action is. Our negotiations are just for show."

"Is that ship armed?"

"I don't know, but I'm guessing a hyper-powerful anpar sling is a pretty good weapon. You can unilaterally fling someone out of the galaxy, from where they can never return to bother you again. Wasn't that the main reason the Exchange requires bilateral input?"

"Shit."

I showed him the images of the ship that had been in Reida's information. His dark eyes roamed the lines of the projection.

"It's huge. I've never seen anything this big."

"More than three thousand on board."

"But we are many more than that. Surely we can contain them."

"If it came to a conflict, maybe, depending on what sort of weaponry they have, but right now they're talking. These are the people who built the Exchange. They're not going to be stupid enough to turn up here and start a war. I suspect they're more dangerous when talking than they are when shooting." Aghyrians had a reputation for their ability to sow discord. Look at what they had already done to the negotiations.

"Then what do they want from us?"

I shrugged and added another question. "How many have they left behind where they've come from?"

Devlin said, "What have they learned while they were there?"

Veyada asked, "Who did they meet while they were there?"

We looked at each other. Veyada was not easily shaken, but the look in his eyes disturbed me. Academics often spoke of potential alien civilisations. So far, every civilisation the Coldi had found in their explorations, no matter how remote, had been traceable back to Aghyrian space travel. There had been a couple of waves of Aghyrian colonisation. At first they sent only seeding probes. The Pengali were part of that wave, as well as some of the highland folk of the Mirani mountains. And the Kedrasi. Earth even fitted in that time period. Later, they had sent people. Indrahui was a colony from this era. Ceren had been hit in all of the waves.

But what about truly alien civilisations?

Thayu came into the hub. "Why are you two still sitting here? I thought you'd come to bed."

"I can't really sleep with this going on."

We showed her the image and the text. She stared at the projection. "Fuck."

"Yes, you can say that again."

She sighed. Spread her hands, let them fall again.

Thayu didn't swear often. She came into the hub and sat next to Veyada. "Well, what are we going to do now?"

We were silent for quite some time, thinking, considering all the options. There wouldn't be much time left before we'd need to go for the next round of talks with the *zeyshi* delegation.

I said, "I'm thinking we should probably create a very large fuss."

Thayu gave me her *uh-oh, it looks like you have a plan* look.

"I'm going to call an emergency meeting of the assembly."

"You can't do that."

"No. But Ezhya can. He will call an emergency meeting once I show him this. He's on his way here."

"No, Cory. He's a party in this negotiation. If he calls a meeting, the claim will be judged to be invalid. You should go to Delegate Akhtari."

"And she is not a party?"

She said nothing. Raised her hand to her mouth. Breathed in deeply.

Eventually, she said, "This is going to be huge."

"Yes."

Veyada said, "To be absolutely correct about it, we should go to see Delegate Ethvos or Delegate Namion." From Kedras or Damarq respectively. They also held veto rights, and Delegate Namion was a right pompous arse, but the perfect person for this sort of thing. "I'm sure we'll have no trouble getting either of them to call an emergency sitting."

As usual, Veyada to the rescue. "All right, let's go right now then."

But even "right now" required some preparation. I copied the translation to my reader, and while Veyada was getting ready, went to speak to Eirani, who was coming up the stairs carrying a blue shirt. "No, no, Muri, you're not leaving the apartment in this state. People would think you were a beggar. You have to change that smelly shirt, and your hair is a right mess."

"But—" I spread my hands, but Eirani had already gone into the bedroom. I slouched after her, heaving a sigh. Arguing against Eirani was useless and she was probably right.

"Just hurry up, right. There is not much time."

"Time will wait for proper preparation. If you look improper, people will remember you for your poor appearance rather than your words."

She was probably right about that, too.

So I sat on a chair and while she was untangling my plait, I snipped off the few stray hairs that still grew on my chin. After multiple treatments to kill off the hair follicles, there weren't many left, but I would probably need to go back one last time before my face was as smooth and hairless as that of other *gamra* men.

When she was done, and I had changed into a fresh shirt, Eirani brought the jacket and ceremonial belt. "It will be a big day in meetings," she said to my protests—the jacket was really hot.

And she was probably right about that, too. I rose and slipped my arms into the jacket while she held it up.

"There, that's better." She held up a mirror and I looked at myself, all ceremonial and proper, with my red Domiri earrings glittering in the light.

"Do be careful for Raanu," I said. "There is going to be a lot of trouble in the assembly today and I can't be certain that no one will shoot at the apartment again today."

Her eyes widened. "But Muri, they've just replaced the window."

"If that's all that needs replacing, we're doing fine. Seriously, though, keep Raanu away from balconies and windows, and stay off them yourself as well. I'd hate something to happen to you."

She nodded, her face solemn. "Raanu likes helping me downstairs, so I'll keep her there."

"Evi and Telaris will stay here. Do ask them for any help, no matter how small. If you see something strange, tell them immediately. Oh, also, Raanu's father is on his way here."

She nodded again. "What about the lady? Does she need to come downstairs as well?"

Had she ever even mentioned Xinanu's name? "Only if necessary. If she asks where we are, tell her that everyone is busy, which is true. She'll know about the meeting. If there is a security situation, include her, but don't give her any information that she doesn't need to have."

"Who is going out with you?"

"Everyone who can legitimately hold a gun, except Evi and Telaris."

She nodded, her expression grave. "I don't know what you're doing, but sometimes you scare me, Muri."

Thayu had come into the bedroom and she laughed. "Only sometimes?"

15

DELEGATE ETHVOS lived in the same building as we did, so we decided to try him first. Veyada and I went to the door, while the others waited, and were briefed on security matters by Thayu. Sheydu looked relaxed and confident; Nicha, too, thank goodness, but Deyu and Reida looked out of sorts and nervous. Deyu kept checking the light duty gun that Thayu had given her, since they were not licenced to carry heavier weapons. Reida's dark eyes kept following everything that happened in the group, as if he was determined not to make any more mistakes.

It was as if the pair of them had been kicked into realisation that this was it. If they behaved well and did a good job, they could stay for the rest of their lives.

The delegate was at home, and his housekeeper, an ancient Kedrasi man whose red hair had completely faded to pale pink, let us through into his office. I was glad to find the delegate home, because I liked him a lot better than Delegate Namion. Kedras tended to cycle their diplomats through the representative position, and Delegate Ethvos had replaced the previous occupant of the position last year. He was, however, a veteran of *gamra* and considered in high regard.

The delegate was also an older man, and a fair bit of grey had crept into his red hair. While we settled at the table, the old servant shuffled around bringing juice and biscuits.

Delegate Ethvos took one look at our material, and especially the image of that huge ship, and said, "This needs to go before an emergency meeting of the general assembly."

I didn't even need to ask him to call it.

The look in his sand-coloured eyes was serious. "If I call the meeting, I'm going to ask you to present this material. No doubt you know a good deal more about it than I do."

I nodded. "I'm fine with that." I'd addressed the full assembly a few times. It was a bit nerve-wracking to see all those thousands in the stands, but if that was the worst thing that could happen to me, I'd be laughing.

"This is a very explosive issue. You should take extreme care with the wording of this speech. It could get nasty if you're not careful."

"I think it's already nasty. We've got Tamerians running through town, and one has already been shot. No one knows who's hiring them either."

"I agree, but you do not want the fights to spill over into the general assembly."

"Is there ever fighting in the general assembly?" The meetings were so formal, so formulaic that I could hardly believe that.

"Not often, but it does happen. The worst thing that could happen right now is if the assembly disintegrates. This discovery will bring a lot of pressure on Delegate Akhtari to resign. We do not want that to happen."

"But I think—" *she should resign over this*. She should probably have resigned years ago.

He held up a tattooed hand. "Because when that happens, the assembly will remain paralysed for too long while elections are held. Asto will want to have a candidate. They've never held the position of Chief Delegate, because previously the seat of the assembly would move with the position of Chief Delegate." And none of the non-Coldi delegates could visit Asto, so moving the assembly there was out of the question. "Since it has been decided that Barresh is a permanent seat of the assembly, that objection has been removed. The situation is perfect for Asto to push forward their choice, and they will. And you will understand why a lot of other people will object to that."

I nodded.

"So when this information goes to the assembly, be careful not to stir up too much anger. Very careful."

———

"He is right," Veyada said when we were out of the apartment. He had that tone in his voice that spoke of his experience of guarding *gamra*'s most powerful leader. "There are a hundred reasons why Chief Delegate Akhtari should resign, and a hundred and one why she shouldn't be allowed to. The assembly will ask for her resignation. We should do our best to prevent that from happening."

"Probably. But I think people asking for her resignation have a point. I don't trust her."

"Would you trust Delegate Ayanu more?"

"Crap, no."

"There is your reason," Thayu said. She flicked her eyebrows.

"All right. But it may not be in our power to prevent it. Any bright ideas about how to prevent two thousand people from asking for her resignation?" Because really, that wasn't up to me. And anyway, I was much too tired to have bright ideas. "Sure, I could be really careful and try not to accuse her directly, but the fact remains that she is Aghyrian and she has never come clean about her involvement with Federza's group. The assembly has a right to know what's going on there, especially in light of what we're about to tell them—"

"Pronouns," Veyada said.

"What do you mean?" What the hell was he talking about?

He explained. "I watched Ezhya do this time and time again. When the situation is serious, he drops the formal pronouns and uses colloquial ones. Not only does it make people listen and take notice, it also gives them the feeling that they're being actively included and they're a lot more likely to listen and do as they're being asked without objection."

"But these aren't Coldi people." What was more, Asto wasn't a democracy, not by a long shot, and what Ezhya said was pretty much law anyway.

"I know, and it may not work, but it's worth a try."

At this point, anything was worth a try. Veyada was absolutely right in saying that Delegate Akhtari's resignation would paralyse the assembly at a crucial time. Oh, hell, I thought she should resign, but I could be made to agree that right now was not the best time for that to happen.

"So what, I talk to the full assembly using *nyo* pronouns?" Those were colloquial, the most common pronoun form since it was the default at Hedron and in Coldi spoken by non-Coldi people.

Veyada shook his head. "*Dhoya.*"

What? "Those are for intimate friends."

"Intimate friends, and very serious situations."

Well, that was not what I had learned, but I'd take it from the expert. Seriously, this language was shifting under my feet. How could I be expected to keep up with it? And did he really want me to speak to the entire assembly using *dhoya* pronouns? If Delegate Akhtari wasn't going to resign, she was going to have a fit instead.

Maybe that's the point, Thayu said. I swore she was secretly laughing at me.

All right, all right.

————

With that process set in motion, we went to the accommodation of the *zeyshi* Aghyrian delegation to see who would turn up for today's preliminary meeting.

With all the things that were going on, we got to the apartment late and the delegation already sat at the table, with the refreshments that the *gamra* staff had brought. They had poured themselves some tea and looked relieved when we came up the stairs.

"No one here yet?" But that was evidently clear.

"I was wondering if we understood the time wrong," Nayu said, holding a cup. She was wearing a pristine white *shayka* with tiny gold flecks woven in, and looked very traditional and very out of place. As it was customary with *zeyshi*, she used *nyo* pronouns, and yes, I could see why Ezhya would use *dhoya* forms. The *nyo* form was bland. It was just about as inoffensive as one could make it, and emotionless as a result. Using it would ruffle some feathers of the *gamra* officials, but would do little else. Everyone heard *nyo* pronouns on the streets and the courtyards and in the corridors of the *gamra* buildings every day.

Dhoya pronouns would make people sit up and take notice. In a good way, I hoped.

I asked the delegation, "Nicha was supposed to come here this morning. Have you seen him?"

"Oh, yes, he was here briefly. He told us that you were coming, else we would have gone for a walk."

"Have you heard anything from the others?"

Nayu snorted. "Those people wouldn't let *us* know if they're not going to turn up."

I ignored the barb. "They'd let someone know, and that someone would let you know. This is *gamra*. We're not into favouritism."

"No?" Sadet snorted. She wore a dark blue *shayka* today. Her hair hung loose to her shoulders. It made her face softer. "It seems that something is going on, and no one cares to tell us what it is. There are all these people walking past our apartment and standing out there gawking at us. Also, the Exchange doesn't work half the time and there were some guards out the front of the building this morning who said that we couldn't go out."

"You shouldn't need to go out. If you need something, let the caretaker know and it will be brought here." I'd explained that before.

"We're not allowed to go for a walk?"

"You are, but you may be asked to turn back or show your identification at any time. Security does things for reasons that are not always clear to us."

Sadet snorted. "It's worse than in our city."

Nayu said, "Anyway, where are the others? I thought we had a meeting this morning? It's not just you that's supposed to be here. Where is that Trader? Where is the crazy witch?"

Damn it, did she really need to talk like that?

All her rudeness is in the pronouns, Thayu reminded me through the feeder.

Yeah, I'm already in favour of taking Veyada's advice.

To the delegation I said, "I don't know where the others are." I was going to tell them that I had yet to sleep, and wasn't up to keeping up with everyone's appointments, but I sure as hell wasn't going to complain. "The Trader and Delegate Ayanu live on another part of the island. They may simply be late. Let me ask my security if they have heard anything about where they are."

I went into the hallway, where Veyada was shaking his head. "You know you are the most incredible bullshit merchant I have ever come across?"

I raised my eyebrows. "It works." I'd rather talk nonsense than be beaten to pulp.

We went a bit down the stairs, where Sheydu and the two youngsters sat on the balustrade. Sheydu was giving an instruction on a selection of goodies that she had produced from her pockets and laid out on the floor. Explosives for blowing up walls, explosives for opening doors, explosives for creating a diversion. Sheydu loved it, as long as it went bang. The bigger the bang, the better.

But when we came down, she jumped down from the balustrade with more grace than people half her age, and swept the entire lot off the floor and into her pockets. Lesson over.

She gestured, *Listen now*.

Nicha had been sitting on the stairs with his reader and he got up.

The rest of us gathered around. Veyada sat on the steps; Thayu leaned against the balustrade. I ended up standing in the middle. I began, "I have no idea what's going on. I expected Federza not to be here. We'll have to find out where he is, but we don't have much time for that. I'm really surprised about Delegate Ayanu's absence."

"Maybe she is also asking for an emergency meeting," Nicha said.

"No," Sheydu said. "I have it from reliable sources that Ezhya is dealing with her." There was a kind of smugness in that sentence that chilled me. *Dealing with* in Coldi understanding often involved guns.

"Then what are we supposed to do now?" Nicha said.

Thayu said, darkly, "Go home and go to bed?"

If only. Wouldn't that be wonderful? "I suppose we better tell the *zeyshi* what we know. Better than that they hear it for the first time from someone else."

Nicha grumbled. "I went to the Exchange this morning and got clearances for all of the delegates to use the *gamra* system. Does this mean that I've been wasting my time?"

"No, not at all," I said.

The *zeyshi* probably wouldn't be allowed in an emergency meeting so Nicha's efforts meant that they could follow the meeting from anywhere within the complex. I didn't think that the public gallery was open for emergency meetings. There had been only one such meeting since I started working for *gamra*, but it had been held while I was at Asto.

Nicha said, "Do you need me today, because . . ." He gestured at his reader.

Xinanu? I met his eyes.

"No, not yet. She's just feeling bad. But I'd rather be there than be accused of not caring."

"All right." Poor Nicha.

Nayu came to the door of the meeting room. "I don't know what's going on, but the Exchange has just shut us out again—"

My reader pinged. I slipped it out of my pocket.

A message from the official *gamra* channel. *Request the attendance to an emergency meeting of all delegates.*

There it was.

I showed the message to Thayu.

Sadet was watching us with an expression of suspicion. "What's going on?"

"I'm afraid we've been called away immediately."

"See? There is something going on."

"We have been called to an emergency sitting of the assembly. We have to attend. I don't know if you can come."

"I think they should," Veyada said. He sounded like he was serious about it, too.

"But what if the meeting is closed to all outsiders?"

"I'll explain at the door." He seemed confident that he could get the delegation in, so they went downstairs to get ready. Did they need weapons, Sadet wanted to know. Sheydu said bring some and wear armour and they went into a little bit of discussion about weapon types and what would be acceptable.

Sheydu sucked in a breath once Sadet had gone downstairs with her fellows. She exchanged a look with Veyada.

They got some serious stuff, huh?

Damn, what did she think was going to happen at that meeting? Wherever I turned, there seemed to be an ever-increasing escalation of firepower. When I started working in Barresh, I would be shocked by the sight of a single gun, and now Thayu wanted me to carry one.

"Any news from Federza yet?" I asked Thayu.

She shook her head. Her eyes met mine in a worried look.

"Maybe we should send someone to look for him."

"Why did he ever leave the apartment? I offered him a safe room."

"The guards said that he'd been picked up by some *gamra* guards."

"And we didn't check that, did we?" What if they had been *Tamerians* in disguise? I wouldn't have thought it possible, but after tonight I could believe anything.

"We had no reason to doubt it."

"Damn it. We have to find him." If anything happened to Federza, it was my fault. I shouldn't have let him leave.

"Don't worry. He'll have received the call for the meeting as well. He'll have to be there."

The delegation members came upstairs. Nayu was the only one who wore nominally normal clothes, although I could see the glint of armour underneath her tunic. Sadet wore a skin-fitting suit with built-in armour and pockets for things that required antennas and wires. She eyed Sheydu as if matching her in strength. I had no doubt that Sheydu was the superior. The other three were all in dark clothing. Their non-descript gear made me think strongly of the Asto army. I had to push that thought away. It would be ridiculous if this delegation contained army people, wouldn't it? Well, *wouldn't it*?

But damn it, last year, during the upheaval caused by Ezhya's absence, Ezhya's second had fled to the *zeyshi* warrens. Who was to say where the army had its ties? The reason that Coldi had little conflict between groups within their population was that they had ties and networks everywhere.

I was trying to eliminate Delegate Ayanu's influence from my association. If I was truly Coldi and I found this influence in my association, I would first secure it to make sure it didn't feed into places I didn't want it to go, but then I would embrace it.

Instead, these sorts of thoughts *Would the army be involved with the zeyshi?* upset me and still, after many years, managed to take me by surprise. If Asha Domiri was smart—and frankly the man scared the shit out of me—then he would have ties with the *zeyshi*, end of story.

Was it then safe to assume that the *zeyshi* Aghyrian claim was a move by Asto's Inner Circle in disguise? I didn't think so, but frankly this stuff made my head hurt.

We left the apartment not much later and walked as a large group in the direction of the assembly hall. Many other delegates were going in the same direction and the courtyards and passages hummed with an air of excitement. The monsoon was starting to build. Fat clouds with dark grey bases cast huge shadows over the island and surrounding marshland. When a cloud alternately blocked out one sun and then the other, the light grew eerie and wan. Even after having lived here for a couple of years, it always creeped me out a little when the clouds did that. The faint and lifeless light somehow suited the graveness of the occasion.

The air was humid and I was sweating before we'd gone far.

The foyer of the assembly hall buzzed with activity. Groups of the minor delegates and their staff—and I was still coming to terms with the fact that I was no longer a minor delegate—waited outside the main doors to the hall, which were still closed.

Not all delegates were equally prepared. Some went in their day-to-day uniform; others were perfectly dressed for a general assembly meeting. People looked over their shoulders at us. There were fifteen of us and Veyada and Sheydu at the front of our group cut an imposing picture. Maybe some people even recognised one or the other of them. Rumours already went around that I was *the man who stole security guards off Ezhya Palayi*. And got away with it.

Was Ezhya here yet?

Then again, if he was, people wouldn't be standing here in a relatively relaxed fashion. They'd have been herded into a corner of the hall by his new guards. I thought. Or maybe Ezhya would be a bit late, as was his habit, to come in at the time that his entry caused maximum disturbance and would be noticed by everyone.

Asto officials were strutting peacocks.

I'd thought this so often that, when we were last in New Zealand, I'd had to go and find a peacock for Thayu to watch. I still remembered her face when it put up its tail.

"That's gorgeous," she'd said, and then, "The colours are a bit like my hair." And for the rest of the time of our visit to the zoo, she hadn't wanted to leave the peacock's side. Were they aggressive, she'd wanted to know, and I told her no, they just wanted to bluff their rivals into a corner with a big show of colour. She fed it pieces of bread. I don't think that up to then she had understood what I meant by likening Coldi behaviour to bluff and peacocks, but it was like seeing the light go on inside her brain.

I smiled just thinking about it.

Damn, I loved that woman.

I touched her arm and she, having followed my thoughts through the feeder, gave me that most gorgeous smile of all the smiles in the universe. That smile that said that I could do anything I set my mind to, as long as she was with me.

16

—————

SHEYDU AND VEYADA made a path for us to the doors of the assembly hall. These days, I came in through the main entrance because I'd been given a box in the lower tiers of the hall. Most minor delegates sat on the unassigned benches at the top of the hall and they crowded up the stairs because apparently someone needed to be found to open the gallery doors.

Veyada went to speak to the guards at the door. There was too much talk in the hall for me to hear what was being said. The guard's expression was grave. I didn't think Veyada was successful. He turned back to us. "The delegation can go in the public gallery. They can't come with us."

"That's all right." Frankly I was surprised that they were allowed in at all, even if only because with all of us here, the box would be very cramped.

"The public gallery will be full of delegates." The assembly hall was only big enough for all delegates if absolutely none took any staff and that never happened, apart from ceremonial meetings. "It is a security risk."

"Why don't we send someone with them?"

"I will go," Reida said.

I glanced at Nicha. Did we trust him enough?

He nodded.

"You and Deyu," I said.

Deyu straightened her back and then bowed. The two of them accompanied the delegation to the back of the queue that snaked all the way up the stairs and into the gallery doors.

"Do you think that's a good idea to send both of them?" Thayu asked.

"She's very obedient. She'll keep him in line."

"I hope you're right. Because I'm not feeling his loyalty yet." She glanced over her shoulder. I had spoken to Nicha. Reida had broken with Delegate Ayanu, but Nicha hadn't spoken to her yet in order to sever his ties with her. That part still remained unsettled, and would probably remain so until Xinanu had left our apartment.

We went into the hall, where the main lights were on and people were settling into their boxes and benches. My box was a familiar place for me these days, considering the amount of time I spent in here. I didn't just attend the general meetings, but also a good number of committee and subcommittee meetings.

Thayu took the seat in front of me, Nicha next to me, Sheydu and Veyada behind me. I couldn't see the *zeyshi* delegation from here. Too dark, too many people. There had to be close to two thousand in the hall.

The Asto delegation had just arrived, a knot of people in the box two levels below mine. I spotted Delegate Ayanu, ordering people about. I didn't see Ezhya. He was supposed to have had words with her and she'd come out of that meeting unscathed?

There were also some people in the Aghyrian box, but they were on the other side of the hall. Marin Federza was one of the most easily recognisable people in the entire assembly, because of the way his silver hair reflected the light, but I didn't see anyone who looked like him. If he was here, he would be in that box.

Damn it. Where was he?

Why had he left my apartment with those "guards"?

And who were these new people who would negotiate on behalf of the Aghyrians instead?

A bell rang, and while talk died down, the main lights dimmed, and people took their seats, the door at the back of the central floor opened. Two guards came out and stationed themselves on either side of the door. Then came Delegate Akhtari in full regalia: a heavy brocade coat with wide sleeves in *gamra* blue with gold embroidery on the lapels, a *gamra* blue tunic and blue trousers, both with exquisite gold patterns. She wore sandals to symbolise her status—because she didn't need to run or flee, she could wear sandals. I didn't think those sandals would protect her from what was to come. Hell, I didn't even think I could protect her. I wasn't sure that I *wanted* to protect her, even to save *gamra* from descending into chaos.

She strode across the floor to the speaker's dais, passing under the downward beams of light that made her hair shine like silver. Behind her another group of people entered. The ceiling light hit the bright red hair of Delegate Ethvos. Next to him was none other than Ezhya, wearing his silver temperature retaining suit and red sash. His new guards, also with the sash, fanned out over the hall and took up positions in the first tier of the audience. One stood right below Delegate Ayanu's box, staring at her. She stared back.

Someone in the box in front of us hissed. "What is he doing here?"

I glanced at Delegate Ayanu and her assistants in Asto's box. They were all sitting stiffly, not talking, kind of . . . resigned or nervous. Maybe I needed to reassess my judgement that she'd come out of this unscathed.

Someone on the other side of the hall yelled. I didn't hear what was being said, but the next moment a couple of guards ran out onto the floor into the audience. Ezhya's guards remained where they were, all of them looking at the origin of the sound, but none of them overly concerned. From the location of the sound, I guessed that some of the smaller entities on the other side of the hall objected to Ezhya's presence on the main floor. They made a habit of creating a fuss when he was in the hall.

But Ezhya being Ezhya, he ignored all of it and sat down at the central table anyway.

It was true that he was allowed a more prominent position than usual: one of the speakers' chairs. Normally he used Asto's box, or rather somewhere near it, because he had a habit of wandering through the audience while he spoke. It was also true that the reaction from the guards to protest calls was usually more subdued. I had no idea what sort of rumours went around about the reason for this sitting, but there were always plenty of rumours, most of them rubbish. The past days had been no exception. Tensions were high in the lead-up to the negotiations about the *zeyshi* claim.

Delegate Ethvos completely ignored the goings-on and took the spot a few seats down from Ezhya, separated by a couple of scribes and other administrators with various bits of equipment in front of them.

Whereas Ezhya had six guards with him—he stood at the top of this association after the breakup of his previous security arrangement—Delegate Ethvos had brought a single person onto the floor: a Kedrasi woman young enough to be his daughter, and who, knowing the Kedrasi penchant to employ family members, probably *was* his daughter, who carried his documents and electronics. I'd always admired the absolute cool of the Kedrasi delegates. They were small of stature and commanded no army to speak of; they never postured or threatened; but they could make a lot of impact with a few spoken words.

Chief Delegate Akhtari rose from the table and turned on the light at the dais.

Whatever disturbance had been going on across the hall died down. I could still see a couple of guards maintaining a warning presence in the audience. The benches behind them were packed, and so was the public gallery. I hoped the *zeyshi* delegation had been able to get in, but I had no hope of making them out from where I sat. There had to be close to three thousand people crammed into this hall. Curious, anxious, angry, frightened people.

Delegate Akhtari rang her bell. "Delegates. Welcome to this special emergency sitting of the *gamra* assembly. I call on Delegate Ethvos, who has called for this meeting."

The delegate rose and entered the pool of light that came from the downward spotlights in the middle of the floor. The intense glow made his hair show up brilliant red. He had come prepared and wore his ceremonial robe, complete with the coat that marked him as one of the five prime delegates who were entitled to call such meetings. He stopped before the dais and bowed before delegate Akhtari, who nodded in return, and stepped back from the dais so that he could get on. It was all very ceremonial. My fists were clenched with the long-windedness of it all, but we would have to go through the protocol before I could have my say.

His assistant remained at the table. Kedrasi went about by themselves, without guards or protection. They tended to be rather fatalistic. "If I die, then I die," Delegate Ethvos had once said to me in response to my question about why he didn't use security.

He put his reader on the dais, pulled out the little stool from underneath, climbed on and adjusted the microphone. He was only the size of a young teenager, a couple of heads shorter than Chief Delegate Akhtari and, even when standing on the stool, could barely see over the top of the dais.

"Delegates. We meet here to discuss a grave occasion that has been brought to my attention by Delegate Cory Wilson, whom I will ask to present his material so that we can all appreciate the seriousness of his discovery."

Finally.

I picked up my reader and left the box in the company of Thayu and Nicha. We had to walk down the stairs that went past Asto's box. Delegate Ayanu made a point of looking the other way.

Everyone in the hall was silent as I crossed the floor into the pool of light and to the dais. Sometimes I wondered what sort of reputation I had amongst the delegates. Would they gossip about me being a lot of hot air and no action, or living in Ezhya's pockets?

I put my reader down while Thayu busied herself connecting it to the projector and Nicha took up position next to me.

I used those last moments to consider the pronoun situation. Would I be bold or would I be traditional? Bold or traditional? Bold or—

Thayu gave me the thumbs up.

I made a split-second decision. "Delegates. Every day since the Exchange outage and since my return from Asto, I've been afraid that I would have to come here and make this speech, and every day I've hoped that I wouldn't have to do it."

A murmur of surprise went through the hall. No one ever heard *dhoya* pronouns in the general assembly. In fact, one rarely heard them on the island at all. Delegate Akhtari stared at me in a *what the hell?* kind of way.

But Ezhya looked at me and nodded.

I continued in slightly more formal language. "Over fifty thousand years ago, a meteorite struck Asto. The Aghyrian people, who lived on that world at the time, had little time to prepare because no one saw it coming. They had three ships that were capable of rescuing but a fraction of their population. One of those ships came to Barresh." And as I said that, another realisation struck me: could it be that the remains of that ship lay under the marshes on the eastern side of the main island and that this is what the signal had responded to and what the Tamerians had been looking for in the dark in the reed beds? "A second ship crash-landed on the Mirani highlands. The descendants of those people founded Miran. The third ship was a deep space vessel, fitted out to carry large crews over long distances where the anpar lines wouldn't reach. They were in orbit, but refused to take extra passengers on board. They disappeared after the meteorite impact and were never heard from again."

I gestured to Thayu who switched on the projector. The image of that huge ship was projected into the middle of the hall above every-one's heads, blown up to a construct of light that filled the entire space above our heads.

The audience exploded into gasps and exclamations. I couldn't hear but imagined what they said.

"What the hell is that thing?"

"I bet Asto has something to do with it."

Even I was impressed.

Wow and holy shit. That was a serious ship and the image was serious quality. Normally if you enlarged a projection, detail became fuzzy, but not this image. You could see all the little protrusions and air locks and tubes on the outer walls of the ship. I enlarged the image, and an even greater level of detail resolved from the projection, showing individual hatches and hooks, panels and a million other things the function of which I could only guess.

"This is the ship, and they're back."

By now, all the talk in the hall had died down. Two thousand dele-gates and their assistants listened to me in absolute silence.

"We knew about this ship, in a roundabout way. The Exchange had captured some snatches of random material from the wake of the anpar burst that fried the Exchange and that, we are reasonably sure, resulted from the ship creating an insanely strong anpar line to return to our galaxy. What we did not know was whether this ship was an automated empty shell, or if it was functioning and live. If there was a crew. I can now say that we have proof that it is live, that it contains people who can still communicate with us."

A murmur rose in the hall, many voices with an alarmed tone. I waited until it died down.

"When the ship left all those years ago, a hardline man called Kando Luczon was its captain. In the historical archives of Athyl, there is evidence that even though his ship could have taken on board tens of thousands across a relatively short distance to Ceren, he refused to take extra people on board. While Asto died and was reborn, while the two sets of refugees struggled, almost died out, and resurfaced on Ceren, they chose to leave the galaxy. While a huge amount of time has passed for us, they've been away for four hundred years ship time. The hardline Kando Luczon is still their captain. You may ask me how I know all this. I know this because people have been talking to the ship."

I signalled to Thayu and the projection of the ship made way for a projection of the translated document.

I waited.

While people read, the shouts of outrage and anger increased. More guards streamed into the hall, and lined up on the walkway that ran between the boxes and the upper stands where most of the minor delegates sat.

I let the tumult build for a while.

Thayu and Nicha both stood on either side of the dais, ready to take defensive action if necessary. Delegate Akhtari glared at me across the floor. Her mouth was a thin line. I had always suspected that she knew of many of the dealings of the Barresh Aghyrians, and I increasingly got the feeling that I was correct. She'd known about this. She should resign, and I had promised Delegate Ethvos that I would do whatever I could to keep her in the job.

I couldn't see Delegate Ayanu. People were standing in the Aghyrian box, shouting, but there was too much noise in the hall for me to make out anything.

Only Ezhya sat at his seat, his arms crossed over his chest, perfectly relaxed and *amused*. As his eyes met mine, I swore the corner of his mouth moved up.

The noise showed no sign of dying down. I looked in the dark space at the back of the dais, but couldn't see the bell, so I tapped the microphone, which produced a loud thudding sound and the noise dimmed somewhat.

"I obtained this material from the office of the Asto Delegate Ayanu, who, in turn, obtained it illegally from the office of the Barresh Aghyrian delegate Trader Federza, who, I believe, had the material in his possession in order to raise it with the assembly."

"Nonsense!" someone shouted.

I ignored it. "I would like Trader Delegate Federza to come forward to explain his position."

There was a lot of rumbling in the stands on the opposite side of the hall. Someone shouted, "Stay in your seats!" In a decidedly impera-tive pronoun form.

None of the noise produced Marin Federza.

I tapped the microphone again. An employee rushed forward to bring me the bell that was used for this purpose. Its clear tone rang through the hall.

"Where is Trader Delegate Marin Federza? Can we get someone from the Barresh Aghyrian delegation to comment?"

There was movement in the Aghyrian box but because of the strong light where I stood, I couldn't make out what was happening there.

The man who came onto the floor—and who wasn't Federza—had the typical tall and lanky form of an Aghyrian. He wore the uniform of a lesser delegate: only his tunic was blue, but his trousers were grey. His hair was dark and curly, held back in a ponytail at the nape of his neck. He had a sharp face, with a long nose and thin lips.

I'd seen him a few times in the corridors of the *gamra* buildings, not that I remembered his name, but my feeder said *Delegate Tomar Samari*. The name sounded vaguely familiar.

Thayu added, *Born in Barresh, educated in the Aghyrian complex, has never left Ceren*. One of those indoctrinated kids like the ones we had seen on the train. Oh so attentive, assertive and judgmental, and a little bit creepy, to be honest.

Likely he had always been part of the delegation, but I'd just never had any direct dealings with him. The Aghyrians were usually silent in the meetings and they had to have some sort of hierarchical structure that governed who could speak in which situations. All of which made me more concerned about Federza.

"Delegate Federza is indisposed," he said in a deep voice that belied his thin appearance.

"I would like to see him," I said, again using *dhoya* pronouns.

His brow furrowed as if he was suspicious or unsure of my intentions.

"When the Trader Delegate came to see me, he was afraid for his life. Someone shot at the window of my office while I was meeting him. I would like to know if he is all right."

"He is."

"Then why is he not here to address us?"

"Is the issue at hand about him or about that ship?"

"He came to me to warn me that some people were talking to the ship. He was afraid for his life. I want to see him before I believe that you act in the interest of the general assembly." I abandoned the intimate pronouns for more formal ones.

"Wait a moment. I object to being painted as criminal," Delegate Samari said.

Some people applauded.

Someone else shouted, "You're a liar!" from the back of the hall. "You talked to this ship and were going to keep it secret from the assembly."

And a few other people shouted. An argument broke out in Damarcian on the other side of the hall.

I glanced at Thayu. *Any news from Federza?*

She shrugged. *Not a trace.*

Can you use your security protocol to track him?

I could, but the equipment doesn't scan the Aghyrian complex. There wouldn't be much point.

If that was where he had gone. Damn it, I disliked him, but that didn't mean I wished him ill.

17

——————

AMONGST THE ARGUING and shouting, a man walked down from the higher tiers of seating. Only when he came into the light did I recognise him: it was the Barresh councillor Ramadu, whose daughter had been the subject of Reida's interest and who—I'd forgotten about that—attended *gamra* meetings on behalf of the Barresh Council to coordinate logistical operations.

He reached the bottom of the stairs, spoke to the guards who stopped him there and they let him through. He came up to the dais and bowed to me. "If I may, Delegate."

I stepped down and he went up to the microphone. "Delegates." His deep voice echoed through the hall. "I would like to confirm what Delegate Wilson says. A few days ago, Trader Delegate Federza came to us. He said that he feared for his life and was expecting attacks both from his own kin as well as from the Asto delegation. He was nervous and didn't want to talk about the issue until he could be guaranteed protection. While we were working on that request, I believe some guards treated him roughly and he left again. But before he did, he told us that some of his kinsfolk wanted to keep certain information from the assembly and that he wanted to give this information to us, providing that we passed it onto the assembly. He didn't say what that information was, only that it was explosive and that he wanted copies of it to go to the assembly."

"That is nonsense!" one of the Aghyrians shouted, and a lot of people tried to drown him out.

"Quiet everyone!" This came from Delegate Akhtari. "Let the man speak!"

"This is what I've come to say: that the delegate speaks true about Trader Federza. He was trying to do the right thing." He bowed and left again, walking calmly the way he had come.

Delegate Akhtari's nostrils flared.

A male voice in the back of the stands yelled, "Chief Delegate, I'm thinking you are extremely biased." I had no idea who this was, but oh, that was a very confrontational pronoun. "I'm thinking you're involved with this group that is withholding information from the assembly."

The spotlight on the ceiling was frantically searching the crowd. It eventually found the speaker, a man of the Indrahui delegation. He stood in the stands, his arms crossed. The spotlight made his black skin glisten.

A good number of people in the hall applauded. Coldi, Damarcians, other Indrahui, Kedrasi, even the Hedron delegation, and they normally supported everything that was against Asto—and therefore supported Delegate Akhtari—as a matter of principle. Now they agreed with Asto. There were many more forces in this issue than I could possibly contain. If the assembly voted against Delegate Akhtari, then who was I to think that I could stop it?

From the moment that it had become clear that President Sirkonen's murder was through Aghyrian technology, I had expected this issue to surface. The Amoro Renkati group had been found guilty, but the Aghyrians had remained silent on the issue. They had simply moved their technology to a less visible place. Many people were not happy with that.

All through the problems with the Exchange outage, they had not assisted the operators in re-establishing contact with the network, even though I had no doubt that they could. They'd simply watched as the operators struggled.

I had to confront this issue. Defuse it, if I could, but I didn't hold my hopes up.

I rang the bell for silence, and when the noise had calmed somewhat, I said, "I think the Delegate could have been more subtle about it, but I think the underlying question is valid." It grew very quiet in the hall. "I would like to give Delegate Akhtari the opportunity to comment on it." It also occurred to me that, being the main speaker, I had acquired the chair of the meeting by default.

She glared at me, nostrils flaring. "What is there to comment?" Her voice vibrated with anger. "Have I ever acted in a way that is not in line with the requirements for this office? What my ethnic group does or doesn't do has no bearing on my position."

I said, "I think the assembly would like to hear your unambiguous statement that you are not involved in their talks to the ship, that you knew nothing of the communication that I've just shown the assembly, and that you absolutely hold to your position of neutrality in this matter." Again, I used *dhoya* pronouns.

"Of course I do." She took a deep breath through flaring nostrils. She frowned at me. "What are you on about, actually?"

It was probably the most sincere thing she had ever said to me. I wanted to say, *I'm giving you the opportunity to save your skin*, but of course I couldn't do that. "It is in the assembly's interest that we maintain a unified front. *Gamra* will soon come under threat from outside. We can't let the fact that some of us have been talking to this ship come between us. We are closer to each other than anyone is to the crew of this ship. We don't know what they want. We don't know if they're hostile. We don't know what their claims will be. None of us should be negotiating with them behind the scenes. It's deplorable that some contact has already taken place. That must absolutely stop. If necessary all assembly members should take a pledge of loyalty to this assembly."

"*Iyamichu ata!*" a Coldi voice shouted at the back, and that pledge was repeated a few times. It was originally a battle cry of troops about to go into a fight, a declaration of loyalty to the leadership. It was also very Coldi, in-your-face and confrontational. It said, *Coldi people are ready, why not all of the rest of you?* I wasn't sure that it was helpful, because I got too many accusations that I was a puppet for Asto already.

Ezhya remained impassive at the table. I thought he looked pleased with himself.

Chief Delegate Akhtari came to the dais. Her penetrating voice echoed through the hall. "Delegate Wilson speaks true. We should be determining a response to this issue as a united group. We should be talking about the ship and how we will approach it. This vessel," she gestured at the projection, "This vessel is the greatest threat to us since the time of the wars. We should not bicker amongst ourselves while this ship listens and approaches."

"That is very well, but we want hard guarantees that we can trust you," the Indrahui man said again, continuing with his very direct pronouns. "We want proof that you are not part of this group that spoke to the ship without our knowledge. We want assurance that you are impartial as you should be—"

Some shouts went up in the hall.

"Be quiet!" Delegate Akhtari shouted over the tumult, but the shouting increased.

It came, not just from the rebellious delegates at the back, but also from people at the front, now starting to ask questions, yelling louder to be heard over the noise. She had to ring the bell repeatedly until a semblance of silence returned to the hall. "I would like Delegate Wilson to continue with the proceedings—"

Another shout at the back of the hall—

"Quiet!" Her nostrils flared. "Either apply for permission to speak or hold your silence."

Several people yelled that they would be applying.

Delegate Akhtari stepped off the dais, and I climbed on again. My hands were sweaty. It was up to me to defuse the situation. Ignore the concerns of the assembly, and they would never shut up.

I said, "I hear a lot of concern. The Chief Delegate could allay the assembly's misgivings simply by answering the question: how involved is our Chief Delegate with the Barresh Aghyrian group?"

She snorted. Her cheeks had gone red.

"Of course I am pro-Aghyrian. This is like asking Ezhya if he is pro-Coldi." Her response was very direct and very much out of character. Rattled, I thought. Surely she had to have expected to answer these questions one day?

"I lived in the Aghyrian compound for most of my life. Still have a room there in fact. I grew through the ranks to be their rightful representative and that of the whole of Barresh—"

"—You represent anyone as long as those people have money!" I couldn't see who that was. Probably Pengali.

A fairly large group of people applauded.

Delegate Akhtari continued over the noise, "I've represented all of Barresh, even the people who have done nothing to earn that representation."

Oo—er. She was really losing it now.

Several shouts of protest went up in the hall. Another scuffle broke out higher up in the tiered benches. The guards were running short on people to control the mayhem. If chaos broke out everywhere, there would never be enough guards to control it. I guessed that was why we wore armour.

I rang the bell long and clear. When a modicum of order had returned, I said, "At this point in time it is most important to present a unified face when that ship eventually turns up. We do not want any major disagreements dividing us. We do not want one of the groups siding with one side and one with the other. We do not want both groups of Aghyrians to be fighting each other."

Someone said, "We do not want a Chief Delegate who is going to favour one side or the other."

Delegate Ayanu added to this, "We do not want a Chief Delegate who is going to hand control of our Exchange network or any part of our planet to these people. What do they even want?"

"Who says that any of us have any interest in *handing over* control to them?" Delegate Samari said, his face red.

Delegate Ayanu yelled across the hall, "Then why have you been talking to them in secret?"

"Since when aren't we allowed to speak to our kinsfolk without letting everyone listen in?"

Delegate Ayanu rose and spread her hands in a theatrical gesture. "Since these supposed *kinsfolk* of yours brought down our entire Exchange network once before and I, for one, would like to make damn sure that it doesn't happen again. And oh, there has been this mysterious ship floating about and we've been wondering if it's live or some empty shell of the past, but no, you're already talking to it, never mind everyone else. It would have been nice if at the very least you'd have informed the rest of us that the ship is live and talking to you?"

Delegate Samari snorted. "Certainly, Delegate, all of this is not news to you?"

Delegate Ayanu glared at him, nostrils flaring. "This is not about *me*. It's about the entire assembly, about *gamra* as a community."

Delegate Samari continued, primly. "Tell me, if *you* had been the first to establish contact, would you have shared it with everyone in this assembly? Including entities you don't like, you don't trust and suspect of illegal activities? You wouldn't. In fact, I know that you've had this information in your possession, and you've known about the status of this ship for quite a while. Possibly even longer than we've been talking to it—"

"That's nonsense! And I can prove it."

"Prove it, prove it!"

Others in the hall took up the chant.

Delegate Akhtari was banging her closed fist on the table. "Quiet, delegates! Quiet, or I will be forced to suspend this sitting!" She rose from her seat and came to the dais again.

Someone yelled, "If you do that, we'll just keep talking outside!"

"You will suspend the sitting to do what?" Delegate Ayanu yelled. "To save your name? You are with these people, this secretive sect that closes its doors to other people. You call us *artificial*, but meanwhile you have *breeding programs*?"

Delegate Akhtari gave her a prim look. "That has nothing to do with the matter under consideration. You have been putting undue pressure on some of the key members of the Aghyrian delegation with all these outrageous claims. You have made threats. You have tried to scare our people into telling you what you wanted to hear—whether it was true or not."

"Because you were deliberately keeping information from us."

"We were not."

"You were."

The discussion between the two women descended into a shouting match of mutual accusations.

Thayu glanced at me sideways, her expression disturbed. *I've never seen a meeting get out of hand like this.*

Two major delegates abandoning all protocol and starting mudslinging matches. To be honest, I'd found this sort of posturing quite common, and despite the fact that *gamra* main assembly meetings had the reputation for being boring and staid, I had never experienced that.

Ezhya was still sitting relaxed, with his arms crossed over his chest. It was very unusual for him not to have tried to steal the limelight, but he had yet to say a single word to the assembly.

I looked at Thayu. *Do you think he's letting Ayanu self-destruct?*

"Ayanu has no defensible position in this argument," Veyada said, behind me. "Whatever she is going to do or say, she will be damned by everyone. Yes, it was her right to know about the Aghyrians talking to the ship, but no, she should not have kept that a secret and she should definitely not have used that to try and blackmail the group."

"Is that why Ezhya isn't saying anything in the meeting?" Because he didn't want to become tainted by her bungling or in any way look like he was involved with it?

He'll have his reasons, Thayu said.

Yes, he did, as always.

But somebody had to take control of the situation or this entire assembly would explode.

Delegate Ayanu was saying, "We are merely defending our position and you think we're using unreasonable means to do so?"

I stepped back to the dais, pushed myself to the microphone and said, "Can I bring the meeting to order, please."

There were some cheers and stamping of feet. Both delegates Ayanu and Akhtari gave me penetrating looks. Delegate Akhtari's face returned to her usual emotionless expression. Oh, she knew she'd let herself get carried away. She nodded to me. "Thank you, delegate. I'll take it from here."

"My concerns have not been allayed," the Indrahui delegate said, still standing in the audience. "The fact that both delegates seem to think it's appropriate to argue like children makes me think that both have too much personal involvement. I have no trust that the delegate for Asto tells us the truth. Sadly, I also have no trust that the Aghyrian representative tells us the truth, especially in the light of the fact that the regular representative appears to have vanished. Neither do I have any confidence in the words of this assembly's leader. I think the assembly would agree with me in asking for an explicit statement that she did *not* have any knowledge of her kinsfolk speaking to the ship."

Someone shouted, "Hear, hear!" and others stamped their feet. The low rumble spread through the hall.

Delegate Ayanu rose to speak—

"And we need a declaration from you, too!" someone shouted.

And more people stamped their feet until the whole hall filled with the sound, and they clapped and chanted, but I couldn't hear what they said. Numerous delegates rose from their seats and slowly made their way through the hall until they formed a solid wall around Asto's box. The guards formed a circle around it, with their backs to the box's low walls. The administrative workers inside looked more than a little panicked.

Thayu was frantically checking her reader and then checking the audience.

Delegate Akhtari grabbed the microphone. "Silence, all!"

The sound boomed through that space, over all the noise. People fell quiet and watched.

"This assembly seems to favour those who spread rumours and make false allegations—"

"Then disprove them!"

"Quiet!" She glared in the direction of the speaker, somewhere up in the higher tiers of the audience.

She blew out a breath through her nose which was so strong that it made the microphone pop. And she let a long silence lapse.

"Right then," she said, and her voice trembled with anger. "Take the vote, because I can't work like this. Take your damn vote and see if someone else can do a better job of taming this chaotic, vindictive pack of predators. I've dedicated most of my life to this assembly, but I've had enough."

She whirled around, stepped off the dais and sat down at the table, nostrils flaring.

Oh shit, and I was meant to have prevented this, although, against the wishes of thousands, I didn't see how I could have done that.

The tumult that broke out in the hall was deafening. People yelled and shouted over the heads of others to communicate with people in the stands. Delegates left their seats to talk to their staff. The guards didn't quite know what to do. They were heavily outnumbered.

I gestured to Thayu and Nicha in the direction of our box. We crossed the floor, sidestepping groups of arguing people.

What were they going to vote?

What was the text of the general referendum?

Delegate Ethvos sat with a few administrators at the table, deep in discussion.

The crowd around Asto's box had already evaporated, but the last people now left, too. Delegate Ayanu herself was in deep discussion with some of her staff.

"Well, that is disturbing," Thayu said. "Expected, but disturbing."

Veyada said, "Where is Ezhya?"

"I don't know, I saw him—"

His chair at the table was empty. Damn it. What was he up to?

"He'll be around somewhere," Nicha said. "He's given Ayanu a lecture this morning, so maybe he trusts her to deal with this issue in the appropriate way."

"Ezhya places his trust in someone else in a vital issue? Someone he isn't known to be very close to?" Not likely.

Thayu nodded. My feeder told me that she agreed with me.

"We can't worry about it now." He'd probably turn up at the most inopportune moment, but while it worried me, I couldn't do anything about it.

I took my chair in the middle of the box and the staff all gathered around me.

"The first vote is easy," I said. "I think Delegate Akhtari knows a lot more about the dealings of her kinsfolk with the ship than she can say. I don't trust her and have never trusted her. The vote is warranted, and she won't survive. I won't attempt to help her survive." The more I thought about it, the more I felt this way. This should have happened after the dismantling of Amoro Renkati and the whole business with Seymour Kershaw. Someone should have insisted that the Aghyrians come clean about their technology. Maybe they'd been talking to the ship even back then. Maybe the ship had provided them with the technology. I felt cold.

Nicha said, "So, what? Vote her out?"

"Yes." I didn't normally discuss my voting intentions, but I thought this was important enough to affect everyone.

"She can't stay," Veyada said. "She's lost the loyalty of too many people."

Like Risha Palayi, who had challenged for the leadership of Asto, and lost. I could still see his body on the table in the *zeyshi* warren.

I said, "The problem comes with who should replace her. I don't know that we have a candidate who has majority support, who won't upset any of the sides, and who can step in quickly. That is the real problem—"

The voting bell rang and most of the talk died down.

The screen went white, the *gamra* logo appeared and faded, to be followed by the text, *Does your entity support the current candidate in the office of Chief Delegate?*

I had never seen that text on the screen, although I had known that it was one of the standard voting questions that were spelled out in the *gamra* rules. A vote of no confidence in the Chief Delegate was so rare that it hadn't happened for many years.

A murmur of talk went through the hall. Delegate Ethvos kept saying to be quiet, but it was a lost cause. Every delegate had only one vote. Everyone was talking with their staff.

We didn't need to talk anymore. There really was no viable solution.

The second bell rang.

I pressed *against*.

There was a brief countdown and then the result appeared on the screen. For: two hundred and fifteen. Against: one thousand, five hundred and ninety-three. After more than seventy years in the job, she was finished.

Delegate Akhtari stared at the screen as if she couldn't believe it, as if the cheers and shouts in the hall were in her support.

Then she slowly got up. This was history in the making. This was the woman I'd first seen when I was a boy at Midway Space Station, who'd held the position of Chief Delegate for more years than I'd been alive. The woman who had inspired fear in the hearts of many, who had blasted me at various occasions, but who had, as a result of the behaviour of her fellows, lost more of her credibility with each passing year.

As if in slow motion, she took off the ceremonial cloak and laid it on the table. The light made the gold embroidery glitter. She produced an object on a chain from under her tunic, pulled the chain over her head and put the object on the table, too. It was some sort of access key, I thought. Then she pushed her chair to the table.

She didn't look at anyone, and her face was absolutely impassive.

There was something dignified about her, as she bowed to delegate

Ethvos and walked out of the hall. Her guards wanted to leave with her, but she waved them back.

When the door had shut behind her, people in the hall burst into shouts. Some cheered, some were angry.

Delegate Ethvos rang the bell and said, "In absence of the Chief Delegate, I will chair the meeting. We must now vote for a new secretary as soon as possible. This will be a temporary position pending new elections. The committee will take serious nominations from any members. I call for candidates to come up on the floor."

In Asto's box below us, Delegate Ayanu rose. She left her box and went down the stairs.

A few boxes down, so did Delegate Namion from Damarq. He was on the floor before Delegate Ayanu, with his box being closer to the entry point to the main floor. He was a tall man, with the characteristic Damarcian deep-set eyes and heavy brow. His hair was dark brown with lighter streaks that belied his age. The spotlights in the ceiling made the gold striping on his uniform glitter. He walked straight-backed, holding his hands folded before him.

"Not him," muttered Veyada.

"Not her," Sheydu said in reply, glaring at Delegate Ayanu.

Both lined up before the dais and were joined by a trio of rogue minor delegates who had no chance of winning the position.

Thayu gave me a penetrating look across the box. She made a movement with her eyes.

What?

She flicked her eyes again.

What the hell? She didn't want me to stand, did she?

You'd do a better job than either of them.

"You have got to be joking!"

She gave me that *I'm serious* look.

I would not do a better job. I lack experience—

They don't need experience right now. Look at all the experience seated around the table. They couldn't stop the current mess happening. They need someone who most members can support.

That was true, damn it, but . . . no. Just no. *I don't want to do it. That's final.*

Oh, I understood her motives. Standing for the job was a thing a

Coldi person in my position would do, even if he had no chance of getting the job. As for me . . . no. There was no way.

Thayu said, *It's only temporary. It's good for experience.*

It would be only temporary until a proper election could be held, but damn it, no. "And that's final."

Delegate Ethvos called for silence. He gave each of the nominees a short time to introduce themselves and outline their visions on how to deal with the Aghyrian ship and the situation within *gamra*.

Delegate Ayanu's speech was peppered with terms like *must defend ourselves against invaders*. I had no idea why she thought that this ship was hostile, and it was the first time that I heard anyone refer to the ship as a risk that would lead to an armed conflict. Well, of course it could, but I wondered if there was more behind it than the usual Coldi propensity to posture.

Then she went on about all the injustices served to the Coldi people over the last few hundred years, such as that a person from Asto could never hold the position of Chief Delegate, because the *gamra* head office couldn't move to Asto.

Seriously, that was solved about thirty years ago. Why was she still carrying on about it? Delegate Akhtari had been in office all that time, and it was not as if the position had been open during that period anyway. I strongly suspected there could never be a Chief Delegate from Asto, because someone in the position of Chief Delegate may well be considered higher in rank than the Chief Coordinator, and that was impossible.

Delegate Ayanu went on well over the allocated time.

The more she spoke, the more the anger inside me made me feel hot. Fortunately, quite a few people yelled loud enough to interrupt her. Most of those were not Coldi.

Delegate Ethvos—who was really too timid for the job of chairing the meeting—called everyone to order.

Next, Delegate Namion gave his speech. Pompous arse that he was, he dedicated about two sentences to the Aghyrian issue along the lines of "we will negotiate" and then started pontificating on the significance of the assembly.

People grew bored and started talking to their neighbours.

Behind me, Sheydu muttered, a bit too loud, "Do remember to kill me if he wins."

The three other candidates didn't make much of an impression either. One from Jeveda, a Coldi-settled world, seemed the most sincere. He spent most of his time assuring us that a vote for him didn't mean a vote for Asto. Being familiar with the Coldi associations, I believed him. If there was no clear branch of Ezhya's associations that stretched to Jeveda, then they were truly independent. I couldn't be completely sure until Ezhya returned and, damn it, he was still missing from the hall.

The other two candidates were even less impressive.

Then we were up to the voting.

A successful bid was meant to have a clear two-thirds majority vote, but the first vote was a mess. Delegate Ayanu got most of the votes, but only twenty percent in total. Delegate Namion got only eleven percent, the others even less, because a lot of people abstained from voting.

Delegate Ayanu went up to the dais and blamed the "anti-Coldi" movement and Delegate Namion declared that the assembly didn't really want a solution. According to him, the Aghyrian ship had promised favours to key groups, and especially the Asto army was interested in meeting them out of the public eye.

He might be a pompous arse, and there might not be a shred of evidence behind his words, but his analysis chilled me. He might well be right. Of the Asto-born Aghyrians, it was always said that they excelled at manipulating others. It seemed that these ship people were no different.

One of the minor candidates was made to withdraw and there was another vote, but the result was even more divided if this was at all possible. Officials from both major candidates came around, talking about our concerns and wishes. Several delegations refused to see the opposing party's representatives, which led to heated discussions. The guards had to step in more than a few times.

Then Delegate Ethvos pleaded for more generally acceptable candidates to come forward. Thayu no longer joked about nominating me. She said nothing about it at all. Every time Delegate Ethvos looked in my direction, I felt like he was saying *You were supposed to have stopped this from happening.*

A Barresh councillor was the only one who came forward, but since he didn't gain a lot of votes, and it didn't solve the impasse.

We ended the assembly with a rather lame decision to keep talking about it tomorrow. I thought of the *zeyshi* delegation in the stands. What would they make of this? They had the right to be angry with the proceedings. They'd come here to negotiate, not to watch people play nasty politics.

18

———

"**I** CAN SEE WHAT you're thinking about this democracy process," I said to Thayu when we were leaving the hall. "Don't even say it."

"I don't need to say anything. You know my position on it."

"But tell me what should happen? How should we solve this crisis?"

"Decisively and quickly. The ship will be here. They'll want to speak to someone who is going to be in power and has the support of all *gamra* members."

"That's easier said than done. We're all divided."

"Yes, we have mess and chaos."

"What would you do to solve it then?"

She just looked at me with that *are you kidding?* expression. I remembered during my visit to Asto how Veyada had said *No, any of us would just go in and shoot him.*

In the end, that was exactly what had happened. Not only that, *I* had fired the shot.

Damn, I knew what she was thinking, and her expression said that she knew that I had worked it out. The way a Coldi leader would solve this was simply to walk into Delegate Akhtari's office and seize the position.

I wanted to say, *I can't do that. It flies in the face of democracy.* But democracy was not something the Coldi held in high regard anyway.

They chose order over democracy. Their system of government was about as undemocratic as they came, but it worked. What we needed now was order. And that thought chilled me. Democracy was failing.

I left the hall in the company of Thayu, Veyada, Nicha and Sheydu, who guided me through the throng of delegates making their way to the door. Everywhere around us people were talking about the candidates. I caught snatches of conversation, mostly what they disliked in Delegate Ayanu.

"Well," Sheydu said when we were in the foyer. "I'm not sure what that achieved."

And we all felt like that, and no one was willing to say it. We were now further from a solution than we'd been coming in. We'd gone in to talk about the Aghyrian ship. We came out without a clear leader. It pained me to see Delegate Ethvos swamped with all the work of documenting the session and keeping the delegates from attacking each other. He got landed with the job when the only thing he had done was call the meeting. He was clearly uncomfortable with the job.

"We should send out someone to check on Federza," I said. How many times had I said that today?

"If he was discharged from his position as Aghyrian representative, there would have been no way for him to attend the meeting," Veyada said.

"That doesn't stop me wanting to know if he is all right. Besides, he still represents the Trader Guild."

"True." He gave me a puzzled look. There was that Coldi callous appearance again. Federza was not in my association, so I should leave the finding out if he was all right to the people who were. Save, of course, that he wasn't Coldi and didn't have an association, and that he had been very frightened of some of his own kinsfolk and damn it, I wanted to know if he was all right.

Thayu touched my elbow and gestured with her eyes behind me.

I turned around and there was Ezhya, just coming out of the door with his entourage. Well, where did he suddenly spring from? He certainly hadn't been in the hall for the second half of the meeting.

He spotted me and diverted his guards in my direction. There was something very purposeful about his actions. The way I read it was that he'd given up on the meeting, gone to do something else and had come back because he wanted to see me specifically.

That's probably pretty close to the truth, Thayu said.

Seeing him, surrounded by hundreds of other delegates who already accused me of being in his pocket, was not really helpful right now, but I couldn't avoid talking to him.

I made the *outside* signal, hoping that he would recognise it.

He did. We wrestled our way through the crowd. I with Thayu, Nicha, Sheydu and Veyada, and he followed behind. I didn't recognise any of the guards he had with him. There was a hard-faced woman who looked like a younger version of Sheydu and a couple of men with the typical guard body shape: tall and broad-shouldered. I'd become so used to seeing Natanu, Veyada and Sheydu there that it was very unsettling. Both Veyada and Sheydu kept their faces impassive and acted absolutely professional to the men and women who had replaced them.

We left the building through the arched entrance. There was a little courtyard park outside, surrounding an area of paving, where people were now streaming across on their way home.

Ezhya went into the park. A couple of junior delegates scurried off a garden bench to make way for him.

We sat down, surrounded by guards.

"It's good to see you again," I said. It was strange but each time I saw him, I felt like I had to re-establish where I stood and what I could and couldn't do. Today, he seemed even more distant than usual. I longed to ask him why he had left the meeting and what was going on with him and Delegate Ayanu.

He took my hand and held it in a warm grip. There was something intense about his manner that disturbed me. I didn't know how to begin.

He said, "I heard say that the move to hold the emergency meeting was yours."

"I don't know if it achieved anything." *Useless* would have been a better term. I'd been powerless to stop what we all feared.

"Of course it did. Some people have been keen to wrestle the assembly from the stranglehold of the Aghyrians for many years."

"Others would have argued that they provided a balance."

"Chief delegates always provide a balance, because they're rarely ever Coldi."

"What about Ayanu?"

"She has no chance."

That had a frightening sound of finality about it. Was that because he'd "deal with" her?

At this level, "dealing with" usually involved death.

He continued, "There are too many who distrust her. No matter how many times she stands, she'll be voted down again and again from within the Asto delegation."

I still didn't quite get what he was hinting at. "Has she been trying to expand her loyalty networks?" Or perhaps calling in favours, from people like Nicha and Reida.

"She was directly tied to Taysha." And of course we all knew what had happened there.

As I'd guessed, this was still part of the ripple effect through Coldi society, a result of the reshuffles at the top. Cut loose from her association, Delegate Ayanu had found herself floundering and searching, in need of guidance from a superior whom she no longer had. Instead, she made a grab for a higher position elsewhere. But since she was no longer in Ezhya's association, she would never succeed.

I nodded. I understood. The reshuffle at the top even affected people outside Asto.

"What are you going to do with her?"

"I'll talk and we make an arrangement."

"That will involve her retirement?" I cringed as I said that. *Retirement* also often involved death, often by suicide. Coldi society didn't deal with loss of face very well.

"We will suggest it strongly to her."

"What about the negotiations?" With two major parties out of the running, we might as well start all over again, except we couldn't afford the time because of that ship out there.

"What about them?" He scratched his chin in a *so what?* gesture.

"You're not concerned? There is a dangerous ship coming this way, people want to talk about who really owns Asto, we are without leadership, one of the major delegates is about to lose her job and this doesn't worry you?"

"If they arrive, if they find us important enough to talk to, we will send negotiators."

"*If?* They will arrive."

"We'll see." Again with that laconic shrug. I couldn't believe that he didn't care.

And when he said *we*, did he mean Asto or *gamra*? For him probably Asto.

"When they arrive, the issue of what they want will be between them and the Inner Circle."

"But what about . . ."

"*Zeyshi* rebels have nothing to do with it. They may live in the aquifers, but they pay for none of their upkeep and do no maintenance. Thanks to our water authorities their lives have become much better, but for those who do not pay their dues, there is no room at the table."

I named the originator of the proverb. "Dezhya Azimi, administrator of Beratha."

"I see you'll soon be able to give my administrators a run for their money. If only they knew that proverb, there would have been a lot less trouble."

Was there even more trouble than I knew of? But I didn't ask any further. He had just shown me a very rare glimpse into the running of Asto. I was sure I needed to know it for some reason, even if I didn't know yet what it was. "You suggest you want to bypass the *zeyshi* if the ship turns up? Neither of the parties might be happy with that."

"We'll see." Again, an unusually laconic answer. "We certainly don't think anyone from off Asto has a right to negotiate over our land."

Fair point, and one I had expected him to make. Coldi were extremely pragmatic and didn't value the emotional attachment to history.

They simply didn't recognise the right of other entities to have a say in a matter that concerned Asto, and weren't interested in negotiating the *zeyshi* claim because they believed the *zeyshi* had no basis for their claims.

And that was it. Clear-cut for him. It was pointless trying to engage him in discussion over the *gamra* leadership. He didn't really care because it wasn't in his associations. That was entirely the problem that non-Coldi entities had with Asto. And I was reluctant to tell him off for not showing any interest, because he wasn't stupid and would have realised the importance of the meeting; so there had to have been another reason that he'd left midway through, and I was quite through with *reasons* right now.

It would just be awesome if everyone put their cards on the table and was honest with each other.

"Has my daughter been keeping you on your toes?" Total change of subject. A much more comfortable one, I had to admit.

"She seems to have struck up a friendship with my housekeeper. She's been helping in the house."

"Good. A bit of manual work won't do her any harm."

"Oh but Eirani makes her do her study work."

"And she actually does it?" He laughed. "Maybe I should borrow your housekeeper."

"How is Natanu?"

He gave me a sharp look. "Are you developing telepathic skills these days?"

"Um, no. Just wanted to know how she was, seeing as she's not here." Nothing had happened to her, had it?

"Do you ever feel that your life is being taken over by women?"

I had to stifle a snort. I could imagine Natanu the dominatrix with a whip standing in the hall of Ezhya's apartment.

"Another girl," he said.

I stared at him, and then I understood. That was why he wanted Raanu out of the house for a bit. "Well . . . congratulations. I'm honoured to be informed." And I was. For all that their public lives were so open, high-ranking Coldi kept their families, even the compositions of those families, well hidden.

I tried very hard to imagine Natanu looking tenderly at a baby and I just could not.

It seemed that all of a sudden, everyone was having children. I loved Raanu and I could just about see a little girl running around our apartment. I didn't understand why Thayu was stalling, and Ezhya's news reminded me uncomfortably that the negotiation was still open and that Menor was expecting a reply from me.

I was dropping stitches. I changed the subject again. "Why don't we go to my house and you can check your daughter's progress for yourself?"

I expected him to say that he was busy, but to my surprise he agreed and the combined group started walking. We talked about trivialities, the building activities on the island, Raanu's study work and the fact that I'd promised her to go out to the sand bar where the marsh met the sea.

Ezhya asked me, "What is 'surf'?"

I'd used the keihu word because I didn't know if Coldi even had a word. Asto's oceans were poisonous, and no one came near them.

I explained, and he seemed intrigued by the concept of "surf" and that you could ride boards in it.

"But you have to be able to swim." Something that most Coldi could not.

"I can swim. I must try this 'surf'. It sounds interesting."

It was the most absurd thing ever. Here we were in a major crisis and he seemed obsessed with an outing to the beach. Next thing he would be saying that we'd go to the beach so that he could see this "surf".

And meanwhile, I was burning up inside with frustration because he seemed to skirt around all the major issues and wanted to talk about trivialities.

We arrived at my apartment, where Evi and Telaris stood at the door, perfectly professional, and unflappable about the sudden influx of high-level security. They met Ezhya's new guards with silent hand signals.

In the hall, we met Deyu, who had already evidently come back from the meeting before us. I hoped Reida had been with her. She nearly fainted when seeing who was with us.

"Oh!" She snapped into a subservient position and Ezhya acknowledged her with a tap on her shoulder.

He was very good at that, connecting with his people, no matter how fleetingly.

But the moment everyone was inside and the door shut, the atmosphere of apparent levity evaporated. Ezhya's guards sprang into action. Two of them went straight into the hub. One took up position inside the main door. Two inspected the living room.

Eirani just came out of the hallway with a trolley full of tableware and almost crashed into one of the men, bristling with armour and guns. She gave a little squeal and then her eyes met mine.

"Oh, Muri, I didn't see you. I was wondering what all these people were doing in here. It's almost time for dinner."

"Be at ease," Ezhya said, in keihu, because he was that type: a man who had to learn every single language that was out there.

Eirani looked at him wide-eyed. She *had* to know who he was, but today, she was acting very much like the innocent housekeeper. At some point in the past, she had been a spy, too.

Damn, I was starting to see ghosts everywhere.

Thayu and Veyada followed the guards into the hub. Their colleagues had evicted Devlin from the bench. He stood just inside the door, looking distressed.

"I tried to tell them . . ." he began.

"It's all right, Devlin."

I would have to talk to him about not giving up his position so easily, but this was probably a legitimate reason. Probably the reason that Ezhya had come with me: his guards wanted to use the hub in a place where they weren't tracked as much as in their accommodation. The guards were bent over a screen, looking at a map of Barresh showing the streets on the far eastern side of the main island. I knew what they were looking for.

"There is nothing there," I said. "We looked. Tamerians were also looking for it."

"Tamerians?" Ezhya said, his voice dark.

"Hired by the council."

He frowned and said nothing for a while. He was probably catching up on some sort of communication through his feeders. After silence, he said, "This worries me."

Yes, it had worried me, too, but I'd not had the time to do anything about it.

The guards were speaking in low voices and in code. Thayu interjected and said something about frequencies. I wondered why it still surprised me that even after having spent so much time with them, my companions could still say things that so utterly went over my head.

Ezhya said to me in a low voice, "That thing they are looking for? The thing that caused the resonance in the Exchange? That is the transponder of the ship that originally came to Barresh."

I faced him, meeting the golden glow of the light reflecting in his gold-flecked eyes. "All those years ago?" But damn it, I had suspected that this was the case. "It's probably hidden under the ground. If it's still functional."

I sensed something dangerous under the surface. He hadn't come here for a chat. He had a plan, and I wasn't sure if I was going to like it. Then again, it was not as if *he* cared about people liking his plans.

"Oh yes, it's functional. The old Aghyrians were the most perfect builders of machines. Imagine building modern equipment, but instead of building it from cheap materials, you'd make it out of the best and most durable materials in existence. That's what they did. They fiddled with their designs until they were perfect. We are still discovering artefacts that they made. Especially in the Crystal Wastelands, there is not a place you can dig that you won't find something. The prized and easily discoverable items have been picked off by bounty hunters, but that leaves the buried material, which is often in much better preserved state. If, as I suspect, the wreckage of that ship sank into the muddy ground in Barresh, the ship itself will have mostly corroded away, but the transponder will still be intact. It's a passive beacon, contains no energy source and has no moving parts. I don't doubt for one moment that it still works. That big ship out there has located the beacon—"

"It has probably known where it was all along."

"I don't think so. When the ship left, those two beacons weren't were they are now."

True. "But there is nothing left of their civilisation for the Aghyrians to come back to. They'd be interested in the people. Maybe in returning to Asto."

"Maybe, but do we know that for certain?"

"Well, of course not."

"I'll take it one step further. These are highly dangerous people. We know that these people in that ship have been in communication with some interest groups in Barresh and probably others that we don't know about. The Mirani settlement almost failed because of the sheer divisiveness of the Aghyrians ways. They're not here to negotiate. They're here to sow discontent and pit sides against each other. They create conflict so that we are distracted and not all our efforts will be geared towards keeping an eye on them. They're already doing that. What we witnessed in the assembly hall is part of their strategy. Make us argue with each other, so that they can continue to do what they want. We know that this happens in Aghyrian society. It's probably part of their culture, but not of ours."

I nodded. "Until they show up and formally reply to our messages, though, is there much we can do?"

"There is."

He leaned back, away from the control panels. The light from the controls reflected in his eyes, turning the gold flecks blue. He looked utterly in control.

We were alone in the room. Thayu had left, Devlin was gone. Two of Ezhya's new guards stood in front of the door, their backs to us.

This was it. He had me cornered.

"I would like to impress on these people, no matter where they've come from or what they think of us, that we do not deal kindly with fools." The intensity in his voice made me feel cold. "As for the negotiations, I have no time for useless chatter with people who fancy themselves important. Because they are not important, and because we are facing the biggest threat to our society we have seen in many lifetimes, or the biggest opportunity we have seen in many lifetimes. It's up to us to make the best of it. We cannot afford to waste any time bickering amongst ourselves. This threat is not going to be solved by talking to *zeyshi* louts or arrogant fops who think far too much of themselves. As an aside, I don't see why either should have as much say in these *negotiations* as they do. The whole thing has turned into a bickering fest. It's a farce and a joke."

"It has, but it's up to us to get the talks back to a situation where trust between the parties is restored."

He snorted. "No. We don't. We're withdrawing from the table."

"But—" My heart was hammering. What about my position? I spent all of the past year organising these negotiations. Damn it, he paid most of my stipend, how could I continue my job? How could we hold negotiations about Asto's land without Asto representatives present? How could he counter the claims if there was no one there to argue the case? The assembly would see Asto's absence as an admission of guilt. They would rule in the *zeyshi*'s favour. "Heavens, why? I don't understand."

"We've got important things to do. This negotiation does not concern us."

"What sort of things are you planning to do?" That was a pretty direct question and one I would never have dared ask him as little as two years ago.

He gave me an intense look and rose from the seat. "It's time to move. Get ready for a small journey. Pack a small bag. Bring your lady spy and Veyada."

"Where are we going?"

"I can't share that."

"When?"

"Now."

"But I . . ." I held up my arms. If I suddenly disappeared what sort of message would that send to the assembly? "For how long?" *What the hell is going on?* But I had to play with him, because I had no other option. Because he had the ultimate power and was the most absolute of rulers. Almost every process at *gamra* fell or stood because of him. But if there was one thing non-Asto candidates appreciated about me, it was my stupidity in challenging him, and my ability to get away with it. "I'm afraid I don't understand. You pay me to facilitate the negotiations and now that everyone is here for those negotiations, you withdraw from the process."

The guard at the door looked over his shoulder, giving me a wide-eyed look at the directness of the pronouns I used. They were indeed far too blunt. And I was far too tired to care.

His mouth twitched. Coldi didn't smile for reasons of politeness or friendliness, and I swore a ghost of a smile went over his lips. It irritated me. I thought I was used to being played with, but every now and then people, and especially Ezhya, managed to pull a strange surprise on me.

He said, "I pay you. I have decided. Pack a small bag. Hurry up. We have a narrow departure window."

And that meant something to do with orbits and big military ships hiding in the depth of space.

19

S HIT.

I left the room in search of Eirani to pack me a small bag. What did one bring for a small trip that may or may not involve deep space travel, gunfights, death and all-out war? Especially the latter worried me. Not simply because of the terrible consequences of war and my severe doubts that even the Asto military had any chance of winning it. I also worried that if Ezhya escalated this into an armed conflict, then much of my theory about how Coldi society worked was wrong. That was of course an utterly silly thing to be worried about, but I'd spent so much time telling people that this was why Coldi society worked that my reputation was tied up with it.

A bunch of additional people had come into the hall and stood talking in an atmosphere of tenseness. The newcomers carried nothing except their weapons, and wore grey or black clothing of a utilitarian type. While some of them were talking to a pair of Ezhya's guards, most of them watched every entrance of the hallway.

I knew the signs: they were all Asto military. Potentially high-ranking.

Some of them glanced at me while I crossed the hall, but most didn't even look.

I couldn't see Eirani or any of the other staff and wasn't sure whether to frighten her by calling her to come upstairs. Would she understand the situation at play here?

Thayu followed me into the bedroom.

"Do you know what's going on?" I asked her.

She returned a question. "Has Ezhya ever been free with his information about his plans?"

Guess not. "I don't like this."

"I didn't like your trip to Asto either. I also didn't know what was about to happen when we left."

True. "Yes, but in that case *I* knew. Now I don't. Tell me that you know and that it's all right. I don't need to see the exact plans. I just want to know that you know about his plan and that it's the right thing to do."

She gave me an incredulous look and spread her hands. "You're distrustful about all the wrong things. Have you forgotten that you're talking about the Chief Coordinator of Asto? You trust Federza and not him?"

Whoa, Thay', no need to get so angry. "I do trust that Federza is telling the truth, much as I dislike the bastard, and yes, I'd trust Ezhya in an instant if only I knew what he was doing."

"He's at the top of all of Asto's society. There is no need for you to know what he's doing. That's trust for you. That's how our system works. I would have thought that having taken part in it for so long, you'd understand at least that much." Damn, she was furious.

I had no time to discuss my concerns. There were voices in the hall just outside my bedroom window.

Eirani hadn't turned up yet, so I pulled a bag out of the wardrobe and put some random things in. I felt stupid, never having had to pack by myself. I didn't even remember where half the things were, or what I should bring. Thayu stood by the door, apparently already packed. She said nothing while I rummaged around and her face had that *you don't really know what you're doing* look. She was right, I didn't know what I was doing. I didn't know if she knew what we were doing.

"I'll get Veyada to take your things from the office."

I frowned at her. Where the hell were they taking me?

"Are you ready?"

"Yes. Maybe."

She met my eyes in that intense look that unnerved me so, but she said nothing. As I followed her into the hallway, and amongst the guards that snapped into action, I thought about the time that our main concern was picking a seed donor for our child. I hadn't thought that wanting to be a mother was a whim, but right now, it felt that way to me. Thayu was happiest when she could be a high-level military spy.

The guards and soldiers in the hallway were all business, blank faces and roving eyes.

Veyada stood talking to Ezhya in a low voice. Veyada carried a fabric sleeve over his arm that held his ceremonial white lawyer's robe. He met my eyes in a *have you got your formal clothing?* way. I did.

I didn't see anyone else in the hall. Not Eirani, not Nicha and not his two young *zhayma*s. There were soldiers standing in the entrance to the upstairs corridor. They'd probably told the staff to stay in their rooms.

One of the guards opened the door and the whole group set into motion.

Veyada fell back to accompany me.

I said to him on a low voice, "I'm worried about Nicha. I would have liked to take him."

"He's needed here to keep things under control."

"He's still fragile." And he would remain so until Xinanu left.

"I think he will be all right. He has his sister with us and enough support to climb back to his former self."

"It's not uncommon for *zhayma*s to be related," Thayu said on my other side.

I glanced at Veyada. "Are you related to Sheydu?" I had never been able to work out their relationship.

He gestured, *yes*, and then after a while, he added, "She's my mother."

His face went blank when he said that. Clearly there was some unresolved issue in that family as well.

So I ended up taking Thayu, Veyada and Sheydu, and Thayu assured me that she would leave Nicha, Deyu and Reida instructions on how to protect the house.

As I had expected, we went in the direction of the station, but there was no train waiting for us, only more black-clad army personnel.

Next to the station was a small jetty, and at the bottom of this a boat ramp and some mooring posts. A flat-bottomed marsh boat waited there, with two more guards. The vehicle seemed brand new, with a silver barrel for a jet engine so large it dwarfed the driver at the wheel. That looked like a pretty damn powerful beast.

Ezhya's guards greeted these unfamiliar soldiers, and they held the boat steady while we climbed in from the jetty. Like most of its kind, the boat had some benches—this one had three—and there was an area with a table at the back near the engine, where the boat's owners would clean fish, judging by the briny smell. This area now held an impressive rocket launcher, its base secured to the legs of the table.

The vessel would take a crew of at least six, and was bigger and sturdier than similar vessels that often tottered past the *gamra* island while I sat staring out the window of my apartment office.

The bench in the very prow was taken by Ezhya's guards with red sashes, armour and two guns each. Ezhya and Veyada sat on the second bench, while Thayu and I took the last one. Soldiers sat down on either side of us with humourless, emotionless faces. To think that Sheydu and Veyada had been like that not so long ago.

Looking at Veyada's back—he was explaining something on the screen to Ezhya—I reassessed my thought that he and Sheydu had been severely demoted by becoming part of my association. I'd been wrong about that. In his previous position, Veyada would never have been able to talk to Ezhya in this way. In fact, Ezhya's new guards were all around the periphery of the ship, peering out over the water on high alert. They obeyed, but didn't speak to their boss on an equal basis. Not to be in someone's association freed a person from having to be overly referential to another person. That was an interesting thought.

The driver brought the engine to life with a powerful roar. Seated on the bench in front of it, I could feel the air suck into the jet and pull at my hair and clothes, as if I were standing in a hurricane. The guards at the front pointed *that way*. The driver yelled an exclamation that got lost in the roar of the engine when he gunned it. The air was sucked out of my lungs. The boat flew forward, barely skimming the water, bouncing over reed clumps. I'd been in these jet boats before, but they were nothing like this. This boat was a monster, and probably belonged to those new commercial fishing operations that went far out onto the marshlands to fishing grounds that may or may not be across the border, and may or may not be subject to frisking by Mirani border patrols. Guess that was why they needed the engine. Hell, it was fast, it was powerful, and it made us soaking wet. The low windshield at the front of the seating area did nothing to stop the sprays of mist that exploded over us every time the bow slammed into the water.

We'd gone a while when I realised that we weren't going to the airport or even to the main island. It was too noisy and windy to ask Thayu. She sat huddled in her insulation suit with the collar pulled up over her ears. Like most Coldi, Thayu didn't like water.

Strangely enough, Ezhya and Veyada continued their conversation as if they were sitting on the couch in my living room.

Where are we going? I asked Thayu, risking the possibility that Ezhya's guards or the soldiers would get a fix on the feeder's output, which would allow them to get into our network.

Thayu spread her hands. *She* clearly didn't want to use the feeder. She gestured with her eyes in the direction where our listening equipment would be in our living room, had we been in the living room. I gestured *all right*.

The message was: be careful, wherever they were taking us.

So I said nothing and watched the reeds, lily fields and occasional islands with megon trees and their drooping branches whiz past.

After what seemed like an eternity of bumping and sheltering from sprays of water, the reeds became sparser and some areas of blinding white glared at the horizon—the sand bar that separated the marshes from the ocean. A bunch of darker shapes lay a bit further offshore, bobbing on the waves.

All right, I got it now. This was why Ezhya had feigned interest in "surf" and "ocean". I should have known.

When we reached the beach, it turned out that the dark shapes were aircraft, and they floated quite a distance offshore. A handful of small dinghies lay on the beach, and a few more were underway to the ships with supplies on board. These were not the same ships I had seen at the airport a few days ago. Just how many of those military ships were there in orbit?

I looked up. Billowing clouds hung on the eastern horizon, but directly overhead I could see the sky. Of course there would be no sign of Ezhya's armada. They'd be well out of range of the scanning equipment, probably hanging around at a LaGrange point while pretending to be pieces of debris. When the engines idled, the electromagnetic emissions from the ships were very weak. They could easily have been there for a long time.

Or they could secretly have come this way under minimal power, waiting for their opportunity.

A boat approached the beach where we were standing. It raced through the surf and slid onto the beach, with the driver displaying more water and boat related skills than I had ever seen in a Coldi person.

He came out and greeted Ezhya, demure and proper. Ezhya's guards helped turn the boat around and climbed in. One of them dropped to his knees and inspected the space under the benches. Satisfied, he made a small gesture for Ezhya to come in. These people left nothing to chance.

This boat wasn't big enough to take all of us, and we waited on the sand while it went out to the ships.

The sand was soft and white, and the crash of the surf on the beach reminded me of the summers I used to spend with my parents on the bay, where our holiday house was right at the beach. Sometimes Thayu and I had come here with my surfboard. Apart from the occasional fishing crew, no one else ever came here. I would enter the water and Thayu would lounge on the beach. Sometimes we would make love under the bright sun.

The dinghy had churned up the white sand, leaving deep gouges in the surface. When it came back, it hovered straight up the beach, and we had to climb in while avoiding the powerful intake from the engine.

We headed for the closest ship, where I could see Ezhya inside, putting on some sort of green suit. A soldier came to the doorway when the dinghy approached. She grabbed the rope the boat's driver threw to her, and pulled the boat close to the floaters of the ship. Thayu jumped out and helped me into a storage hold full of crates and boxes. There was a door in the metal wall to the right. I followed Thayu into a cramped cockpit, where the pilot sat studying Coldi text that scrolled over the screen in front of her. She turned around briefly, greeted Thayu—subserviently—and continued her work without showing any sign that she had noticed me. Thayu pulled me into the bench behind the pilot.

I sat down, looking over the pilot's broad shoulder. A chill crept over my back. Had I ever realised how little Asto cared about anyone with status in *gamra*? It wasn't *their* system, and Coldi were extremely practical. If it didn't affect them, they had trouble mustering interest in the subject. Even the Chief Delegate would fall entirely outside their associations and wouldn't have any feedback into their system.

Ezhya and Veyada came in behind us.

". . . have no time for that," Ezhya was saying.

"We can't stop them tracking." Veyada wormed himself between the back of our seat and the narrow seats behind us. He sat down.

Ezhya also sat down and did up the seat belts. One of his guards joined us.

There were some thumps on the floor behind us. The pilot spoke to other crew through the microphone. The tinny voice that drifted through the loudspeaker spoke entirely in code. Something about flight directions, I gathered.

The door of the vehicle shut with a thump.

The pilot swiped the comm screen and called up the flight diagnostics. The craft was at ninety-five percent of carrying capacity, ninety-six percent readiness, fuel was at seventy-six percent and the outside current that made the ship almost invisible was off. That was a measure taken for the sake of lowering fuel consumption. It was not really necessary in Barresh anyway.

I'd had a few flying lessons, because Ezhya wanted it—and this was pretty much the extent of my knowledge. Once you were in the air, it was easy, he said. I hadn't gotten to that part yet, and to be honest, it sounded pretty damn scary to me.

For a few moments, no one spoke. The diagnostics on the screen crept up. The pilot moved her hand when readiness hit ninety-nine percent. The low hum of the engine increased.

Hundred percent.

The engine roared into life.

I was pressed into my seat. A glimpse of the marshlands shot past the window, followed by a view of the sky and then a wider view of the marshlands. The sky again. What the hell was the pilot doing? Rolling. Twisting. Turning. My stomach didn't like it at all.

I glanced at Thayu in the seat next to me, who knew of, if not understood, my discomfort. She put a hand on my leg, very discreetly, where the people behind us couldn't see this little admission of weakness. Right now, I wasn't feeling very strong. I was human, weak and fallible in the face of this display of military might.

Fortunately, the craft evened out and rose straight into the air. The sky turned dark blue and then black. The glow of the atmosphere receded.

By now, the pilot was busy again with her comm screen where the messages in code scrolled faster than I could read. She turned on the visual screen on the wall. This surprised me a bit, because the one previous time I'd come to an Asto military ship, they'd blanked out all the visual input.

The screen now showed me an enhanced view of one of Ceren's little moons. Behind it hung a multitude of little dots that could have been stars or asteroids, but I knew them for what they were: a veritable armada of ships.

Holy shit.

I glanced over my shoulder at Ezhya. He met my eyes squarely.

Never underestimate Asto. I didn't know how many times I needed to be reminded of that fact and yet their sheer military might surprised me every single time.

"Do you really believe that the risk warrants this reaction?" I asked him.

"These people have the technology to travel outside the galaxy. They have maintained a coherent society for all this time. According to their logs, only four hundred years has passed since they left, but that's still a remarkable time to have maintained social coherence. Most societies fall apart every hundred years or so. The captain is the same as the heartless man we know left behind many people to die on Asto. I could not believe it is the same man, but it seems this is the case. Four hundred years isn't that long. Already Aghyrians live longer than any of us. They may have developed immortality for all we know, but we can't ask them. They won't talk to us directly. To them, we're products of their science. Not real people. Beneath them."

The contempt in his voice disturbed me.

Then a thought: the Coldi didn't know how to react when someone considered them inferior. They might not even know how to react when threatened by someone with considerable military might.

Since Asto was so much bigger than most *gamra* entities and nobody considered the Coldi inferior, the situation simply never arose.

As we came closer, the true size of the armada resolved from the shadow of the moon. There were at least thirty large ships. Some were the classic box shape for deep space travel, others were long and narrow and huge. There was one that looked like it had a habitat with artificial gravity. A space station, really? How long had it been here? Why was he showing me this now?

The screen before the pilot showed how a locator beam was guiding us from one of the large craft, one of the long and skinny ones.

The closer we got, the more the thing grew in size. First it took up most of the screen, and then we could see only portions of the ship, and those portions were ever zooming in, while more detail resolved. This thing was massive.

We flew into the shadow of the craft, where the pitch-darkness was broken only by the occasional pinprick of light on a piece of equipment or maintenance hatch. A square opening marked the surface ahead. Strong floodlights came on when we approached, casting harsh shadows both inside the dock and the surrounding part of the hull.

The downward camera gave us a view of the inside of the dock. Entry was through the ceiling. I could see people moving inside. *Walking*, yet the ship had no rotating habitat. Our ship hovered above the opening and eased through the invisible wall that separated the dock from the void of space. The windows glowed orange with the heat as we passed. As soon as we had gone through, up and down resolved from the multitude of directions that I'd felt while in space.

"Artificial gravity?" I glanced at Ezhya.

Thayu was watching with wide eyes. The military was secret not just from us, but from Asto's citizens as well. She loved this sort of stuff.

Veyada, though, would have seen it all before, and he was talking to Ezhya as if he came here every day.

The pilot engaged the downward jets and the ship eased down on the floor of a huge hall. One of the guards inside the cabin undid his safety harness, rose and opened the door to the cargo hold.

Ezhya was also getting up from his seat.

I was itching to ask questions, but I'd learned that any Coldi who was familiar with Asto military might didn't just keep the knowledge hidden from the public, but most military operations were never talked about, even amongst people who should know. We were to get no explanation of what this ship and the other ships were doing here. Even Thayu and Nicha disliked talking about what little they knew with me. To ask questions would be considered rude.

We left the cabin for the cargo hold, where the outside door had just been opened and the gangplank was zooming out. The air inside the big ship was too hot to be comfortable, and smelled of hot metal, and a kind of industrial smell that I couldn't place.

We followed Ezhya down the gangplank. A couple of people waited there, all in desert-pink military uniform.

They greeted Ezhya with subservient expressions, and maintained those expressions for the rest of us, even though we probably didn't deserve it. I was quite hungry, and itching to ask what the point was of all this. Ezhya gestured a few code signals to the ship people, some of whom I deduced to be of high rank.

Then he said to me, "Come."

20

———————

HEART THUDDING, I followed Ezhya out of the hall. I sensed Thayu close behind me, so she must have surmised that she was allowed as well. Veyada was likely to follow close by, too.

Surely Ezhya was finally going to show me the reason why I had to come here.

From the arrival hall, we went into a corridor with a spongy floor that felt sticky under my feet. I frowned at Thayu, but she looked as bewildered about the material as I felt. I didn't dare open the feeder. The level of surveillance was likely to be extreme.

Every soldier we met snapped into a subservient position to the point where I would pick up immediately if one person failed to do this. This was how Coldi saw if everything was in order: if a high-ranking Coldi person entered a room, the only people who didn't look down should be equals or superiors.

Ezhya took us up a winding staircase with only enough room for one person. He opened the hatch at the top and climbed into a dark room. We followed him. It reminded me of going to the bridge of the military ship that had taken us to Asto.

But the dark room where we came out wasn't a ship's bridge. We stood on an elevated walkway that stretched into the darkness. Little blue lights illuminated small spots of it. The ceiling overhead curved as if we stood in a huge cylinder. I surmised that we were in the core of the ship, in the engine room, or whatever it was that gave the ship such a long, narrow shape. Beneath our feet lay a number of huge metal tubes which disappeared into the darkness on both ends.

Was this the legendary military sling? I couldn't believe Ezhya would show that to me.

"The main problem with this Aghyrian ship is that they won't talk to us directly," he said over the low hum of the engine or ventilation system. I took a moment to realise that we were continuing the talk we'd started aboard the shuttle.

"How much contact have you had with this ship?"

He didn't answer that, but I figured it was quite a lot.

"Are they coming this way?"

Thayu had stopped a little bit behind us. Well within earshot, I believed, but far enough to give us the illusion of privacy. Veyada had probably gone to do Veyada-things, and I assumed that Sheydu had remained aboard the shuttle.

Ezhya said, "They know about the Ratanga cluster." Again not answering my question directly.

The Ratanga cluster, of course, was the part of the galaxy arm where we were, and where Kedras was, and a couple of other inhabited worlds within a single jump of each other. The world of Damarq, the main node of the Exchange network, lay in the middle of this cluster. It was the beating heart of the Exchange network, of *gamra* and all the civilised worlds.

A pilot had once assured me that when you jumped an anpar line, it was extremely hard to find where you had come from without specialised navigation equipment. Even when using the gravitational centre of the galaxy as a reference point. In the fifty thousand years that had passed in this galaxy since the ship had left, positions of stars would have shifted enough to completely throw the ship's navigation off-course.

Finding Asto in the galaxy would not have been easy. But they had found it.

Ezhya continued, "If they decide to target an attack on the Exchange system, they could knock out communication to all the Ratanga worlds before a single warning system would trigger."

I nodded. It was a weakness of the Exchange, and one no one was sure how to defend against it, simply because there had never been a need to do so.

"I am not going to allow a repeat of what happened last time."

I wanted to ask him if he thought that a fleet of military ships would prevent it, but that was surely a dumb remark. He was about to show me something about this installation. I leaned both elbows on the balustrade and looked down at the curves of the metal tubes that ran under the walkway. There were control panels at regular distances along the tubes, consisting of a little box with yellow and blue lights set on a panel with buttons, or something similar—it was hard to see in the low light.

Ezhya leaned on the balustrade next to me. Even though the temperature of the air was, as was customary for Asto, the level of a hot summer's day, I could feel the heat radiating from his skin. Wow. I knew that the Coldi's lowest body temperature was a little bit under forty Celsius, but wasn't sure of the upper limit.

He said, "The fact that we've been working on a transportable one-way Exchange core has to have been the worst-kept secret of *gamra*."

"Yeah. I guess."

"Well, this is it." He gestured at the tubes underneath us.

My heart jumped. Well, what the hell, he *did* show me.

"It's not that new anymore, or, for that matter, secret. It's not particularly elegant, it's not refined or small, and it still requires the presence nearby of a secondary ship, but here it is."

"We could have used that when I went to Asto."

"Yet, you did not, because my staff were under strict instructions not to reveal it to anyone not authorised. And they did not."

"Even if using it would have been to your benefit."

"Yes. Even so." He interlaced his thick fingers. "I wasn't there to authorise them."

Fair enough. That was Coldi loyalty for you. "Why are you showing it to me now?"

"Because I need you to see it."

Dumb question, Mr Wilson.

"Because I need you to use it."

Thayu took in an audible breath and turned sharply to us.

"As I said, the people on this Aghyrian ship will not speak to us directly. This man called Kando Luczon, and his crew, regard us as an inferior class of humans, having originated in their experimental facilities. So I'm sending someone I trust not to come with underlying political agendas on behalf of an ineffective group that fancies itself important." He flicked his eyebrows. Whoa, that was one of the most sarcastic jokes I'd heard from him.

"I'm guessing I am that someone."

"You may be guessing correctly."

Holy shit. My heart was hammering.

"This is why I want you to see this. I want you to understand that we will defend our home world against these people until the very last person left alive. I want you to understand that we regard the attack on our Exchange as hostile, and that we will consider further attacks hostile actions. I want you to appreciate that we have considerable means to stop these people. They're only three thousand, and we're not afraid of them."

Evidently. "But they could bring a lot of knowledge that would be to the benefit of all of us."

"They could, but history is not in favour of the option that they will share it."

"Have they not left their technology behind for you to use?"

"That was because they had no choice. They had to leave. They would have taken all their technology with them if they'd had the chance. They still consider the technology theirs. They consider *us* their creations, to do with as they wish."

His eyes met mine when he said that. The seriousness in his expression sent a chill down my spine. If up to now I hadn't believed the strength of his feelings on this subject, I certainly did feel it now.

Coldi were no one's property, and no one within any of the *gamra* worlds would stand for the idea that they were. If anything—if the *gamra* worlds knew about this—that attitude would galvanise support behind him. We were treading on very, very dangerous ground.

While he explained to me the principles of the sling in layman's terms, we walked slowly over the elevated walkway. The basic operation of the sling was that this giant ship had both the strength and precision to generate a one-sided anpar line without the need of an anchor node on the receiving side. The ship itself did not move, but it provided the means for other ships to jump.

We came to a spot where the tubes fed into a huge torus-shaped chamber. It was quiet here, from which I surmised that the machine was not currently operating. I had a sneaking suspicion that it was probably not safe to stand here during operation.

When he finished explaining, he led us out of the room, down another staircase. The doors at the bottom were full of warnings. We went into a little room where we changed into protective suits of a heavy material that I suspected were shielding for radiation. A crewmember gave us facemasks and breathing apparatus. The air inside the tanks was, as everything related to Asto, uncomfortably warm. Fortunately, the suit was fairly loose, but I still felt drops of sweat run down my back.

We went through a kind of air lock into another large room that resembled a factory hall but didn't appear to have a well-defined floor and was probably designed for operation in zero-g conditions. In the middle hung a giant concrete bunker encased in a metal framework. The surrounding air was so misty that, with the haze and the scratched surface of the facemask's visor, I couldn't see the bottom.

"We store a micro gravity-well in here," Ezhya said, sounding muffled inside his mask. "This is why this ship has gravity. Mind you, the vast majority of the space inside that bunker is taken up by distribution shields and other protective and gravity-diffusing measures, otherwise we couldn't stand here. The size of the well is no bigger than a grain of sand." A touch screen encased on a sleeve of clear material sat on the upper balustrade railing. It came to life with a tap of his glove, displaying a squiggly line readout.

I stared at that bunker. Was he really saying that it contained a very small black hole?

"The gravity well is our shield and energy source at the same time. With space shielding, the problem is getting rid of excess heat. We simply feed it into this chamber and the gravity well absorbs the heat, or ionised particles, or anything that collects on the shields. It produces a massive amount of radiation. Also, when the highly energised particles hit the well's event horizon, they sometimes have so much energy that they split into matter and antimatter. If the matter particle drops into the well before the antimatter particle, it produces a tiny amount of antimatter. It would be a tiny speck on the nail of your little toe, but that's what powers the sling, and the ship's engine, and all the equipment you see in here. It is vital that this ship keeps moving, and the more stuff that hits those shields, the more energy we'll have. This is the ultimate war ship."

The statement barely concealed the underlying horror. The "more stuff" that might hit the shields could be fire from enemy weapons, but also entire enemy ships. "Why are you telling me this?"

"This is technology that we developed independent of the legacy left to us by the Aghyrian people. When I send you to speak to them, I want them to know this. I want them to know what we can do—what we won't hesitate to do if necessary."

Yes, this was typical Coldi bluff. My understanding of them, on that issue at least, had been correct.

We toured several other parts of the ship—mercifully without further need for those protective suits—each containing some marvel of technology that I'd never known existed, most of them for military use. I asked few questions, realising the special position I'd been granted to see this. Thayu was quiet, but I was certain that she absorbed each word Ezhya said.

At the end, Ezhya led us back to the docking area. The shuttle that had brought us was gone—had it gone back to Barresh? And where was Sheydu?—and in the middle of the floor stood a simple sleek vessel.

It looked like a transport shuttle but it was my bet that it had been extensively modified inside. The door stood open.

"This is where I leave you," Ezhya said. "I'm sending three of my guards with you."

Our eyes met. I didn't have the heart to remind him what happened last time that I went with some of his guards.

"The lady can go with you, too; you need a *zhayma*. But none of them can go with you into the Aghyrian ship."

"I'm all right to go alone if they want to talk with me."

He nodded, silently, in a *this worries me* kind of way. "You will *have* to go alone, seeing as they won't accept us anywhere near their ships. It pains me that I'm not giving you enough time to prepare, and I'm unable to give you any more support. The launch window is quite narrow."

"All right, then, let's do it."

He dug in his pocket and handed me a feeder, metallic black to resemble Coldi hair. "Take this. I will use it to stay in contact with you for as long as I can, but the Aghyrian ship blocks all communication. Once you're inside, you're on your own."

I took the feeder from him and lifted it to the back of my head. The tentacles latched onto my hair and climbed up until the bottom of the "body" settled on my skin. The customary burst of warmth came with shards of Ezhya's thinking. I suddenly realised he'd used *dhoya* pronouns on me for most of our discussion, and I hadn't even noticed.

And as we walked up the shuttle's gangplank something else occurred to me: he wouldn't have asked for my help if he hadn't run into some sort of insurmountable problem.

Of course he wouldn't, Thayu said while we went into the ship. *And do you notice that it's not like him to stay behind while others do the work? And that we haven't met my father yet?*

Damn it, she was right about both observations, and they left me deeply cold inside.

Inside the cabin, the pilot already sat at the controls, and two others were on the seats behind the pilot's.

We sat down and one of the seconds came to help us with the elaborate seat belts that went so tight around my belly that it became hard to breathe. Over the top of the seat belt went a thick cover that was so heavy that it felt like it stuck to my skin. The material was squishy and the soldier tucked it in around me, and strapped the material around my legs. I guessed visiting the toilet was now no longer an option. I was also getting really hot. How long was this flight going to take?

I was still hungry.

Thayu's face looked paler than before.

"All ready?" Ezhya said from the door.

"Ready," one of his soldiers repeated.

Ezhya retreated and the door shut with a thud that enclosed us in a bubble of warm and stuffy air. The ceiling vents came on, blowing warm but dry air over my face.

The pilot was busy talking to the comm operations. He wore a military uniform with a couple of gold dots on his chest. Quite a high-ranking pilot, I guessed.

Thayu looked at me from her restrained position. *Only higher rankings get to use the sling.*

That made sense.

Why doesn't the pilot use one of these suits?

She didn't know, but I could feel through the feeder that the thought disturbed her.

What about Veyada and Sheydu?

She didn't know.

The floor of the craft vibrated with the roar of the engine. The forward viewscreen showed the hall outside, where people were retreating from the craft. The vibration increased in strength. Slowly, we rose into the air and then moved forward in the direction of the gaping void of space. Sweat trickled down the side of my face. It irritated me, but I couldn't wipe it away, since my hands had been strapped in and I was covered in a gel-filled suit.

Something made a zooming sound in the cabin. From both side walls came two sliding doors that closed the area between us and the pilot. Ah, I saw. The craft wasn't usually kitted out to take passengers and only the front of the cabin was pressure controlled. Where we sat was not. Hence the suits.

I glanced at Thayu.

This is going to be safe, isn't it?

If it's not, it's too late now.

I like your optimism.

The roar of the engine increased and I sensed movement, although it was hard to tell in which direction.

"We're off," Thayu mouthed.

Good luck to us.

21

T HE CABIN HAD NO window, and no data stream told us where we were. It surprised me how claustrophobic that was, in addition to the pressure suit that made me feel hot. There were also, I noticed with rising panic, no barf bags, and I felt with increasing certainty that I was going to need one.

But when I closed my eyes my vision faded to be replaced with an image of Ezhya facing me.

"What the hell?" I opened my eyes again and tried to sit up but I was too tightly strapped into my seat. I could only see the closed partition in front of my seat and even that I didn't see very well because my vision had gone blurry. "Thayu, are you still there?"

"What's the matter?" I could hear her voice well enough, but I couldn't see her, because again I was seeing Ezhya instead. He looked at me sideways while walking through a passage with metal walls as in the ship we'd just left.

"I'm seeing—"

Ezhya's voice cut in. "This is a new development in feeder technology."

Now feeders could infringe on our vision and not just on our thoughts. Great. Wearing one of these, you'd never again have any privacy. What if you needed to go to the loo? Oh, I forgot, Coldi observed no privacy in that quarter either.

"My apologies if it distresses you, but it's the quickest way to brief you on our involvement with the Aghyrian ship while you're travelling. There are some things you need to know before your arrival."

Oh yes, here it was. All those things I hadn't been told that would put me in mortal danger and that, if I'd known prior to departure, would have made me think twice before going. How did they expect me to do my job like this?

On the other hand, it was not as if I'd ever had any choice in the matter.

Damn it, why did I always get myself into these situations? Moreover, how could I get myself out of them? Preferably alive.

"The material you obtained from Trader Federza's office was part of a conversation the Barresh group of Aghyrians had with the ship. But we were the first to speak with them and were the first to have visual contact with the ship."

"I'm gathering that did not go well?" The Coldi propensity to posture made them terrible negotiators. This feeder Ezhya had given me had some nifty technology. As well as visuals, it included the function of a regular feeder.

"I can see what you're thinking, but we were not the aggressors."

"What the army's intentions were is of less importance than how their actions were perceived by the ship." I couched my observations in careful terms. On occasions like this I was unsure what my status with him was. On the one hand, he controlled my life with a single command. On the other, it seemed to amuse him that I would say things no one else dared tell him, and often I felt that this was indeed my function.

"I understand that. The dignitaries at *gamra* seem to think that the inhabitants of this ship are benevolent."

"The official line has been that we've assumed nothing until the identity of the ship could be established. It had been acting like an auto-operated random piece of debris." And, if the Coldi had known otherwise for quite some time, why hadn't *gamra* been told?

"The current situation developed quickly. Their captain, Kando Luczon, is a vindictive man. By all tests we've been able to run, he is the same captain who condemned tens of thousands to their deaths because he would not take extra refugees on board. They've been to another galaxy. They've probably made enemies there. They are not here to negotiate, but they are here to take. But I'll show you so you can judge for yourself."

Ezhya had arrived at a small room where all the walls were taken up with screens and other electronic equipment. Scrolling text flickered over the screen. A serious-faced man sat behind the controls.

At a sign from Ezhya, he hit a button and all of a sudden I was in the control room of another ship. This was a slightly larger vessel than the one I was in, maybe one of those that accompanied us. Three people were at the controls, a pilot and two copilots. Instead of the darkness of space, a blaze of light was coming in through the front viewscreen. The entire viewscreen was taken up by some sort of structure: the outer skin of a ship, and the light came from the craft's flood lights hitting the hull of this giant ship and reflecting back into the cabin. The crew were silent, staring at the screen, where features on the outside of the ship outside slowly scrolled past.

Their faces showed up as pale ovals, wide-eyed.

One of the copilots pointed. "That's the front of the engine chamber."

Another nodded. I realised that they were probably in possession of the same plan as I had seen in the material from Federza's office.

The copilot asked, "Are those weapons?"

"You'd expect a ship like this to be armed," the pilot said.

"At this size, what can possibly make any kind of impression on that ship?"

"A small shuttle, full of explosives, flown into the dock."

"They'd have to be an impressive kind of explosive—"

"Contact," someone said.

The viewpoint swung around. There was a fourth person in the cabin—this instantly made the ship bigger still, because if there was a fourth person at the controls, there would be another three people on board. No way Coldi would travel here without a complete association.

This fourth person sat behind a comm station. Lines wriggled over the screen in front of her.

"We're getting a response from the ship."

"Any way of knowing if it's an auto-responder?"

"Not at this stage."

"Send another ping," the main pilot said.

Her hands went over the controls.

A moment later, another burst of wriggles zigzagged over her screen.

"Whoa!" She pushed her earpiece down. "That was loud."

"What was it?"

"Some sort of pulsating tone."

"Any idea what it means?" one of the copilots asked. She looked over her shoulder, turning her back on the main viewscreen, which, at that very moment, flashed red. The glow lit the cabin.

"What the hell!" the main pilot yelled.

Various alarms started beeping in the cabin. Lights flashed on the controls.

The second copilot was frantically searching through information screens.

"Anything damaged?" the pilot asked.

"The link to base is out."

"Re-establish it."

She gave him a *what do you think I'm doing?* look.

The comm officer said, "I'm getting an incoming signal."

"Decode."

"I'm trying. Doesn't make any sense so far."

"Is it auto-generated?"

"I don't think so."

"Send out our handshake beacon."

"I tried; it's not going through—oh, wait. I'm getting a response now." She read on the screen for a while, her face lit blue from below. "They're talking about right of way, and Aghyr. Damn, it looks like it is the old ship."

"The very same one?"

"It seems so."

"Is anyone alive on board?"

"I don't know. Can't tell. My infrared scans are being blocked."

"Try sending the stripped code."

She worked for a bit on the screen, scrolling down, checking menus. Then she said, "Code sent."

They waited. No one spoke. The only sound in the cabin was the hiss of air from the recycling vents.

I wondered what code they were talking about. Obviously they knew a lot more about the ship than we did. With the vast wealth of data excavated on Asto, that shouldn't surprise me.

Then, the comm officer took in a sharp breath.

"What?" the pilot asked, but at that moment, a low tone filled the cabin. It grew louder and louder. The sound pulsed, and I knew that pulsing.

"Turn it off!" the pilot screamed.

"I'm trying to!" the communications officer yelled.

The pilot rose from his seat and reached for her controls.

The recording stopped abruptly to make way for a recording of an outside camera. A couple of smaller ships approached the huge Aghyrian behemoth against the backdrop of the blackness of space.

My heart took a while to calm down. What had happened in the other recording? Why did it cut out all of a sudden?

A voice said, "Get ready to launch."

"Ready."

It went quiet again. The small ships moved oh so slowly along the side of the large ship.

A tinny voice said, "Establishing contact." And a bit later. "Package sent. Standby."

More silent time went by. Some sort of protrusion on the large ship slid into view. It looked like a viewing port with windows. I found it strange that they would use windows. Screens were so much safer.

And then, suddenly, that pulsing low tone again.

Voices shouted. The smallest of the ships disintegrated.

I stared at the debris floating soundlessly through space.

Ezhya came back in my vision. "None of the crew of those missions survived. The ship used the sound to destroy our vessels."

We'd heard that sound in Barresh. I remembered the way it had made the air in my chest vibrate, and how I'd been afraid that the building would collapse. A wall had already collapsed.

But what did they think I could do against a long-distance weapon like that? I was a diplomat. I could do words. I didn't do weapons.

"We want you to talk. They've communicated with us," Ezhya said. "We need to re-establish that contact."

Re-establish? "When did that happen? After the attacks or before?"

"Before. We exchanged some communication."

And obviously, something had happened there. In the usual infuriating fashion, layers of the truth were being peeled back.

"Yes, something went wrong. That's why you're going there."

Funny. I would have sworn that this was part of a plot to get rid of me. "I'm not sure what I can do if the situation has deteriorated this badly already. I presume that I will be fully briefed before I start doing anything." Because even now, I wasn't getting the full detail.

"You will. We'll need to convince them that you're not Coldi. We will be sending your image, with all your bio-diagnostics. They seem to attach importance to someone's biological heritage."

Well, that made me really feel safe. Damn it, why did they think we could make a difference?

"Why not just threaten them with weapons?" Damn, they had a *black hole* aboard one of their war ships. They could suck the entire ship into it if they wanted.

"It will become clear to you when you arrive."

Well, I bloody well hoped so, because so far, I was not impressed.

The view flicked off and I was left to stare at the inside of the mask. One glance aside at Thayu revealed that she looked as worried as I felt.

I couldn't do anything with half-baked information.

I understand, Ezhya said in my thoughts. *Believe me, I understand. But we need to be extremely careful with what information we let out.*

Just what kind of damage could, for example, the Aghyrians do to the Asto army? They didn't even have any kind of organised army, let alone equipment.

Unless they—no, I wasn't going there.

Unless they hired the Tamerians—no, I wasn't going there either.

Damn it, damn it.

I was pressed into my seat, which meant that our ship was quickly gathering speed. I had no idea how far we still had to go before the large ship would engage the sling, and with each second that passed the shuttle gathered speed, and I liked this less and less.

I was sweating in the suit. I wanted to get out of here. I was never much good at being in small spaces, and I didn't think that I could be of any use to the Asto army.

Still, the shuttle gathered speed. I was being pushed into the back of the seat, with the weight of the gel-filled bag on top of me.

Faster, faster and faster. The weight of that thing was getting very uncomfortable.

Damn. Did they know how weak and fragile I was compared to them? I tried to lift my head in order to look at Thayu, but I could not. How many gees was this ship pulling?

Very uncomfortable.

I saw spots. Damn it, I was going to pass out.

Voices echoed through my mind, but I couldn't make out what they said or even if it was just the pilot talking or if people were trying to talk to me. I was merely struggling to breathe.

Thayu!

I sensed her warmth, but if she was anything like me, she wouldn't be able to move.

And the ship was still accelerating.

The world turned white.

For a moment that was all I saw. A bright light. For all I knew I could have died and gone to heaven. I didn't really believe in heaven, but if there was evidence, I could be convinced otherwise.

But this wasn't heaven.

The rainbows kind of gave it away. The colours sliding back into place, as they did after an Exchange jump.

I took a deep breath, and another one. Air flowed into my lungs. It was still too hot and stuffy and smelled of Coldi sweat, but I'd never experienced anything more beautiful.

Someone was taking the mask off my face. My vision was blurry. An impossibly warm hand touched my cheek.

"He's waking up." That was Thayu's voice.

I was sure I hadn't lost consciousness. Or had I? Was I making a habit of passing out at least once for every trip I went on?

I tried to speak, but my mouth felt dry.

Where the hell were we?

Someone put a thin object in my mouth. I recognised what I hoped was a straw, and sucked. Water.

Green-coded, hopefully, although it would probably burn me if it wasn't. I drank. The water was lukewarm and tasted metallic, but wonderful. My vision was still dubious. I could make out shapes where people were, but not their faces.

Someone leaned over me and the hot gel-filled bag was lifted off me. The breeze was so cold that it made me shiver.

"You're soaked through," Thayu said.

I ran my hand over my shirt. She was right. "Everything in these ships of yours is too hot for me." I hoped I hadn't wet myself. The smell was just sweaty, so I guessed not.

"Where are we?"

But at the same time, I noticed the front viewscreen. The barrier between us and the pilots had rolled back into the wall and I could see into the rest of the cabin.

Most of the viewscreen was filled with star-spotted sky, but a couple of bright white specks floated in the middle of the screen.

"Where are we?"

"Two jumps away from the Janto cluster. There is a large star to the right of the field of vision. No habitable or useful worlds."

There often weren't any around these large stars. They were too unstable and too short-lived to have planets that had evolved enough to harbour life.

"Is there more than one ship?" To be honest, it looked like there were many, ten or fifteen at the very least.

"Those are ours," Thayu said. "We'll be with them soon. Eat something."

She passed me another jar with a straw. I didn't really feel like eating, but it gave me something to do, and likely there would be no time for eating once we arrived at our destination. I sucked on the straw and immediately recognised the bland taste of Asto army supplies. There were only a few meals from their arsenal I could eat, and during my two-week trip from Ceren to Asto, I'd tried them all, even mixed them to avoid the tedium, and still managed to get so thoroughly sick and tired of them that even now I couldn't stand the taste.

I shuddered.

I finished the jar, though, and lay back, dozing, until I noticed that I was being pulled forward off my seat. The craft was engaging its brakes.

I made an effort to stay awake, but I dozed off anyway.

When I woke up, the ships on the viewscreen had come a lot closer and it was clear that there were more than just a couple. The closest ones resolved into recognisable shapes, mostly of the square, blocky deep-space variety. Others were smaller. There were also one or two of the arrow-shaped type that would contain acceleration tubes, as on the ship where I'd left Ezhya. Wait—all those dots in a separate group to the right were ships, too, and I could make out at least four more of the long ones in that group. And then all those little specks . . . Holy cow.

I'd thought that the ships I'd seen in orbit at Ceren were an armada. I'd been wrong. *This* was an armada.

How many of those ships were there? Each of those workhorse square ships would have a crew of a few hundred. The larger ones would have thousands. The big arrow-shaped ones . . . I hated to think how many they had on board. Tens of thousands at least. There were hundreds of ships here, and as we came closer, more and more resolved from the shadows of the bigger ones.

Population numbers were pretty much the same on Asto and Earth, both about five billion, both having been much larger in the past. But counting off-planet . . . I'd wondered about that before and the thought of the vast size of the Asto military made me sick. How much of Asto's military personnel lived their entire lives in space and were never counted as inhabitants of the planet?

"What the hell are all those ships doing here?" I said in a low voice.

"This is a substantial part of Asto's fleet. You are not supposed to have seen this." Thayu's voice was like a soft breath at my shoulder. She had obviously been awake while I slept and I'd missed some briefing.

"Certainly, but there would be enough fire power here to destroy ten alien ships."

"You don't know that. Knowing where it comes from, it could be pretty much indestructible."

"Could be. Where is this Aghyrian ship anyway?"

She pointed ahead.

I squinted at the armada, and at the darkness of space behind it. Couldn't see anything.

"You're not seeing it?"

I shook my head.

"Think big."

I did, and lines linked up against the darkness of deep space. The shape I had seen on the material stolen from Federza's office resolved from the faint glimmers in space. I knew why the edge of the armada cut off so abruptly: because the rest of it was *behind* the ship.

"Holy crap."

Thayu nodded. "It's so dark that it absorbs all light. It's very, very hard to see. This is a true deep space vessel."

"This is the same ship they built all those years ago?"

The pilot said, "This ship is five hundred years old by their time, more than fifty thousand by ours. We've traced back their anpar lines and think they may have come from the Renzha galaxy." This was the Coldi name for the Andromeda galaxy.

I couldn't stop staring at the massive shape that was barely visible behind the armada. I'd been wrong again. There was certainly a lot of fire power here, but a behemoth like this could easily swipe all of those insignificant little ships aside just by its sheer presence. Hell, most of those square-looking military ships would probably twirl around uselessly in the ship's anpar wake. Holy-fucking-shit. "Why is the ship still here? Certainly if they wanted they could easily jump to another place."

Ezhya said in my mind, "Actually, it's not so easy. We disabled their drive, although we're not quite sure how it happened. We're keeping them in position with our network of Exchange slings."

I wondered how many of those arrow-shaped ships there were. I could see seven from my position.

"There are fifteen," the pilot said.

There were a lot more of those ships than I expected. Sometimes it was a wonder why not every inhabited world was in Coldi hands.

Ezhya said, "There would be no point trying to take over every world. A network like that would fragment soon, and we'd end up with a situation similar to the current one. Except all our competitors would be Coldi as well and they'd be much harder to fight than, say, Damarcians."

Well, that . . . reasoning had me floored, actually.

Every time he did this, I was amazed at how the deeper Coldi psyche was different from ours, how much I still had to learn, and how much I would probably never understand.

What would philosophers on Earth call that way of thinking? Post-expansionism?

First, people went all gung-ho on expanding their influence into space, increasing their numbers like crazy. But like the Roman and the American empires before them, every empire must crumble and fragment. Here was Ezhya showing a deep understanding of that, and acting like it, because you can't hope to keep control over an empire that size, and the enemy you may end up facing could well be your former family.

That was what maturity in colonisation looked like, not just in space but everywhere, and that the countries on Earth hadn't achieved by a long shot.

That might be why many of the entities in *gamra* were reluctant to engage too deeply with Nations of Earth.

A civilisation didn't know how primitive it was until it had a chance to look back and see the mistakes of the past.

I felt like I'd just been taken by the hand and shown a glimpse of a hundred years into the future.

22

———————

A JUNIOR OFFICER came with a set of dry clothes for me, and she showed me to a tiny bathroom to put them on. I was still feeling a bit wonky, and the lack of gravity definitely didn't help. Neither did the bland meal which sat like a brick in my stomach. They must have been semi-prepared for me because they had clothing that was both in my size and in *gamra* colours.

Thayu came in to help me and told me to hurry up because we were about to enter a larger ship's hold and people were waiting for me.

By the time I'd changed, the shuttle was in the dock, and the hold door was open. A junior officer waited outside to accompany us wherever we needed to go.

Another military docking hall, another ship, and no sign of a second ship carrying Veyada and Sheydu. And everyone seemed in a hurry, so there was no time to ask. We followed the officer through the corridors, pulling ourselves along using railings on the walls.

The "people" who were waiting for us turned out to be a swathe of military suits, gathered in a room at the back of the ship's bridge. All those faces, stiff, disturbingly alike with regulation ponytails, were thoroughly unfamiliar to me.

I glanced at Thayu. Her father was commander of the army. I'd never been able to work out if he was the only commander, but previously I would have guessed that he was, since he had been moved up as Ezhya's second. The new feeder Ezhya had given me had to help with maintaining the strength of that bond.

Asto military leaders were always at the scene of the most serious conflict, which made me wonder where he was and why he wasn't here. Maybe I'd been wrong about his position in the army.

The room was quite small, insignificant and stuffy, as with all Asto ships. There were no outside screens, and the lack of up or down or any kind of direction made me feel queasy.

I wasn't sure that this was such a good idea. Coldi were thoroughly impervious to motion sickness, but unfortunately I didn't share that feature.

There were seven people, all kind of floating along the walls, where there were railings for this purpose. They were not a complete association because of the way they separated when Thayu and I came in and made room for us.

I picked out the highest-ranking officer from those in the room by the way the others positioned themselves around her, or at least I thought the officer was female, because with Coldi it could be darn hard to tell.

The higher-ranking officer gave a brief nod when I came in but she said nothing. A glance at her earrings established that she was Domiri, and that probably earned me the nod.

"I am Shazayu." Her tone sounded like I was supposed to know from her name who she was.

Help me, please? I asked Thayu. But Thayu had taken up the subservient position. I didn't tend to do *sheya* greetings unless I absolutely couldn't get away with not doing it.

She gave me a curious look, and a brief and tense silence passed in which no one appeared to be sure what to do. Clearly she had expected some sort of acknowledgement of position from me.

"I'm here as a non-Coldi negotiator." I hoped this would allay her concerns about how I fitted into their scheme. I wanted to shout that they didn't need to establish my position, but my earrings clearly suggested otherwise.

A junior officer in plain dark clothing floated around the room, bringing containers with what I presumed were drinks. He didn't offer me one, so I presumed they were red-coded.

The others all took a container and the tense situation relaxed for a bit, but looking around the seven military suits, I didn't think it had resolved. What a weird atmosphere hung in this room. Maybe they didn't know what to do about me; and, really, in that case, it was up to me to take this situation by the horns and turn it around. Bluff and bluster was what they expected. Their instinct didn't react to me, but my behaviour could substitute for that to a certain extent.

"My information tells me that you are standing for the position of Chief Delegate," Shazayu said.

What. The. Hell. Did you tell her that? I glanced at Thayu but her face maintained that blank expression that Coldi did so well.

"That is news to me. Right now, the *gamra* assembly is in turmoil. If for some reason I end up with the position, rest assured that it will be temporary. I'm not interested in the job."

She nodded, and seemed to relax a little. Hell, how isolated were these armed forces ships?

It was my guess that she was probably more concerned about how the position of Chief Delegate fitted in the military associations, also considering the fact that I was a member of her clan, than anything to do with *gamra*. As long as the *gamra* secretary was not Coldi, there was no problem.

Two other two top brass officers stole curious glances at me. Not quite meeting my eyes, but getting very close.

There was a short and uncomfortable silence. They didn't like this, oh no, they didn't.

"Apparently, I'm here to negotiate on your behalf. I'm supposed to be briefed about the most recent details of the situation." And it would also be nice if someone could be a bit clearer about the plan and what they wanted me to do. All these silences unnerved me. These people unnerved me and their behaviour was just weird.

"It's a matter of urgency," Shazayu said.

"I understand that."

"I don't think you do."

"Then explain it to me, because I cannot negotiate unless I know what's going on." And by hell, something was going on, and I was getting very, very uneasy about this.

"Coming here, you asked questions about our engagement with this ship so far."

"I always ask lots of questions. That's what I do."

"We're keeping the ship trapped in this locality. They've escaped us twice, but now we've disabled their drive by counteracting the energy buildup. You asked why we don't just shoot them."

"I'm guessing you're a bit hesitant about shooting at something of which you do not know the strength. You want to make sure that when you shoot, it will have the desired effect. Also I guess you'd rather talk with these people to see if they have anything valuable on offer."

"That was our thought. At the first location where we caught up with them, we established contact. They have been reading our communications. The Exchange is as open as an Outer Circle bar, and it's easy to tap in. We knew they were doing this and hoped it meant that they had gained an understanding of our society."

"Are they really as good with languages as the rumour says they are?"

"Yes, they are. Quite extraordinary. These people are genetically indistinguishable from the Barresh Aghyrians, but they are more difficult to deal with."

I was asking myself *Is that possible*, but of course it was. "That sounds like you've spoken with them."

"We have."

"You spoke through the radio?"

"At first, yes."

"You went to their ship?"

"A small shuttle. Eight aboard."

I really did not like her little hesitant silences and the fact that I needed to ask everything. She seemed . . . disturbed, damaged almost.

"I'm guessing they were shot at?"

"They did not come back."

Now we were getting to the meat of the story. "This was the contact you had with them before the images of hostility we've seen on the other recordings."

She consulted briefly with the officer next to her, who gestured, *Yes*.

"The recordings you saw were of the parties we sent to retrieve them."

That part suddenly made sense. "Did you try to talk to them?"

"We did. They responded by jumping away from us. We followed, asked for the return of our people. They said their genetics were interesting, and sent us a document that went into great detail about how we were the descendants of the sixty-four couples that they left on Asto in preparation for colonisation of worlds with hostile climates, never thinking that they might need those characteristics to survive on their own world."

I would have started feeling sick here, if I wasn't feeling nauseous already. "Did they say anything of the fate of those people you sent?"

"They did not. We asked them for details. We brought in more ships. And they jumped out of our reach again. So we called up experts in anpar travel. We devised a plan, a sling network to trap them and disable their drive. When we found them again, we put the plan into action and that's where we are now. The ship is not talking to us."

"Have they made any demands?"

"No. They've stated that they won't talk to us because we're inferior. We're not real people."

"Because they produced the Coldi race?"

"Because they think they own us."

"That's why you want me, right?"

"Hopefully they will talk to you."

"You want me to go there and negotiate for the freedom of your envoys?" If they were still alive.

"That's it."

Shit. I should have known that it was something this. Coldi were bad at negotiation, but they couldn't shoot, because . . . yeah, why? They normally didn't care all that much for a few lives if it was to the benefit of Coldi society. A cold chill went over my back despite the stuffy and hot air. "Can I ask who these hostages are?"

"You wouldn't know any of them, except one: Asha Domiri."

23

———————

OLY SHIT AND fuck on a fiddlestick.

Thayu let out a small squeak when the officer mentioned her father's name, very uncharacteristic for her.

Thay'?

Her face had gone white and her eyes were wider than usual. It was the first time, ever, that I had seen her display any emotion in relation to the man who was her biological father. She had even locked him inside a safety bunker when we were in Asto, and she had discussed his ambitions for the top job in a detached manner

Cory, please?

The earrings that dangled on both side of her head glittered with the same blood red stone that I wore. I had no idea how she saw the colour—Coldi didn't see red—but it was significant for them. It was a ruby, the Domiri clan colour. I belonged to the clan. Asha was the clan leader.

Then it struck me that this was also the reason why everyone was keeping the issue quiet. Coldi being Coldi, they had thought nothing of their leader going over for talks, because that was the way Coldi did business. But take out Asha, and the entire army would again go through the resettlement of positions that we'd just seen with Risha and Taysha on Asto. A whole army incapacitated through infighting.

And that—I felt cold—might even have been the Aghyrian aim. They studied Coldi society. They knew how to deliver a crippling blow to it without firing a single shot. And it could be that Ezhya had asked me, in a roundabout way *Go over there and find a way in which we can hit them back.*

Shit indeed.

Our meeting with the top officers was finished. Some of the officers that I hadn't been introduced to slunk from the room like pink-uniformed ghosts.

Their un-unified and somewhat hesitant appearance now also made sense to me. With Asha gone, cracks were already appearing in the loyalty networks. People were not sharing things as they should because they could use knowledge to their advantage later.

They could keep the current structure in place for perhaps a little longer, but Asha's absence was a vacuum that people felt a pathological need to fill.

"We have a shuttle waiting for you," Shazayu said.

I glanced sideways at Thayu. She nodded and had that *I want to come* look on her face. Yet she must know that she couldn't.

"Have you had any contact with the ship recently?" I asked.

"We've sent them a message with information about you and your genetic print."

I wasn't going to worry about how they obtained that, even though my conscience told me to do just that. There *was* no privacy when Coldi were concerned. I should have been used to that long ago. There would have been plenty of opportunity for them to collect this material. "Have they replied? Do they indicate that they will let me board?"

"Not yet. They're likely to have their own scans that they have applied to us in the past."

"Who is to say that they're not going to shoot us to pieces like they've done with the other two ships?"

"Nothing, except we've let them know that we have the capacity to destroy their ship."

Except of course the big ship and the Asto military's sling ships had antimatter and gravity wells on board that would likely wipe out the entire fleet if the containment fields around those energy sources was breached. Any attack on the ship might well backfire. And no one *knew* if they were capable of destroying the Aghyrian ship. No one knew what kind of weapons they had.

Damn it. This mission was even more stupid than going to Asto to try and rescue Ezhya's position. "I'm going to have to go in with some assumptions. I'm going to assume that if they wanted a conflict they would have already started one. So either they want to talk, but maybe not to you; and I'm also going to presume that the presence of all these ships is not truly keeping them here, but they're playing along, just to see what they can get out of us. Or they're waiting for some parameter—"

"—a second ship turning up?" Shazayu asked.

"By my reckoning, they would not need to wait if they have additional ships. If this ship can jump here, then others could do the same. If they're waiting for something, it's likely to be something that they don't control, like the alignment of stars. Alternatively . . . The Aghyrians used their own genetic material to create you, didn't they?"

"Yes, as far as I understand." She raised her eyebrows. "Why?" Coldi did find it distasteful to be referred to as an artificial race, but I was going to have to address it.

"If they share a lot of their genetic material with you, they may share some of the same characteristics."

Her frown deepened.

"Supposing all the *gamra* entities banded together and hired an army of Tamerians for a stand-off against Asto—"

"There aren't enough Tamerians to make an impression on our army."

"You don't know that. And supposing there were. Just suppose." I knew Coldi weren't very good at taking hypothetical situations seriously and this was going to be a stretch for her.

Thayu frowned as well. "I don't understand what you're getting at."

"Just wait. Let me make my point. Supposing Asto is under threat and the enemy is clearly stronger. What would Ezhya do? Would he flee? I don't think so. Would he pretend to be more than what he is?"

Shazayu looked at me sharply.

"Because that's what Asto does best, isn't it? Looking bigger than they really are. I have, for example, no idea if all the ships I've seen surrounding the Aghyrian ship are real, are war ships capable of inflicting damage, are the entire fleet or are only part of the fleet. And I'm not even considered to be an enemy."

It seemed that Thayu got what I was aiming for. "Do you think they could be bluffing?"

"I wouldn't be surprised if they were. Add up the facts. They haven't said what they're doing here. They haven't contacted *gamra* even though I'm sure they're aware of it. They have just given the local Aghyrians some empty and unconnected information with half-hearted promises. If they really had so much powerful technology, would they have come back here in the first place? They consider us primitive and not worth the time, so there must be a reason why they want to come back. My guess is they're pretending to be all-powerful. My guess is that the Exchange sling is probably the only thing they've got. If they were really that powerful, they would not let themselves be captured like this."

Shazayu said, "I hope you're right. I think they're waiting for us to give them an excuse to destroy us. And then they will move to Asto."

"What is there for them? The Asto they left was a green planet. Today, it's desert. The oceans are poisonous. The climate's too hot for them. The land will no longer support its people. Asto farms in space. It buys food from Ceren. Why would they want to come back?"

"Because it's Asto."

It was a strange thing to say for a hard-nosed military officer, and more sentimental than I was used to from Coldi. Underneath all the bluster, they were very protective of their world and aware that its previous inhabitants could return and demand a share in its control. "We won't know until we talk to them. So let's go. I just want to be sure that this is all the information you have and there are no further nasty surprises to come. Did Asha, for example, send any communication before he was supposedly restrained?" If he was still alive.

"The ship only lets out communication approved by them."

So that was as I thought. I hoped to hell that I'd now finally been given the last pieces of information.

A junior crewmember arrived with two flight suits of the type I'd sometimes seen pilots wear. The suit had a mask and a harness for two small air tanks.

"For emergencies," Shazayu said.

A junior officer showed us into another room where we could change.

I floated in the air, trying to find a place to hang my suit while I took off my onboard overalls. In my experience so far, everything to do with the Asto army required an extraordinary amount of changing clothes.

I didn't find a hook for the suit, so Thayu held it for me, while I fumbled to take off the overalls.

"I don't think it's fair of them to ask you to do this," Thayu said. I was surprised at how angry she sounded.

"They clearly ran out of options." I was doing my best to stay calm and to quell my stomach, but the latter wasn't working very well. My hands were clammy and my face sweaty. When I took off the top part of the overalls, the air from the vent made me shiver. Again the shirt that I wore underneath was soaked in sweat.

Getting changed in zero-g is not easy, and the tight rubbery suit didn't make it any easier. I ended up holding onto a wall railing while Thayu pulled the material over my feet.

"Are you holding up?" she asked me, while doing up the fastening at the front.

"Compared with what we're facing, I guess I am. But I could be better."

"What you're facing, not we. I'll try to stay with you for as long as I can, but ultimately, you'll have to go into that ship alone. It worries me."

"It worries me that Veyada and Sheydu were left behind somewhere, probably kept back by Ezhya, but I wish I knew where they were."

I hugged her. Her breath made a cold spot in my neck. I stroked her face. Her skin felt warm and dry.

Last time we'd been in danger—although not nearly as much danger as I was facing now—I'd had the opportunity to sleep with her one more time. We didn't have that luxury now. And in hindsight, the problems we had faced back then were a pale shade of what I was facing today.

We left the room where a pilot—I was starting to recognise the markings—was waiting for us. The man took up the subservient position for us, and Thayu tapped him on the shoulder.

While we pulled ourselves through the corridors, he explained to us that he could only get to within a certain distance of the ship. "Any closer and they start to make threats. We will fly to this distance and announce you. If our previous experience is anything to go by, they will guide us into the ship. Or it may be that they want you to come alone and you may have to pilot the pod. I understand you have some flying experience?" He didn't meet my eyes, according to protocol.

"Um . . ." I did have some experience, but it was in a winged craft in the atmosphere and it had been with an experienced pilot sitting next to me. I had zero experience in zero-g flying.

Thayu said, "I can pilot the pod. Let me come."

The pilot turned to her but didn't meet her eyes. "They seem cued to our genetic material."

"I can hide behind the engine shield."

"No, Thayu. That's not in place for nothing."

"Hmm, it may be good to have another person on the pod if it comes to that." This was Shazayu behind us.

"No, Thayu, that would be dangerous."

"And what you're doing is not dangerous?"

I spread my hands and let them fall again.

"If you are captured on that ship, I want to be with you."

There was no persuading her, and Shazayu didn't seem to think that it was as bad an idea as I did.

We returned the docks, where the same shuttle that had brought us here waited for us.

We climbed on board. Inside the cabin sat two copilots, different ones from the crew that had come here with us. These were lower-ranked crew, I was sure. Both pilot and copilots were expendable. Their loss would not upset too many loyalty networks.

Great.

We strapped in our seats. There was no need for the gel-filled bags or the partition.

We also had the luxury of being able to see the front viewscreen.

The cabin went dark the moment we left the dock, with just blue light from the screens lighting the pilots' faces. The shuttle moved past the side of the ship like a fly hovering over a horse's back. Then the pilot pulled us out of its shadow and we crested the army ship. In the corner of the viewscreen I thought I spotted some kind of weapons mount before it vanished from view.

The Aghyrian ship came onto the screen, massive, silent and dark.

For a long time, no one spoke. The incredible size of the ship stunned us all into silence. It was one thing seeing it on a screen, but another seeing it from a tiny ship in the middle of space.

For a while, we described a curved path towards the ship.

Soon, the hull of the ship took up most of the forward viewscreen. The pilot enlarged the view. Smaller protrusions dissolved from the larger mass showing increasing amount of detail. A lot of the outer protrusions looked weathered, some even bent as if they had been hit by space rocks or debris.

An airlock entry door scrolled over the screen, a square opening with an inner ring that looked extendable. A yellow sign on the outside proclaimed a mysterious command in a type of script I was unfamiliar with. Oh, I could see that it was Aghyrian, but written in such a way that with my limited knowledge of characters, I couldn't make sense out of it.

I made note of all these protuberances, collecting pictures of detailed features on the hull.

"I'm sending a signal now," the pilot said.

The screen in front of him showed a waving line in green.

He waited, his hands over the controls, ready to react. Afraid of another burst of destructive sound? Awaiting total obliteration?

The wriggling line suddenly disappeared. "They're receiving us." He blew out a breath.

We waited, occasionally looking at each other. I reached out and touched Thayu's hand. She looked at me, love obvious in her face. Not so long ago we'd been talking about a family. Today we faced death.

Nothing happened for a very long time. Various features of the outside of the ship scrolled over the viewscreen. Wow, some of those panels were terribly scratched. Not really a condition I'd like to fly in.

Then without warning, the controls went dark. A zooming sound filled the cabin. I was pressed in my seat.

"They're pulling us in," the pilot said. "I've lost all control over the ship."

I looked at Thayu. This was it.

24

WE MOVED AT quite a high speed but remained at roughly the same distance from the ship as we had been.

The pilot fiddled with the controls but from where I sat it didn't look like he had much success in bringing them back to life. One of the copilots was trying to contact the main fleet on a separate system that still appeared to have power.

But after a while he announced, "All the outside links are jammed."

Thayu had linked the outside visual feed to her reader and was watching the structures scroll past, while occasionally tapping the screen. She wore her thought sensor and I presumed she was taking notes.

Then we started moving towards the ship. We entered the shadow side, out of the harsh light of the giant star. It was pitch dark here. Thayu used her sonar to get an image, but the quality and resolution dropped considerably.

"There," the pilot said.

The dark surface with various protrusions was broken by a huge open bay. The opening was square, several ships across, and dark inside apart from some blinking lights in the depths.

This appeared to be where we were headed. When we hovered over the opening, a laser-like shaft of light pierced the darkness, coming from within the ship. It became visible only where it hit some kind of barrier of vapour. It swept the mouth of the docking bay and found our ship. An indistinct pattern of light blue spots flashed over the pilot's screen.

"Diagnostics," Thayu said.

"They send a huge bunch of frequencies all packaged in a highly targeted beam," the pilot said. He had his head turned to a screen to the side of the main viewscreen.

No one spoke in the cabin while the blue light tracked over the outside of the craft. I clutched the armrests of my seat. Thayu was studying images of the docking opening on her reader, making notes and comparing things. The screen showed the recorded graphics enlarged to the point of blurriness. She looked busy so I didn't ask her what she was doing and she didn't volunteer information. This was Thayu in her element.

The copilot at the back was also looking at something on the screen. Some kind of text. I thought he'd said that the system had been fried.

Thayu briefly met my eyes. She put a finger to her lips and gestured with her eyes at the big ship.

It looked very much like this was another data-gathering operation. But I didn't understand how they communicated back to the army ship. A chilling thought: was I but a pawn in their game? It looked like they had a plan, and Coldi plans usually involved guns and explosives. I, Thayu and three junior officers were going to take on a ship of thousands? What were they thinking?

The ship descended into the maw of the opening. It was dark in here. A lot like the Coldi ships, actually.

"How huge is this place?" I couldn't see a floor, only platforms that floated in the air without anything to hold them up. I couldn't see the walls and I couldn't see other ships.

Thayu had pulled up the diagram that we'd gotten from Federza. She was tracking something with her finger. The image zoomed in, showing a three-dimensional framework of lines that described the shape of the ship. I found it really hard to make much sense of these images.

As we slowly moved into the hold the vastness of the place overwhelmed me. I could only see brightly lit platforms hovering in nothingness. The sides of the cavity were well out of view.

We slowed down a lot.

There was a clang against the outside of the ship. The ship settled on the surface of one of the hovering platforms and we settled in our chairs. There was *gravity* here.

"We're in," the copilot said to whoever was still listening.

A moment later, the pilot said, "Outside air is declared safe."

"What do we do now?"

"Wait, I guess."

We waited. Sweat rolled down my stomach. Thayu was still annotating her images. I wanted to ask her what she was doing, but she made an Indrahui hand gesture that she had learned from Evi and Telaris. *Quiet*.

Then the screen lit up with large blue letters.

Your envoy can exit the vessel. Leave weapons behind. The language was quite stiff, as if they'd learned Coldi from listening to *gamra* meetings.

Thayu nodded to me.

This was it, then.

I rose from my seat. I felt heavy. Probably the ship was running on Asto gravity and it was a bit more than Ceren or Earth.

Thayu gestured, *Be careful*. She tapped her arm to indicate the gun she wore there, but I couldn't see how she would even know if I was in trouble. All the electronics in my suit had gone dead. I couldn't update on anything that happened to me.

This was such a stupid expedition.

Damn, Thayu.

With the pilots in the cabin I didn't know if I should kiss her, but I wanted to. She looked so . . . I was going to say vulnerable, but that was an Earth reaction. Thayu's expression wasn't one of Coldi vulnerability. It was one of determination. As always, they had a plan. They had asked me to come because the ship people would allow us in here, but I was not a negotiator. I was a decoy. She was going to try and free her father by force.

She just looked at me and shook her head slightly, as if even though our feeders weren't working, she knew what I was thinking and wanted me to stop thinking those things because others might be able to see them, too. Not that I knew how, but people always said that my thoughts were easy to deduce. It was scary.

So I hugged her and she hugged me back and I hoped that whatever she had planned wasn't too crazy, but knowing her, it probably would be. After all, she'd had us flying on giant drones into the sunrise over Athyl during our last adventure. I wasn't even armed this time.

The outside door opened. A waft of warm and humid air spilled into the cabin. It had a very distinct Coldi scent: that of wet stone.

Standing in the door opening at the top of the gangplank, I looked into a massive hall. The ship stood on a small platform that hung in the middle of a huge empty space. There was no light in the hall except a soft glow around the platform, and no sign of movement. I stepped off the gangplank onto a hard, metallic surface. The sound of my footsteps vanished in the vast space. I walked past the side of the ship, but found nothing of importance. Nothing that attached the platform to the invisible walls or any other structure that would allow us to get off this thing. Nothing on the other side either. Great, what now?

There was a rumble behind me. I whirled around, but it was only the pilot of the shuttle closing the door.

Well, this was kind of . . . anticlimactic. How to neutralise an enemy: plant them on a platform suspended in thin air without any means to get off. Then let them sit there and ignore them. They would never need to talk to us again. Maybe Asha and the others were on a similar platform in the darkness where I couldn't see them. Maybe, to add insult to injury, Asha watched us landing and getting out of the ship, knowing what would happen but unable to warn us.

That was an unsettling thought.

All our plans about readiness to escape in case things went wrong now seemed thoroughly ridiculous. Never mind I had taken Thayu and the pilots. There was no way we could get out of this ship if we wanted to. Having lost all control over the shuttle, the pilot could do nothing. So, what was I supposed to do now? Wait here? Feel like an idiot?

But then something started happening: a group of three specks of light came floating down from somewhere above. When they came closer, it became clear that they were people, but their appearance was eerily ghostlike. I was looking for signs that this was a projection, but when they came closer it was clear that they were real, live people. They eyes moved, studying me and our shuttle. They were tall and lanky like the Aghyrians in Barresh. Two of them wore identical shirts: grey with red trims. I figured they were guards or assistants. Both had long dark hair tied back in buns. The person in the middle had white hair and wore a dark blue outfit. With his pale eyes, he looked a lot like a full-blood Mirani aristocrat. Even more aloof than Federza. His face bore some wrinkles but from my experience with older Aghyrians, he could be anywhere from seventy to a hundred and twenty years old, like Delegate Akhtari. Or maybe four hundred years old. This man might well be the captain, Kando Luczon.

They floated down until they stood on the platform. They towered over me. One of the guards was a woman. The old man had penetrating green eyes with which he studied every part of me. His face remained impassive.

I bowed, hoping that bowing was something they would understand.

The old man gave a sharp command.

Before I could reply, the two guards approached me on each side. I slowly straightened and remained still, not wanting to provoke them, but also not wanting to make them think that I was afraid. One of them held a small device against my neck. I held my breath, expecting a sting of a needle, but it didn't come. He withdrew the device and showed it to his companion, who nodded and then nodded again to the white-haired man.

He said something to the pair and they fell back again, and then he said in passable Coldi, "You interest me." He used formal pronouns.

From close up, his face looked older than I had thought at first.

"You are Kando Luczon?"

He laughed and it was a rude sort of laugh that set my teeth on edge.

"Kando Luczon," he repeated, the sounds much sharper than I had pronounced them.

The Coldi language lacked harsh sounds. One of the comments I always got if I returned to Earth was that I pronounced s as z and t as d or th.

"I come in peace," I continued. I used formal pronouns, but if he'd been a person at *gamra* I would use professional ones to indicate that I thought he was being rude. That nuance would be lost on him. He might only know the formal words and their associated noun declensions.

He laughed again. "Peace through a thousand war ships."

"The ships are not mine."

"Yet you came on such a ship."

"The ships belong to Asto. They want to resolve this situation without conflict. The ships are out there in case there is a conflict. The ships are here to stop your sling crippling our Exchange."

He laughed again, and then there followed an uneasy silence in which he studied me, his expression intense. I found it hard to believe that this was the same man who had seen Asto destroyed. That he could still talk to us. That he and his crew had left the galaxy, that they could build an anpar generator that could span that sort of distance reliably.

The two crewmembers who had come with him both stared into the distance. Listening to instructions? Studying the shuttle?

He didn't look like he was going to say something so I continued, "As you can see, I'm not Coldi. I have been asked to come here because I've studied different people and their customs. I'm a negotiator. I'm interested in hearing your story." I was doing my best "clueless diplomat" impersonation and if Thayu had been standing next to me, she'd be rolling her eyes.

"Yes, you are interesting."

I wondered what that scan device to my neck had revealed about me. "I'm from a different type of people who are not related to the Coldi race."

He let another silence lapse, while he regarded me with a kind of *are you, now?* expression. Then he said, "Come."

Without warning, he stepped off the platform into the air. I just managed to keep myself from grabbing his arm to stop him falling. He turned to me, standing in midair, and gave me a *what?* kind of look. "Have you not seen localised gravity fields?"

I hesitated. If I said no, he might consider me dumb and might not elaborate.

"We have . . . something like this." I was trying to wrack my brain over what example I would cite if he asked. Hell, localised gravity? Of course, the gravity well I had seen in the large army ship.

But that was Asto military and highly secret—

No, Ezhya had shown it to me for a reason. That reason was obviously that he wanted me to bluff. He might have known that the ship had something like this. It would show up in their gravity field scans.

I stepped off the platform, holding my breath as if jumping off a dive board into the water. As soon as my feet had left the surface of the platform, all semblance of gravity disappeared.

Whoa. I almost went toppling, except where there was no gravity, there wasn't any toppling. The shuttle standing on the platform gave me a good indication of which way was up, but I wasn't feeling any of that.

One of the guards took my arm while I was trying my best to recover my dignity. *Don't behave like a dunce, Mr Wilson. It does not go well with bluffing.*

Damn, this really made me feel like I had a bad bout of vertigo. I guessed a bout of puking also wouldn't do wonders for the relationship, and thinking about puking was a really bad thing to do while I was trying to keep my stomach calm. I could taste that revolting liquid meal in the back of my throat.

Stop it, Mr Wilson.

After the two guards had dragged me along for a while, I noticed that while there might not be any gravity, my feet seemed to "stick" to an unseen point in the air, which allowed me to stand up. Every time I made the action of putting down my feet, that "stickiness" returned.

In this manner, we "walked" through the air. A breeze wafted from somewhere above us and this seemed to be where we were headed.

We came past a number of similar platforms. Some were empty, others contained small craft of the type I had seen before, the distinctive low-slung shapes that were carved in stone panels in the aquifers of Asto and in the history archives of Barresh. Judging by the shape, they were surface-to-orbit craft, with streamlined shapes and powerful engines. Others I had never seen before: oval-shaped things that were all cabin and virtually no engine, and dark, arrow-shaped craft that may or may not be fighter craft.

As we progressed through the hall, the platforms started to become tilted until most of them hung at right angles to the direction I had thought was up.

We came to the side of the hall, most of which was made up of cranes and platforms pointing in all different directions. One platform, facing the same way as we did, contained a stack of crates, while the next hung at a 90-degree angle, but there were cranes on the platform whose chains also hung at the same angle. The platform behind that was upside down, but a small craft stood on it, adhering to the upside-down surface like a gecko. That alone was enough to give anyone vertigo.

I saw no activity on any of these platforms.

We made for a gallery-like shelf. When we stood on the metal surface, and its gravity had re-established a sense of direction, I figured that the darkness of the hall might not be a matter of choice. Added to the impression I got from the unfixed damage on the outside of the ship, I wondered how many crew this ship still had. Maybe the situation was different from what I had expected. They had been away for four hundred years, had not found anything, and they had elected to come back. They were limping, almost dead because of disease, interior feuds or something else. They held Asha as hostage because they feared that vast army that was watching them, and other than the sling, they not only had no weapons, but no people to man them. This was an action of desperate people.

From the gallery we went into an opening to a corridor. Here the direction of gravity suddenly changed sideways. Whoa. I held onto the railings that seemed to be set in the middle of the floor for that purpose. We stepped onto a platform that moved down and came out into another passage. Down or sideways, I'd lost track of the directions.

This passage looked like a type of service corridor. There were little alcoves in the walls with screens and workstations. I couldn't help but stare at the slim designs and how much they resembled the latest technology designs on Earth, and thinking that would surely have to be a coincidence. The text on the screens was very different, and so was the way that images detached themselves from the screen and floated to the next screen, flapping like a butterfly.

In this passage, we also met the first other crew of the ship: a couple of men and women in muted grey clothing who worked silently and efficiently at the workstations. They used some sort of thought or iris sensor, even though I couldn't see any, because they didn't type.

They looked up while their leader passed, and followed his progress down the passage with their eyes. None of them said anything, and the captain didn't acknowledge any of them. When he had passed, they averted their eyes and kept working, not looking at us either.

Something about that behaviour made me uneasy. They'd been travelling through space for four hundred years, and for the first time someone from outside the ship came on board. One would think that it would make people curious, at the very least.

At the end of the passage we came out in a wide room with a floor that was black and smooth as glass. In the middle stood a semicircular couch. The far end was taken up by a bank of curved viewscreens which displayed the outside of the ship and, beyond that, all the white specks that were the Asto army's ships.

Captain Luczon invited me to sit on the couch.

I did. The seat covering felt rubbery and soft, and my suit stuck to it. The two crew who accompanied us had taken up positions at the door. I felt utterly naked and vulnerable without Thayu or Veyada or Sheydu.

"I will talk to you because you are not one of them." He used very formal pronouns.

"I'm interested in your story. How you have returned here, what you have discovered on your travels and what you have to offer."

His green eyes looked me over in a kind of uncomfortable *I bet you are* silence. Maybe he had expected to be grilled over the people they were still holding.

We'd get to that subject later. "My name is Cory Wilson. I represent the entities of *gamra*, which is—"

"I know what it is."

Another uncomfortable silence. Was he going to give me the opportunity to establish a friendly discussion, or was he going to be rude?

"How do you know who I am?" His speech rattled with unpleasant tones and set my teeth on edge. I could imagine so well how Coldi bluff would have gone down with him. How well his replies would have gone down with Asha.

"We know about you through the historical archives that have been excavated over the years. There are wall carvings, but people have also found working equipment and documents that can still be read."

"At Asto, after the disaster?" He raised his eyebrows.

"In the aquifers. Geologists say that the heat of the impact lique-fied a good deal of the surface. A layer of molten rock sprayed over the surface, enclosing the waterways. The heat turned the water into steam, and with nowhere to go, the water turned into ice under pres-sure. This kept the tunnels open. When the surface cooled, the water returned to its normal state. Because much of the old civilisation was buried, quite a lot has been preserved." Some of it was just really hard to reach, because it was encased in rock.

"In any of those documents, have you come across the name Waller Herza?"

"*I* haven't." It seemed an odd thing to ask. "There is a lot of Aghyrian history and I admit I'm not a specialist in the field." Federza might know who this person was. It was absurd that I was speaking to someone who might have known the legends of those archives person-ally. Absurd and invaluable. "Is this person of value to you?"

"You can say that again. I should very much like to see what his projects have come to."

"I hope you realise that you can't travel to Asto." I wasn't going to enlighten him about my recent trip. "Asto is closed to all except Coldi, because it is too hot for other people."

He tilted his head. "Except it's not really, anymore, is it?"

Damn, he'd probably heard that from the Aghyrians. I had to admit the truth. "It's changing."

Then I had an odd thought. Of course Aghyrians could have told them about the changing climate as soon as they had established contact with the ship, but I guessed that travelling back here from outside the galaxy required some preparation, and they couldn't turn up the moment that the first changes were reported to them. What if Captain Luczon and his crew had already known? If there was some sort of beacon at Asto that warned these people that the climate was changing? Those Exchange hiccups had been happening for years.

Ezhya's voice sounded in my thoughts. *They're not here to negotiate. They're here to take.*

"Indeed. The climate is changing rapidly." He looked smug.

"Do you wish to return to Asto?" My heart was hammering in my throat. This was not going well. This man didn't want to talk. He wanted to dictate his terms and I had no doubt that he was fully aware of the value of the hostage he had. And he was not going to chat about where he'd been and what they had seen there.

"It is why we've returned. These people, these war ships out there are wasting their time." He gestured at the bank of viewscreens that lined the walls and where Ezhya's army fleet was visible as small specks. Watching this ship. Keeping it here, they said.

"They're defending their world."

He snorted. "It's our world. Those fake people don't belong there. They try to stop us, but won't be successful. Nothing can stop this ship."

"There are five billion people on Asto. It's their home. They have worked for generations to make the world what it is."

He laughed. "What it is? It's pile of slag and rubble, that's what. If you want to know what it should have been, had these people been smart enough to actually do a decent job, I'll show you."

He lifted his hand. The room darkened and the bank of viewscreens against the back wall turned uniform black. A large round shape materialised on the screen. A planet, seen from space. I recognised the shape of the continents, if not the green expanses of the land, the forests, the fields and the snow on the mountains. The ocean was azure blue and not yellow. The glow of the atmosphere blue and not white. The scores and cracks that so clearly marked the surface today were barely visible.

Captain Luczon said, "That is what we had. This is what Asto should look like."

As I watched the former beauty of Asto roll past, noting towns and villages, I could only think that Ezhya should see this. Thayu should see it. In fact every adult and child on Asto should watch this.

"It will never be like this again," I said, my voice hoarse. All those towns and settlements. All those people. How many had died on that day? I'd known of course, but it was one thing knowing about it, but another altogether seeing it before your eyes.

The view flicked to another image, this one a bit further away. And then a streak in the sky, as I realised with horror what I was looking at. They had recorded the whole disaster, but had not offered help? They had not evacuated as many people as the ship could carry?

The streak grew bigger and brighter until I could make out the flaming ball that formed its front end, until I could see how it glowed when it hit the atmosphere, and seconds later slammed into the planet. The shockwave made the image waver. A huge fireball erupted, engulfing the planet, followed by roiling clouds of dust with streaks of fire within.

The planet became smaller and smaller, barely recognisable and shrouded in dust. That was how the ship had left it.

The screen went dark again to be replaced by a grainy image of Asto today: a planet of pinks and yellows, damaged, scarred, badly overpopulated. How had they obtained that? But I thought I knew: those old unregistered satellites that hung around both Asto and Ceren looking like bits of space junk. The ones that had upset the Exchange when responding to the ship's commands.

Captain Luczon was studying my face with an intense expression. "Looking at these images, I don't think these people have done so well, haven't they?"

"They don't need to. The Coldi quite like Asto as it is." In fact, the changing climate unnerved a lot of people greatly. They were afraid of an influx of visitors that might overrun their world. And with their population control measures, they were managing their resources well enough.

He scoffed. "It is a poor effort. They should have done better. We will do better for them."

"If you can so easily return a planet to health after a disaster like that, there are thousands of worlds where you can live."

"True. But none of them are ours. Asto will be green again."

25

———

THAT STATEMENT chilled me. Through all of the time that I'd been here, he'd shown little emotion, no empathy with the people who had died, and a bucketload of contempt for the Coldi.

Even if we all agreed that a climatic engineering project was necessary, he was not a person I'd want to put in charge of it, let alone a project that involved the lives of five billion people.

He lifted a warning finger. "Asto is ours. I want to see it again. I'm an old man. Is it such a strange request that want to see my home world green and healthy again?"

"The planet is inhabited. The current inhabitants won't see the benefit. They're numerous and smart." I cringed to talk about Ezhya in this way. "They are very capable of carrying out large projects if they see the need." Terraforming? I was sure Coldi could do it.

"Then why haven't they done it?"

"Because they are happy with the way the world is."

"Impossible."

"Talk to them, and they will explain. They can vary their body temperatures to suit the climate."

His nostrils flared. "Can they eat rocks, too? Can they breathe poisonous air?"

Damn, he really hated Coldi. One would almost think that there was more behind it than the fact that Coldi now considered Asto their world. "On that subject, you're restricting the freedom of a couple of people who came to talk to you before. You're probably aware of the status of one of these people, and of the fact that the structure of Coldi society depends on this person."

"They were rude."

No, they were bluffing. "They were acting according to their custom, as are you and I."

"They were still rude."

"You are holding this person so that his capture will have the maximum effect on the people and ships that outnumber you, and you hope the disruption will give you a break so that you can jump out of this siege."

He gave me a *so what if I am?* look.

"That's not going to work. Keeping this person here won't end the siege and it won't diminish their vigilance. Not only that, but the moment they have established a new leader, the hostages on your ship will have lost all of their value." This was exactly why so many high-ranking Coldi committed suicide: because their lives lost value when they lost their position.

Not a flicker of unease went over his face.

"You have the negotiating chips in your hands right now. Wait much longer, and the advantage is gone, and that army out there will have no hesitation in opening fire." I had no doubt that this would happen. The trouble was that if that happened, I would likely still be on board this ship.

"I'm ready. I may not have any personal weapons, but I have weapons that are much more interesting than that. This ship carries antimatter. If they breach the containment field, they're gone."

"You'll be gone, too. You won't ever see Asto."

"We have other engines, and if necessary we'll jettison the anti-matter, and jump before it hits any of your ships. We are not crazy."

"The Asto army has a second armada in our system. Really, I'm not here to talk about acts of war. The lives of millions are at stake—"

There was a thunk elsewhere in the ship that made the floor vibrate.

Captain Luczon turned his head sharply to the door. It seemed his two guards had collapsed. At that moment someone dropped from the ceiling. Hell, that was Veyada, whom I'd last seen several transfers ago.

Captain Luczon took something from his pocket—

"Watch out, Veyada!"

Another thump, and there was Sheydu, who grabbed the captain from behind and lifted him straight over the back of the couch. He made protesting noises, but she clamped a hand over his mouth. Then she unclipped her gun and before I could say anything, fired.

"No!" I rose.

She gave me a strange look.

"That man is the original Captain Kando Luczon who left Asto at the time of the meteorite strike."

She looked from me to the captain, slumped in her arm.

"That's a pity, because he's an arsehole. I should have used a higher setting." She lowered him to the bench, where he hung sideways against the armrest. His hand twitched.

I hoped she was joking, but damn, with Sheydu I never knew.

Thayu came running up to me. She squeezed my arm in a gesture of warmth. "Quick, Cory let's go and find my father."

"Find him? Do you know how big this ship is?"

"Come." She turned around and made for the room's exit. A couple of Aghyrian crew came running the other way, and Thayu stunned all of them.

Into the corridor. She turned sharply to the left.

"How do you even know where we're going? We might get lost."

"You're kidding. They gave us a map."

Of course that was what she had been doing when we came in: cross-referencing the spots on the map with the plan.

I did my best to keep up with her, but she was running fast. "Thay', not so quick."

She stopped briefly to let me catch up.

"How did you even get here? What about Veyada and Sheydu? They weren't even on board the shuttle."

"Just because you couldn't see them doesn't mean they weren't there."

"True."

"We have to hurry. This diversion is only going to last for so long. The old man will probably wake up soon."

"He's the original captain."

"The one who refused to take people on board?"

"The very one."

Her eyes widened. "Did you get anything out of him?"

"Not really. He was being stubborn. He showed me images of Asto as it used to be. He wants to return Asto to how it was."

"So that they can make a claim." Her eyes flashed anger. I had judged the Coldi reaction well enough.

At the end of the corridor we came to another gravity switch. Thayu had obviously been here before and ran straight up the wall. I stumbled after her. This was seriously weird. I wondered why they kept changing gravity like this.

We ran out the corridor . . . into a void with no gravity.

Whoa.

I stopped too late, lost my footing and floated into the empty space. "Thay'!"

She had managed to hold onto the end of the corridor. She was receding quickly as I floated away from her. Moving my arms or legs made no difference.

"Hang on."

She jumped—completely in the wrong direction.

"No, Thayu."

How were we going to meet up now? The hall was huge. It would take ages until we were on the other side.

But she was coming closer and closer still. Hang on, had she just calculated in her head where to jump so that with all the forces that acted on the ship, she would catch me?

Her hand grabbed mine, the skin warm and dry. We sped up with a jerk pulled along by her momentum.

"Sorry," I said.

"We needed to get to the other side anyway. The map doesn't tell me about all the gravity changes."

We floated through the semidarkness, occasionally pierced by a shaft of light.

What was this place? The entire walls were covered with something that looked like a honeycomb that emanated a soft blue light from within. Each individual cell was a—a pod, with a person inside. It looked like—no, it was—a hibernation station. Thousands upon thousands of people in pods.

"Shit, look at that," Thayu said. The soft blue glow silvered her face.

"I think we have just found the crew."

We had reached the other end of the hall, and I grabbed onto a railing along the outside of one of the pods.

We floated there for a while, looking around.

The pods were arranged in layers, heads facing the hall and feet attached to the ship. The arrangement stretched above and below us all along the walls, broken only at places where there was an entrance. Each pod contained one person. The closest one was a woman, next to her was an adolescent man and then an older man, all ages and genders randomly mixed throughout. Each lay on a surface that resembled white foam, covered by a half-tube of see-through material that was warm to the touch. Every person wore a mask that covered nose and mouth. A small tube led from the bottom of the mask into the bed of foam.

If I looked through the cover and moved my head, the edges of objects became strangely distorted as if the empty space in the pod was filled up with a clear fluid. Something inside the pod emanated soft blue light, but I couldn't see where it came from.

"Do you think it was necessary for the passengers to be inside these pods to jump the kind of distances this ship has been doing?"

Thayu gestured *no idea*. "I wonder how long they've been in here."

"Or why they are in here and why he hasn't woken them up."

"Or whether they have ever been woken up."

That sent a chill through me.

Maybe the ship hadn't been to another galaxy. Maybe they'd just floated around aimlessly, with the crew dormant, until they'd fetched up back here.

"But then why would the captain be awake?"

"Because someone needs to crew the bridge."

"Why hasn't he woken them up?"

"Those are the big questions, aren't they?"

Far too many questions than I felt comfortable with. All I could say was that I didn't trust that captain. He could be hiding that the ship was more powerful than he made it out to be, but he could also be hiding a desperate situation.

The ship could be a decoy, a Trojan horse type of venture aimed at dealing us a blow from a powerful civilisation across galaxies.

Or they could simply be curious and homesick.

Their mission could have failed completely.

And for me, there was no way of knowing which applied.

Damn it.

And I was meant to make sense out of this, to hand *gamra* the conclusions on a platter, and tell them what to do.

These people *were* going to end up in Barresh. Who would we trust with the liaison between them and the rest of us? How could we keep them isolated so that they didn't start to infiltrate different groups, giving them tidbits of technology, as we had seen with the Barresh Aghyrians?

Or maybe once they were on the ground, it would turn out that their mission had failed and the technology they shared was old and hadn't been added to for four hundred ship years.

It was up to me to make that call.

"Come, we have no time for dreaming." Thayu was not really the person in my association that I could discuss this with. She was practical, and I loved her for that, but for long discussions about society and philosophical questions, I needed Veyada, and I was counting on him to have some useful insights.

Later. Much would be said about this later.

We floated past, pulling ourselves along by the edges of the cubicles.

We came to a different section that was closed off by a giant container of see-through material. We hovered in front of the glass looking at the rows of pods hanging there.

Thayu pre-empted my question. "Don't ask me why these people are in here. I don't know."

I could see nothing different about the people, except . . . "They're all women."

Young women, too.

"They could be breeders," Thayu said.

I was reminded of the pregnant woman I had seen in the *zeyshi* warren on Asto.

"Aghyrians are obsessed with breeding and genetics."

"Seems like that."

I couldn't tell if any of the women were pregnant because of all the coverings.

"According to my map my father should be in a passage that leads away from this hall."

"How do you even know where he is?" I thought the big ship jammed all communication.

She gave me a sideways look. "That's the big question, isn't it?"

"You know how many times you've said that today?"

"Sorry, but some details I'm not allowed to discuss."

"Thay'." I held her back. "When did you become a military spy?"

She gave me that blank look that she did so well. The blue light from the pods reflected blue-green in the gold flecks in her eyes. She was so gorgeous, so deceptively quiet, so dangerous.

"My father does dangerous things. He knew I would likely do dangerous things, too. At my birth, he had a tracker implanted in both of us, so that if either of us was ever in danger, we could rescue the other. My father loves me very much, no matter what you think."

I cringed. "I don't think anything. Your relationship with your father baffles me. That's all."

"There is nothing to be baffled about. My father and I treat each other as protocol says we should. We don't need to communicate through regular channels. And I probably shouldn't tell you this, but I work for the Inner Circle, not the military."

Which, because of her father being Ezhya's second, was pretty much the same thing.

"I'm sorry. I didn't need to know that." Breaking through the protocol always left me feeling guilty. Had I been Coldi, and had I actually understood these relationships, she would never have told me.

She touched my cheek with a gloved hand. "Hey, I love you because you're always doing unexpected things. Life is never dull with you."

Geez, thanks, Thay'.

She unclicked her gun from the bracket on her arm. She didn't offer me a weapon, probably judging me a menace in zero-g, and probably being right about that. She grabbed my arm with her free hand and pushed off. We floated across the vast empty space again. I was glad for the infallible Coldi sense of direction, because I had no idea even where we had come from.

She took me into a passage that led out of the hall. It was quite dark here, but fortunately, gravity returned.

Both sides of the passage were lined with medical booths, each with an empty pod. There were rails on the floor, a main track in the middle of the passage with side tracks to each bay, where the pods sat.

I stopped briefly to look inside the pod. It had an odd chemical smell. There was none of the white foamy stuff. The bottom of the pod was taken up by various pieces of equipment.

"Come on." Thayu was waiting for me.

I followed her to the end of the passage where a glow of light came from an opening in the floor. Thayu stopped at the very edge and knelt. There was another gravity change here, but she didn't use the railing that stood at the edge.

I began, "What—"

She placed her finger against her lips.

I crawled to the edge of the opening and looked in. Whoa. What would have been a sheer vertical wall became the floor. Inside the well-lit room, a woman was tending to a handful of pods, walking from one to the other, while the blue light glowed over the face of the occupants—wait, the person inside that one had a broad face with a flat nose with flaring nostrils. He had a curved mouth with dark lips and thick black eyebrows. His hair—black and straight—was tied at the back of his head in a ponytail.

I didn't recognise the face, but this was a *Coldi* person, not Aghyrian.

I mouthed to Thayu, "Is that one of ours?"

She gestured, *yes* and *wait here*. She was turning down the beam intensity on her gun while balancing on the point where gravity shifted. Then she jumped over the edge into the room.

I lay on the floor in the passage and waited, staring at the ceiling, feeling naked without a weapon. Hopefully Thayu wasn't going to need my help.

This close to the gravity shift, I could feel shimmers of weightlessness, but the rubbery suit the army had given me felt like it was made of the ultimate non-slip material.

The sound of a discharge echoed from the room, and another one and a little later a third one.

Thayu ran back to the entrance. She reached out a hand for me, helping me over the gravity change and into the room.

The woman who had been checking the pods lay motionless on the floor. She wore the same grey uniform as the others, and disconcertingly she had golden curly hair much like mine. She carried no weapons that I could see.

"Help me with this thing," Thayu said.

She stood at one of the pods, staring into its blue glow of light. The occupant was Asha Domiri.

Shit.

"How do I turn this thing off?" Before her, against the side of the glass covering was some sort of control panel where lights blinked and fine lines of light and Aghyrian script lit up.

"Have you tried opening the lid?"

"I don't know what's inside and what keeps him sedated." She sounded distressed, panicked almost.

I knocked on the cover. It made a hollow sound. "I think there's air inside." The pod looked a bit different from the ones inside the big hall. The light wasn't as evenly distributed. "I think they were still going to add the fluid." I found a clip along the edge that might be used to close the lid. I fiddled with it, but couldn't figure out how it opened.

I said, "We don't have any time. How about you shoot it?"

She gave me a dubious look, but then took out her gun, dialled the beam to narrow. She crouched and pointed the weapon so that any charge would go through the canopy and back into the room. She fired. The cover glowed briefly but didn't break. She dialled the strength up and tried again. The charge hit the top of the canopy. An orange stain spread through it, pulsed and faded.

"Damn it." Thayu bent over the cover. A spark crackled—

I yelled, "Watch out!"

The cover shattered in thousands of little pieces that flew out like a spray of water and fell like molten globs of glass on the floor. Thayu had shielded her face, but two pieces stuck to the sleeves of her suit.

Molten globs of glass . . . That was a strange coincidence. I saw similar globs of glass on the carpet in my office, on the bed in Marin Federza's bedroom. The Tamerians wouldn't have been in contact with—damn, certainly I was dreaming. Seeing ghosts everywhere.

Thayu yanked the other coverings off her father, scattering bits of glass. Underneath, he was wearing a pyjama-like grey suit. She peeled off bandages and straps from his wrists and ankles, pulling off drips and tubes. The screen of the unit was flashing in yellow.

Then she had him free from all attachments. She waited, panting.

"We may have to carry him," I said, and I tried not to worry about the other six people. I pulled the gun from her hand. "Let me start on the others."

That she let me take it was a measure of her distress. As I turned to one of the other pods, she said, "Come on, you can wake up now." It pained me how her voice cracked.

I fired. The orange stain spread over the cover. Then I used the barrel of the gun to let the spark escape. The glass blew out.

I was pulling away all the tubes and plaster attached to the man inside when there was a great gasp behind me. I turned around just in time to see Asha roll on his side and vomit a great gush of green stuff. It went over the bed of squishy foam and onto the floor.

The man I'd just freed was gasping, too. He exhaled a spray of green stuff through his nose and then vomited as well.

Freeing all the other guards was a messy business. By the time we were done and the last of the guards had woken up and was puking his guts out, Asha was walking around, retrieving his and the guards' clothes, belts and weapons from a bin between two of the pods.

I asked him how he had ended up here.

"We went to negotiate, but they were never interested in anything we had to say," he said, his voice still hoarse. "We came into the docking hall and they stunned us as soon as we left the craft."

Attacking a leader who came to talk was considered extremely rude. That said, if I had to be honest, I thought that this had been a bad, predictable and dumb miscalculation on his part.

That's because the Coldi never need to negotiate with anyone of the same strength who doesn't understand their customs.

Still, if Asha found out how few people there were awake in this ship where he had let himself be captured, it would be a cause of severe embarrassment.

Or more likely it would be a cause of affront.

All the guards found their clothing and most of their gear in the bin and were happy that none had been stolen. Thayu had to re-stun the Aghyrian woman. "We had better go now, because if I have to do this again, I'll probably kill her."

We went to the control room where we found Veyada and Sheydu, now in the company of a group of about twenty crewmembers, all seated on the floor. Aghyrians, all of them, many young women. The captain sat on his chair and Sheydu held a gun pointed at him. He was staring at his knees while holding his head.

Veyada raised his eyebrows when he met my eyes. His stance relaxed a bit when he noticed Asha. Asha's guards went to help Sheydu guard the crew.

The man himself went to Captain Luczon. "You insulting bastard." He grabbed the captain by the front of his shirt—

"Wait," I said.

Asha turned around and gave me his *you insignificant worm* look. Bluff, I had to remind myself.

"There have been many misunderstandings." My heart was thudding. Every now and then, I had this odd feeling that he was going to challenge me in a fight, which I would utterly, utterly lose.

Asha snorted. "The only thing I need to understand is that he authorised an attack on a peaceful delegation. No misunderstandings necessary."

"I agree that was not a smart move, but maybe they felt threatened."

"Well, they should have." Then he turned to Captain Luczon and yelled in his face, "I only need to give the word and the army outside will attack. Your insults know no boundary."

The Captain didn't react. He continued to meet Asha's eyes in contempt. And Asha's abrupt and aggressive replies were really not helping.

I said, "Let's all ease off and cool down. I'm sure we can find a solution."

Asha went to his group and I retreated to the other side of the room, where Veyada stood. The screens behind him showed scrolling text.

He noticed me looking at it. "He has reopened the communication channel."

"That's something at least."

We were silent for a bit. Asha's guards had started searching the crew. Sheydu stood next to the captain. I blew out a sigh through my nose.

"I guess you don't like this either?" Veyada said.

I shook my head. "We need to get out of here. If this was supposed to be a take-over of the ship, it was much too easy, and I'm afraid he'll spring a trap on us."

He nodded. "I wonder when the rest of the crew are going to turn up."

"We've discovered where they are."

He gave me an *oh?* look. "I guess the news isn't good?"

"That depends. There are thousands of them. They're all in stasis pods in a giant hall just behind this section. Probably still using the same techniques as they used for the buried children." Those pods had lasted and kept their occupants alive for more years than one could comprehend. The last one had been found a mere hundred and fifty years ago, a young woman who had gone on to become one of the great Aghyrian teachers and mothers.

"Is this the state in which they travelled?"

I spread my hands. "No one knows. The old man is telling me some story about being old and wanting to see Asto one more time. He's upset that the Coldi haven't brought Asto back to the way it was before. I'm disturbed by his contempt for the Coldi, to be honest. He is also surprisingly unsentimental in other respects. He never mentioned the rest of his crew. For all I know, they might have been asleep since leaving Asto."

"I gather you don't trust him."

"Don't trust him?" I laughed before returning to seriousness. "But what I fundamentally don't understand is why he allowed this siege to happen if he's really as vulnerable as he says. It would have been much easier to be honest. He could have communicated with *gamra* that he needed help, or that he wanted to re-establish contact. Instead he talks to certain groups only, and they're instructed to keep those communications a secret."

Veyada said, "I'm guessing the army's presence spooked him."

"Or he's not as vulnerable as he makes out, because he's been talking to the Barresh Aghyrians."

"Talk does not require weapons."

"I'm thinking that he was hoping that the Aghyrians would be all-powerful and was hoping to get some help from them." I could just about imagine Federza telling them all sort of half-truths and coming under fire when reality came out.

"Maybe. It's all speculation."

True.

The old captain still sat motionless in his seat. Never mind how many crew he had, he could probably kill all of us—including himself —with the press of a button or a command in his head.

"We're going to have to assume that we've got control of the situation and have to make a decision what to do with him and his crew and the ship."

We thought about that for a while. Thayu and Sheydu were helping the soldiers search the captives. A female prisoner held out her hands and when Sheydu patted the bottom of her drab uniform, she touched Sheydu's armour with an expression of curiosity on her face. Sheydu straightened.

The woman said something in Aghyrian and held out her hands again.

Sheydu gave her a puzzled look and continued searching while the captain looked on with his impassive expression. They didn't look like the actions of hostile people. I just couldn't get a handle on them.

Next to me, Veyada said, "If he wants to see Asto, why not let him see Asto?"

I turned to him. "Do you think Ezhya and *gamra* would be fine with having this behemoth with untold technology in the system and no clue what these people are capable of?"

"I'm not talking about the ship. Just him."

"Leave the ship here?"

"Under guard, of course."

"Do you think he would leave the ship that's been his home since he was born?"

"That's his decision. We can maintain this stalemate indefinitely, if that's what he wants. If I were him, I'd take the hand we offer him."

Except I didn't think that it was so simple, but leaving the ship and its thousands of dormant crew here would be a good start. Anything was better than a show of weapons. It also gave the army more time to analyse the ship's capabilities. More time to gain an understanding of each other.

I asked him, "How confident are you that the army has really disabled the sling?"

"Ask Asha."

The man himself was talking to Thayu, who—and this continued to disturb me—stood in the subservient position. Thayu was his daughter for crying out loud.

I joined them, refusing to play the game of superiors. Asha met my eyes, nostrils flaring.

"Everything in order?" I asked him coolly. Let's play the game of bluff.

"At least the old man restored connectivity to the main fleet."

"Then we should think about going back to our shuttles. Do you think we'll be let out?"

"We'll shoot our way out if necessary. I'm keen to leave."

Asha's absence brought the army's power structure into danger. *That* was what had been at stake here. For all I knew we were all trapped here until the old man could be persuaded to press the button on the mechanism that released us.

"I'd like your assessment of the situation, especially with regard to threats. Do you think we're in control of the situation?"

He flicked up his eyebrows. I didn't know what that was supposed to mean. Damn it, every time I thought I had this man worked out, he threw me a curveball. "The crew is in stasis. There are over three thousand of them. We have found only thirty-one running the ship."

"I've seen the stasis chamber. What is your assessment of why they're in stasis, how long they've been in there, when the captain intended to wake them up—"

"Or *whether* he intended to wake them up." There was a serious, penetrating look in his eyes. Here was another person I should never underestimate.

"You're thinking that the captain has forcefully retained his crew?"

"It seems that way to me. Otherwise he would have woken them up and gotten them to man the battle stations once we turned up."

Damn, yes, he was right about that. "He says he wants to visit Asto."

"No way."

"What about him alone? Coming with us, on our ships?"

He flicked his eyebrows. "And leave this abomination here?" A flicker of interest went over his face.

"Well-guarded. Are you absolutely confident that you've got their sling contained?"

"Reasonably confident."

"But not one hundred percent?"

"Look, I know that it's hard to stomach for diplomats and other talk-fest enthusiasts at *gamra,* but military matters never come with a guarantee."

Whoa. Definitely something going on there. I glanced at the other military people. There were seven, a complete association. Which meant he'd gone in here like Ezhya had come to Barresh before the Exchange outage: alone with a complete association of personnel, not as the head of that association.

And was probably regretting it. He wanted to go back to his people as soon as possible, and I should take him there. Instability of Asto's troops was the last thing we wanted.

"I'll stay with my troops and guard this ship," he said, "if that's what Ezhya wants. We'll even retreat from this ship if that helps us honour our agreements. The fact that these people violate rules of negotiation doesn't mean that we should, but if they pull a trick like this again, there *will* be shots fired."

26

———————

I WENT TO CAPTAIN Luczon's chair. He looked slightly less woozy and his green eyes focused on me as I stopped before his chair and bowed.

"We have decided that we can take you to Asto, if you wish."

He raised white eyebrows. "After all this, you're going to let us pass? I thought you would have more objections than that."

"You alone, on our ships, to negotiate. This ship stays here."

"Hmmm."

He said nothing for a while. His face was impossible to read.

"We're also happy if you want to send an envoy, if, being the captain, you prefer to stay with the ship—"

"No. I'll come."

That was quick.

"I need to inform my crew." He made a move to get up, but Sheydu, with the gun next to him, shifted ever so slightly. The captain eyed her. "If you call off your fighter."

I made the Indrahui hand gesture for *fall back* and Sheydu retreated.

He rose, still eying Sheydu suspiciously. He muttered something under his breath in Aghyrian.

He shuffled across the floor and the soldiers who stood guarding the group of crew moved aside for him to pass. He kneeled amongst them, speaking in Aghyrian. I hoped Thayu or someone else would be

smart enough to record his words so that we could get them translated. Seated in the middle, he looked like a father speaking to his
children. They all listened, wide-eyed. Occasionally, one of them asked
a question, always in a subdued and timid voice. I remembered that
quiet obedience from the Aghyrian children I had seen on the train in
Barresh. It unsettled me. Was he only a captain, or a leader, or given
god-like status? Was he their father?

Thayu, on the other side of the group, was definitely making a
visual recording of this. We'd go over it and analyse it, pass the
recording onto the experts in behaviour and they'd tell us what they
thought. Not Coldi people but Damarcian academics who looked at it
with fresh eyes.

Then the captain rose and came back to us, without looking back
once to the crew he was going to abandon.

I said, "Some people in our group are very keen to get back to our
fleet as soon as possible. Do you want to pack a bag with some
clothes?"

He gave me a blank look.

That was right. Had he ever left the ship in his life? Had he ever
travelled anywhere? Had he ever felt the breeze on his skin or heard
the rustle of leaves on the wind.

He again went to the group of crew and spoke to a young woman.
She rose.

"Can she go to my cabin?"

Asha's guard jerked his head. A junior member of the association
left the room with her.

We remained in a tense situation. No one spoke. The Coldi
guards held their guns and walked around the group trying to look
impressive, but to me it looked like they weren't certain what to do. I
had no doubt that they'd have been much happier with an armed
battle. Have a shootout, settle the score, move on. That was the
Coldi way. Standoffs and an uneasy peace was not. *Negotiating*
was not.

The young woman and the guard came back. She carried a case
that she put next to the captain.

Ah, I saw, he was of the type who expected to be served. "Do we
allow him to take two servants?" I asked Veyada.

He pursed his lips while thinking. I could follow his likely line of thinking. More people would increase the risk. But by having more people, we could learn more things, too.

I had an idea. I pointed at two random people in the group, a middle-aged woman and a young man. "You, and you. Come with him."

I didn't know why I chose those two. It might be the worst decision I made, but it beat letting him choose his companions and later ending up with accomplices.

Both came without complaint. The young man picked up the case with the captain's luggage.

Ready to go. None in the group of crew showed any reaction.

What a strange people.

It was a short walk through the passage, past another gravity change into the big hall. As soon as we entered, shafts of lighting came on from all around the walls, piercing the dusty air. It allowed me to see a greater portion of the hall than before. It was really strange to see the platforms hanging at random angles that bore no relationship with the next platform.

Captain Luczon made one of the landing platforms turn up with a wave of his hand. That was how it was done. I tried not to take too much notice of the dust on the surface.

The first stop was the shuttle that had brought Asha here. He and his guards got off before the platform zoomed through the hall to our shuttle.

The pilot must have been in contact with the other pilot, because the engine was idling, the outside lights on, and the door was open.

I went up the gangplank first, followed by Thayu and then Veyada and Sheydu guarding the three Aghyrians.

We all found seats and strapped in for the journey. The pilot was going through his pre-flight routines when suddenly he said, "Oh, wow!"

Displays of emotion were rare in Coldi military, so I looked over his shoulder to the viewscreen in from of him.

Floodlights had come on in the hall, showing its vast size. There were hundreds of floating platforms, many with small surface to orbit craft, some fighters, too. The opening through which we had entered the ship was one of four. This was massive.

The captain sat behind me, sandwiched in between Veyada and

Sheydu. His face remained impassive. No doubt he wanted us to see this.

All external controls on our shuttle had been removed. The trip to the fleet's command vessel was a short one. As soon as we set foot outside the shuttle, an officer came to me to say that Ezhya wanted to speak with me. He took me to a small comm room where he gave me an earpiece and let me sit on a stool surrounded by equipment, no doubt much of it highly secret. Apparently I had acquired some degree of military clearance.

The feeder that I still wore in my hair combined with the earpiece to project Ezhya in the room with me in a fashion that was so realistic that I had to resist the temptation to poke him to check.

I told him what we had found. He seemed only mildly interested in the images of Asto before the disaster. He was more interested in the ship's military capability. Overall, he seemed not unhappy with my meagre efforts.

He was about to sign off and let me get on with returning to Barresh when I remembered something.

"The captain spoke of someone I've never heard of. Do you know who Waller Herza was?"

"He asked about him?"

"Yes, is that strange?"

"Well, no. Kando Luczon and Waller Herza were both in the employ of the Aghyrian government, in the research and colonisation division. Kando Luczon took his ship to other worlds and left colonists on those worlds. He wanted to modify the worlds so that they resembled Asto. Waller Herza had a different approach to the process. He wanted to breed people that were versatile and could adapt to many different environments without the need for extensive climate modification. He was the 'father' of the Coldi race. According to most of the historical texts, those two men hated each other with the passion of a burning sun."

Oh, now a lot of the captain's comments made sense.

And I was taking this man into the stronghold of the products of his archenemy? Great. Just great, Mr Wilson.

———

I returned to Thayu, Veyada and Sheydu, Captain Luczon, and his two shy companions. They were waiting with a higher-ranked flight crew to take us back to Barresh. We would have to make the best of this situation. Keep him talking, keep him away from militant groups.

Back to Barresh and the slew of domestic problems I was facing. Was it wishful thinking that Xinanu would have had the baby while we were away and that our association would be free to speak to each other as normal in my apartment?

That Marin Federza had simply been on a trip and had resurfaced?

That *gamra* had elected a sensible person to replace Delegate Akhtari?

That the Barresh council had realised its errant ways in employing Tamerians and had apologised for doing so?

That both Aghyrian groups had realised that they were facing a much stronger opponent and that they had decided to work together?

That Thayu had agreed to use Menor and that we could at least move ahead on that front?

Dream on, as they said.

Most importantly, we were going back to Barresh where the serious negotiations over Asto were about to begin, with a participant who could throw a very large spanner in the works.

The *gamra* assembly would probably hate me for the next few years to come, but whatever Captain Luczon had up his sleeve, I couldn't see how I could have handled it differently.

———

Thank you for reading Changing Fate. The story continues in Ambassador 4: Coming Home, where Captain Luczon causes no end of trouble.

Be a champ and buy Ambassador 4 direct from the author in ebook, print or audio.

ABOUT THE AUTHOR

Patty Jansen lives in Sydney, Australia, where she spends most of her time writing Science Fiction and Fantasy.

Her story *This Peaceful State of War* placed first in the second quarter of the Writers of the Future contest and was published in their 27th anthology. She has also sold fiction to genre magazines such as Analog Science Fiction and Fact, Redstone SF and Aurealis.

Patty has written over thirty novels in both Science Fiction and Fantasy, including the *Icefire Trilogy* and the *Ambassador* series.

pattyjansen.com

BOOKS BY PATTY JANSEN

MORE INFORMATION:

PATTYJANSEN.COM

For a complete list of books, scan the image below with your phone.